"Rowe is a paranormal star!" ~J.R. Ward

Praise for Forever in Darkness

"Stephanie Rowe has done it again. The Order Of The Blade series is one of the best urban fantasy/paranormal series I have read. Ian's story held me riveted from page one. It is sure to delight all her fans. Keep them coming!" ~ *Alexx Mom Cat's Gateway Book Blog*

***

Praise for Darkness Awakened

"A fast-paced plot with strong characters, blazing sexual tension and sprinkled with witty banter, *Darkness Awakened* sucked me in and kept me hooked until the very last page." ~ *Literary Escapism*

"Rarely do I find a book that so captivates my attention, that makes me laugh out loud, and cry when things look bad. And the sex, wow! It took my breath away... The pace kept me on the edge of my seat, and turning the pages. I did not want to put this book down... *[Darkness Awakened]* is a must read." ~ *D. Alexx Miller, Alexx Mom Cat's Gateway Book Blog*

***

Praise for Darkness Seduced

"[D]ark, edgy, sexy ... sizzles on the page...sex with soul shattering connections that leave the reader a little breathless!...*Darkness Seduced* delivers tight plot lines, well written, witty and lyrical - Rowe lays down some seriously dark and sexy tracks. There is no doubt that this series will have a cult following. " ~ *Guilty Indulgence Book Club*

"I was absolutely enthralled by this book...heart stopping action fueled by dangerous passions and hunky, primal men...If you're looking for a book that will grab hold of you and not let go until it has been totally devoured, look no further than *Darkness Seduced.*"~*When Pen Met Paper Reviews*

***

Praise for Darkness Surrendered

"Book three of the Order of the Blades series is…superbly original and excellent, yet the passion, struggle and the depth of emotion that Ana and Elijah face is so brutal, yet is also pretty awe inspiring. I was swept away by Stephanie's depth of character detail and emotion. I absolutely loved the roller-coaster that Stephanie, Ana and Elijah took me on." ~ *Becky Johnson, Bex 'n' Books!*

"*Darkness Surrendered* drew me so deeply into the story that I felt Ana and Elijah's emotions as if they were my own…they completely engulfed me in their story…Ingenious plot turns and edge of your seat suspense…make *Darkness Surrendered* one of the best novels I have read in years." ~*Tamara Hoffa, Sizzling Hot Book Reviews*

***

Praise for Dawn at Birch Crossing

"*Dawn at Birch Crossing* is m-a-g-i-c-a-l! Hands down, it is one of the best romances I have read. I can't wait till it comes out and I can tell the world about it." ~*Sharon Stogner, Love Romance Passion*

"*Dawn at Birch Crossing* is contemporary romance at its best…. There was not a moment that I wasn't completely engrossed in the novel, the story, the characters. I very audibly cheered for them and did not shed just one tear, nope, rather bucket fulls. My heart at times broke for them. The narrative and dialogue surrounding these 'tender' moments in particular were so beautifully crafted, poetic even; it was this that had me blubbering. And of course on the flip side of the heart-wrenching events, was the amazing, witty humour….If it's not obvious by now, then just to be clear, I love this book! I would most definitely and happily reread, which is an absolute first for me in this genre." ~*Becky Johnson, Bex 'N' Books*

"*Dawn at Birch Crossing* is an amazing story of love and life…I literally laughed out loud, cried and cheered…. Dawn at Birch Crossing is a must read and must re-read." ~*Jeanne Stone-Hunter, My Book Addiction Reviews*

Darkness Reborn

***

The Order of the Blade
Book Five

Stephanie Rowe

Darkness Reborn

ISBN-10: 1479387185

ISBN-13: 978-1479387182

Copyright © 2012 by Stephanie Rowe.

Cover design © 2012 by Peter Davis. Cover design and layout by Peter Davis at www.loszombios.com. Cover photos courtesy of iStockphoto.com.

All rights reserved. No part of this publication may be reproduced, disseminated, or transmitted in any form or by any means or for any use, including recording or any information storage and retrieval system, without the prior written consent of the author and/or the artist. The only exception is short excerpts or the cover image in reviews.

Please be a leading force in respecting the right of authors and artists to protect their work. This is a work of fiction. All the names, characters, organizations, places and events portrayed in this novel or on the cover are either products of the author's or artist's imagination or are used fictitiously. Any similarity to real persons, living or dead, is purely coincidental and not intended by the author or the artist.

For further information, please contact Stephanie@stephanierowe.com

Dedication

There are no words to describe the depth of my appreciation for Janet Juengling-Snell for all her help and support on this book, and with all my books. Thank you, Janet, for everything. You are the BEST!

Acknowledgements

Special thanks to my core team of amazing people, without whom I would never have been able to create this book. Each of you is so important, and your contribution was exactly what I needed. I'm so grateful to all of you! Your emails of support, or yelling at me because I hadn't sent you more of the book yet, or just your advice on covers, back cover copy and all things needed to whip this book into shape—every last one of them made a difference to me. I appreciate each one of you so much! I want to give a huge shout out to all my beta readers, who turned this novel around super-fast so I could get it out to my readers. You guys are the BEST! I also want to give a huge shout-out to all my Facebook friends, who supported me so much during the writing of this book when I was sure I would never get it done. Special thanks also to: Jeanne Hunter, Sharon Stogner, Jan Leyh, Summer Steelman, Teresa Gabelman, D. Alexx Miller, Holly Collins, Janet Juengling-Snell, and Phyllis Marshall. There are so many people I want to thank, but the people who simply must be called out are: Denise Fluhr, Dottie Jones, Alencia Bates, Emily Recchia, Rebecca Johnson, Nicole Telhiard, Denise Whelan, Tamara Hoffa, Jean Bowden, Linda Watson, and Ashley Cuesta. Thank you also to the following for all their amazing help: Judi Pflughoeft, Deb Julienne, Courtny Eskew,Julie Simpson, Mary Lynn Ostrum, Shell Bryce, Jacqueline Wilson, Jodi Moore, Christine Mabry, Casey Harris-Parks, and Amanda Tamayo. You guys are the best! Thanks so much to Pete Davis for such an amazing cover, and for all his hard work on the technical side to make this book come to life. Mom, you're the best. It means so much that you believe in me. I love you. Special thanks also to my amazing daughter, who I love more than words could ever express. You are my world, sweet girl, in all ways.

Chapter One

Sarah Burns clutched the steering wheel tighter, her hands shaking so violently she could barely grip the leather. She swallowed, her mouth parched, sweat beading on her forehead as chills wracked her, the attack from last night taking a brutal toll on her body.

As she sped along the twisted mountain road, she watched the sun dropping lower and lower in the sky, and a cold fear gripped her. *Please God, don't let the sun set yet.*

She grabbed her phone and dialed the same number for the thousandth time that day.

Her grandmother answered on the first ring. "We didn't find him, Sarah."

Tension rippled through Sarah, and the fresh bruises on her body began to throb even more. "It's almost sunset," she whispered, her throat still raw from screaming all night, from the clawed hands that had gripped her throat so ruthlessly, trying to cut off her cries for help. "You have to find him."

"We've looked everywhere. We have no idea where his lair is."

His lair?

Tears burned in Sarah's eyes. Yesterday, her brother Jacob had been sleeping in his bed on the porch, a charming eighteen-year-old who had sworn to protect Sarah and his grandmother against the hell that stalked them, determined to be the man who would stand up and be their protector. He still blamed himself for failing to protect her seven years ago, even though he had been only eleven at the time, and he'd ruthlessly committed his life to making sure no one ever got to her again. He'd been so eager to have his dream and to become powerful enough to protect her against the monsters that hunted her. Jacob, her protector, her guardian.

They had all believed he would do it.

Last night, she'd heard him tossing and shouting as he had the dream battle that would either turn him into a Calydon warrior or kill him.

Jacob had survived it, and he'd woken up with the brands on his arms that marked him as a Calydon, a warrior who could turn into one of the deranged monsters that had been hunting their village and Sarah's kind for so long. Some Calydons took years to go insane. Not her brother. One night. *One night* was all it had taken for him to turn against Sarah, and the fact she loved him gave him the power to truly destroy her.

And now, he was somewhere in the woods around their village, waiting for the sun to set so he could track down Sarah and finish what he'd started last night. "Nonny, we have to find him before dusk. As soon as it's dark, he'll come after me again—"

"We have to go inside now, Sarah. We can't be caught outside after the sun goes down. There's nothing more we can do." There was a loud thud, the sound of the door slamming shut as her grandmother began to set the nighttime safeguards, which included bolted doors, talismans, and spotlights that lit up the yard like it was midday.

Sarah bit her lip as she looked around the SUV she was driving. Glass windows. Metal siding. No protection. Nothing to help her. "I can't die," she said, dread filling her as the sky began to glow with the pink and red of a glorious sunset. Sunset had been a nightmare her whole life, a beautiful image preceding endless nights of danger. Tonight, it held a far more deadly promise than it ever had before. "You know I have to live. *I have to.*"

"Sarah." Her grandmother's voice was firm and unyielding. "You survived last night. You'll find a way to survive tonight, if they find you again."

"Oh, they'll find me." The sun dipped lower in the sky, only the top crescent visible across the mountain range. She took a deep breath, fighting against the fear and the dizziness, her head still throbbing from the beatings. Nausea churned in her belly, the aftermath of using her powers so violently all night still hitting hard. "You know they will."

"Then you survive." Her grandmother's voice was fierce. "You do whatever it takes."

Sarah covered her mouth against the urge to break down and cry, to beg for someone to help her, for the sun to suddenly, miraculously zoom back up into the sky, for a reprieve. She never cried. She never bemoaned her fate. She simply accepted it and closed her heart to any kind of weakness. But last night had broken through her emotional shields. It had been hell far beyond what she ever could have imagined, and the thought of going through it again... She looked down at her arms, at the bruises and claw marks on her skin, and she shuddered. "Nonny, I don't know if I can get through another assault. Last night—"

"Is over. And tonight won't last forever. You only have to survive until dawn."

An owl moved in the trees, making Sarah jump. How many minutes until night hit and they found her? She punched the gas, making the truck leap forward. Her view of the sunset disappeared as she drove deeper into the woods, the trees closing down on her like a canopy of death, trapping her.

The wheels on the SUV spun as she drove further and further away from Akara, the village that was her home, trying to put as many miles between it and herself before sunset struck. The further she was from Akara, the longer it would take for her brother to get to her once he woke up. Every muscle in her body was aching, pain was shooting through her back, and the chills were getting more violent. "I didn't get a chance to heal from last night," she said quietly. "I don't have much power left."

Her grandmother was silent for a long moment. "You didn't go to the fountain this morning to restore your powers?"

The fountain in the burned out section of their village had been standing for over a thousand years, filled with water that gave the gift of life to Sarah, but the flow had been getting weaker and weaker over the last several years. "The fountain was dry, and I didn't have time to try to dig out the water. I had to leave. I had to try to make Nashoba before dusk." But she wasn't going to get there in time. "I'm still three hours away from it." Nashoba was rumored to be a village like hers, and she was headed there to get help in dealing with the creatures haunting Akara and to find a new source of water. She'd tried to contact people there, but had come up empty. Jacob's turning had made it impossible to wait anymore, and she'd had to take the chance she could complete the drive between sunrise and sunset.

But she had to make it there before sunset, and it wasn't going to happen.

Traffic was a bitch sometimes.

"Sarah." The exasperation in her grandmother's voice made Sarah's throat tighten with fear, because it was the acknowledgement of death, the reality that there was no way Sarah could sustain herself through another night like the last one if she hadn't rebuilt her defenses after last night's assault.

They both knew it. Sarah had risked everything to try to make it in time, and the payoff was not happening the way she'd needed it to.

"You keep driving, do you understand?" There was a loud crash from over the phone, and Sarah jumped. It had sounded like the deadbolt had just been released.

"Nonny! What are you doing?"

"I'm going back out there. When they start hunting, they're going to find me before they find you."

"What?" Chills rippled down Sarah's arms at the thought of her grandmother heading into those woods to take on the creatures who had tortured her all night. They didn't want Nonny. They wanted Sarah. There was no reason for Nonny to throw herself in their path. "No! Don't! You'll never survive." Sarah heard the scrape of wood and knew that her grandmother had just pulled open the heavy door that barred the nightmares. "Nonny! Stop!"

"You're more important than I am," Nonny announced, like some damned martyr.

What was wrong with her? Martyrs weren't cool! "Oh my God, Nonny! What kind of statement is that? Go back inside!" Sarah wanted to scream with frustration as she heard the tap of her grandmother's feet on the front porch stairs. "They'll kill you!"

"As long as it takes them three hours, it's worth it," her grandmother declared. "I've got a few tricks of my own. I'll knock them on their asses a few times before they can get to me."

"God, no!" The devastating weight of loss swept through Sarah like a chasm of emptiness. There was no way she could handle it if her grandmother was killed. Nonny was the only person left in her life that mattered to her, and the thought of her dying... *No.* Sarah's trembling became more violent, the pounding in her head more intense as waves of despair crashed down around her. "Nonny, stay inside! It won't help me if you die. It will break me. I need your faith and hope to make it."

"That's a bunch of bullcrap, Sarah. You have plenty of hope and faith of your own. What you need is time, and I'll give that to you."

"Nonny!" she shouted, wishing she could swing the vehicle around and handcuff the stubborn old lady to the bed and never let her go. She would, if she could get back there in time. But that was impossible, so all she could do was cajole, threaten and beg, hoping to get through her grandmother's thick head. "Don't you dare do this! I'll find a way. I always do."

Nonny's footsteps crunched on the gravel as she walked down the driveway. "You survive tonight, do you understand? You're the only hope, Sarah. The only one, by God."

"I don't have hope or faith anymore," she retorted. "It's gone, and if you die, then I've really got nothing left." Her brother and his crew had taken the final shreds of hope from her last night when Jacob had walked up to her and jammed his claws into her throat. Having her beloved brother turn on her had shredded her faith in life, in humanity, in goodness. Without faith and hope, she would die, because those elements were what gave her soul life.

The beatings last night hadn't been about killing her with violence. It had been about breaking her soul by having those she loved beating her, and by forcing her to use her powers to hurt others. The way to destroy her was to strip her of all hope and faith, because those emotions were what sustained her. Without it, she could not exist, and if she didn't exist...

God, no, she couldn't think like that.

She rubbed her neck, bile churning at the feeling of those five puncture wounds, at the reminder that the brother she loved more than anything had led the assault on her last night. One of the best ways to destroy her was to force her to use her powers to hurt others, especially those she loved. It was devastating to watch men she'd once known and loved suffer and die at her hands, and each time she'd done it, another part of her heart had died.

She had so little hope and faith left after what had happened seven years ago, and last night had almost destroyed her completely. Another night like that? She knew she didn't have the resources to survive it. "If you die, I have nothing left, Nonny. You're the only thing left in my life I can believe in. I can't do it without you."

Her grandmother swore. "You'll die if they get you tonight, and you'll die if I get killed? What kind of crap is that? Toughen up, Sarah. I won't sacrifice myself if you're just going to roll over and give up just because the night gets a little rough!"

"I'm not going to roll over! Don't sacrifice yourself!" Sarah jammed her foot on the gas, ignoring the sweat streaming down her temples, the nausea roiling in her belly, and the aching of her body. "I'll survive tonight. I'll find a way. Just go back inside. Please, you're all I have left, Nonny." Her voice broke, and she had to fight to hold back the tears.

Seven years ago, everything she believed in had been destroyed when the man she had loved with all her soul, who she'd known since childhood, had turned on her after becoming a Calydon. He'd murdered her parents. He'd slaughtered their baby girl, tearing her from Sarah's arms as she fought to protect her. And then he'd come after Sarah, his eyes blazing red as the demon consumed him.

Grief filled Sarah at the memory of her husband sprawled on the ground, crawling toward her to get in the final killing blow before he died, his life bleeding from him, spilling into the earth like black poison into dust.

To stop him, she'd killed him. She'd murdered the man she'd loved, and he'd killed almost everyone she cared about. The old anguish flared deep and agonizing again, brought to life by her brother's turning on her. If she couldn't trust those she loved, who could she trust?

The debilitating emotions she'd fought so hard to suppress for so long swelled inside her: the despair, the hopelessness, the doom, all the feelings that would finally destroy the soul that had been dying for the last seven years.

She rubbed her hand over the scar on her stomach, from the blow that had nearly killed her. The eleven months in the hospital with nothing to do but obsess about Mason's betrayal, her unforgivable failure to protect her daughter, and the loss of so many who she loved so dearly. The loneliness and guilt had been overwhelming, and Sarah knew her spirit would have broken if it hadn't been for her grandmother sitting by her bed, haranguing her relentlessly to survive for one more day.

To lose her grandmother now? Her only rock? Sarah knew it would be more than she could take. "Nonny. You can't sacrifice yourself for me. You can't!"

"Bullshit, Sarah. Of course I can. It's your time to step up, and it's my job to help you. Your life is worth more than mine. Godspeed, child."

"Nonny!" Sarah gripped the phone frantically as the line went dead. Her hand shaking, she frantically dialed again, and it went right into voicemail. "No!" She screamed her denial, her anguish, her protest useless in the empty cab of the truck.

Her damned curse, her blessing, her fate, whatever name you attached to it, had stolen everything. And now it was going to take her grandmother, the woman who had held Sarah's broken body, refusing to let her die after the man Sarah loved had attacked her and killed their child.

Sarah couldn't do it without her grandmother. She knew she couldn't. It wasn't simply her life that her brother had been trying to take from her last night. It was her soul, her hope, her faith, the very things that gave her power.

Nonny was the only light left in Sarah's life, the only beauty, the only sign that there might be something good in this God-forsaken existence she'd been cursed with. Without Nonny, there was nothing left inside Sarah. No hope. No faith. Nothing.

The darkness closed in around Sarah, and a sudden chill rippled down her arms, a knowledge so ingrained in her that it told her exactly the moment the sun had set.

It was now.

She had a sudden vision of her stubborn grandmother strutting out of the village, her chin raised defiantly and her leather sandals whispering silently across the ground as she headed into the nightmare of claws, demons and hell beyond what anyone should endure.

Dammit! She would not let that happen. "No!" Sarah slammed on the brakes, and the SUV skidded across the asphalt. She shoved the door open and leapt out, her battered bare feet aching as they hit the pebbles. She raised her arms to the sky, and closed her eyes, tapping into the very depths of her soul.

She pictured her brother, and she let her heart bleed with the pain of his betrayal. She allowed her heart to fill with her love for the little boy she'd raised after their parents had been killed. She recalled the tone of his voice, that deep tenor that was so like their father's had been. She imagined herself standing above his bed while he was a sleeping teenager, praying he would be spared.

She opened her connection and her soul to Jacob, begging him to find her before he spotted their grandmother, tapping into the blood bond they shared and her immense love for him. *Jacob. I'm here. Come find me. I'm almost to my destination, and you'll never get me then. You have no time to waste. Come find me, now!*

A cool breeze teased over her skin, the hoot of an owl drifted through the woods, but there was no response from Jacob. He hadn't noticed her yet. What was he doing? Killing Nonny? *Jacob!* She screamed his name—

Suddenly, his face appeared in her thoughts, and she felt the cold ripple of his presence in her mind, utterly devoid of the jovial warmth that had been a part of him for so long. She stared into his vibrant blue eyes. The anguish and wisdom in them was so heartbreaking that she *knew* she was looking into Jacob's eyes in that very moment, and that there was still awareness and humanity in them. Dear God, it was after sunset and his eyes were still blue. "Jacob?" Desperate hope leapt in her chest. "You're okay?"

Then his eyes began to glow red, that violent, punishing crimson of death and hate, and she felt her heart shatter again at the loss. Dammit. She should know better than to hope, because losing it was far more devastating than never feeling it in the first place.

Jacob let out a roar of fury. Violent heat burst over her, and she knew he'd targeted her location. He was coming after her. The race had begun.

He wouldn't notice their grandmother now. He would be focused only on hunting Sarah. Yay. Happy day. There was nothing like forcing an assassin's attention onto yourself to reinforce the fact that it's just *not* a good day.

Sarah shut him out of her mind, determined to block their connection enough to make it difficult for him to track her. Last night, she hadn't been ready to block him, and he'd found her the moment the sun had set. But now, she was ready.

Sarah closed her eyes and carefully reinforced her mental shields, trying to block her location from the brother that she'd been so connected with her entire life. It felt cold and empty not to have his warmth a part of her, but it was also a relief, a realization that maybe she had some control over how this played out.

How long could she hold him off? Not three hours. Not when they had always been so close. But maybe there was hope up ahead, around the next bend. Every minute gave her a chance, every minute gave her grandmother a chance.

Her heart thundering, Sarah dove back into the truck, hit the gas and took off into the woods.

How long would it take for him to reach her? Since he was a new Calydon, his teleporting range was still limited, and he would have to make a series of leaps to catch up to her. Had she contacted him before he'd found Nonny? Would his need to kill Sarah be strong enough to get him and his team to forego easy prey? *Please, Nonny, be safe.*

And would Sarah be able to survive another night at his mercy?

She looked down at the cracks in her skin, like a porcelain doll about to break, and she knew the answer was no.

But she'd have to find a way to change that to a yes.

* * *

Crack.

Sarah jumped at the noise that sounded like a lightning bolt exploding into a tree trunk by the side of the road, right next to her. It had been almost two hours since she'd let her brother connect with her, two terrifying hours when she'd flinched at every sound, wondering how long she had.

Ten minutes ago, she'd started to hope she was going to make it. She was only an hour away from Nashoba. Forty-five miles. That was all—

Crack.

She jumped again, her adrenaline surging. That sounded too close.

Too real. She frantically looked to the left, searching the forest for the red glow of eyes stalking her. She saw nothing but the dark expanse of woods.

Crack. The sound was ahead of her now.

Crack. Behind her. *Crack.* To the right. *Crack.* To the left. The night began to bombard her with the sound of Calydon claws digging into tree trunks.

Okay, she definitely wasn't imagining it. Not anymore. They'd found her. They were here. All around. How many were there? One that was teleporting from tree to tree, or dozens of them, leaping along beside the truck? How many had her brother brought to destroy her?

Sarah poised her hand over the button on the dash, knowing she would have only one opportunity. "Come on," she muttered to herself. "Time this right." She had to strike before they attacked, but she needed to wait until they were all close enough to be affected. She had one chance to catch them unprepared.

As men, they were smart and talented.

As monsters, they went on instinct and gut, and her only chance was to be smarter than they were.

She turned off her headlights, leaving only her parking lights to illuminate the isolated road as the SUV raced along, trying to lure her attackers into a sense of safety. The night seemed to come to life, swelling around her like the hand of doom, ready to suck her into its depths, offering all the advantage to the beasts hunting her. The blackness was terrifying, a nightmare from her youth—

No. She could handle this. She could do this.

Sarah gunned the gas, straining her eyes for that red glow that would tell her where they were. The trees were black specters, striking at the night as the wind took their branches and knifed them across the void.

A dark shape fluttered across the road, and she almost hit the button—

No. An owl. She'd almost moved too soon. Sweat dripped down her forehead at the close call, but she didn't dare take a moment to wipe it away. She had to be ready.

Her only chance was to strike when they didn't expect it. The impact of artificial light was limited, and if they had time to defend themselves, her assault would be powerless. Her only infallible weapon was her own powers, but the cost to her was too great, especially if she had to hurt her brother...

She jutted out her jaw, and fierce determination swelled through her. *No. She would not let them win.*

Then she saw what she'd been looking for: two small red circles glowing at her from a tree ahead, the eyes of a demon watching her. Another set to the right. A third on her left. She grimaced, realizing they were all around her. Her brother couldn't have done the stereotypical male "I-never-ask-for-help" thing and come alone, could he? No, he'd brought the whole damned posse with him. Damn Jacob and his overly social tendencies.

The Calydons were all around her, just like last night. Panic swelled in her throat, and she fought it back, fighting against the urge to be pathetic and terrified.

Terror got her nowhere, and dammit, she had somewhere to be in the morning.

Sarah fixed her gaze on the undulating shadow poised on the tree trunk, those red eyes watching her so carefully, tracking her progress. He was preparing to time the attack with flawless precision.

Yeah, well, so was she, and she was the smarter one, so odds on her. Or not, but positive thinking was supposed to accomplish *something*, right?

Her finger trembled over the button. Ready. Waiting.

She forced her foot off the gas, slowing down, so they would think they had more time and get careless in their attack. Her instincts were screaming at her to floor it, to try to outrun them, but she knew she couldn't. This was her only chance—

Then she heard it. *Click click click.* The rapid triple click, the only warning their prey ever had. *Click click click* from all around her, from each one as they prepared to attack.

Game time...Now!

Sarah jammed her foot on the gas, and the vehicle exploded forward at the same moment that the night filled with black shadows leaping off the trees, right at her. She had a split second of raw horror as she saw that bottomless mouth and the twelve-inch claws coming at her—

Screw being afraid. "Leave me alone!" She slammed her finger down on the button, and the floodlights on the roof of her truck burst to life, lighting up the dark woods as if the angels themselves had unleashed heaven's blessings onto the night.

The night screamed with their agony as the light burned them, and she swerved to the left as one catapulted past her in a helpless free-fall, his wail of agony like the worst suffering in the bowels of hell.

She heard the thud of its body crashing to the asphalt behind her, rendered helpless by the light that he hadn't had time to shield against. Others hurtled past her vehicle, their equilibrium destroyed, the night filled with the scent of their burning flesh. Thud after thud of creatures that used to be men hitting the asphalt, screaming in agony.

Nausea and regret at the harm she had caused flooded Sarah as she fought to regain control of the SUV as it careened across the road toward the woods. "Come on!"

The vehicle finally obeyed, and she realigned it, jamming her foot on the accelerator the moment she had control, hurtling up the dark road again. Guilt burned at her as she drove away from the bodies, leaving them to rot and die from her attack. Although the backlash wasn't nearly as severe as if she'd used her own power to hurt them, the cost was still significant. A bad-ass warrior she would never be, as convenient as it would have been to have that be her professional calling.

How many more were going to be in the next wave? And how soon? She knew they were coming, because she hadn't seen her brother go down. As long as he was still alive, he would be able to track her and bring them straight to her—

"Sarah." The low male voice rasped in her ear, and she yelped, hit the brakes, and whirled around.

Her brother was sitting in her backseat.

Her stomach dropped, and raw terror knifed through her when she saw the blood red glow of his eyes, filled with the promise of death, torture, and a night of her begging for mercy she would never receive. His tousled blond hair was the same as it had been before his change, but his black tee shirt was torn and his skin was stretched taut across the bones of his face, like the demon within was about to break right through his skin. "Jacob, don't do this—"

He lunged over the backseat at her, his claws bared as he went for her throat.

She lunged for the door, but there was nowhere to go. Nowhere to hide. No mercy was coming for her tonight. Only hell.

Chapter Two

Even with his chest heaving from exertion, his weapons burning in his hands, steam rising from his bare torso from the humidity, and the earth ruthlessly torn up from the battle, Calydon warrior Kane Santiago wanted more.

He needed more.

He needed to keep going until sheer, raw exhaustion dragged him ruthlessly into the sleep that wouldn't come, until he was so drained that he couldn't think any more.

Kane had been driving himself relentlessly for eleven days straight, but it hadn't been enough to chase away the gaping void trying to consume him. It had been coming at him for months, this great pit of darkness, stalking him at every moment, but now it felt like his entire soul had been sucked from his body and thrust into a bottomless void of blackness.

He didn't know what was coming for him or how to stop it. He didn't have answers. All he had was a scarred body that looked like an artist had used his flesh for a canvas and a knife for a paintbrush, and a thousand unanswered questions about a past he didn't remember.

Kane's skin looked like ancient designs had been carved into it, but no one on this God-forsaken earth could explain why he had them or what they meant. Kane's memories of his life began five hundred years ago, the day Dante Sinclair, the now-deceased leader of the elite team of Calydon warriors called the Order of the Blade, had hauled him out of the gutter. How old had Kane been that day? Thirty? A hundred? Two hundred? How had he ended up there, covered in body art of the most brutal kind?

He had no idea, but the story carved on his body and the enormity of the blackness hunting him made it clear that there was shit he needed to know about his prior life, and he was running out of time to do it. In his five hundred years as an Order member, he'd spent every day fulfilling the Order's mission to protect innocents from rogue Calydons, grimly willing to sacrifice one innocent to preserve the greater good, but no matter how hard Kane fought in defense of the Order's moral code, it still hadn't filled that void inside him, an emptiness that had been taking on a decidedly violent taint lately.

The void he could live with. The uncontrollable need to inflict violence on others without justification? Not so much. That shit had to stop, and now.

The air in the southern Oregon woods was thick with moisture, rich with the scent of earth saturated by the rain that was too cold for this time of year. Thick fog was rolling in fast, sucked in by the dance of the heat and cold. The air Kane was breathing was alive with vibrant energy, and yet all he could feel was the endless free-fall of his spirit into the bottomless chasm of darkness.

"These guys were serious shit." Caked with sweat and blood from the battle, Ryland Samuels crouched beside one of the two rogue Calydons they'd been hunting for the last eighteen hours, deadly bastards who had put up a hell of a fight before Ryland and Kane had taken them down. Usually two-on-two battles were weighted so heavily in favor of the Order of the Blade that they lasted less than a second—but once they'd finally found the bastards at sunset, the two rogues had kept Ryland and Kane at max capacity for over two hours before the good guys had won.

The fact that the battle was so tough was bizarre as hell because the rogues had been so underdeveloped physically that they couldn't have been more than eighteen years old. They'd been only a month or two past the dream that had brought them into their powers as immortal Calydon warriors. No rookie should ever have been able to put up that kind of battle against elite warriors who had been saving the world for over five hundred years.

And yet they had.

Which meant the Order needed to find out what they were, where they were from, and why they were both rogue. Rogue Calydons were bad shit, and the odds of two Calydons going rogue as a team almost nil, so the Order needed to make sure that these two were an anomaly, and not a trend.

Ryland hooked his machete under one of their wrists and raised the dead warrior's hand. "What's with the manicure?"

Ten-inch claws protruded from the tips of the Calydon's fingers, still covered in Kane's blood from when it had tried to cleave his heart out. "Maybe they came up from Hollywood," Kane said. "You know how those fancy Californians are all bailing up to Oregon nowadays. How the hell would I know what his deal is?"

Ryland narrowed his eyes at Kane's aggression. "You seen it before?"

"No. Calydons have weapons, not claws." Kane shifted restlessly as Ryland nodded his agreement. He was unable to settle now that the battle was over. He was on edge, his instincts still ready for more action. He knew they needed to figure out what was up with the rogues who had invaded their territory, but he couldn't focus. All his senses were on overload, telling him that something was deadly wrong. He scanned the woods, hunting for a clue, but came up with nothing.

Ryland dropped the kid's wrist. "What's your deal, Santiago?"

Kane whirled around to face his teammate, his adrenaline leaping at the tense undercurrent in Ryland's voice. "What?"

Ryland flashed him a grin that didn't reach his pitch-black eyes. "I'm the one who's supposed to be on the edge of going rogue, not you. You planning to snap so you're the next one who has to be cut down to save the world, instead of me?"

"I'm not going rogue." Usually, a Calydon went rogue only after bonding with his *sheva,* the woman destined to be his soul mate for all eternity. The bond between them, once completed, was destined to turn him rogue and destroy both of them and all that mattered to them once all the stages of bonding were completed. However, a rare few turned into mindless, killing machines even in the absence of a *sheva.* Expectations were high that the moody Ryland would soon fall into the latter category, but Kane had his shit together. "I'm fine."

Ryland rose to his feet, his well-muscled bulk innately aggressive. His black jeans and t-shirt had been shredded mercilessly from the fight. "Don't lie to me, Santiago. There's no room for that shit between us."

The black brands in Kane's arms burned, and he fisted his weapons, a set of doubled-spiked flails with spiked balls spinning on the ends of the steel chains. The clang of the metal balls cracking against each other jerked Kane's attention to them, and he suddenly realized how close he was to launching himself at Ryland.

He was ready to strike first against his own teammate? Kane swore and sheathed his weapons. They vanished into the air, returning to the brands on his arms that were an exact match for the weapons they housed. He held up his hands in surrender. "Stand down. I'm good."

Ryland sheathed his own weapons, taking the temptation away from both of them. "Shit, man. You're off, big time."

"I—" A sound caught Kane's attention, and he turned sharply. "Did you hear that?"

"What?" Ryland went still, and the air hummed as both Calydons reached out into the night with their senses.

For a moment, Kane heard nothing but the skittering of rodents' feet, the hoot of owls, and the crackling of the earth as it drank in the moisture from the night.

Then he heard it again.

A woman's scream. Unending terror and pain. The roar of a spirit fighting desperately and hopelessly for its very survival.

The sound went straight to Kane's core, ripping through his shields like a burning knife into his heart. His whole body vibrated in response, adrenaline raging with the need to find her. To protect her. To save her. Kane spun around wildly, almost desperately, trying to pinpoint the sound and determine where it was coming from. It was bouncing off the trees, echoing in the air, coming at him from all directions, like an assault of agony. "Fuck!"

"What?" Ryland strode up beside him. "I don't hear anything."

"How can you not hear that?" She screamed again, eviscerating every defense Kane had. He had to go. Had to find her. Had to save her and find out who she was. *She needed him.* Black light flashed above the brands on his arms, a loud crack split the night, and then Kane's weapons appeared in his hands, the glittering steel ready for battle.

"What is it?" Ryland called out his own machetes with a crack and a flash of black light. "I'm picking up nothing. Tell me what you got."

Kane shoved his teammate aside, his entire soul howling with the need to find the woman. "Where are you?" he bellowed, his voice echoing into the night.

No response. Just the ominous echo of silence. Was she dead?

Uncontrollable grief ripped through Kane at the thought of her being dead, a loss so severe he went down on his knees, gasping for breath. He braced his hands on the earth, his fingers digging into the moss, fighting against the crushing blackness, the loss, the shredding of his innermost core—

Help me. The desperate plea invaded his mind, a woman's voice filled with pain, anguish and betrayal.

Kane's head snapped up, instantly alert. She was alive! His entire being vibrated with rightness at the sound of her voice. He lurched to his feet as her anguish shredded his mental shields and consumed him. *I hear you.* He sent out his reassurance, his iron strength, showing her the immense power he offered.

There was no relief from her. Just another stab of pain that knifed all the way to Kane's gut. *Hurry. Please hurry.*

Son of a bitch! Kane focused every fiber of his soul on her, and his entire existence honed in on those words, on her voice, on her spirit, on her very being.

Then he located his target. He knew where she was. *I'm coming.*

Kane didn't hesitate. He didn't pause to question the intensity of his response to her or ascertain what he was heading into. He didn't even take the time to grab his teammate and take Ryland with him. He just locked onto her location and dematerialized, using her desperation as his only guide as to where he needed to be.

* * *

Sarah felt her soul disintegrating into a thousand pieces as she clutched her hand over the wound in her side. Strewn around her on the road were dozens of dying Calydons, she had destroyed. Her chest ached, and her heart felt like daggers were digging their way through it. She'd killed them all. Every last one.

They'd kept coming, one by one by one, goading her into attacking them to stay alive, forcing her to take one step closer to the death of her body and her spirit. Fever burned, her head ached, her vision was blurry, her mind numb with the horror of what she'd done.

There was one more assailant left. The one who was there to bring her down. The one who had been waiting to make his move until she was so worn down that she would have no more defenses.

"Go away," she whispered, her throat so raw from screaming that she could barely make a sound. "Please don't do this, Jacob."

But there he came, prowling around the end of her SUV, her blood dripping from his claws. Her younger brother's blue eyes were glowing blood red, bottomless pits of torment and violence. His tee shirt was spotted with her blood, his jeans torn. On his arms were the violent black brands in the shape of a sickle, too thick and too dark for a Calydon who'd come into his powers only two days ago. He was so much more than he should have been.

Dammit! How could he have succumbed the way the others had? This was her *brother*. Around his neck glittered the talisman she'd given him when he was sixteen, hoping it would be enough to keep the monster at bay. There it hung at his throat, taunting her for thinking she could save him, that somehow, this time, love would be enough to protect a male from the curse. "Come on, Jacob! Be stronger than this!"

He growled, an unearthly, inhuman sound that brought back nightmares of the night Mason had attacked. She scrambled backward, instinctively reaching for the baby that was no longer there, the one she hadn't been able to protect. Her hands closed over air, and for a second, she panicked, then reality came crashing back on her. There was no baby this time. It was just her, and her brother. "Jacob! Dammit! Don't do this!"

Something flickered in those red eyes, a flash of blue, and she realized he still had a chance. He wasn't lost entirely. "Jacob! Don't let this consume you! You're stronger than this—"

He stopped his approach and stared at her, his body coiled to attack.

She froze, afraid to trigger him. "Jacob," she urged. "It's me. Your sister. You love me."

Silence hung between them, and her heart began to pound with hope. Would he come back? Would he—

He attacked, launching himself at her.

She screamed, but she had no chance to get away before his claws sank into her stomach. Sarah gasped as pain rushed through her, and she saw the promise of death in his eyes. She knew she had no choice. Once again, she had no choice. "Damn all of you!"

He lunged for her heart, and she unleashed the white light buried within her. Her skin radiated out into the night with such intensity that the entire forest glowed.

Jacob screamed and stumbled off her, covering his eyes as his skin began to blister.

Sarah gasped as the backlash of her powers hit her. Pain knifed through her, and she clutched her stomach, gasping at the agony slicing through her. She fought to cut off her powers and end her attack before she could kill him, shoving aside the intense heat radiating from her, yanking it back into her and away from her brother.

Jacob was sprawled a few yards away, writhing as the light burned him. Sarah trembled, and tears streamed down her cheeks as she looked at the man she loved so dearly, dying in front of her. She pressed her palm against the wound in her belly as the shakes and nausea overwhelmed her. Hollowness began to fill her, a bottomless abyss of nothingness. *Death.* It was coming for her, ready to decimate the final shreds of her soul.

No! She couldn't succumb. She had to find faith again. There had to be something worth living for, something good inside her. Desperate, she searched her heart for something to believe in, but there was nothing there. Just the betrayal of her brother, the loss of so many she loved, the truth of so many lives she'd taken. There was nothing left to hold onto, nothing to pull herself out of the pit that was consuming her.

Jacob's eyes met hers, and she saw in them too much life. Horror welled through her as she realized that in her attempt to avoid killing him, she'd cut off her attack too soon. He wasn't debilitated enough. He was going to attack again.

Sarah watched in disbelief as Jacob began to drag himself toward her, his red eyes fixated on hers. "Don't," she warned. Frantically, she searched the woods, desperate to try to find another option, a way out. It couldn't end like this! "Don't do it."

He uncurled his claws, and tears filled her eyes. How could he be making this choice? Wasn't there anything left of the human being he used to be? Of the brother she once loved? She knew he'd been chosen for her, because the betrayal by her own brother was the final blow that would eviscerate every last shred of hope and faith from her soul. "Oh, come on!" she shouted at him. "I'm your damned sister, Jacob! You're a better man than this!"

Jacob didn't even hesitate, dragging himself closer and closer to her, the inexorable approach of doom. Was he too weak to teleport, or was he forcing her to watch his approach on purpose, to have each inch of progress destroy another part of her soul?

As she watched him, her heart began to fragment, piece by piece, the strings that had been barely holding it together for so long finally breaking. Weakly, she managed to raise one hand in warning, letting white light pulse from her palm. "I'll kill us both," she whispered.

His eyes glowed with excitement. "I know."

He knew. He was willing to sacrifice himself just to see her die. How on earth could he have been conscripted like this, turned so far from the person he used to be? "Dammit! I won't let this happen!" She fought to sit up, and dizziness sent her back down to her side as she struggled for breath. *Come on, Sarah! Fight!* She shoved herself up on her elbows. "Jacob—"

He jammed a claw between her shoulder blades and knocked her back toward the earth. Pain barreled through her, and the dark chasm inside her grew larger, threatening to overtake her—

Then she felt it again. That warmth in her mind. That protective male energy. She hadn't imagined it? It was real? Was there really someone out there who could help? *Hurry. Please hurry.*

I'm coming. The male voice was so fierce and furious in her mind that sudden hope flooded her like a great burst of sunshine.

Jacob froze, his hand suspended in midair over her throat as if he'd sensed it too.

"Someone is coming to save me," she whispered, her throat too dry to do more than rasp out the words, the deadliness of the stranger's voice reverberating through her. "Run, Jacob, before he gets here. He'll kill you." She had no doubt of that. She'd felt the violence pulsing through the stranger, and knew he wouldn't hesitate.

It was great, of course, to have some protector descend upon her like a gift from the heavens, but this was her brother, after all, and she didn't want him to die. There had still been flashes of blue in his eyes. He still might reclaim himself. She had to give him that chance. "Get out of here, Jacob!"

But he didn't retreat, and his forearm tensed to strike—

The night burst with sudden energy, and a huge Calydon warrior materialized beside her SUV. His torso was bare, covered in scars. His shoulders were tremendous and wide, and his fists were clenched around a pair of deadly spiked flails. He was strength and power, consumed with a ferocity that made the night thunder. He met her gaze, and for a split second, she felt the world grind to a halt, as if time had literally stopped from the force of their connection.

Then his gaze went to her trembling hand, where she was pressing so weakly and desperately against the wound in her side. Intense, violent fury darkened his face, and his body vibrated with aggression. She saw him fixate on Jacob, who was still crouched over her, his claws poised over her throat. The two warriors stared each other down, and she knew Jacob was trying to decide whether he could kill her before this warrior reached him.

Sudden terror consumed her, a sense of overwhelming loss at what would happen if these two warriors engaged. Everything was being held in the balance, dependent on the outcome of that moment. Both men had to live. *They both had to live.* She knew it with sudden certainty, with everything she had. "No, Jacob," she managed. "Don't do it—"

But before she could finish the words, Jacob slashed at her neck. The new warrior bellowed with rage, and he materialized at her side just as Jacob's claws raked across her throat. He jammed the flail in Jacob's chest and flung her brother into the forest as she grabbed at her neck, gasping at the pain.

Jacob landed with a thud, then scrambled to his feet and bolted into the darkness, fleeing to preserve his life and attack her another day. She grabbed the warrior's ankle as he started to fade to go after her brother. "No," she gasped, terrified he would finish off Jacob. "Let him go."

He looked down at her, and she saw the aggression and violence in his dark eyes, a jolting reminder that he was a Calydon warrior, a male she couldn't trust, an unpredictable enemy who would turn on her at any moment, the creature born to be her very downfall.

Stunned, she let her hand fall from his ankle. How could she have forgotten what he was? How could she have forgotten the lessons she'd learned so brutally? How could she have let herself be consumed by the relief she'd felt at his arrival?

The moment he sensed what she was, even on a subconscious level, he would kill her. There would be no way for him to stop himself. It was why he and all the other Calydons were created: to destroy her and her kind.

His eyes were black now, but they would soon turn red. They always did.

It was nighttime now, the kind of dark, moonless night that was the playground for his kind. She was alone with him in a stretch of forest, miles from humanity, still helpless from the punishment of using her powers against Jacob and the others. She had no defenses. No resources. No way to survive him when he turned on her.

But as the aftermath of her powers began to take over her, and the fever set in, she knew that without him, she wouldn't survive either.

* * *

She was dying.

Kane could feel the ebbing of her life force as her hand fell away from his ankle. Urgency coursed through him, and he crouched beside her, his Calydon instinct to hunt down her attacker vanishing in the face of her fading spirit. He put his hand over her side and swore when she tried to jerk away from him. "No, no," he said quietly. "I won't hurt you."

But there was terror on her face. Not random fear of what he was, a member of the Order of the Blade with a fearsome reputation. No, there was wisdom and a grim acceptance of reality in her blue eyes, as if she knew who he *truly* was. As if she had the answers he'd been seeking his whole life. Shock shot through him. "You know who I am," he said fiercely. "Who am I?"

"You're a Calydon," she rasped out, her voice hoarse, as if she'd been screaming for days.

A Calydon? That was all she saw? Disappointment coursed through him, the same loss he'd experienced so many times when he'd thought he had a lead on his past. How could he have been wrong this time? It felt like she was seeing right through him to his core.

"Go away," she whispered. "Now."

And leave her dying? He was almost insulted that she would even suggest it. He had no idea who she was, but he was consumed with the need to keep her safe, to protect her. "No."

Kane pressed more firmly against her belly, trying to stem the flow of blood. She was burning up, and what looked like hairline fractures were streaking across her skin. Tremors were shaking her, and he could see the wildness of pain in her eyes. "Tell me how to help you." He wanted to pick her up, but she looked so fragile, like she would shatter into a thousand fragments if he moved her. Damn. He had no concept of how to be gentle. He knew how to fight the bad guys, not how to handle someone so delicate she looked as if she would disintegrate in his arms.

She shook her head and tried to roll onto her side away from him, as if she were going to try to get up. "Just let me go. I think I can make it."

No chance was Kane letting her go. He carefully grasped her shoulders. The heat from her skin burned his fingers, and he swore at the intensity of it. What the hell was happening to her? "I can feel your spirit fading," he said. "Don't lie to me."

Her gaze flickered to him, vulnerability etched on her face, and for a moment, her shields fell. In that split second, he felt the true depths of her anguish, a torment that filled her soul, the burden of responsibility so great that it was destroying her. The black void within him surged in response, recognizing the pain within her, and he grimaced, struggling against the sudden onslaught of emptiness.

Her eyes widened. "What's wrong with you?"

"Nothing." He fought it back down as her body began to shake even more violently. She fell back to the ground with a thud that sounded like her skin had cracked even more, and she couldn't suppress a small moan. He instinctively reached for her, but she tried to scoot away from him.

"I'm here to help you." Refusing to allow her to reject his aid, he gently grasped her shoulders. What was she seeing when she looked at him? He was a damned hero to most people. The only ones who looked at him in terror, like this woman was doing, were the rogue Calydons when they realized Kane was going to cut them down. But he wasn't going to hurt her. There was simply no chance, no matter who she was. The urge to keep her safe was more powerful than anything he'd ever felt. It reverberated all the way to his soul, his need to protect her. She was safe with him, and he knew it, but she was still looking at him as if he were there for the sole purpose of killing her. "Why are you fighting me?"

She closed her eyes, and he felt the pulse in her energy as she fought for her life. "Because you'll have to kill me if you stay."

"Fuck that. I don't kill women." But the moment he said that, he knew it was a lie. He'd killed women before. Not many. Not with pleasure. But because the mission that drove him was bigger than the life of a single innocent, and as an Order member, he'd made an oath to protect humanity at any cost. But he wouldn't hurt her. Never her. Never this woman in his arms, whose blue eyes looked at him as if she saw to the very depths of who he was, in a way that no one else ever had.

"I'm different. You won't be able to stop yourself." Then another tremor shook her, and she gritted her teeth against the pain.

"Son of a bitch." Fuck her resistance to him. There was no way he could leave her like this. He could help her. He knew he could. He felt it in the very fiber of his being. He had a connection to her, one that went past his scars to the part of him that held his secrets. Something in the depths of his soul recognized her, but he didn't know what or why or how. All he knew was that he would lay down his damned life to protect her. The need to keep her safe was beyond anything he'd ever felt in his life.

Carefully, so gently, trying not to scare her, trying to make her understand he was there to help, he lifted her onto his lap, supporting her against his chest. "Tell me what to do," he demanded. "Tell me how to help you."

She shook her head, her eyes beginning to glaze. Desperation filled him, a sense of gaping loss consuming him. He was losing her. He knew he was. Because she wouldn't trust him to help her. "I'm not a damned murderer," he said. "Tell me what to do!" He couldn't keep the fierceness out of his voice, couldn't suppress his frustration with his inability to help her.

She closed her eyes, and said nothing. She was shutting him out. Seriously? She was going to risk death instead of accepting his help? What the hell? "What's your name?" he said urgently, trying to connect with her, to get her to trust him in time.

Sarah Burns.

Her voice was the faintest whisper in his mind, and rightness filled him at the intimacy of it. He leapt on the chance to connect with her, wrapping his spirit around hers and trying to warm her coldness. *My name is Kane Santiago. I won't hurt you. I swear it.* He took her hand and set it on his chest. *Can't you feel it?*

Her fingers curled into his chest, and electricity shot through him. He sucked in his breath, shocked by the intensity of her touch, by the current rippling through him. His entire being leapt in response, and the dark void trying to consume him roared in rebellion as his spirit turned toward Sarah, as if she were a great light that could hold off the darkness.

He knew in that moment that he needed her, on levels he couldn't even comprehend. She was his salvation, his hope, his only chance to defeat the monster trying to chase him. "Sarah!" He hugged her more tightly against him, demanding her response. "Tell me how to save you!"

I need your faith.

My faith? What the hell was that all about? How was that going to save her? *Where are your people? Do you have a healer I can take you to?* He didn't bother to ask about a regular doctor. He'd sensed that she wasn't completely human. The richness of her spirit was too intense, too compelling. The air was lush and rich around her, as if she filled the atmosphere with life. As if she filled *him* with life.

Her voice grew fainter in his mind. *Tell me something worth living for, Kane. Make me feel it.*

Something worth living for? Son of a bitch. That was the one thing he had no answers for. He knew only death. He knew only loss. He lived with a void, violence and an empty past.

Why do you get up every morning? Why do you decide to breathe another breath? She arched in his arms as another convulsion took her. *What do you live for?*

Kane swore. *I don't know. Answers. I want answers. I refuse to die until I find out who I was.*

She gasped in pain, and more cracks appeared in her skin.

Okay, so clearly not what she'd been looking for. Son of a bitch! What the hell did she want from him? All he did every day was protect the world from monsters, save innocents from a hell worse than death. That was his job, and now, here he was with one woman dying in his arms and he couldn't stop it?

Her relief cascaded through him, and he felt the warmth of their connection in his mind. *You save innocents, Kane. That's what matters to you.*

Fuck, yeah, I do, but that's not what I live for.

Tell me about someone you saved. A child. A woman. An innocent. Let me feel it. Show me something good to believe in. Her body started to shake more violently, and her eyes rolled back in her head. *Now,* she gasped. *Now, Kane, now!*

He didn't get it. How would a story help her? But he didn't care. He tried to think back to all the times he'd gone to battle, all the deaths he'd caused, trying to remember one of the innocents he had saved. All he could recall was the death, the destruction, the carnage he'd left behind. The blood on his hands—

Seriously, Kane? Sarah's voice was weaker now, barely audible. *That's what you give me when I ask for faith? That's all you have? I thought you had more...* Her energy grew fainter, colder, and he felt her distance herself from him. *You gave me hope. You were my last chance. Hope dies...*

He was losing her! Kane swore, searching his mind for something worth remembering in his damned life. A child flashed through his mind. A small child. *A baby boy.*

Anguish arced through her, and she gripped his arm. *A boy? Tell me. Tell me.*

He couldn't remember. He just had an image in his head of a child. *Brown hair. Dark eyes.* Something caught in his gut, something important, a gnawing certainty that the child was important. Who was it? Why couldn't he remember?

More, Kane. How did you save him? Show me his innocence. Sarah's voice was urgent, desperate, and he knew they were out of time.

He swore, unable to remember any more about the child. Frantically, he tried to think of another. *I—*

Sudden movement caught his attention, and Sarah's original assailant materialized in front of him again. There was a rush of heat, and then another ten Calydons appeared, teleporting from hell knew where. Kane's weapons burned with the need to attack, but he couldn't risk engaging.

Sarah needed his help, and he wouldn't abandon her to fight.

The Calydons lunged at him. Kane immediately pictured the spot where he'd left his teammate and dematerialized, taking Sarah with him.

Chapter Three

Ryland spun around, his weapons ready as Kane appeared behind him. Ryland's gaze immediately went to the woman in Kane's arms. Sarah's eyes were closed, her breathing shallow, her heartbeat too damn faint. "What's going on?" Ryland asked, moving into a battle stance before Kane even spoke.

Kane didn't waste words. "Tell me a fairytale. Now!"

"What?" Ryland stared at him as if he'd gone insane. "What are you talking about?"

"She needs to hear a story of angels, goodwill and redemption. I got nothing to offer. Talk to me."

Ryland glanced down at the woman, and something in the hard lines of his face softened. Kane was shocked by the transformation on Ryland's face. The warrior was always angry, always on the edge of violence, fury, and lack of control. And yet there was something on his face, an easing of tension, an expression of actual humanity as he looked at the woman in Kane's arms.

Kane instantly tightened his grip on her. "She's mine."

"Fuck that." Ryland strode across the earth right toward Kane, ignoring Kane's growl of warning. "How in hell's name did a bastard like you find an angel?"

Kane swore as Sarah groaned in his arms. He pulled her more closely against him, trying to infuse her with his strength. "I need a story of angels, you dumb ass. Not compliments about her."

"Shit, man, don't you get it?" Ryland looked up at him, and for the first time since Kane had known him, the warrior's eyes were green instead of the bottomless black pits they always were. Was that Ryland's real eye color, not the black they'd always been? "She's an angel," Ryland said quietly, almost reverently. "The real deal. Put her down. You aren't worthy of holding her. None of us are."

"An angel?" Stunned, Kane looked down at Sarah. Her dark brown hair was tangled around her shoulders, her face ashen, tight lines of suffering around the corners of her mouth. Her throat was still bleeding from the attack, and more blood was oozing from her side. There were bruises all over her throat, and she was trembling violently against him. Protectiveness surged over him, and he knew it didn't matter what she was. Right now, she was a woman who was dying in his arms, and he had to stop it. "Tell me a story of redemption, Ryland," he said quietly, trying to soothe her with the tones of his voice. "Without it, she dies."

Ryland immediately went down on one knee, and bowed his head, a show of respect so far from the rogue warrior he always was. "My mother," he said quietly. "She was the most beautiful soul that ever graced this earth."

Kane was stunned by the raw emotion of Ryland's words, of the depth of reverence in his voice. Ryland was a cold killing machine, who cared only about following his own path, about revenge, about his own brand of justice. He was a warrior who felt nothing, who saw no beauty, who had no depth to his soul other than death, pain and anger, and yet his sincerity about his mother was so evident that Kane could feel the other warrior's emotion. "Son of a bitch, Ryland," he said softly, staring at the warrior he thought he knew. "Who the hell are you?"

Ryland's head snapped up. "Don't swear in her presence, you bastard. She's a fucking angel, and deserves far more than a piece of scum like you or I could ever offer her. Don't ever forget it."

Kane. Sarah's voice melted through his mind, and he swore at how weak she sounded.

Listen to Ryland. He's telling you about his mother. Kane knelt in front of Ryland, meeting Ryland's grim face. "Talk, Ryland. Fucking talk."

"My mother died trying to keep me safe," Ryland said urgently, looking at Sarah. "I'll never forget the blood, the way she screamed when the—"

Kane hit Ryland in the side of the head. "What the hell's that? How is that a story of hope and faith?"

Ryland's eyes darkened to black again. "She's my mother. She is all that was good in this world."

"She died? How is that good?" Jesus, did the man have no sense of humanity? Even Kane knew there was no hope and faith in a story about dead mothers.

"To save the sorry ass of her fucked up son, yeah," Ryland snapped.

"That deserves a chorus in the heavens by the angels themselves."

Kane. Sarah's fingers moved weakly, and he caught her hand. *It has to be you. I can't feel his emotions. Only yours.*

Shit. His emotions weren't the kind that could save an angel, or anyone else for that matter. Kane looked at Ryland, desperate. "Help me, man. The feel good story has to come from me, but that's not my thing. I got nothing."

Ryland met his gaze. "Dante. It has to be Dante. Tell her about Dante."

Sudden grief poured through Kane at the thought of their leader who'd been assassinated so recently. "I can't—"

I feel that, Sarah said. *You loved him. Tell me. Who are you thinking about?*

Jesus. Emotions? She wanted him to talk about his emotions? He was a male. He didn't do emotions—

Ryland's machete was suddenly at Kane's throat. "You will get in touch with your emotions if I have to carve them out of you. You give the angel what she wants. Now."

Kane swallowed, the blade drawing blood as he met the eyes of the one man who understood how much it had broken him when Dante had died. *Dante Sinclair saved my life, Sarah. He found me in a sewer, left for dead. I was covered in scars. I was a violent, deadly bastard ready to cut off any hand that tried to help me, and he didn't give a shit.* Kane ground his jaw against the sudden swell of emotions, against the memories of that day when he'd been down in the rotting sewage, with no idea of what he was, who he was or how he'd gotten there. He could still recall that aching sense of loss and emptiness inside him, nearly crushing him with the void.

When Dante had reached out and extended his hand to him, it had been a lifeline Kane had never forgotten.

He saved you? Sarah's fingers tightened in his.

He stared at her fingers curled so desperately in his hand, at the first sign of strength he'd seen from her. Her hand was so small, so slight, so vulnerable compared to his callused palms that were twice her size. The need to protect pulsed through him, and he clasped his hand more securely around hers, cherishing her small, vulnerable outreach. *Yeah, he did. Dante gave me hope when I had none. I didn't deserve it, Sarah. I was covered in scars, and my weapons were still bloody. I'd killed someone. Maybe many. We don't know. But Dante didn't care. He hauled me out of that rancid stink, and he offered me a chance to start again. I'll never forget that.* Emotions burned in Kane's chest, grief for his leader that he hadn't allowed himself to acknowledge since Dante had died. He'd shut it down, like any halfway decent warrior would do, and as hell was his witness, he knew why he did it.

It sucked to feel this kind of pain. He didn't want to think about Dante being dead. He just didn't.

Thank you, Sarah whispered. *That's beautiful. Your love for him is so powerful.*

Love? Fuck that. What was love? He honored and respected Dante, yeah, but there was no man love between them. Kane shifted uncomfortably, knowing that if love was what she wanted him to describe, he had no chance. He wouldn't know love if it stabbed him right in the eye.

Ryland jabbed him with the machete. "Don't be an ass. Pay attention to the angel."

The angel... Kane looked down at Sarah, and saw the faintest trace of a smile at the corners of her mouth. Her eyes were still closed, her body still trembling, the cracks still visible on her skin. But that smile. That faint, barely-there smile hovering at the corners of her mouth struck something deep inside him, something he'd never felt before, a soul-deep sense of rightness, of connection, of knowing that he'd done right, that he'd helped her.

He sifted his fingers through her tangled hair, needing to touch her. Her eyelids fluttered and then opened a sliver. Her eyes were a brilliant blue, like the sky on a clear summer day when the sun owned the earth and there was no one he had to kill. "Sarah," he whispered, her name like a gift of salvation on his lips.

Her trembling fingers closed around his hand, and the rest of the world fell away until it was just them. *No one has said my name with such reverence in so long,* she said. *It sounds beautiful the way you say it.*

It is beautiful, Sarah.

She smiled faintly, and her fragility tore at his heart. "Kane," she whispered, her voice so raw and scratched that something inside him cracked. "Tell me what you see when you look at me."

"What I see?" He could feel her desperation, and knew that she was still searching for more positive energy to cling to. God, this was taxing him to his limits. He could slay a thousand demons for her, but feed her stories of hope and faith? He had no foundation for playing that role.

Ryland leaned closer, his shoulder bumping against Kane's as he peered at Sarah. "Tell her that she has eyes more radiant than the turquoise feathers of the hyacinth macaw as it takes flight across the Brazilian landscape, with the sun reflecting off its wings."

"A Brazilian landscape?" Kane stared at his teammate in shock. "Are you kidding me? Aren't you supposed to be nearly insane, almost rogue and a veritable bastard?"

"This is an angel," Ryland whispered reverently. "Don't you get it? She's why there's any good left on this earth. All goodness comes from the angels. Without angels, it's only darkness." He bowed his head to Sarah. "We honor you and serve you."

Sarah laughed softly, and she brushed her fingers over Ryland's shoulder. "Thank you," she said quietly.

Kane froze, his muscles going rigid the moment he saw her touch Ryland. Sudden fury burned within him as Ryland shuddered from the touch. A fierce possessiveness surged through Kane, and the brands in his arms vibrated with the need to unleash his weapons and take down his teammate for getting so close to her. "Back off," Kane said quietly, unable to keep the threat out of his voice. "Now."

Ryland lifted his head and met his gaze. Defiance flared in Ryland's eyes. "You don't get to claim her, Santiago. She's a gift to everyone." Ryland's fingers tightened over the handle of his machete. "You will not clip her wings and drag her into your personal hell."

Kane. Sarah's voice was urgent, and she gripped his arm. *I need you. Now.* Her body was shaking again, and her face had paled.

Fierce protectiveness surged through Kane, and he didn't give a shit about Ryland anymore. Sarah was what mattered. Only Sarah.

He hugged her more securely against his chest, as if he could protect her with his body. He would be the one to tell her what he saw when he looked at her, not Ryland. He didn't have stories about love and hope, but this question he could answer. "When I look at you," he said fiercely, "I see a woman who has fought bravely to save herself. A woman with courage, who, despite all that she's dealing with, still has the ability to fight for hope and faith." He tightened his grip on her as her eyes fluttered open and she met his gaze. "I have no hope in my life," he admitted. "I kill to save the world, an endless spiral with no answers, and yet you touch my soul in a way I didn't know was possible."

Kane. She set her hand on his arm. *That's beautiful.*

He felt himself falling into the blue of her eyes, tumbling so fast he couldn't stop himself and didn't want to. He took her hand in his, tangling their fingers together. "In you, I see a beauty and a purity that exists nowhere else in this world." He didn't just see it. He'd felt it from that first moment, a depth to his soul that he hadn't accessed in so long. "I don't know anything about you," he acknowledged, "but you're like this burst of humanity into my soul that I never thought I would feel."

Sarah's eyes began to glisten with unshed tears. "You have such passion," she said. "I forgot what that was like." She rested her palm against his cheek, her fingers still trembling.

Rightness cascaded through Kane, and he set his hand over hers, holding her palm against his skin. The moment stilled, intensity filling him with such desire and need for her that it physically hurt. He could feel the thud of his heart in his chest, the rush of blood through his veins, and the burning of fire in every cell of his body. It was agonizingly painful, as if his entire being was fighting to come alive, to tear down the walls that had kept it locked down for so long.

He swore, tightening his grip on her as the darkness that had been chasing him for so long roared to life, trying to suck him away from this place that Sarah had brought him to. Agonizing loss assailed him, terror at losing this sense of humanity she'd given him. He didn't want to retreat back into a place where he didn't feel, where he couldn't hear his own heartbeat. He wanted to stay in the light with Sarah.

Her eyes widened, and she tightened her grip on him. "What's happening to you?"

"I don't know," he rasped out, fighting at the onslaught of darkness, against the void struggling to consume him. It felt like the closer he got to connecting with Sarah and his humanity, the stronger the darkness inside him became. A battle for his soul.

"It's happening again, isn't it?" Ryland was beside him again, his face intense. "What the hell is it, Santiago?"

"I don't know." Kane's back bowed from the pain, and his soul screamed in protest as the blackness swirled through him. "Son of a bitch—"

The air pressure shifted, and Kane instinctively threw himself over Sarah, reacting to the threat even before he'd had time to register what it was. He pinned her to the ground as a sickle careened through the air and slammed into his shoulder, right where her head had just been.

Ryland leapt to his feet with a battle roar, while Kane shielded Sarah with his body as dozens more weapons hurtled through the air, slamming into his back in an attempt to harm her. "What the fuck's going on?" He cradled his arms around her head, blocking her with his shoulders as he shouted at Ryland. Sarah curled beneath him, accepting his protection and burrowing into the shield he was offering her.

"Remember those honeymooners from Hollywood?" Ryland grunted, as if he were striking hard against the assailant.

Oh, yeah, Kane remembered the rogues with the manicures. "Yeah, why? Did they come back to life or something?" He grimaced as another blade slammed into his back, and he tucked Sarah more tightly under him, trying to cover every inch of her trembling body. He needed to get up and help Ryland fight, but he couldn't move away from her. Every blade was coming for her, not him. Outrage surged through him at the realization that their assailants were trying to attack *her*. Who the hell took on an innocent woman?

"Apparently, they have a big ass family and the reunion is here," Ryland said.

Damn. More rogues? Where were they coming from?

It's my brother, Sarah said, her face buried against Kane's chest. *He's trying to destroy me.*

Your brother? And to think I always wanted to know who my family was. Kane turned his head slightly, and saw that it was the same warrior who'd been after Sarah when Kane had first arrived on the scene. How had he found them after Kane had teleported?

But it wasn't just the one guy. He'd brought a dozen warriors with him. All of them with red glowing eyes, unfashionably long claws, and the same intensity as the two rogues that had been such a tough take-down before. Kane itched to fight them, but he knew he couldn't. His number one priority was protecting the woman in his arms. "We need to bail, Ry." There was no way they could engage and keep Sarah safe at the same time.

Ryland didn't bother to answer. He just continued to defend Sarah and Kane with his weapons as he stepped on Kane's ankle to create body contact between them. "Go!"

Kane instantly dematerialized, taking Ryland and Sarah with him. But as the woods disappeared, he met the gaze of Sarah's brother, and saw in them a glittering truth.

The bastard would be right behind him.

* * *

Tears burned in Sarah's eyes, as Kane teleported them away from her brother. "He's not going to give up," she told Kane, her heart aching at the thought.

"Your brother?"

"Yes. He's the one tracking me. The others don't have the blood connection to me, so they can't track me without him. It's Jacob." Sarah felt the strength that Kane had given her when he'd shared his emotions with her begin to fade, chased away by the visceral reminder of Jacob's betrayal.

Dammit. No! She couldn't afford to be weakened. She had to stay strong. Faith and hope were all she had to sustain her. Fighting against the nausea, she opened her eyes to focus on Kane, to let him fill her world the way he had a few minutes ago.

He was looking past her, searching the woods he'd taken them to. His jaw was whiskered, his eyes blazing with lethal determination as he rapidly assessed their situation, engaging in urgent discussion with his teammate as the two warriors evaluated their options.

Kane was pure elemental Calydon, with his huge muscles, the black brands on his arms, and the gaping emptiness inside him. She'd felt Kane's void all the way to her core. As empty as her brother was, Kane was all that, and so much more. There was nothing left of who he might have been: his humanity and warmth was so buried. All that remained was the monster, the shell, the demon that possessed good men and turned them into creatures of death, destruction and betrayal. Kane was everything that she'd feared for so long. He was the epitome of the creatures that had stolen everything from her. He was her greatest nightmare, and she was trapped in his arms.

And yet, in his embrace, tucked against his bare chest, she felt safe. As if he'd erected some tremendous shield that could keep the danger at bay. She should fear him. For heaven's sake, he knew she was an angel. Both men did. And yet neither one of them had moved to hurt her. How was it possible? Was there more to them than the deadly creatures she'd grown up defending against?

But even as she asked the question, she knew the answer was yes. The depth of Kane's pain was extraordinary, so tremendous that it had touched her heart. A man with nothing but emptiness and death in his soul wouldn't be capable of feeling such pain. She wanted to heal him, to help him, to give him relief.

Sarah's chest tightened at the realization, at the gift that he offered her by making her want to help him. It had been so long since she'd wanted to reach out. She'd been focused only on her survival and doing her duty, and she hadn't had the energy or inspiration to help or heal anyone else for so long. Until Kane.

He looked down at her, and a smile flashed across his face. "Nice to see you looking conscious."

She smiled, her heart warming at the way his face lit up when he looked at her. "I think you can put me down."

"No chance." He actually tightened his grip on her. "What's the deal with your brother and his buddies? How can they teleport? Why do they want to kill you—"

Her brother flashed beside them, grabbed her and then began to dematerialize again, snatching her right out of Kane's arms. Her skin lit up in self-defense before she could even think about it, the white light bursting over the clearing in a blinding attack. Jacob swore and dropped her, but before she'd even hit the ground, another one of Jacob's teammates grabbed her and started to disappear. She took him out, and then another, and another and another. So fast, milliseconds between each grab and attack. She had no time to regroup, no time to heal, just more death, more pain, more—

"Come on!" Kane flashed beside her, yanked her out of another male's arms and dematerialized.

She didn't even know where he took her. Didn't even know where they landed. The agony was too intense from the aftermath of using her powers to harm and the weight of her brother's betrayal. It all had hit her too soon, when she was barely recovered from the last time. The cost ate away at her, ripping through her humanity, eviscerating the very part of her that gave her life. The pain in her head was crushing her like a vise, her skin fragmenting, her blood boiling over, burning through her veins, poisoning her body.

"Hang on, Sarah," Kane ordered. "Don't die on me, sweetheart."

Even through her pain, Sarah almost laughed at his command. The man had so much to learn about angels and women if he really thought that order was going to work. Then her body began to convulse, and she forgot about everything but trying to stay alive.

* * *

Kane swore as Sarah's body spasmed in his arms. With her brother tracking them so closely, he had no time to stop and help her. He had to keep them moving until he could get far enough ahead to stop. "Don't let go of me," he shouted at Ryland. "We need to keep going."

Ryland's face was grim, and his fingers dug into his arm as Kane flashed them to another spot. They'd barely materialized when he teleported them again. And then again. And again. A dozen times, in a myriad of directions, until his senses were screaming from overload and strain.

He didn't dare wait or delay, knowing he needed to create a tangled web long enough to give them breathing room. Again and again he took the three of them, his body bowed under the strain. He felt Sarah weaken in his arms, drained by the effort of dematerializing and then rebuilding.

Kane finally stopped by a stream, a hundred miles from where he'd begun, a place in southern Oregon he knew well from years of training as an Order member. The woods belonged to Quinn Masters, one of the most deadly Order members alive, and it was his acreage that they used to train. In these woods, they were on Order turf, even if the rest of the team wasn't actually present.

Kane gently lowered Sarah to the damp earth, and Ryland dropped beside him, his head bowed as he fought for breath.

"Damn," Ryland gasped, his hands braced on the ground. "You should hire yourself out for kids' parties. You'd make millions. That was impressive, Santiago. I had no idea you could do that."

"I'm a talented guy. What can I say?" Kane set Sarah down and scooped water out of the pure stream, ignoring the trembling of his own muscles. He'd never attempted anything like he'd just done, and quite frankly, he was damned pleased he'd managed to do it without leaving body parts strewn all over Oregon. "Drink, Sarah." He propped her up and eased water into her mouth, relieved when he saw her swallow. *Sarah. Concentrate on me. Just hang in there a little longer.*

He felt a flicker of a response from her, but no words. Shit. She was too far gone. Urgency thrummed through him. He had to get her alone, get the space and time to heal her. "Here's the plan," he said as Ryland shoveled the cold water over his own head. "I'll drop you at the mansion, and you alert the team. I'll give you ten minutes to assemble them, and then I'll come back there and stay. Our pursuers will land at the mansion and keep going if I'm not there, so let them go through the first time. When I'm back and the bastards show up, we'll be ready."

Ryland nodded grimly. "Good. I hate running. Let's take these fuckers down." His eyes flickered toward Sarah. "How's the angel?"

"Not good."

Ryland met his gaze, flecks of green in his dark eyes. "I can't believe you're the one who can help her. Lucky bastard."

Kane grinned. "It's because I always go to church on Sundays."

Ryland snorted. "Hah. You've shed more blood on hallowed ground than any of the rest of us. You should burn in hell for even touching her."

"You can take that up with her when this shit is done."

"I will." Ryland's eyes darkened, and he set his hand on Kane's shoulder. "I don't like bullies who try to hurt angels. Let's bring these bastards down."

"You got it."

Kane.

His heart jumped at the soft voice, and he looked down at her, hoping to see her looking at him, but her eyes were still closed, her body limp in his arms. *Sarah?*

Don't kill my brother. He has to live.

Kane grimaced. *Sweetheart, he's the one who's bringing those assassins to you. He has to be stopped.*

Her agony filled him, slicing through him like a great wall of pain. *No, he has to live. Promise me.*

The intensity of her voice was so strong, Kane knew he couldn't say no. *I'll try, but if I have to choose between you and him, it's going to be you.* He wanted to offer her the world, but he wouldn't lie to her. If he had to make a choice, there was only one decision he would make.

You're my only hope, Kane. You're all I have. Her eyes flickered open, and he felt his soul stop at the anguish in those blue depths. *Please.*

He swore, and looked at Ryland. "She says her brother has to live."

Ryland grinned, respect flashing in his eyes instead of the aggravation Kane had expected. "That's just like an angel, isn't it? Wanting to save the man who's trying to kill her?" He slapped Kane's shoulder, his amusement fading. "This chick is so going to get fucked up hanging out with us, Santiago. We need to get her away from us as soon as possible. I won't destroy an angel."

"Yeah, me either." Kane tucked Sarah more closely against his chest. Tremors were wracking her body, and he knew that they were almost out of time. Could she even survive the next fifteen minutes that he had planned for her?

She had to. He would make sure of it.

Chapter Four

Kane stumbled as he materialized for the second time in the courtyard of Dante's mansion, the former abode of their deceased leader that had become the working headquarters of the Order of the Blade. Ryland caught him as he almost went down, his black eyes blazing. "We're ready."

His head still spinning from the magnitude of energy he'd had to expend to keep teleporting himself and Sarah, while ensuring their safe recovery each time, Kane looked around and felt intense relief fill him at the sight of the Order of the Blade surrounding him. His boys had his back, as they always did for each other.

Almost the entire team was assembled, weapons out, battle stances engaged. Ryland. Quinn Masters, their acting leader until Dante's replacement could be identified. Gideon Roarke. Thano Savakis, with his damned arrogant grin that hid a lethal talent that far surpassed the thirty-five years he'd been alive. Elijah Ross, who had finally begun to put on weight since his ordeal. Zach Roderick and Gabe Watson rounded it out. All accounted for except Ian Fitzgerald, who had vanished several weeks ago, carrying the body of the woman who looked like his dead *sheva*. No one had been able to find him since, and that wasn't good. Ian was a dedicated team member, and to have him disappear without a trace was an indication of something being seriously wrong.

Standing with the team were two new additions: Drew Cartland, Dante's son, who had more powers than any rookie should and his uncle, Vaughn McIntyre. Drew was a major concern for the team: as the son of their former leader, one of the greatest warriors ever, he should have fit in with the Order smoothly, but there was also something ominous lurking beneath the surface that had them all on alert, watching him carefully. Was it the residual contamination from the battle they'd had with one of the founders of their race, or was it something more ominous?

Beside Drew stood Vaughn, the kid's protector, a deadly fighter with a heritage he refused to reveal. It was a daunting crew, and Kane grinned. Good luck to the playboys from Hollywood. Everything was about to change.

Quinn's swords were out, his body tense with readiness for battle. His dark hair was spiked and short, and his brown eyes were blazing. "Ryland filled us in," Quinn said. "Anything else you can add before they show up?"

"They won't be weakened by all the teleporting I just did," Kane said, shifting Sarah in his arms to tuck her more securely against his chest, preparing against her brother showing up and trying to snatch her again. "They'll have been taking turns teleporting the rest of the team, so they'll all be fresh. The leader is the one who can track Sarah. He has to be stopped."

"No," Sarah protested, lightly hitting her fist against Kane's chest. "Don't kill him. Jacob has to live."

Quinn met Kane's gaze, and the two men exchanged silent agreement. There would be no way to hold her brother since he could teleport. They didn't have a lot of options.

Kane. Sarah touched his face, and he looked down, grimacing when he saw how vulnerable she looked. Her lips were almost blue from lack of circulation, and there were so many cracks on her skin it looked like a puff of wind would fragment her. *I will die if he dies.*

Kane felt the truth of her words, and he swore. It was one thing to do his best to honor the fact she loved her brother and didn't want him to die. That was admirable, as Ryland had said, but it wasn't going to stop him from doing what he had to do to save her life. If, however, killing her brother meant she would die... "Shit, Quinn, we have to keep him alive—"

There was a shift in the air pressure and Jacob flashed beside Kane. He started to dissolve with Sarah, and her skin flashed white as she knocked him on his ass. Kane struck instantly, cracking his flail against the side of the younger warrior's head, trying to knock him out without actually killing him. The Calydon stumbled, and then regained his balance. His eyes burned with red fire, and Kane knew the kid had decided to engage instead of just stealing his sister.

Excellent. That was exactly what he wanted. A fight. If the kid was fighting, he wasn't going to be trying to disappear with Sarah, and it gave Kane more options to deal with him.

The night filled with the crack of Calydon weapons exploding.

Hell descended upon them as Calydons appeared out of thin air, attacking the Order with such intensity that four Order members were down within a second. They were back on their feet instantly, but the mere fact the newcomers had gotten the jump on them said much about the quality of their opponent.

"Hot damn," Thano shouted, a shit-eating grin on his face. "This is going to be fun!" He let out a Tarzan battle cry and then charged into the fray, swinging his halberd like a crazy man.

"Take her out of here, Kane," Quinn shouted as he cut down one of their assailants. "We've got them."

"Not yet." Sarah was shaking violently in his arms, her life force so weak that she wasn't even holding onto him anymore, but Kane couldn't leave until Jacob had been shut down, or the kid would follow them.

Jacob leapt to his feet and charged them. Kane swung his flail at the same time Ryland hurled his machete. Their weapons sandwiched Jacob's head with a sickening crack, and the young warrior fell to the ground and didn't get up.

Kane and Ryland exchanged grim glances. There was only a slim chance at best that the kid could recover from that. They'd crushed his skull. Mission accomplished to keep Sarah safe, but to keep her brother alive?

Shit.

A roar of fury arose from Jacob's team, and Kane covered Sarah with his arms as he blocked a dagger hurtling toward her head. "Get her out of here!" Ryland shouted as he spun to engage.

"Jacob!" Sarah tore herself out of Kane's arms with unexpected strength. Kane grabbed for her, missing her as she raced across the manicured lawn and fell beside her brother. Tears streamed down her cheeks as she collapsed beside him, twisting at Kane's gut. Shit. It was his fault. He'd done that. He'd caused it. Seeing Sarah's grief suddenly made the "sacrifice one to save many" feel like a philosophy he could no longer stand behind.

"Jacob," she sobbed, taking her brother's hand and pressing it to her heart.

Kane had to look away, his own chest tightening as her grief filled him. It made him think of Dante, of the lives he'd taken in the name of duty, of the tears that had been shed when the Order had finished doing what they had to do.

One of the rogues saw Sarah and hurled his spear at her. "Sarah!" Kane shouted in warning as he tried to dematerialize to get to her before the weapon did.

Sarah didn't even look up, she was so intent on her brother's state, and Kane's body tingled but nothing happened. Too drained? Now? What the hell? *"Come on!"* He summoned every last ounce of strength he had and teleported himself. He materialized right beside Sarah a split second before the spear would have hit her. The spear plunged deep into his chest, piercing his heart, and he swore as he went down beside her.

The pain was brutal, and he felt the last of his reserves rush to protect his heart from the injury.

"Get out of here," Ryland yelled again. "Now!"

Kane rolled onto his side as Ryland blocked a steel arrow headed toward Sarah, quickly assessing the situation. Even though Jacob was down, his team hadn't abandoned the battle. If anything, they were even more aggressive now, as if they realized this was their last chance at Sarah because they couldn't track her without Jacob. The Order had formed a ring of protection around Kane and Sarah, but there were too many attackers, coming too fast, with the one goal of getting to Sarah. Shit. They were out of time.

"Sarah," he growled, as he yanked the spear out of his chest "Take my hand."

She looked over at him, and he was stunned by the absolute devastation in her eyes. The anguish, the loss, the betrayal. *Kane. My brother...he's dying.* There was so much vulnerability and fear in her voice that he was overwhelmed with a need to protect her, to relieve her pain. Then, as he watched, her eyes rolled back in her head and she collapsed.

"Sarah!" Kane lunged for her as three Calydons broke through the ring of protection and charged toward them. Three others disappeared from sight on the outside of the circle, and he knew they were going to teleport inside, directly to Sarah. His fingers closed over hers as a Calydon appeared beside her, already lowering his battle axe toward her head.

The instant Kane felt her fingers against his, he called up all his power to teleport them again. It surged through both of them like an electrical shock, and he felt his body disintegrate as the blade came down toward Sarah's head.

There was a loud crack, and then they were gone.

* * *

Sarah was falling, falling, falling. It was dark. The pain was so intense. And her soul was like the blackest doom, a cavern of hopelessness welling up inside her. Tears bled from her heart, her mind filled with all the images that had tormented her for so long: her baby, her beautiful baby, taken down by the man she'd loved. Her parents, covered in blood, tossed aside by the man she'd given her heart to.

She felt that same despair and grief that she'd felt as she crawled across the wooden floor toward the door, trying to escape from the man she'd trusted with everything that was important to her. The feel of the cool metal doorknob sliding through her fingers as he grabbed her ankle and dragged her back toward him.

Again, she was staring into those red eyes of death and hatred, eyes she'd known and loved since they were toddlers. The man who'd grown up as her best friend, and then become her lover, her husband, and the father of her baby. She felt that anguished betrayal as he threw her down, his blood-stained axe in his hand as he reared back to destroy her—

Sarah. Come back to me.

The voice was like an electric shock, blasting through the memories consuming her. Kindness. Safety. Help. The words bounced through her mind, emotions that seemed so foreign to her, and yet familiar. Like she'd once known them. Like they'd once meant something to her.

Before all the death.

Before her brother had tried to kill her.

Before he'd killed Nonny... Grief surged through Sarah as she suddenly remembered what was clenched in her fist. Her grandmother's necklace, the one she never removed. She'd found it in her brother's hand. He'd killed Nonny. *He'd really killed her.*

Despair flooded Sarah, consuming her, yanking her down. All she'd fought for, all she'd worked for, gone. Taken by those she'd trusted the most. The ones she'd given her life to protect—

Sarah. It's Kane. Come on, sweetheart. Come back to me.

Again, his voice broke through the despair sucking her down. This time, she felt his urgency, his pain, his stress. For her? Was he hurt? Sudden emotion leapt through her, a connection to his soul. Desperately, she reached for it, trying to hold onto him as an anchor, but it slithered out of her grasp, an elusive wisp of hope. She struggled to focus on him, but images of her brother kept floating into her mind. *Kane? Help me. I can't find you.* She tried to reach for him, but she couldn't move her arms, couldn't seem to connect with him.

She felt cold. So cold. Her skin hurt. Hard to breathe. Hard to think. Her mind was getting fuzzy. The light...fading...the flame inside her...the white light...getting smaller...*Kane!* She screamed his name, terrified of what was happening. The light couldn't go out. It couldn't go out!

The minute I heard your voice when I was in the woods, my entire soul came to life.

She struggled to understand his words, to grasp what he was

saying, but her white light grew fainter. *Kane!*

Something warm settled on top of her. A heavy weight. Comforting, strong heat trying to penetrate the deep coldness settling in her body. Kane's body. On top of hers. Surrounding her with his strength. With his power. *Don't you understand, Sarah? My soul has always been this empty void. I can barely feel. I can barely connect with people. I feel so little.*

His aching emptiness touched her, drawing tears to her eyes.

My only mission has been to protect humanity. To make a difference. To save another life. And another. It was all that kept me going.

Sarah felt the truth of his words, the emptiness inside him that had been filled only by his knowledge that he was saving innocents. There was nothing else in him, no heart, no soul, no passion. Just the emptiness of honor and duty.

Until I heard your voice, Sarah. She felt his hands frame her face, and she tried to touch him, but she couldn't move her hands. Couldn't act. Her body felt too heavy, her limbs like dead weights. *When I heard your voice, it was as if something plunged straight past the emptiness inside me and brought it to life. It hurt, and the pain felt so unbelievably amazing. The raw, unbearable emotion of being alive...it's incredible, Sarah. What kind of incredible gift is that? You need hope and faith? You're the one who already has it. You gave it to me the minute you reached out and found me. I won't let you die, because you are the one damn thing in my life that has ever made my heart beat. Do you hear me?* His hands tightened on her face. *You are my salvation, Sarah. You are the first breath of hope I've had in five hundred years.*

Sarah felt his pain in every fiber of her being, and she felt his disbelief, his awe, his raw, untamed, desperate *hope* that she could save him. His emotions plunged deep inside her, awakening that part of her that had lost faith, that had given up, that had abandoned that which gave her life.

The white light inside her stopped fading, hovering in the balance, trying to decide which way to go.

Kane. She reached for him, and this time she felt his face beneath her hands. The moment her fingers touched his skin, electricity leapt through her. Life. Passion. Fire. Hope. It was as if he were the very source of life she'd been searching for. He was her chance. He was the hope for humanity.

He was so close, but still out of reach. She needed more of him. She needed all of him. She needed all he had to give her. The white light flickered, and she screamed in protest, unable to pull herself out of the chasm she'd fallen into so deeply. *Kane!*

You are mine, Sarah. The words were almost violent, thrusting past her shields and assaulting her fading light. Then his fingers tightened in her hair, his body tensed against her, and he kissed her, a kiss that claimed her very soul and offered her his. It plunged deep inside her, past the darkness, past the despair, past the approaching death, right to the light that burned in her very core.

A tiny spark flickered. One spark. One spark of life, of renewal, of hope.

Yes. The word burned deep in her soul, calling to Kane, asking him for all that he had.

Yes. His answer was fierce in her mind, and then he clasped her face and deepened the kiss, an almost violent assault that demanded her response, that allowed no room to ignore him. It was a kiss of ownership and connection, a forced merging of their spirits. It was so full of intensity and strength that it stripped away all her despair, hopelessness, and abandoned faith. Instead, the kiss ignited such passion, yearning and fire within her that it almost hurt.

The kiss was everything she needed. Kane was everything she needed. This kiss was their future, their hope that something good still existed in this life. She flung her arms around him and kissed him back, opening herself completely to him, entrusting him with her very soul... exactly as she'd sworn never to do again.

After her soul mate had murdered her family, Sarah shut herself down to save herself, and now her only chance to survive was to throw her entire being into the safekeeping of the man meant to destroy her.

Sarah didn't hesitate. She just pulled him down and kissed him back with everything she had.

This man, this moment, was worth the risk.

* * *

When Sarah's body softened beneath his, Kane realized she'd accepted his kiss. Passion instantly rushed over him so intensely he could barely breathe. He tangled his fingers in her hair, plunging into the kiss, into the connection, desperate for the relief she gave him.

The void inside him, the one that had been threatening to consume him for so long, raged in fury, refusing to relinquish its grip on him, refusing to lose him to Sarah. It swelled in intensity, trying to suck him down, battling against the emotions that Sarah had brought to life.

It was like a battle between two demons inside him. The dark. The light. The pain. The salvation. Death. Life. Hell. *Sarah.* Every cell in Kane's body burned like acid had been bled into his veins, plunging through him and incinerating every tissue in his body. The more he kissed her and the more he immersed himself in her, the greater the pain. Sweat streamed over his brow, and his body shook from the force of the internal battle being waged within him. "Son of a bitch." He broke the kiss, gasping at the surge of agony ripping through him. Bracing himself above Sarah, he threw his head back, bellowing in fury at the darkness eviscerating him. "What the fuck do you want?" he shouted at the blackness trying to take him. "What the hell is it?"

Kane.

Sarah's desperate voice broke through the darkness trying to consume Kane, and he jerked his gaze down to the woman beneath him. Her dark hair was tangled across the forest floor, her skin ashen, tears squeezing out beneath her thick lashes. His gut tore as he saw the marks on her throat from her brother, the bruises covering her arms. Her body was trembling beneath his, so vulnerable, so fragile, so desperate.

Her eyes flickered open, and he saw anguish in those blue depths. There was so much pain and betrayal in them. Fear. Hopelessness. The extent of her suffering tore right through his gut. "No more, Sarah," he growled. "No fucking more."

Then he lowered himself on top of her and offered every single breath of life he had to give. It wasn't much. Hell, it wasn't much at all, but it had been enough to keep him alive after five hundred years of battle and life-threatening injury. It had to be enough to save her. He was going to make damn sure it was.

He fisted her hair and kissed her again, and this time, he gave her everything. The kiss was intense and ravaging, and he unleashed every last bit of fury, anger, hope, life and passion he had into their connection.

Yes, Sarah whispered. *More.*

You can have it all. Kane deepened the kiss, thrusting everything he had into it. But the moment he opened himself to her, the darkness inside him roared to life, trying to hold him back, trying to stop him from connecting with the beauty of her spirit. The physical pain was brutal, like knives carving off his skin, but the depths of torment to his soul was a thousand times worse. It felt like something was trying to vacuum his spirit right out of his chest. His breath stuck in his lungs, and he fought for air, even as he deepened his kiss, reaching for Sarah with the very soul that the darkness was trying to tear away from him.

Come to my light, Kane. Connect us. I can help you.

A primal scream began to hammer at his mind, the wail of death and darkness trying to overtake him. He knew this was what had been coming for him for so long, and it was trying to take him now. He fought for breath, he fought for sanity, and he fought for his soul, even as he continued to offer himself to Sarah, trying to give her spirit an anchor to hold onto. Their connection wasn't just for her now. It was for him. He felt like her kiss, her touch, her skin were all that was keeping him from being sucked into the void clawing at his ankles, trying to drag him down further and further...

Sarah flattened her palm across his chest, and white heat leapt from her, knifing right into his chest, splitting the blackness away from his lungs. He sucked in his breath frantically, his heart pounding with the violence trying to take it.

He knew then that as much as he was her salvation, she was his. She was his only chance, and he was hers. He had no idea what was going on between them, but he knew that neither of them had a chance alone. They needed more. They both needed more. They needed each other. And they needed it now.

He shoved at her shirt, tearing it over her head. Skin to skin, the rush leapt through him, and Sarah gasped at the contact as he lowered himself back on top of her.

Yes, Kane. Yes. Sarah ran her fingers through his hair, kissing him as desperately as he was kissing her.

He kissed her jaw, her throat, her collar bone, her breasts. Frantic, desperate, a race against death for both of them. He fought to reach for her with his mind, but the darkness was like a shield between them. *Sarah. I can't reach you.*

You have to! This isn't enough!

Kane felt the brush of her mind, and he was suddenly hit with an overwhelming sense of heart-wrenching desperation, despair and failure that he immediately realized was Sarah's. It was so intense it shook him to the core, nearly breaking their connection under the onslaught of the darkness still attacking him. *Shit.* He opened his mind to hers, knowing he needed to reach more than her mind and her thoughts. He needed to access her soul, the life that beat within her. *Sarah. Let me in.*

She clung to him, kissing him fiercely, her lips moving desperately under his as the intensity of their kiss deepened. *I'm trying. I'm not used to making myself vulnerable.*

He swore and pulled back, framing her face with his hands. "Sarah," he growled. "Open your eyes."

Her eyes fluttered open, and his gut seized at the fading light within them. "I will never hurt you. Trust me," he ordered. "Put yourself in my hands, and I swear on my Order oath that I will keep you safe."

She stared at him, and he felt the intensity of her conflict. Terror so deep it was like a cold film coating her spirit, increasing the gulf between them. He swore as he felt their connection begin to falter, as her skin began to get cold. "No!" He gripped her face, searching some sign that he was reaching her. "Come on, Sarah! Now!"

He felt a sudden surge of determination rush through her, and her eyes deepened. "Now," she said. She grabbed him around the back of the neck and pulled him down toward her.

He met her mouth with desperate furor. The instant their lips met, shock reverberated through his head. Violence, anger, despair, death, and light, life, hope, faith. Her emotions, her life force surged through him, yanking him toward her. Rightness exploded through him, a desperate need to connect, and his kisses turned frenzied and uncontrollable. He poured his soul into her, and then he saw it, gleaming faint and white in his mind.

A flame.

A tiny, white flame, fluttering in a breeze he couldn't feel. Her life force, barely holding on. It was calling to him, beckoning to him. A salvation. A sanctuary. A challenge.

His spirit broke away from the darkness eating at him and rushed toward that white light, using it as a guide.

"Yes," Sarah gasped, gripping his shoulders.

"You're mine," he growled, his soul burning with the need for more of her. Her soul, her body, her mind, her entire being. He couldn't get close enough, couldn't touch enough of her, couldn't tighten the bond between them sufficiently as the dark specters screamed in his mind, fighting to hold onto him.

Sarah was his white light. She was his life, his chance, his sanity, as he was hers. He tore off his pants, and yanked off hers, shocked by the feel of her body against him as he settled back over her. Her skin was like hand-spun silk, so soft and smooth against his skin, unlike anything he'd ever felt before.

This kind of beauty wasn't his life. This wasn't his world. Such delicacy, such purity, such passion. He was overwhelmed by the sensations rushing through him, by the depth of the craving pulsing through him as he ran his hands over her body, as he kissed her breasts, her ribs, and her belly.

Sarah shook beneath him, her body still trembling, the cracks still evident on her skin. Anger rushed through him, fury that she could hurt like that. What was he doing thinking that he could save her? He wasn't the man to offer tender love and delicate caresses to a woman. He was violence, he was bloodshed, and he was battle. He was a man without a past, without a soul, without—

"Kane!" Sarah gripped his shoulders, her eyes wide with sudden fear.

He felt it then, the last grip of her soul, leaving her body. "No!" He roared in outrage, and he dropped his hips and plunged his erection inside her, connecting with her the only way he knew how. Violent heat exploded between them, and Sarah screamed as Kane bellowed from the intensity of the connection. White light flooded the night, and Kane thrust again, and again, and again, utterly consumed by his need for her. She clung to him, her fingers digging into his shoulders as she raised her hips to meet his.

Sarah. God, yes, this is it. Kane reached for her with his mind, and this time, he found her. She reached for him at the same time, and their souls met, a fierce connection of such passion and desire, of raging life that it shook him all the way to his very core. He was barely even aware of the darkness screaming through him in rage. All he could feel was the pressure in his chest, the burning of life through his body, life he'd hadn't felt in five hundred years.

He thrust it all into Sarah, into her body, into her mind, into her soul, offering her every last bit of life that he had. He offered her his pain from when Dante had died. He showed her the intensity of his emotions when Dante had pulled him from the gutter. And he bared his soul to her, allowing her to see the gaping emptiness inside him, and the way everything had changed for him the moment he'd heard her voice.

Oh, Kane. Her voice was so tender, so beautiful that his chest tightened. Soft white light flooded him, shining into the very depths of his soul, making the darkness shrink away, screaming in protest. *Thank you for that gift. I will treasure it always. It is safe with me.*

Safe? Safe. He hadn't felt safe in five hundred years since he'd woken up with no past and a body covered in scars. But now, in Sarah's arms, with the beauty of her spirit filling him, he felt like he'd just come home. "Sarah." Her name was like a gift on his lips, and the moment he said it, uncontrollable passion swept through him. He drove once more, and then exploded into her. Sarah shouted his name, clinging to him as the orgasm swept through both of them, igniting the night with a white light so blinding and so intense he felt sure he would never see again.

And that was okay with him.

This moment...it was what he'd been searching for so relentlessly for five hundred years.

Chapter Five

Pinned to the earth by his weight, Sarah grasped Kane's muscular shoulders as he slept on top of her. Her body was still thrumming from the intensity of their lovemaking, by the sheer force of life he'd thrust into her. They'd both crashed the minute the orgasm had taken them, plunging into the healing sleep that would restore both of them.

The first light of dawn had awakened her. Sarah stared in awe as the sky filled with the orange glow of a new day. She'd thought she would never see the light again, and yet here she was, alive. Not completely healed, not safe, but she'd been given the gift of one more day.

Thanks to Kane.

She studied the man wrapped around her, his arms and legs entangled with hers, tucking her into the protective shield of his body. His light brown hair was tousled, the whiskers on his jaw thick, his body still tense even in his healing sleep. She knew that although he was healing himself, he was still alert, and if there was any threat, he'd be awake in a split second.

Warmth filled her at the realization that he was there to protect her. How could this Calydon be her salvation? How could he make her safe? Like all other Calydons, he'd been created to destroy her, and yet he was the one who'd plucked her from the precipice of death, offering her his very soul. All Calydons, those from the Order and those from her village, derived their powers from demon magic. As an angel, she was the one thing standing in the way of demons, making her a primary target for them.

Demons couldn't cross over onto the earth themselves, so they did it through those they could taint, like the Calydons, turning them into their weapons. The village of Akara was closely connected with the

Afterlife, which is why it could support angels, but that meant it was a vulnerable place for demons to try to finally break through. They wanted the village, and they wanted to destroy the angels who protected it. Kane was a Calydon, which meant that his instinct, his nature, was to destroy her. But he hadn't. He'd saved her. How was that possible?

Emotions tightened her throat as she recalled the intensity of what he'd shared with her. How immense had the void within his soul been? It was a gaping emptiness where his spirit should have been. Literally, he had no soul. How did he live like that? It had felt like someone had carved his soul right out of his body, leaving behind nothing but some paper-thin filaments to hold him together.

But then, when they'd connected, it was as if something had come roaring to life within him. His soul? His spirit? She didn't understand how he could seem so empty, and then minutes later, find his way to such incredible passion and emotion. It was almost as if there were two different men inside him. The intensity of Kane's response when they had finally connected emotionally had been so powerful, and it mirrored exactly what she'd felt when she'd made contact with him. How was it possible for there to be something so intense between them? Even with Mason, she'd never experienced that kind of intensity and connection. It had been amazing and powerful, touching her soul in the most beautiful way.

She smiled as she trailed her fingers through his hair, basking in the softness of the strands. Kane was different from Mason. More powerful. More intense. More burdened. It was terrifying, but at the same time, exhilarating and intoxicating.

With a sigh, Sarah ran her fingers down his neck, then frowned when she felt the ridges in his skin. She lifted her head to look more closely, and then her heart broke at what she saw. His entire body was covered in markings carved into his skin. She recalled now seeing the scars when he'd first appeared, but then chaos had erupted and she hadn't thought about it again.

Last night when they'd made love, it had been too dark for her to see them, and she'd been so close to death she hadn't felt them with her hands. His body had been shadows, salvation, and her only hope at life. But now, to see the extent of the damage to his skin... Who had done that to him? Her body went cold at the idea of how much he must have suffered.

Then she recognized the shape of one of the scars on his shoulder blade, and she stiffened. No. Impossible. It couldn't be. She leaned closer, and her mouth went dry.

She propped herself up for a better look, and foreboding filled her when she confirmed her first reaction. Carved in Kane's skin was the same talisman that she'd given to her brother to keep him from being consumed by the curse that haunted all the men in her village. It was the same talisman that hung on the door of every house in her village. It was the same one that had dangled from the neck of her husband as he'd struck down their child.

And it was all over Kane's body, plus dozens more she didn't even recognize. Was he from her village? She went rigid in sudden fear, as memories assaulted her. Of stories told to her as a child, warnings of Los Muerte, the black specter who had haunted the woods. Los Muerte had nearly wiped angels from their village single-handedly six hundred years ago in a violent fortnight of death and destruction. He was the monster that had sired the race of creatures who hunted her even now. The one that nobody could stop. "Oh my God." Was Kane actually Los Muerte? Had he finally returned to finish what he had begun so long ago?

Her heart pounding, her instincts screaming at her to run, Sarah squirmed her way out from beneath Kane, horrified by the desire that licked through her as his arm slid across her belly. Her skin pulsed at the feel of his bare skin against hers, desire racing through her even as panic hammered at her.

Still in his healing sleep, Kane grunted and reached for her, his strong hand wrapping around her ankle. Sarah froze, terrified, waiting for him to rear up and attack her...but his touch was warm and gentle. Reassuring. His thumb stroked her ankle bone, a casual but seductive caress that made longing cascade through her belly.

How could this man be Los Muerte? She'd seen inside him. There'd been no death, no destruction, just the honor of a warrior who had given his life to his mission. Then she remembered the emptiness inside him, the gaping darkness that had fought for him, trying to take him from her. His complete lack of a soul. She'd had to fight for Kane to access enough of his humanity to reach her, and only her white light had created the fissure that had enabled her and Kane to break him free enough to save her.

Frowning, Sarah knelt beside him, a sense of rightness settling on her as he cupped her calf and shifted closer to her, pressing his face against her lap. She touched the markings on his back, tracing the designs as she looked at them more carefully. There was definitely the one she'd first recognized, but there were others that also matched those in her village. The concentric circles that were engraved on the fountain in the old village. The tear drop that was carved into the boulders at the entrance to the old pit. Plus so many others she'd never seen before. All the designs were overlaid, as if whoever had carved them hadn't wanted even a breath of space between the talismans.

Had they been protecting Kane from the demon trying to take him? Or were the talismans the very thing destroying his soul? "What are you, Kane?" she whispered. "What happened to you?"

He moved suddenly, gripping her arm. She tensed, but he didn't awaken. Heat burned in her forearm where he touched her, and she looked down, expecting to see steam rising off her skin.

But there was no steam.

Just a thin, silver line down her forearm.

Fear knifed through her and she yanked her arm back. "Oh, *no.*"

Gone was the brand that had marked her as Mason's *sheva,* a daily reminder that she'd blindly and foolishly opened her heart to the man whose curse had compelled him to murder her family, her daughter, and then try to kill her too. The brand that never let her forget how close she'd come to failing all of humanity by putting her trust in the man destined to kill her. Not just all of humanity, but the one specific person she was meant to protect. Angels rarely knew who they were linked to for protection, but she knew her life force was holding the souls of others. If she died, then they would lose hope and faith, and without that, the soul could not survive.

Mason's brand had served as a constant reminder to never make the mistake of trusting again. That brand, that reminder, was gone. It was gone.

In its place was pure, unblemished skin, marred only by a thin, silver line, one on each arm.

Her heart hammering in her chest, she looked at Kane's arm, at the dark brand on his skin that marked his weapon as a double spiked flail. The handle was a perfect match for the mark on her arm.

She was his soul mate, and they'd completed their first stage of the bond by having sex.

Dear God. *Not again.*

Now she understood why the connection between them had been so intense and powerful. Why she'd been able to feel his emotions and hear his thoughts. Why his touch had been like the very salvation brought to save her life. How could she not have realized it? The mind-to-mind communication? Of course she was his soul mate! But she'd been so caught up in almost dying and the gift of his protection that she hadn't questioned it. She'd just clung to what he offered and accepted it unconditionally, not even taking time to think about what it might mean.

Like the fact she was his *sheva.* His soul mate. The woman destined to be sucked relentlessly under his spell until there was nothing left of her, and death took both of them. She'd barely survived last time. Again? *Not again.*

If he was Los Muerte, then she'd just bound herself to him, giving him access to her soul and her spirit. Giving him the tools he needed to finally destroy her.

"Damn you, Kane." She'd given herself to him so completely last night, accepted his very soul, trusted him as she hadn't dared trust in so long...and it was all a lie.

Frantically, she replayed the rest of their time together. Had they done any of the other five stages of the bond? Sex yes, no doubt about that. What about the others? Trust—had either of them shared one of their deepest secrets or given the other one the power to kill them? No, no, no, she was sure they hadn't. Transference? No, she hadn't called out his weapon. That was definite. They hadn't done the blood bond either. Death—had either of them killed to save the other or offered their life? She grimaced as she thought of the battle outside the mansion, of how Jacob had fallen. Had Kane dealt the killing blow to anyone who'd been about to kill her? Maybe, God, maybe.

Her heart pounding, she stared at the marks on her arms, trying to determine whether there were enough lines to justify two stages of the bond, or whether only one-fifth of his mark was present. No, no, no, there was just the one thin line on each arm, barely any of his brand. That had to be only one stage. Just sex. Not death...which meant Jacob was alive. Relief cascaded through her, quickly followed by wariness. She gulped, looking around the woods. If Jacob was alive, he would be coming for her again. She would need to stick with Kane for protection.

Crap! She couldn't stay with Kane! If she did, the bond would draw them ruthlessly together, until it was completed. Right now, there were still four stages left. She wasn't locked down yet. She could keep him at a distance...but even as she thought it, she felt the surge of desire and need for him. The calling of her soul to his, inextricably bound by the destiny that was calling them together.

"Dammit!" Sarah hugged herself as she stared at the man who had saved her life only hours before, who had made her believe that maybe, just maybe, there was a chance for her and for them. She felt the last vestiges of hope and faith that Kane had brought to life within her begin to fade. Was he the man meant to destroy her? The most deadly monster of them all? A thousand times worse than Mason and Jacob?

She'd been wrong about the two men she'd known her whole life. How could she possibly see Kane's true self when she barely knew him? The *sheva* bond would obscure her ability to do anything but tumble into his arms and under his spell.

She couldn't take the chance. She had to separate from him while she still could. Her need for him tearing at her heart, Sarah forced herself to turn away from him and grab her clothes. She had to get away from him before he sucked her in, before she made the same mistake for the third time, the fatal time.

"I won't die," she said fiercely. "Not even for you, Kane." She yanked her clothes on, grabbed her grandmother's talisman and then took off into the forest, running for her life, running toward the one chance she had left: the village of Nashoba and a community that could save her.

And while she was heading toward Nashoba, she was fleeing from the male that had already touched her heart, into whose safekeeping and strong arms she wanted to throw herself. She'd turned away from the first man in seven years that she'd wanted to trust.

* * *

Kane bolted upright, leaping to his feet as he sprang back to consciousness from his healing sleep. The moment he'd awoken, he'd known Sarah was missing, and panic had instantly assaulted him. The woods were bright, the sun high in the sky, as he spun around and searched the woods for Sarah. Jesus. Where the hell was she? How had he not woken up when she left? "Sarah!" he shouted.

There was no reply. Just the chatter of chipmunks, the twitter of birds, and the sound of the breeze through the trees. *Sarah.* He reached out to her with his mind, and found nothing. Not even a sense of her energy.

She was gone.

Wrongness and loss plunged through him, so intently that his weapons appeared in his hands, ready to attack. The dark void swelled inside him, clawing at him, trying to take him. "Fuck off," he growled.

He didn't know what was after him. He had no damn clue what it was, but he knew that Sarah had held it at bay. Sarah had been his anchor, his salvation. He had to find her. He *would* find her. Fierce commitment surged through him, a need to find the woman who had plunged through the emotional void he'd had for so long. He wanted more of her. He wanted to feel her spirit tangled with his. He needed to know who she was, what was after her.

Kane immediately tapped into his preternatural instincts, searching his surroundings for the residual taint of violence or conflict, but there was none, which meant Sarah hadn't been hurt or taken from him. Excellent. She'd left on her own...

Damn.

She'd left him on her own? He didn't like that. He didn't like that *at all.* Why hadn't she felt the need to stay wrapped around him, breathing in the fullness of their connection until life finally forced them apart? Wasn't she feeling what he was feeling? She had to be. There was no way it was one-sided. He'd been intimately connected to her last night, and he knew damn well that he'd rocked her world.

So why had she left? The instinct to find her and keep her safe was urgent and compelling, and it sent life and purpose surging through Kane. She was why he was alive. He knew it in his soul. He'd spent five hundred years protecting humanity, but his mission as a member of the Order of the Blade had never coursed through him with the rightness and strength that he was feeling right now.

Sarah was his mission. Sarah was his past, his present and his future. Sarah was his, and he was going to claim her now—

Then he laughed softly, realizing that he had no idea which way she'd gone. Her spirit still lingered, and a faint white haze drifted through the trees. Her signature, covering her trail so he couldn't track her. *I will find you, sweetheart, and I promise you, it won't take long.*

He inhaled deeply, breathing the white mist into his lungs. It drifted through him, loosening the grip of the darkness trying to consume him. He had a sudden memory of that white light slicing through the blackness in his chest, and he looked down at it, expecting to see a white mark on his skin.

Then he went utterly still in shock. On the left side of his chest, just above his heart, was a two inch circle of unblemished skin.

The scars were gone.

Stunned, Kane ran his fingers over the skin. The skin was so hot he jerked his hand off, his fingertips instantly charred.

But there was no doubt: the skin was smooth in that spot. Perfect. Unmarred. Five hundred years of scars and unanswered questions, and Sarah had changed it.

Sarah had the answers he'd relentlessly pursued for five hundred years.

Anticipation rushed through Kane, and he lifted his head, searching the woods with the intense, focused resolution of a warrior on a mission.

She had run from him, but she couldn't hide. "I will find you, Sarah Burns," he promised.

And then he would have answers.

For the first time in five hundred years, he had a lead on his past. Excitement and hope leapt through him, and he began to lope through the woods in pursuit of the woman who had given him what he'd been seeking his whole life.

* * *

When Kane finally returned to the mansion after failing to find Sarah, the scene was grim. The gardens were destroyed, and the bodies of dozens of Calydons were strewn across the lawns. Their twelve-inch claws had vanished, but the black brands on their arms remained. There was no doubt they were Calydons, though they were unlike any he'd ever seen.

Assorted members of the Order were collecting them on the patio, a pile of assassins that really didn't match the violets planted next to the stone bench. Lily Davenport, Gideon's *sheva*, and the world renowned expert on Calydons, was kneeling beside the pile of bodies, studying the brands on one of the fallen males.

"Did any escape?" Kane asked as he walked across the churned up grass toward his team.

Quinn tossed another body on the pile and nodded. "Just before dawn, all the ones still standing teleported away." He scanned the horizon, the bright blue sky of morning. "I don't know if they'll be back or not. Lily's never seen them before and doesn't know what they are."

"I know what they are," Lily interrupted. "They're Calydons. I'm trying to figure out their lineage, since they're different than you guys. I think they're a small enclave, which is why there isn't much about them."

Kane grinned at Lily, once again thinking how much better it worked for the Order now that Lily was on their team, instead of exposing them to the world. A woman with that much information about the Order needed to be kept close, and the fact she was Gideon's soul mate had made her a valuable asset. "Have you figured out where they're from?" He suspected that if he found their place of origin, he would find Sarah.

Lilly shook her head. "Not yet, but I'm working on it."

Kane grimaced with frustration. "Let me know when you do."

"You bet." She bent over one of the dead warriors, snapping a photograph of his brand.

"Where's the girl?" Quinn asked, looking past Kane for Sarah, who, of course, wasn't there.

Kane ground his jaw, still annoyed that he'd slept right through her taking off on him. Had he really been so knocked out by the sex and intimacy that he'd passed out like that? Apparently. He shoved his hands in his jeans pockets. "Yeah, well, I lost her."

"You what?" Ryland strode up, his body streaked with blood from all the battles. His muscles were flexed and tense, and his eyes were coal-black with adrenaline. "You lost our angel? Even though she has a team of assassins hunting her? How is that going to keep her safe, you bastard?"

Kane narrowed his eyes, his brands burning with the need to call out his weapons in response to Ryland's possessiveness about Sarah. "She took off on me."

"And you let her?" Ryland swore. "I'll find her. Jesus, Kane, an angel dropped into our lap. You don't fucking blow that assignment."

Kane flexed his hand. "She's mine," he said quietly, barely able to contain his aggression toward Ryland. Ry was always on edge, but usually it didn't affect Kane. Today, it was grinding under his skin, making him want to engage. "She is my responsibility."

Ryland moved into Kane's space, his eyes blazing. "Fuck that. You lost her. She's anyone's now."

"She chose me, and we both know it." Kane met Ryland's gaze, and let him see his commitment to Sarah.

Ryland stared at him, and then swore. "You slept with her? You defiled an angel?" His machete flashed into his hand with a crack of black light, and Kane instantly called his out as well.

"Hey!" Quinn moved quickly between them. "Stand down. Now."

"What's going on?" Thano Savakis sauntered up to them carrying a peach latte, despite the Order's attempts to get him to switch to a more testosterone-appropriate drink. "Don't tell me the Order finally decided to self-destruct and no one invited the new kid on the block?" He propped his elbow on Ryland's shoulder, completely ignoring the danger of the situation. "Just because I'm not old, cynical and bitter doesn't mean I don't appreciate a good internal feud over a woman. So, tell me, who slept with whose chick? Was it behind the bleachers or in the back of a station wagon?"

Ryland didn't move, and Kane held his ground. A sudden, ominous burst of raw pleasure hit Kane at the thought of attacking his teammate, and he tightened his grip on his weapon. "Bring it on, Ryland."

Ryland stiffened, and Thano immediately whooped and shoved Ryland to the side. "Dudes, you guys are taking this way too far. Kane, what the hell's got your panties in a twist? You should see your face right now. You look like a ghoul from a bad horror movie."

Kane felt the seriousness underlying Thano's easy tone, and he became aware of the violence streaming through his muscles, of his burning need to attack Ryland. "Shit." He took a sharp step back, immediately sheathing his weapons. He would have struck first against Ryland, and this time he'd come a hell of a lot closer than he had in the woods. What the hell was that about? Yeah, it was standard operating procedure to be ready for Ryland to come unhinged, but never Kane.

He and Ry had an understanding. They were both fucked up, but they would never direct it against each other. Until now.

Ryland turned his dark gaze on Kane. "Santiago," he said quietly, still gripping his machete. "There is something seriously wrong with you."

Kane met his gaze. "I know, man."

Ryland nodded in acknowledgement, as Quinn and Thano stepped aside, giving them space to resolve it. "What is it?"

Kane tapped the smooth patch of skin on his chest. "I'm changing."

Ryland's eyes widened, and Thano and Quinn immediately came over, not even pretending that they hadn't been listening.

"Wow, you have nice skin," Thano said. "I had no idea you were so delicate."

Kane eyed Thano. "Shut up."

"Never." Thano grinned, but his eyes weren't laughing. "What is it?"

"Damned if I know, but Sarah has answers. I think it happened because of her."

"Then we find her," Quinn said. "You're treading an edge right now, Kane, and we can't afford for you to go rogue. If Sarah affects that, then we need to find her." He gestured at the pile of Calydons on the ground behind him. "These guys are serious shit, and we need to stop them. Seems like she'll have info about them as well."

Kane ground his jaw as he looked past Quinn at the warriors on the ground. There were only ten, and yet most of the Order were sporting serious injuries. "What are they, the next generation of Calydons? The young bucks here to take us out?"

"Apparently." Gideon walked up, the body of Sarah's brother tossed over his shoulder. "This one is still alive. He's in a coma, but he's alive."

Kane swore, immediately thinking of Sarah's safety. "The minute he wakes up, he'll teleport and track down Sarah. We won't be able to hold onto him."

Gideon met his gaze. "It's a chance we have to take. He's our only lead. We don't even know where these guys are from."

"No—" But even as Kane protested, he remembered Sarah's words that if her brother died, then she would die. But if he lived, he would kill her. Son of a bitch. There was only one choice. "I'll find Sarah before he wakes up."

Ryland walked up beside him. "I'm coming with you."

Kane stiffened. "You think that's a good idea?"

Ryland grinned. "I'm the only one strong enough to take you down if you go rogue. So, yeah, I think that makes it a damn good idea that I go with you because you're not exactly roses and bunny rabbits right now."

"I'm not going rogue," Kane shot back, but even as he said it, the bare spot on his chest burned, and the darkness swirled inside him.

"Yeah." Ryland met his gaze, and nodded once. No further exchange was needed.

"I'm in," Thano said, his green eyes flashing with determination. "You need a young guy along to take on these kids. You old guys will run out of stamina."

Gideon and Quinn nodded their agreement. "We'll search from this end," Gideon said. "Lily will research it, and we'll monitor Jacob and try to get info from him."

Kane nodded. A three-pronged attack was good. One way or another, they would find Sarah.

"Stay in touch," Quinn said. "I have a bad feeling about this deal."

"Yeah, me too." But as Kane thought about what it had been like last night to connect with Sarah, to bury himself inside her and open himself to her so completely, he knew that wasn't the whole truth. He had a bad feeling about the mutated Calydons, but as for Sarah? All good... except for the fact she'd taken off on him.

That still bugged him. It was hell on a man's ego to give a woman the best loving he could, and then have her bail without a word. But her actions also intrigued him. She might be fighting for her life, but she had the courage to do what she felt was right, and he liked that. A lot.

He was fired up as hell to find her again. What answers did she have? Would she be his salvation, or bring him to the doom that had been stalking him for so long? He rubbed his hand over the smooth spot on his chest, wondering whether the missing scars were a good sign, or a bad one.

He needed to know, and he was going to look forward to getting the information from her. He grinned, adrenaline racing through him at the challenge Sarah had presented to him by bailing on him. What would she say when she saw him walking up to her? Would that same passion and desire still be there?

Or would it be even stronger?

He had a feeling he knew the answer. What had ignited between him and Sarah was only the beginning.

Thano raised his eyebrows. "What's that shit-eating grin for?"

"You'll never know, rookie," Kane said as he raised his arm for his teammates to grasp. "Let's go. I know where to start the search." Thano and Ryland set their hands on his arm, and he dematerialized, taking them right to the truck that Sarah had been driving when he'd found her.

Unless the truck was unregistered, he would know everything he needed to know about her within about five minutes.

Two minutes later, as he stared at the spots where a license plate should have been on the back of her truck, Kane had his answer about how hard it was going to be to track her down.

The game of cat and mouse had begun.

Chapter Six

She was almost there.
Almost there.
She could make it.
Come on, Sarah.

Fighting for consciousness, Sarah maneuvered her rented Jeep onto the well-hidden, dirt road to her village. The trees blurred in and out of focus, and the sounds of buzzing filled her ears. Dammit. She'd waited too long to come back.

She needed to come back at least once a week to restore her powers, but she'd waited almost two weeks since the night of Jacob's attack and Kane's rescue before coming home. She'd refused to abandon the hope that she could find help outside the village, and she'd been avoiding coming back to a town that didn't have her brother or her grandmother anymore.

She'd been so devastated when she'd finally made it to Nashoba and found a burned out village that had been long abandoned. There was no sign of a fountain of water to restore her, and the houses were boarded up. She'd visited three other sites where earth angels were rumored to live, and they were all burned out, stripped of the magic that could keep her alive.

Her powers dwindling fast, she'd had to return to Akara to recharge. Her drive home had been burdened with the grim possibility that her village might be the last functioning enclave left. She didn't know of anywhere else to find resources. Her trip had been a bust. She'd failed in her quest, and now it was almost too late to save herself.

The vehicle bounced over a rut, and the Jeep careened toward a tree. She yelped and yanked the wheel back to the left, barely avoiding a head-on collision with a massive pine. "Concentrate, Sarah."

She gripped the steering wheel and leaned forward, trying to concentrate on the winding road. The pavement seemed to blur in and out of focus, and she fought for control, straining to see the white marker for the turn-off...

There! She hauled the Jeep to the right, bouncing over the rocks as the vehicle shot down the road, relief cascading through her. She was almost to the village, almost to the fountain, almost home. See? She'd timed it perfectly and had everything under perfect control. The fact she was dizzy, weak and hallucinating because she needed to restore her powers so badly? It was merely an indication of how she had efficiently maximized her resources to get the most out of her trip, not an indication that she was desperate and spiraling out of control. Not at all.

Yes, so she might have utterly failed to come up with a secondary source of support while she was trekking around the countryside, but she was an efficiency goddess in knowing exactly how long she could push it. Go her.

She hit the gas, the tires spewing gravel as she peeled around the corner and burst out of the woods right into the center of the almost-abandoned village. The sight of her grandmother's house hit her hard, and tears filled her eyes as the enormity of her loss filled her. The lavender cabin with its yellow trim and massive collection of colored-glass wind chimes was such an anomaly in a town of rustic cabins, but Nonny had never cared. She did what she wanted and thumbed her nose at anyone who disagreed.

Just like how she'd walked outside after dark to find Jacob.

"Damn you, Nonny," Sarah whispered as she clenched the steering wheel, jamming her foot on the accelerator, knowing that she had no time to grieve. She had to get to the fountain, or Nonny's sacrifice meant nothing.

Ruthlessly shoving aside her tears, Sarah kept driving, right through the center of town. Most of the stores were boarded up now, and the pots of flowers in the town green were just old, dead strands of flowers from last summer that no one had bothered to repot.

The white church was silent, the bells no longer pealing the hour, plywood nailed up over the stained glass windows she'd loved so much as a child. There were a few people gathered on the front porch of the Spur & Cask, the general store that had once been the focal point of the bustling eastern Oregon town. Today, it was the only place still open to get groceries or news, but just walking inside gave the aura of a past dying out. One that would be completely destroyed once Sarah was dead.

This was her town, the place she'd grown up with friends and family, a place that had survived near destruction hundreds of years ago, and clawed its way back into the living. The town had been rebuilding piece by piece until the last ten years, when the cycle had begun again.

Now, it was almost dead again. Sarah was the last angel still living there, and there were so few people who even remembered what the village had once been.

Loneliness aching through her, Sarah drove past the closed-down theatre and down the dirt road to the older section of the village, the one no one bothered to go to anymore except her. As she passed one of the outlying cabins, she saw a door open. Out onto the sagging porch came Javier deLeon, one of the old guard who had once patrolled the streets at night to keep everyone safe. She'd heard stories about his legendary strength from the days before she was born, but today he was simply old, gray, and wrinkled. He was the man who spoke to no one and who lived on the outskirts. People left food on his porch, but it was never touched, and no one knew how he managed to feed himself.

But onward he lived, year after year, never faltering over that precipice of death that he'd seemed to be on for decades.

Javier's long hair was split in two braids which trailed down his back in gray and white ropes of gnarled mess. His skin was dark, as if he'd spent years in the Oregon high desert sun and paid the price. A cold chill rippled over Sarah as he watched her pass by, his black eyes riveted to her Jeep.

He always watched her. Never spoke. Retreated when she reached out.

She raised her hand in greeting, and to her shock, he gave her a single, solitary nod, not taking his eyes off her. The chill immediately shifted to a cold that went all the way to the marrow of her bones. Why had he acknowledged her *now*? What had changed?

But as she glanced down at the hairline fractures fissuring over her skin, she had a bad feeling she knew: it was because Javier sensed she was dying.

Crap!

Her hands shaking now, Sarah pulled the Jeep up beside the crumbling mound of rocks that had once been the center of the village, a majestic fountain of life and hope. The tires skidded on the dusty earth, too dry for this time of year. Coughing at the billows of dust, Sarah yanked off her seatbelt, grabbed the door frame and pulled herself out of the seat. She landed on the parched earth, and her legs gave out instantly, her knees crashing to the rocky ground.

Sarah gritted her teeth as she braced her hands on the earth, her palms burning from the impact. "Come on, Sarah," she muttered. "All you have to do is get over to the fountain. It's really not that difficult."

Almost glad that Nonny wasn't there to give her grief for letting herself get this weak, Sarah crawled over to the fountain. She grabbed what was left of the crumbling stone wall, heaved herself over the two-foot barrier and landed in what used to be a pool at the base of the fountain.

Ten years ago, it had been filled with cool, pure water that would have seeped into her skin from the moment she landed in it. Ten years ago, all she would have had to do was collapse right now, submerge beneath the water and let it restore her.

Today, there was just the dry, crumbling rock that had once been the bottom of the fountain. Gritting her teeth, Sarah pulled herself across the basin to the statue in the middle, a sculpture that now looked more like a decaying leper than an angel. She braced herself on the bottom of the statue and reached up into the small bowl that used to overflow—

Her fingers touched dry rock.

No water. Not even a trickle.

Damn! It had been almost dry when she'd left, but there'd been dampness. Now, it was bone dry. "Come on!" She had not allotted time to actually run out of water completely. She needed water *now*.

Sarah grabbed the statue and hauled herself to her feet to look inside. The opening that water had been flowing through for a thousand years was *dry*. "Oh, man. This isn't good."

Sarah shoved her fingers inside. Dry. "Oh, come on!" She grabbed a small rock, a fragment from the angel's toe, and clenched it in her fist as she leaned against the fountain, using the crumbling tower to hold her up. She hit the opening with the rock, trying to chisel it to make it bigger.

The opening crumbled beneath her assault, getting wider and wider, and still no water. "Oh, crap. Seriously?" The rock fell out of her hands and clattered to the ground. "Dammit!" Tears of frustration burned in her eyes as she turned to retrieve it, and then she saw a shadow move in the woods.

She froze, straining to see into the shadows of the forest. "Nonny?" There was a dark shadow, a quick movement, and her heart started to race as she saw the muscled bulk of a Calydon. Of course it was a Calydon. Who else ran around in the woods of Akara these days?

Aching disappointment and loneliness arced through her at the realization that it would never be Nonny sneaking up on her again, and she fisted her hands against the grief, trying to steel herself. For two weeks, she'd fought to control her sadness, and she had to continue to keep control. Every minute she was in town, she was in danger, and she couldn't afford to get killed just because she was too upset to concentrate on staying alive.

She had to focus on the movement in the woods, on the scout that had noted her arrival. It was daytime, so they wouldn't attack, and some might even be close to their normal human selves, but she knew she'd just been spotted.

She'd have to leave town before nightfall and pray they didn't track her. How long could she keep sneaking into the village during the day and getting out at night before they figured out how to follow her? Not long. She knew it wouldn't be for much longer. And if they caught her tonight? Yeah, she'd last maybe five minutes. Tops.

Which meant she had to find the damn water *now*. Her jaw jutting out in determination, she grabbed another rock and began pounding at the fountain. Her fingers were bleeding, and the rock slipped out of her aching grasp again. Sarah groaned as she watched it clatter across the pebbles, and slowly sank to her knees, leaning her head against the side of the fountain. She closed her eyes, the warm rock rough against her cheek as her body trembled. "This is ridiculous," she muttered. "It would be so anticlimactic to die sitting next to the fountain that is supposed to save my life. I'm really not this pathetic, am I?"

"See what happens when you have sex with a guy and blow him off? It never ends well to break a guy's heart."

Sarah whirled around at the sound of the male whose marks still burned on her arms.

Standing behind her, his shoulder propped casually against the crumbling frame of one of the old buildings was Kane Santiago, a smug expression on his face. His torso was bare, showcasing the myriad of scars across his strong body, and his jeans hung low over his hips. With his hair tousled and spiky, the sun gleaming from behind him, his shoulders broad, he looked exactly like the savior who had plucked her from death and gifted her with the very depths of his emotions. But with his scars so vivid and raw across his body and the hard set to his jaw, he also looked exactly like Los Muerte himself, come back to life.

* * *

Sarah had no time to fear him. No time to worry about the talismans on his body. She just needed him. "Kane," she gasped, unable to keep the relief out of her voice.

His gaze swept over her, and his cocky amusement fled, replaced with that same intense protectiveness she'd seen before. "What can I do?"

She gestured at the fountain, her hands trembling, blood oozing from her torn up fingernails. "It's supposed to have water. I can't get it."

She couldn't keep the desperation out of her voice.

Kane strode across the crumbling village square and vaulted effortlessly into the fountain. He crouched beside her, his face intense and all-business. "Where does the water come from?"

She almost cried with relief. He didn't bother with silly questions that wouldn't help. He'd instantly realized the danger of the situation to her, and he was focusing on what mattered. "From the earth. But it's not rising."

Kane set his hand on her hair, a tender, soothing gesture that made her want to cry as he studied the fountain. His gaze was sharp and clear as he scanned it. "It's usually in the bowl?"

She nodded. "I tried to chisel through the opening, but I couldn't get very far."

Kane stood up and peered inside the bowl, then he shot her a look of respect. "You got pretty far."

The tension began to ease from her body now that Kane was here. She wasn't alone. She had help, and quite frankly, she was too damned desperate to worry about whether that help was in the form of the world's greatest lover or the world's most deadly demon-tainted mass-murderer. If the man could get her water, then he could have whatever past he wanted, at least for the moment. "Well, I've always been known for my rock-chiseling skills. It's a girl thing."

He raised his brows. "Impressive."

"I know." She grimaced, unable to keep all of the trembling out of her voice. "Unfortunately, my skills seem to be declining. I couldn't pull it off."

"I got it." He crouched beside her, and pushed her hair back from her face, his gaze intense. "But do me a favor and don't take off on me again. It was a bit of a pain in the ass trying to track you down." His voice was hard, but beneath it was an undercurrent of vulnerability, a man who had so much to lose and so much at stake.

Like she was going to argue right now. Anything to get his help. Besides, it wasn't as if she was going anywhere at the moment. "Yes, I promise not to crawl the entire two inches away from you that I could manage before I crumble to the earth in a pile of sheer exhaustion and impending death."

Amusement flickered over his face. "I swear, there's nothing like saving a woman from death twice to make it easy to manipulate her."

She rolled her eyes. "You can't manipulate me. I made that choice because you look like some lost puppy dog at the thought of losing me, and I felt bad for you. And because I'm too weak to move anything but an eyelash." Despite her flirting, she couldn't suppress her discomfort at having to rely on him. She hated to put herself in a position where she would be in trouble if he turned on her, but she had no choice. Not right now.

He cocked an eyebrow at her. "You pitied me?"

She pressed her hand to her forehead, trying to quell the pain thudding through it. "Exactly."

"Pity?" Kane grinned, even as he set his hand over hers and pressed lightly. She was startled to feel a surge of energy from him. "Well, damn, woman. I think that's a first. I was hoping for raw, unbridled lust keeping you hopelessly begging for another kiss from me, rendering you utterly incapable of doing anything but fantasizing about me and my incredible lovemaking skills."

As his touch took away some of the throbbing pain in her head, Sarah shivered with desire, his words evoking memories of their lovemaking. Oh, the man had no idea what he did to her. She thought of the brand hidden beneath her long sleeves and stiffened, trying to pull away from his touch. Dammit. She had to remember to keep her distance, because the bond would try to pull them together. She couldn't afford to complete any more stages and tighten their connection, making it more and more difficult for her to protect herself from him when he finally turned. "You won't win me over—"

"No." He gave her a long look as he grasped her shoulder, not letting her escape from him. "I can't imagine anyone could, but right now I'll settle for not having to spend another two weeks tracking you down." He gestured to her. "I might have to get a little violent with the fountain, so I want to move you out of range. Can you walk?"

She shook her head, not even bothering to try to come across as some powerful woman. He'd seen her at her worst. She had nothing she could prove to him. "Not so much, no."

"May I?" He held out his arms, and she almost laughed at his attempt to look harmless.

How dangerous could it be for him to carry her a few yards? Surely she could manage to resist her attraction to him for a few steps, so that he could help her? Of course she could. She might be throbbing with desire for him, but she was also an emotionally stunted and damaged woman. She should have no trouble calling upon that trauma to resist the temptation of being in his arms. "Yes, sure, you can move me."

"Excellent. I've been wanting to feel you up for weeks." He slipped his arms under her and scooped her up with way too much ease, his biceps bulging as he stepped over the crumbling wall.

"Don't be crass. I'm not that kind of girl." But damn, she couldn't stop the swell of desire that cascaded through her at the sensation of being held in his arms. Suddenly, all the intensity that had erupted during their first encounter raged to the surface again. Her skin felt hot, her belly pulsed, and her whole body began to vibrate.

Kane stopped and stared at her. "Son of a bitch," he said softly, staring at her with such sensual desire that she felt like he was about to ignite every cell of her body. "What is it with you?"

She pulled her sleeves over her hands and shook her head. "We had a night of great sex, and there's a little residual stuff going on. That's it."

"No, it's not." He bent his head and pressed his face to her hair, inhaling deeply.

Sarah stilled, her heart thundering at the intimate gesture. It felt amazing to be in his arms again, to feel his body surrounding her like some great shield. She'd wondered how she could have made love with him so recklessly, and now she knew. It was abundantly clear just how thoroughly he unraveled her defenses. He stripped her of all sanity and logic, and made her burn with something she didn't even understand. Suddenly, all the weakness that had been haunting her fled, replaced with something powerful and strong. Life? Hope? Excitement? Things she hadn't felt in so long.

Kane pulled back, and something flashed in his eyes. Pain. Hunger. Lust. Tension. Slowly, without another word, without asking permission and without bothering to see how she felt about it, he hoisted her in his arms, crushed her against his chest, and kissed her.

The moment his lips touched hers, something inside Sarah came roaring to life again, just like it had before. The hunger she'd seen in his eyes filled her, sweeping through her like some great storm trying to wrench her off her feet and thrust her up into a raging inferno of desire, lust and passion.

She couldn't stop herself from kissing him back, from wrapping her arms around his neck, from breathing in the sheer force of who he was. His energy and life force streamed into her, surging past the tears and breaks in the fabric of her soul, plunging right to her heart. She clung to him, kissing him back every bit as fiercely as he was kissing her, afraid to lose the feeling he gave her. He was life, he was light, he was courage and strength, everything she didn't have on her own, everything she needed.

With a growl, Kane shifted her in his arms so that she was facing him, her legs on either side of his hips, her breasts crushed against his chest. His hands dug into her butt, his mouth almost violent on hers as he kissed her back. It was as if all the intensity from that night had never left, despite two weeks of absence and the fact it was broad daylight.

She fisted his hair, her heart thundering as she kissed him. God, it felt amazing to be held and kissed, like she was alive and breathing for the first time in years. Her skin was on fire, the blood racing through her, her body trembling with such desire that her stomach actually ached with need.

Jesus, Sarah. Kane locked his arm behind her shoulder blades and plundered her mouth, his kiss so deep and so passionate it was as if he were trying to find her soul and strip it out of her body.

But as she kissed him, she felt the kiss begin to change. More passion, more darkness, more violence surging through him. His arms began to tighten around her, almost too tight, almost crushing the breath out of her. Adrenaline raced through her, along with a tremor of fear. Los Muerte. The name whispered through her mind, as the darkness of Kane's spirit began to close around her like a thick, dark cloud of violence and death—

"Hey!" A firm hand slammed down on both their shoulders. "Cut the crap, Kane. Can't you see the angel's in bad shape?"

Sarah jumped and tried to pull back, but Kane just locked his hand behind her head and cut off her retreat, claiming her with one final kiss of pure possession. It wasn't until he'd decided they were done that he finally allowed her to break the kiss, his brown eyes staring at her with fierce ownership as he pulled back. Lurking in his eyes was that darkness, a pulsing void trying to take him, to consume him. Pain flickered across his face and he grimaced, showing her that he was feeling the same agony that he'd felt when they'd been making love.

"Kane—" She started to reach for him, and then she was hit with violent weakness. It flooded back into her now that the kiss was over, and she lost her grip on his shoulders, her fingers too weak to hold on.

"Shit, Sarah." Kane cursed under his breath as he tightened his grip on her, holding her securely against him.

"I'm okay." She leaned her head against his shoulder and squeezed her eyes shut, fighting to breathe. Her lungs felt tight, and it was hard to get oxygen. Kane's kiss had flooded her with energy and life, but the moment it had ended, the weakness had come crashing back, even worse than before. "I just need the fountain." Or a kiss, apparently, though that rejuvenation had ended the moment the kiss had. Maybe she needed to kiss him relentlessly and never stop. Maybe that would save her life.

"I'm on it." Kane gently set her down, and crouched beside her, running his hand gently through her hair. "Stay here. We'll get the damn thing to work."

"We?" She leaned her head against the stone, struggling to breathe, to get air into her lungs. Okay, she was no longer amused at how weak she was. This was definitely pushing it a little bit too close. But how was she supposed to know that the water would dry up and some overly-tempting testosterone factory would show up to seduce her with his kisses?

"We. My team." Kane jerked his head to the left, and she managed to turn her head enough to see what he was pointing to. Two massive warriors were standing beside them. One of them was the dark haired one she remembered from the other night. His pitch black hair was shaggy and unkempt, and his face was dark with fury. Ryland, the one who knew she was an angel.

Fear rippled through her as Kane stood up to face them. "You remember Ryland Samuels," he said, not bothering to look away from her face. "He has a crush on you, but don't get too excited about it. He's a veritable bastard who has never once brought a woman roses."

Ryland strode over to her and crouched in front of her. "I'm here to serve you," he said intently. "You tell me what you need, and it's yours. You honor us with your presence."

Her heart tightened for the emotion on Ryland's face, for the raw, almost unbearable pain in his eyes. God, she wished she could help him. There was so much grief and anger within him, so little humanity left inside. "Thanks," she whispered, her voice so raw it hurt to say any more.

"Hey, enough with you guys trying to impress the girl," the other warrior said, his dark brown hair cut in a short style more fitting of a guy in a Polo shirt than a male with a long, hooked spear clenched in his fist. "Let her choose between you guys herself." He winked at Sarah, a cheerful flirt that she knew instantly was designed simply to annoy the other two, and she almost smiled.

Who would dare antagonize men like Kane and Ryland?

"Thano Savakis." Kane jerked his thumb toward Thano as the three of them strode across the courtyard toward the fountain.

She could feel the determination from all three men to get the fountain working, and the faintest flicker of hope drifted through her. Was there really a chance? Could they do it?

"Thano thinks he's smarter and funnier than he is," Kane said as he vaulted over the wall to the fountain. "Don't get too attached because we're likely to take him out at any time."

"You'll never be able to take me out," Thano retorted cheerfully. "You're way too old for a hot youngblood like me."

"Fuck that," Ryland snapped. "You're not smart enough to stay alive. You'll never make it to a hundred."

Sarah's heart tightened with longing at the easy camaraderie between the men as they circled the fountain, talking in low voices as they inspected it. The affection had been evident in Kane's voice even when he'd been giving them grief, and she could sense the commitment they had to each other.

What would it be like to have strength like that at her back? It reminded her of too long ago, before the people she'd cared about had all died.

Kane turned his head suddenly and looked right at her. *Sarah.*

His voice was like a warm strength curling through her mind, and she couldn't stop the sudden burn of tears. *What?*

You're not alone anymore. I have your back. Even Ryland does, though I'll have to kill him if he makes a move on you.

She stared at Kane, at the massive, deadly warrior who dwarfed the fountain that had once been so big, and she felt the honesty of his words and she wanted to cry with relief. She wasn't alone. Regardless of who he once was, or who he might become, right now, in this moment, she could count on him, and that was an unbelievable gift.

But even as she began to relax and feel good about trusting him, she felt the slither of something dark inside him, beneath that rugged commitment. It was the kind of evil, tainted darkness that had destroyed so many, so brutally, for so long.

Kane's eyes narrowed, and she felt a sudden surge of the violence inside him. *What do you know about me?*

Dear God, what could she say? Was he really Los Muerte? *I—*

"Got it." Ryland shouted from the back side of the statue. "This is the spot."

Kane turned away then, sparing her answers she wasn't ready to give...for now. But she'd seen from the look on his face that he wasn't going to let it go. He was going to demand answers, and as she rubbed her hand over the brand on her arm, she knew there were things she simply couldn't afford for him to know.

Chapter Seven

The darkness inside Kane was getting worse with each passing moment. It had been getting exponentially stronger since he'd first walked into the village of Akara two hours ago, waiting for Sarah's return. He rubbed the back of his neck restlessly as he knelt at the base of the crumbling fountain, studying the crack in the rocks that Ryland had pointed out. He felt like his skin was peeling off his body, like the scars were made of acid, burning through his skin.

What the fuck was going on?

Ryland set his hand over the crack at the base of the statue. "The air is damp here. There's water beneath the ground."

Kane tested the air, and a cold blast of damp air hit him. It sizzled against his palm and he pulled his hand back. Across his palm was a blood-red streak, as if he'd been lashed by a burning whip. "Shit."

Ryland's dark eyes met his, and he flipped over his hand, showing Kane that his skin was clear. Not a mark.

"Thano."

The third warrior placed his hand over the crack. "It feels damp," he agreed. "Definitely water under there." He pulled his hand back and showed both of them. Again, not a mark.

The three warriors exchanged grim looks, and again, that cold, threatening energy seemed to swell inside Kane, like a chisel trying to crack his soul. Astronomical pain slashed through him.

Worse now. Getting worse. Why was he different from Ryland and Thano? What the hell was going on? He closed his fist, refusing to get dragged down into fixating on it. His mission was to get Sarah water, and then he could deal with everything else. "Let's get this damned fountain out of the way then."

"Wait." Sarah's desperate voice interrupted.

"What's up?" Kane turned to look at her, and the moment he saw her again, he felt like he'd just been sucker-punched by his first sighting of her in over two weeks. She was leaning against the crumbling wall, her face pale and weary, but her eyes were brimming with fire and passion.

Jesus. *She was real.* Ever since the night he'd met her, he'd had her only in his mind, trying to piece together what she really looked like, trying to figure out exactly what that whirlwind night had been about. He'd seen her only in the dim light, so his memories were of how she felt beneath him and what her voice sounded like. He could still remember the white light fading in her soul, and the beauty of her spirit as she'd flooded him when the darkness had tried to take him.

She'd become almost a fantasy, a phantasm who'd blown into his life in the night and vanished by morning. With each day that had passed, it had been more and more difficult to hold onto the details of who she was, and with each day, the void in his soul had become stronger and stronger, until it felt like there were a thousand pounds of weight crushing his lungs, making it almost impossible to breathe.

He didn't sleep anymore, unwilling to relax his safeguards against the onslaught inside him. His only mission had been to find Sarah. He'd been consumed by the need to locate the woman who had wiped out some of the scars on his chest and made him feel alive for the first time in five hundred years. He'd felt pain when he was with her, yeah, and darkness, but she'd also made his soul come screaming to life, and that was worth all the pain and torture in the world.

And now, after two weeks of frustration and dead ends, he'd found her. She was real. *Real.*

Her hair was ash blond, like the color of sunshine breaking through a storm cloud. Her eyes were an even more radiant shade of blue than he'd remembered. But she looked delicate and fragile, so pale she seemed almost translucent. Her hands were trembling, and dirt was caked under her fingernails. He swore under his breath as the need to protect her raged to the surface, but he forced himself not to move toward her, afraid to spook her before he'd gotten her settled.

She'd taken off on him once, and he could not allow that to happen again. He needed to handle the situation better this time. Right now, she needed his help, and he was going to give it to her. He needed to save her ass quickly, and then get her alone where he could solidify his position in her life so she didn't leave him.

"Don't destroy the fountain," she said. "It has special properties."

Kane grimaced at the several thousand pound tower of stone. Not move it? "You like to make things difficult, don't you, sweetheart?"

She managed a small smile. "You wouldn't adore me so much if I made life easy for you."

"Yeah." Kane eyed the fountain, trying to figure out a solution that didn't involve decimation. "True, but you're a serious impediment to my need to be violent and destructive."

Her smile faded, and he felt a surge of fear from her. "Do you really feel that way? Violent and destructive?"

At her sudden tension, Kane swung around to look at her, dropping the pretense. "It's part of who we are, Sarah," he said honestly. "It's what makes us able to save the damn world on a daily basis. I'm no angel, not by a longshot." He wouldn't lie to her about what he was, about the violence that was pulsing inside him, about the life he'd been leading for so long.

She bit her lip, and he felt her sudden withdrawal. The moment she pulled back, the void inside him roared back to life, fighting to consume him. He almost staggered from the force of it. There was no pain this time, just a sense of utter blankness. Death? Son of a bitch. What the fuck was going on? One minute he was consumed with a void that felt like the steady approach of death, and the next minute, there was such violence and pain tearing through him that he wanted to rip off his skin and let the demon loose into the world. Death versus life? Life was a demon, and death was death? Was that what was going on inside him? Because if so, he opted for door number three, whatever that might be—

Another wave of vast emptiness hit him, and it felt like his spirit was getting sucked into an arid dust bath, draining the life from his cells one by one by one.

"God, I love that angel perspective," Ryland said reverently, pausing with his machete in his fist. "She wants to save every damned thing, doesn't she? Even an old fountain. Can you imagine living that way? Fucking beautiful."

Thano raised his brows. "Dude, we need to get you some therapy. There's no beauty in your world. There's only violence and bad attitude. You don't even know how to notice beauty."

Ryland glared at him. "Fuck off, rookie."

Thano just grinned and held out his arms. "You can stop pretending you don't want to hug me. I can do the man-hug thing without losing my raw, manly sex appeal. Everything is beautiful, and all that, right?"

"Thano," Kane muttered, bracing himself against the pain trying to tear him apart. "Stop fucking around."

Thano and Ryland both turned toward Kane, and Thano's grin dropped off. "What the fuck is wrong with you?"

"I don't know." Kane's head was spinning, and he felt like he was losing his equilibrium. He braced his hands on the ground and bowed his head, straining to keep his balance and his focus. His skin felt cold, and his muscles felt like they were sluggish and heavy, like he was lodged in a pit of quicksand—

Kane. Sarah's hand landed on his bare back, and a shock of energy ripped through him.

Don't move, Sarah. Stay with me. He went utterly still, centering all his attention on the feel of her hand against his bare skin. The softness of her touch. The heat of her hand. The life beating within her. Slowly, ever so slowly, he felt the grip that the void had on him begin to lessen. The world stopped spinning, and his muscles began to fire again. The pain began to start again, but he didn't give a shit about that. He'd take the pain over what had just happened. Was that death? Was he a sliver away from dying? Because that's what it felt like.

He took a breath, then turned to look at Sarah. Her face was still streaked with the hairline fractures, and she was so pale that she looked like death itself. Ryland and Thano were each supporting one of her arms, and Ryland's arm was around her waist, holding her up.

For a split second, the ancient male instinct roared through Kane at the sight of the other two males touching his woman, but then Ryland shook his head once. "Don't do it, Santiago. We're saving your ass, so back the fuck off. Control yourself."

His heart thudding with the need to attack his friends, Kane looked at Sarah instead, focusing on the intensity of her blue eyes. Ryland was right. They were holding Sarah in position so she could touch Kane and bring him back. Why did her touch make the void disappear and bring the pain and the darkness to life? *What are you doing to me, Sarah? Why do I react like this around you?"*

Uncertainty flickered in her eyes, and she shook her head. "I don't know."

She was lying. He knew she was, and that realization burned through him like acid. "No lies, Sarah. No damn lies."

She stiffened at his tone, and Kane saw Ryland move closer, trying to put his body between Kane and Sarah to protect her. Thano touched Ryland's arm in warning when Kane tensed, and Ryland froze, partially blocking Kane's access to Sarah.

No one moved, the tension so thick that it felt like one wrong breath would make everything snap. Violence rolled through Kane, a raw need to rip Ryland apart and make him pay for being too close to his woman. Kane felt his upper lip curl into a snarl, and Ryland tightened his fist on the machete. Kane immediately called out his flail, and Ryland raised his blade.

Thano swore and slid his arm over Sarah to pull her away, and Kane instantly pressed his flail to Thano's throat. "Don't fucking take her away from me," he growled. His voice was harsh and raspy, almost unrecognizable, and he felt Sarah suck in her breath.

Black spots began to dance through his vision, and Kane called out his other weapon. Ryland and Thano instantly did the same, and then all three men were armed, with Sarah in the middle.

"I think you should go, Sarah," Thano said, his voice grim. "There's something seriously fucked up happening right now."

But Sarah didn't move. She just looked up at Kane, searching his face desperately as if trying to understand. Then suddenly, more quickly than any of the men expected, she darted in front of Thano, putting her throat right in front of Kane's flail.

Kane swore and sheathed his flail instantly, jerking his hand back as Ryland and Thano grabbed for her—too late, because Kane would have already killed her by then if he'd wanted to.

"Jesus!" Thano grabbed Kane's arm and shoved him back, while Ryland grabbed Sarah and spun her away, shielding her with his body.

Darkness rolled through Kane at the sight of Ryland yanking Sarah away from him, and he lowered his head, glowering silently at his teammate as Thano set his hands on Kane's shoulders and shoved at him, ordering him to stand down.

Kane ignored him, his gaze riveted on Sarah as she turned in Ryland's arms. She raised her chin and met his gaze, her blue eyes blazing with audacity and...something else. No longer fear. Smug satisfaction. Relief.

"I knew you wouldn't hurt me," she said, her voice full of such relief it went right to his core and peeled away at some of the darkness inside him. "I knew I could trust you." Then she smiled, her face so radiant that it felt like he'd just been blinded by heaven's rays.

"Jesus," Ryland muttered. "That's why you did that? To test him?" Ryland looked almost ashen, which was astounding for him. "Sarah, he's a bastard on the edge. We all are. He was right when he said he's not an angel. Don't believe in us, and sure as hell don't test us by jumping in front of our weapons to see if we'll pull the blow."

"Speak for yourself," Thano said. "I'm completely angelic. It's the new wave of the Order."

Kane didn't reply to the banter, stunned by what had just happened. He was still shocked by that sight of Sarah on the other side of his flail

when so much violence had been streaming through him. He stared at Sarah, trying to comprehend what had just happened. *Why did you do that?*
I had to know.
He still didn't get it. *Know what?*
Her smile faded. *Whether you were going to try to kill me now, or whether we have time.* Grim reality darkened her eyes, and she began to sag against Ryland, as if it had become too much in her weakened state. *You can't fake instinct, so now I know.*
I would never hurt you, Sarah. Never. The words burned inside him, a raging ferocity that tore him out of Thano's arms. He strode across the rubble toward Sarah, ignoring Thano's attempt to restrain him and Ryland's warning to back off.
You know that's a lie, Kane. Didn't you say no lies? Pain flickered in her eyes, pain and weariness. *No lies between us.*
Kane caught her just as her legs gave out. He swept her out of Ryland's arms and into his own. *If there are no lies between us, then tell me why I respond to you like this. You know.*
Sarah collapsed against his chest, her body trembling. *I do know.*
Something vibrated through Kane, a desperation so intense it almost shook him to his core as he stared down at her. "You know who I am?" Sweet Jesus. His heart began to pound, his blood roaring through his ears as his grip tightened on her. "Do you know who I am?" he repeated. "Do you?"
She looked at him and nodded. "I think I might, but I'm not positive." She touched his chest, flattening her palm over the smooth patch of skin. Her touch was like a burst of heat through him, igniting the coldness that had been trying to consume him for so long. Desire ricocheted through him like the rippling heat from the high desert sands. Her eyes jerked to his, and he saw the same sudden awareness of the heat between them. "I might be wrong."
"Who?" Holy shit. Was it over? Was he finally going to find out who he was? He pulled her closer, his entire being vibrating, coming alive for her. He cupped her hips, pulling her closer, needing more of her, as if she could reach inside him and release whatever had been locked up for so long. "Who am I, Sarah?" He was vaguely aware of Thano and Ryland moving closer, but he didn't care. He could barely breathe, could barely stand, the intensity of his reaction was so strong. He was consumed by the woman in his arms, by what she knew, by what she did to him, by what she could offer him.
She slid her hands on either side of his neck, rubbing her hands over his skin as if she needed to touch him as much as he needed to

consume her. "I'm not sure you want to know, Kane."

Her gaze met his, and it was so full of emotion and passion that raw, heated lust tore through him. Not just lust. A roaring, living need to connect with her, kiss her, touch her, and bond with her. He pulled her closer, breathing in her air, wanting more, wanting to know every secret she had. She had the answers to everything for him, everything. He almost fell to his knees, so desperate was he for all she had to offer. He gripped the back of her hair, pulling her face close into his. "Sweet Jesus, woman. Tell me who I am—"

"What in God's name is going on over here?" A raspy voice bellowed out from behind Kane.

Sarah let out a yelp of surprise as Kane turned around to see an old lady hobble out of the woods wearing a rainbow-striped tee shirt and a pair of camouflage pants, and she was carrying the largest damn set of bow and arrows he'd ever seen in his life.

She raised the arrow and aimed it at Kane's head, right between the eyes. "I never gave permission for my granddaughter to be involved in a four-way with three men who have more muscles than the Hulk on steroids. Is this what happens when people think I'm dead? Sex orgies? Really? Put the girl down, you over-sexed mass of testosterone, or I will shoot you in the head that actually has the brains." Then she lowered the tip of the arrow, aiming right at his crotch. "Or maybe I'll start with the other one."

Ryland and Thano went still beside him.

"Wow," Thano said, sounding awestruck. "That's a real woman. If she were seventy years younger, I'd get down on my knee and propose to her right now."

Kane turned his body so he was blocking Sarah from the arrow. "Sarah?" Kane leaned closer to Sarah, brushing his lips over her ear. "Do you know her?"

"Kane." Sarah was staring past him at the old lady. Her fingers dug into Kane's neck, and he realized she was shaking violently. Her voice was trembling. "Do you see an old woman with a bow and arrow? Or am I imagining it?" Tears were brimming in her eyes, and there was so much grief in her face that he felt something inside him crack.

The void that had been trying to consume him vanished, and he felt a burning pain in his chest. Void and emptiness, or pain and violence. Nothing in between. He felt like he was losing his freaking mind. "Sarah. What's wrong?"

"I'll give you three seconds," the old lady yelled, "or this arrow is going right in your family jewels, big guy."

Thano snickered, and Kane called out his flail and held it over his crotch, not taking his attention off Sarah. "Tell me what's going on," Kane urged. "You want me to take her out?"

"Take her out? Really?" Sarah grabbed his arm, bursting into tearful laughter. "She's really there? I'm not imagining it?"

"Shit, yeah, she's there. Who is she?"

But Sarah didn't answer. She was already out of Kane's arms and racing across the rubble. Kane swore and took off after her, knowing that she was going to make it only about ten yards before her legs gave out from weakness.

He was wrong.

She made it only eight.

But he was there to catch her anyway.

* * *

Sarah gasped as Kane swept her up and carried her toward her grandmother. She tumbled out of his arms, clinging to her grandmother as tears poured down her cheeks. "Nonny!" She hugged her tightly, unable to believe she was holding her grandmother. "You're alive."

"Damn straight I am." Nonny hugged her back, her thin arms like wire wrapping around her.

"But how?" Sarah pulled back, searching her grandmother's wizened face, trying to understand how she was still there. "Jacob had your talisman in his hand. You never take it off."

"I didn't take it off." Nonny's wrinkled face suddenly looked old for the first time Sarah could remember, as true sadness filled her eyes. "He ripped it off my neck. I think he couldn't bear to see it when he killed me."

Sarah bit her lip, betrayal welling up inside her again. How could Jacob have been ready to kill their grandmother? She understood why he was trying to kill her, but Nonny? There was no reason for that except for the sheer, raw high of killing. "How did you stop him?"

"I didn't." Irritation flashed in the old lady's eyes. "He was just rearing back to kill me with his sickle when you called him. He dropped me and disappeared."

Sarah stared at her grandmother, stunned by her story. "It worked? I distracted him from killing you?"

"Yes, it did." Nonny glared at her. "You scared the shit out of me, girl. Never call the bad guy to your doorstep again, or I'll have to take a switch to you."

Sarah started laughing, the relief was so great. She'd done it.

All that she'd suffered had been worth it because she'd protected her grandmother. "Don't ever sacrifice yourself to save an angel again. We'll beat you every time."

"Hah," Nonny scoffed. "Look at you, so weak you can't even stand up. Why haven't you restored yourself?"

"The fountain's dry. Kane and the others were just working on it—"

Nonny barked with irritation. "They weren't doing anything. They were just standing around." She looked past Sarah and eyed Kane, who was still standing right behind Sarah, barely giving her any personal space at all. "Who the hell are you anyway?"

To Sarah's surprise, Kane bowed to her grandmother. "Kane Santiago, at your service." He brushed his hand through the air, indicating behind him. "And these are my compatriots, Ryland Samuels and Thano Savakis." His eyes blazed with fierceness and satisfaction as he looked at her grandmother. "We're Order of the Blade, and we've come to help your village."

"Order of the Blade?" Nonny stared in disbelief. "Why on God's green earth would you come here?"

"Because we protect the earth from rogue Calydons, and you've got yourself a problem with them, don't you?"

Sarah stiffened, realizing that she'd never thought to ask Kane why he was there. She'd been so caught up in the intensity between them that she hadn't even thought logistically about the fact that he'd appeared in her village out of the blue. Damn! Had he really come to find the Calydons? She couldn't let Kane find out what was going on in the woods. The Order would destroy everything. They would kill her brother. "We've got it covered," Sarah said quickly, her heart pounding for the safety of the men who had gone rogue. She didn't want them dead. She just wanted them stopped, and she wanted herself to live. That was very different than the team slaying of all the "bad guys" that the Order would do.

"Like hell we do, Sarah. We're in serious shit here, and there's no point in pretending we're not," Nonny said. A genuine smile burst over her face, and she slapped Kane's shoulder. "Welcome boys. We've been waiting two thousand years for you. It's about damned time."

"Wait—" Sarah grabbed her grandmother, and pulled her to the side. "They're Order, Nonny," she whispered. "You know what that means—"

Nonny ignored her and looked right at Kane. "You think you can squeeze water from stone, young man?"

Kane glanced back at the fountain. "Yeah."

Nonny met his gaze. "You do that, and you can stay. Sarah needs a man like you."

A conspiratorial grin flashed across Kane's face. "It doesn't appear she agrees with you, but I do." He grinned at both of them, then turned away, gesturing at his teammates to meet him at the fountain.

"Nonny," Sarah hissed at her as Kane headed toward the fountain. "Didn't you see his scars?"

Her grandmother raised a well-plucked eyebrow at her. "You think I'm blind? Of course I saw them. The man's covered with them. Why? Do you find them abhorrent? Because personally, I think the man's obvious sex appeal is enhanced by his badges of suffering." She smiled fondly at Kane and the others. "I always liked a man who'd seen the grittier side of life, and I think it's awfully judgmental that you are repulsed by them."

"No! God, no. Of course I'm not repulsed by him!" Sarah grimaced when she saw Kane grin, and her grandmother chuckled. Damn Nonny for making her say that. Sarah lowered her voice and leaned closer to her grandmother. "It's the shapes of the scars. Didn't you see them?"

"Of course I saw them." Nonny rolled her eyes again. "Again with the questions about my eyesight? Do I suddenly look old to you or something?"

"No." Sarah wanted to strangle her grandmother. "It's just that, what if they mean—"

"Mean what?" Kane turned back to them, his brown eyes boring into both of them. "You know what my scars are? Both of you?"

Sarah saw the anguish in his eyes, and suddenly she wasn't certain anymore. How could this man be Los Muerte? He'd averted his weapon instinctively when she'd moved in front of his blade. Los Muerte's instincts would be to kill her. But then again, there was no mistaking the darkness within him... Dammit! "I don't know—"

"Yes, you do, Sarah," Nonny said. "You know exactly what those scars are."

Kane met her gaze, waiting. He wasn't waiting for her grandmother. He wanted to hear it from her. But what was she supposed to do? Tell the man who'd given his life to protecting innocents that he could be the biggest assassin of them all?

Nonny broke the silence. "Save my granddaughter, and we'll talk," Nonny said, her eyes blazing fiercely. "We've been waiting for you, young man. Even Sarah."

Satisfaction gleamed in Kane's eyes, and he nodded once, accepting Nonny's promise. "Not as long as I've been waiting for you." He settled his gaze on Sarah, his voice so heavy with meaning that her body ached in response, and Nonny let out a low whistle and muttered something about the legal levels of testosterone in a man.

Sarah collapsed back against a rock as Kane turned away, her skin flush with heat that had nothing to do with the morning sunshine. Damn him. How could he affect her that way?

Kane caught up with Thano and Ryland, and the three men got to work. Nonny eased Sarah to the ground while Kane and the others began tearing apart the rocks beside the fountain with their hands. The rock seemed to crumble beneath their iron grip, and as Sarah watched the thousand-year-old structure succumb to their strength, she began to fully understand the power of these men.

Of the male whose mark was still on her arm.

The warrior who, despite the intensity of how he made her feel, seemed likely to be the demon who had come back to the village for the singular purpose of being her ultimate destruction. A shiver rippled over her, and she hugged herself, leaning against her grandmother for support. And as she watched his muscles bunching with the effort of unearthing water for her, she couldn't keep herself from wanting even more of him, like a lamb rushing straight into the lion's gaping jaws.

"Dear God," she whispered. "What have I done?"

* * *

Luc Acostos whipped his head up as the breeze carried to him the scent he hadn't smelled in over six hundred years. He froze, his claws buried in the animal he'd just slaughtered, claws that had long since stopped retracting during the day. His muscles tensed and he swung around, frantically scenting the air as he tried to track it. Was he imagining it?

He breathed deeply, then caught it again. That same scent of earth and humanity, of the sulfuric taint of demon and the lily-of-the-valley blessing of purity beyond words. "Jesus!" He leapt to his feet and bolted through the woods, moving so silently and so quickly that even the animals didn't notice him pass by. He brushed a deer with his hip, and the animal hadn't even managed to lift its head to look around before he was past.

Faster and faster he ran, his legs pistoning as he vaulted over underbrush and dead trees, ducking past branches, leaping over boulders. His heart was pounding, his mouth dry, adrenaline screaming through him as he sprinted straight toward the scent he'd locked onto, desperate to get there before it dissipated—

There!

Luc slammed to a stop, his body becoming as still as death as he waited in the shadows, frantically searching the cluster of people around the fountain that he'd finally succeeded in drying up.

His gaze went right toward the tallest male, the one cleaving at the earth beside the fountain with his spiked flail. "By hell's angels," Luc whispered, staring in disbelief at the warrior who was covered in scars.

It had to be him.

Every cell in Luc's body was screaming in response, fire burning through him so intensely that black smudges crept over his arms. It was the black taint of the hell he'd been tormented by for the last six hundred years, the one that made his skin scream with agony every minute of every day. The poison that bled through his veins, eating away at his insides like the slow onslaught of death that would never give him the mercy of actually coming for him. The agonizing thud of his heart, like a dagger being ripped through the tissue each time his heart beat. But the emptiness in his soul was a thousand times worse than the most brutal physical pain it was possible to suffer.

Was it all over now? Was it finally going to end?

Luc watched the warrior, his heart thudding with agonizing anticipation as he waited for the warrior to turn around. To see his face. To *know*.

The warrior stopped suddenly, going utterly still. Slowly, he turned his head, scanning the woods near where Luc was hiding.

No shit? He'd sensed him? Luc stilled his heart, going into complete stealth mode.

Still gripping a massive chunk of rock, the warrior slowly straightened up. With a flick of his fingers, he got the attention of the other two, and all three men began vigilantly scanning the woods. The air began to hum as they reached out with their preternatural senses. The women on the ground near them went still, and suddenly they were looking around as well.

Luc smiled, knowing that they would never find him. No one could. Not unless he wanted them to. *Turn around. Show me your face.*

The warrior dropped the rock and spun around.

Luc froze in stunned disbelief as recognition ripped through him. It was Kane Santiago. The prodigal son had returned. Raw, dark elation tore through Luc, and he dug his claws into his own palm, drawing blood.

Kane turned his head sharply, staring directly at Luc's hiding place.

Luc swore as the warrior seemed to stare right at him. Could he really see him? If he could, that could mean only one thing: their connection was already rebuilding itself. Kane was coming back to him.

A slow, satisfied grin spread across Luc's face as he looked into the male's dark eyes. Eyes so dark they could be from only one place: hell.

Luc's hell.

The hell he hadn't been able to escape for six hundred years. The one that would never release him, until he found his replacement. Luc grinned, knowing that he'd found him. *Welcome to hell, Kane. You owe me a lifetime, and I'm going to take it from you.*

Kane shouted sharply, and sprinted straight toward him.

Luc swore and whirled around, bolting into the woods. He let the forest swallow him up, running hard until there was no sound from behind him. Slowly, he eased down and turned to face the direction of the old village, where Kane Santiago had come back to him.

Luc held up his hand, and watched his flesh disintegrate into wisps of black smoke. The spirals of smoke circled in the air, twisting around, gaining power. "Tonight," he said aloud. "I will come for you tonight."

Then the rest of him dissolved into smoke, and he tore through the woods, a lightning-fast streak of pure evil that left behind a trail of death before he slithered through a crack in the earth and disappeared.

Chapter Eight

Gideon scowled when he walked into the dungeon in the basement of Dante's mansion and saw the only person on earth who mattered to him sitting too damn close to the bastard who had almost killed one woman already. It didn't matter that Quinn and Elijah were also in there, armed and within about two inches of Lily. He'd seen Jacob try to kill his own sister, and Gideon wanted him nowhere near his woman. "Lily," he said, unable to keep the edge out of his voice. "What are you doing with Jacob?"

His soul mate looked up at him, her face glowing with that same intensity that she always had when she was acquiring information. As the world's leading expert on Calydons, Dr. Lily Davenport was in sheer heaven living at the mansion and becoming the Order's most important intellectual resource.

Damn, she was beautiful when she was working. Her blond hair was tumbling around her shoulders and her eyes were a lively green, so different from when he'd first found her, nearly broken after two years of imprisonment at the hands of a psychotic bastard. "I sedated him," she said cheerfully.

"You did? Why?" Gideon strode across the room, nodding at his teammates even as he blew by them. He set his hand on Lily's head, entwining his fingers in her hair, needing to reassure himself that she was safe.

"He was waking up," Quinn said, backing up just enough to give Gideon space, but not venturing far from Jacob's side. Quinn's dark hair was tightly cropped, and his customary black tee shirt was stretched tight across his upper body, showcasing exactly how strong he was. Not that it eased Gideon's mind. There was no one he trusted to protect Lily as well as he could.

"Jacob hadn't even fully regained consciousness before he started to teleport," Quinn said, his brown eyes gleaming and focused. "So I knocked him out until we could figure out how to hang onto him long enough to interrogate him."

Lily rolled her eyes. "If you guys keep hitting him in the head like that, there will be nothing left in his brain for me to learn from." She held up a syringe. "So, I sedated him."

Elijah's face was dark, his body shifting restlessly as he stepped away from Lily and paced the room. Elijah's green eyes were clouded and turbulent, his brown hair ragged and unkempt, and Gideon knew the warrior was still treading too close to the edge that had almost done him in.

"I don't agree with Lily's approach," Elijah said. "We're a race of violence, and that's how we need to handle him. I don't like that she figured out how to knock us on our ass and fuck with our minds by making us sleep." He eyed the syringe with suspicion and distrust. "That should be destroyed. Now. And why are you trying to figure out how to manipulate us, anyway, Lily?"

Lily looked at him calmly, her face soft with understanding. They all knew what Elijah had gone through. "It won't work on you, Elijah,'" she reassured him. "You're too old and powerful. Jacob is only eighteen, and he's got a lot of humanity still left in him. You're way beyond my reach."

"It's not his age that makes Elijah immune," Quinn interrupted, spinning his sword restlessly in his hand. "It's the fact he's Order. It's the fact we're all Order. Shit doesn't work on us that works on others. Never has."

Gideon grinned. "True. We are a bunch of bad asses."

"Not funny, and not true. Not anymore." Elijah stalked across the room and looked out the window that looked down at the courtyard behind the mansion. "We almost got taken out by that kid out there, who's only eighteen years old. We're not indestructible. The world is shifting, and we're playing catch up."

Gideon knew that Elijah was referring to Drew Cartland, Dante's son, who was training with Gabe and Zach. Elijah was correct that there was shit going on that they hadn't seen before: males that were stronger than they should have been who went rogue for no apparent reason. The Calydons who had invaded their domain with their claws and teleporting ability made it damned clear that they had some new challenges to deal with.

Gideon looked at Lily. "Any word on who these guys are? On what their deal is?"

"No. Not yet." Lily picked her computer up off the small table beside her. "I've found some anecdotal reports of clawed Calydons from about two thousand years ago. There are rumors that some of the original Calydons, the ones who were turned by that demon-tainted water, had claws, but I can't find any kind of real evidence, and there have been no reports since."

Gideon crouched beside Lily and studied her notes. "So, we've got throwbacks to two thousand years ago? Where the hell are they coming from?"

"They're young kids," Quinn said, nudging the comatose Jacob with his blade. "This kid hasn't been alive for two thousand years. These are new ones."

Elijah leaned on the metal cot, bracing his hands beside Jacob's head. "Who the fuck are you?" he whispered, his voice laced with threat and urgency. "Talk to us." He swore and lowered his voice, but it was still thick with emotion that ran too personal. "Trust me, kid. You don't want to be the guy who kills his own sister. For hell's sake, let us help you before you make a choice that will haunt you for the rest of your goddamn life."

There was no movement from the cot, and Elijah swore and spun away, striding across the room. Gideon touched his arm as he went past. "We're not going to let him kill his sister."

Elijah's eyes flashed. "Don't make promises you can't keep, Gideon."

Gideon stiffened. "I'm not—"

"Hey!" The door slammed open, and Ian Fitzgerald burst into the room.

"Ian!" Gideon's relief at seeing their teammate who'd gone missing three weeks ago was instantly chased away when he saw Ian's deteriorating condition.

The warrior had been gaunt before, but he looked even worse now. There was dried blood on his shirt, his face was shadowed, and his body looked like he'd lost even more weight. His jeans were caked in dirt, and around his head was a piece of blood-stained fabric, tied into a headband like some teenage bad ass. Shit. The man had been dying a slow death since he'd lost his *sheva* eight months ago, and it looked like death was winning.

At the thought of Ian losing his *sheva*, Gideon swore and tightened his grip in Lily's hair, unable to even allow himself to imagine what it would be like to lose her. His entire body thrummed with sudden adrenaline, and his weapons burned in his arms, ready to be unleashed at any threat to his woman.

Lily touched his arm and looked up at him. *It's okay, Gideon. I'm right here.*

But he couldn't breathe, sucked into Ian's anguish, consumed by the image of being like his teammate, of losing his woman—

Elijah swore and gripped Ian's shoulder as Ian braced his hands on the wall, his ribs heaving as he tried to catch his breath.

"Hell, man," Elijah said. "You look like shit. Where have you been? No one's been able to reach you."

Ian caught Elijah's arm, and stared at the team. "I found her," he said. "I found her."

Gideon stared at his teammate in disbelief, as Lily caught her breath. "Who?"

"My *sheva*."

Gideon swore under his breath, and exchanged glances with Quinn and Elijah. That was impossible, and they all knew it.

"No." Elijah turned Ian toward him, and set his hands on his shoulders. Elijah's face was grim, knowing all too well the delusions that the mind could play. "I killed her, Ian. Don't you remember? I'm sorry as hell that I did it, but I did. You were there. She died in your arms."

"No!" Ian knocked his hands away. "She came back to life. And died again. And now I have to find her before it happens again."

"Ian, she didn't come back to life," Elijah swore, and Gideon saw the tension in his body. Elijah knew what it was like to lose his mind, and he was still on edge most of the time. Only his *sheva* kept him sane, but Ana had gone off with her sister Grace, Quinn's *sheva*, for a trip into town. Elijah had been needed to stay and guard Jacob, so it was the first separation he'd had from Ana since they'd completed their bond.

"That's impossible, Ian," Quinn said. "Your *sheva* died. You don't come back from that. Elijah's right."

"No." Ian lurched to his feet and looked at Lily, his eyes blazing with a clarity that didn't look like a man drowning in his own delusions. He looked desperate and haggard, yeah, but there was a clarity that Gideon hadn't seen in months.

"There has to be a way that can happen. Tell me what she is," Ian said to Lily, his voice urgent. "Tell me how it can happen. I have to find her again. I've been looking, but I can't find her. I don't know where she is." His voice vibrated with desperate agony, and Gideon had a sudden sense that Ian was closer to the edge than he'd ever been before, even when they'd had to chain him up for three months to protect him and the rest of them.

At Ian's desperation and his stark suffering, Gideon felt a rush of hope that Ian was somehow correct that his *sheva* was alive. He wanted Ian to have that chance to be with her, to feel the surge of life that came from bonding with his soul mate. He looked at Lily, who was frowning. "Is there a chance she came back to life?" he asked her. "Is there a way to come back from being truly dead?"

Lily rubbed her forehead, wearily. "I don't know. I've never run across it, but that doesn't mean it can't happen."

What the fuck are you thinking? Quinn's voice pushed into Gideon's mind. *It sucks that Ian lost his* sheva, *but you really think it would be better if she were still alive?*

Gideon eyed his teammate. *You would rather exist without your sheva? You think your life would be better without Grace?*

No way. Quinn narrowed his eyes and paced restlessly, his body coiled with visible tension at the mere idea of it. *But every minute of every day, I think about the fact that our destiny commands that once a warrior completes his bond with his mate, he is destined to lose her, go rogue and destroy everything that matters to both of them. I look at the woman who means more to me than my own life, and I wonder when that time bomb will go off and I'll lose her. Sometimes I can't even think straight because I'm quivering in bloody terror waiting to lose Grace. If Ian escaped that hell and dodged the bullet by having his* sheva *die before he could get attached to her and go rogue, then fuck yeah, I think he's better off.*

Shit. Gideon had thought he was the only one who had those nightmares. He swore and looked at Lily, who was talking intently with Ian, grilling him with questions. *We beat our fate, Quinn. We're all still alive, and we need to remember that. We won.*

For now. Quinn closed his eyes, and Gideon felt the well of raw emotion coming from him. Fear, at the very deepest level of his core. *We knocked destiny on her ass, but we didn't defeat her.* He opened his eyes. *You, me, and Elijah are the first warriors in two thousand years not to be destroyed by the* sheva *bond. You really think we're so special? Fate's going to come for us, Gideon, and as God is my witness, as much as I love my woman and would go through hell a thousand times for every minute I have with her, never on this earth would I want Ian to have to find his woman and lose her again, because I know it will fucking break me if and when it happens.*

"Not me." Elijah slowly rose to his feet, his voice commanding the attention of the room. Since he was blood-bonded with Gideon and Quinn, he could hear their conversations unless they were actively blocking him, which they hadn't bothered to do. "I've been through hell and back, more than a thousand times, and it all goes away when I'm with Ana. I don't give a shit what happens in the future, but I'm willing to risk my own soul and every last piece of my heart for another minute with her." He nodded at Ian. "Find your woman, Ian. Find her, and give her everything you have. It's worth every fucking minute of it."

Ian nodded. "I know."

Elijah sheathed his weapons. "I'm going off guard duty. I need to find Ana." He met their gaze. "I can't do this without her." Then he turned and strode out of the room, not even bothering to look back.

For a moment, no one spoke. What was there to say? Gideon agreed with both Quinn and Elijah, and right now, he couldn't even begin to imagine a single second without Lily. Was it better for Ian to never find his woman, or to find her, give his soul to her, and *then* lose her?

Ian was the one who broke the silence. "Alice is my one chance to survive," he said, his voice hard.

"Alice?" Gideon exchanged glances with Quinn. "I thought her name was Catherine Taylor—" He cut himself off when he saw the look of agony on Ian's face. "Or Alice is fine." What the hell was going on? Ian's *sheva*, the woman who had died was Catherine Taylor. Since when did Ian's *sheva* become a woman named Alice? Ian's dark expression made it clear that now was not the time for questions.

"Fuck destiny and what it wants to do to us if we complete our bond," Ian bit out. "That doesn't matter right now. All that matters is that I find Alice."

Quinn looked at him grimly. "But fate's plan for you *will* matter—"

Ian met his gaze. "If I don't get through today, then the future is irrelevant. I have to find her."

Gideon swore when he saw the intense expression on Ian's face. Recognition pulsed through him, because he knew exactly what it felt like to have a singular focus on one woman. There was no other option. Not for Ian. "Then we're with you." He slammed his hand down on Ian's shoulder. "Fuck two thousand years of destiny."

Quinn cursed under his breath, but nodded. His eyes bore into Ian with the grim reality of their lives. "You want me to strike you down if you go rogue, or her?"

The mission of the Order dictated that the *sheva* of an Order member was always killed to prevent the completion of the bond and the triggering of fate's destruction. Order males were so rare and so elite, a critical factor in protecting innocents from rogue Calydons who were essentially undefeatable except by Order, that the female had to be sacrificed to save him. But since the three of them had met their *shevas* and dodged destiny, the rules were beginning to blur.

Ian whirled on Quinn, calling out his weapons instantly with a crack and a flash of black light. He had them at Quinn's throat before the warrior had even reacted. "No one dies. Not me. Not her. Not ever."

Quinn raised his brows, and Gideon grinned, relief cascading through him. *Damn, it's good to see him like this. He's got a mission, Quinn.*

Ian had been without fire, without passion, without life since his *sheva* had died. To see him with a fire in his eyes...damn...it was good. Really good. But hell, if he lost his *sheva* again, would he ever survive it? "Ian, if you don't find her—"

There was a loud noise from the hallway, and Vaughn McIntyre strode into the room. He was Drew's guardian, the man who Drew called his uncle, a warrior who had made it clear that he would defend the youth with his life. Vaughn's eyes were glittering with a faint hint of green, reminding Gideon that although the Order had accepted Vaughn into the mansion because of his relationship with Drew, they still had no idea what the hell he was or who his people were.

"Drew's training has to stop," Vaughn stated without preamble. "The kid tried to kill Gabe today. He lost sight of the fact it was training. He snapped." He stopped in the middle of the room. "I'm taking him away from here. Now."

Gideon shook his head, while Quinn subtly moved into battle stance. They all knew they could not afford to let Drew leave. He was too deadly, too on edge, and too tainted with the spirit of Ezekiel, the madman who nearly destroyed the Order so recently. They had to watch Drew, and carefully. "It's not the training that's doing it, Vaughn. It's Drew himself. He needs to stay here where we can help him manage it."

"Fuck that." Vaughn shook his head. "There's violence in his soul now. It wasn't there before he came here."

"It's what happens when you come into your powers as a Calydon, and it's from Ezekiel, too," Quinn explained. "It's our job to help him manage it—"

"No. I won't let him go down that road. The Calydons are a bunch of crap, and I'm taking him out of here. We can take care of him."

"We?" Gideon went into high alert. "Who? Who are your people, Vaughn? Why would they be able to control him when you think we can't?"

"I'm taking Drew," Vaughn said, aggression thickening his voice. Vaughn flexed his hands, and his skin began to glow with the faintest hint of green as he prepared for them to try to stop him. Gideon swore. What the hell was going on with Vaughn? He'd never seen his skin like that before.

"Hey!" Ian strode across the room and grabbed Vaughn's arm. "What the hell are you? What's up with the green?"

Vaughn's face went expressionless, and he gave no information. As always. "Back off, Fitzgerald. My battle is not with you."

"Do you know a guy named Flynn?" Ian demanded. "Turns green? Violent as hell? His eyes go green like yours, Vaughn. I've never seen anyone else's do that, besides you."

Vaughn went still, staring at Ian. Saying nothing.

Gideon scowled. "What are you talking about, Ian?"

"A man with Vaughn's eyes killed my *sheva*. I want to know where to find him." Ian watched Vaughn closely. "He was a hell of a lot like Vaughn. Do you know where I can find him? He knew Alice, and he might have the answers I need."

Vaughn met Ian's gaze. "How did he kill her?"

"A green disc."

"Son of a bitch." Vaughn broke away and strode to the window. He braced his palms and leaned out, watching the courtyard. Gideon could still hear the clangs of metal on metal as Drew sparred with Gabe and Zach.

"Listen," Quinn said, walking into the middle of the room, taking control back from Ian and Vaughn. "Ian, we've got some serious shit going on right now. I hear you about your woman, but we've got some major issues with these guys and an angel they're trying to kill." He jerked his chin at Lily, who was hunched over her computer and typing furiously. "Lily's working on that right now, and we need to allocate all our resources to this situation, including you."

"No." Ian turned and strode toward the door, apparently leaving. "If I don't find Alice, none of this shit matters—"

"Wait." Vaughn spoke up, not turning from the window. "I'm going with Ian."

Ian whirled sharply around, and Gideon stiffened. "You're taking Drew on a hunt?" The kid was too volatile to take into battle, but Vaughn had always kept vigilant watch on the young Calydon, never entrusting him to anyone else.

"No." Vaughn finally turned away from the courtyard, and there was grim resolution on his face. He looked right at Quinn. "I want your oath that you will take over Drew's training. That you will watch him carefully and monitor every thought in his mind. He's close to the edge, but I don't know what direction he's going in or what's causing it." Quinn was the Order member that Drew had chosen to trust originally, and it was only Quinn that Vaughn truly trusted.

Quinn narrowed his eyes. "I'm not blood-bonded with Drew. I can't get in his head unless he lets me."

"Then blood bond." Vaughn leveraged himself off the window sill, cutting off his own view of the kid. "Drew needs to be protected from himself." He walked over and stood beside Ian. "I have to take care of this situation with Ian, and I can't involve Drew." He ground his jaw, and Gideon felt the intense conflict in the man, his need to address whatever situation Ian had alerted him to warring with the need to protect the youth he considered his son.

"We all have to do what's right for the greater good," Gideon told him. "It's what we do. Take care of your situation. It's what you need to do."

"I'm not Order," Vaughn snapped. "I don't sacrifice one innocent to save millions. Those aren't my values. I don't give a shit about the greater good. That's not what this is about." He jerked his chin at Quinn. "You in or what?"

Quinn nodded. "I'll go get Drew now. He'll help us with Jacob."

Vaughn gave Quinn the briefest flash of a smile, then he turned toward Ian. "Ready?"

Ian slammed his fist into his hand and grinned. "Fuck, yeah." He jerked his chin at Gideon. "We good?"

Gideon glanced at Lily, and she looked up immediately, as if she'd sensed his perusal. She gave him a warm smile that went straight to his gut, and Gideon knew there was no decision to be made. For reasons more complex than Ian was sharing, he needed to find his woman, and they'd all just have to deal with the consequences. If Ian went rogue, they'd do what they needed to do and kill his *sheva* again. But hell, Gideon hoped it didn't come to that. "Yeah, do your thing, Ian."

"Good luck, Fitz," Quinn said. "Keep in touch and let us know what you need."

Ian grinned, his eyes blazing with a life that Gideon hadn't seen in him for eight months. "You bet." He slammed his hand on Vaughn's shoulder. "Let's go."

The two warriors sprinted out of the room, their boots pounding down the hall as they hauled ass out of the mansion, brought together by a shared urgency and two different missions.

Quinn looked at Gideon, a grim expression on his face. "If this goes wrong, we're going to lose Ian for good. He can't handle losing his *sheva* again."

Gideon ground his jaw. "I know." He walked over to the window and looked out. Drew was circling Gabe while Zach watched. The youth had put on twenty pounds of muscle in the last two weeks, amassing strength at a rate far faster than he should have, given how recently he'd come into his powers. He moved with a grace and aggression that was already lethal, and the expression on his face as he stalked Gabe was deadly and emotionless. Gideon felt a ripple of foreboding.

Quinn walked up beside him, and the two blood-bonded warriors studied the scene on the grass. "What the hell's going on, Gideon?" Quinn said quietly. "We have a woman who is apparently coming back from the dead repeatedly, a young warrior who is stronger and more violent than he should be, clawed rogue Calydons who can teleport, and an angel who's being hunted by them. There's too much out of alignment right now that we can't get a handle on. It can't all be coincidence."

"No, it can't." Gideon glanced over at the metal cot Jacob was sleeping on, shackles holding him down. "We've got no choice. We've got to wake him up and get some answers."

Quinn swore. "We can't wake him up. We'll never hold him long enough to get anything from him."

Gideon scowled. "We're going to have to try soon, because I'm not going to sit around on my ass waiting for hell to hunt us down. We need to be ready."

Ready for what, he didn't know.

But they needed to find out.

Chapter Nine

What had been hunting him?

Kane stood at the edge of the woods, his senses straining to track the creature he'd sensed in the woods. Whatever he'd sensed had been the vilest of evil, and it swept through Kane like acid ripping through his tissue. Adrenaline roared over him as he searched the woods with his preternatural senses, trying to get a read on what he'd just seen. It felt familiar, like he'd recognized it, like his soul knew what it had been. But what the hell was it?

"Hey." Ryland jogged up beside him, his machetes clenched in his fists. "What'd you pick up?"

"I don't know—" Suddenly, Kane was hit with a brutal stab of pain, as if a dagger had just been plunged into his ribs and ripped through his skin. "Jesus!" He grabbed his chest, staggering from the sudden pain. The pain spread through him, right through his gut and down his legs, as if it were tearing through his muscles, ripping them from his very bone. Violence spewed through him, and his head was suddenly filled with images of bodies being ripped to shreds, covered in blood, strewn across the barren earth. He shook his head, trying to clear the vision, but it became worse. He could hear screams, the agonizing screams of people being torn from life by hell—

"Shit!" Ryland grabbed his shoulders, holding him as Kane twisted in pain. "What the hell's going on with you?"

"I don't know," Kane gasped—

"Down on your knees, boy!" Nonny was suddenly in front of him, her wizened face blazing with intensity. "Sarah, get your ass over here. Thano, get some water from the fountain. Destroy the damned thing if you have to. Get it now!"

Kane's knees dug into the rocky terrain, and he felt blood trickling down his temple as Thano took off. The visions were arcing though his brain now, the worst carnage and slaughter, horror beyond the imaginable. Violence and outrage spewed through him, along with the need to leap up and kill. He needed to destroy, just like the visions in his mind.

He looked up and saw Ryland crouched beside him. A snarl curled Kane's lip and his flail erupted into his hand. "You need to die, you bastard—"

"Back off, Santiago," Ryland snapped. "What the fuck is your deal?"

"Sarah!" Nonny barked. "Get over here!"

Sarah crawled over to him. "Kane?" Her voice was worried, but the mere sound of it was like an infusion of peace and serenity, ripping through the pain like a white light through blackness.

"Sarah," he gasped, reaching for her. He caught her hand, and yanked her into him. She tumbled against him so hard that their bodies smacked together. The moment Kane held her in his arms, he felt his whole body react in shock to her warmth. "Jesus, Sarah." He tangled his fingers in her hair and buried his face in her neck, trying to concentrate only on the feel of her body against his.

To his disbelieving relief, Sarah slipped her arms around his neck and pulled him close, resting her face against his cheek. Her skin was warm and soft, like this great gift of peace and freedom. But the visions in his head were still there, the violence, the—

No, Kane. Focus on me. Sarah's warmth wrapped through his mind, and he could almost feel her prying his mind from the grip of the visions. *Come back to me.*

Kane honed in on her voice, using the sound of her soft whisperings as an anchor, pulling him back from the edge. Slowly, the visions began to fade, and he became aware of desire pulsing within him, an awareness of the way her body was crushed against his. Her breasts were flush against his chest, her arms holding him tightly, her heart beating rapidly against his ribs. The darkness fled, the violence vanished, and all that was left was Sarah. He gripped her hair and pulled her head back so he could look at her.

Her blue eyes were flushed with worry and desire, sensual attraction that went right to his core. But there was wariness in her expression as well, and he knew it was because she'd sensed the extreme violence within him. Her eyes looked haunted, and her skin was ashen. Suddenly he was furious that he'd been distracted from getting water for her. when she was in such dire straits. "You need the fountain."

Sarah's gaze left Kane's face and went to his forehead, and her brow furrowed in concern. "God, Kane." She touched his head, and pain shot through him. He became aware of the pain again, and the blood cascading down his face. He was bleeding, even though nothing had hit him? What the *hell?*

Not that it mattered, not with Sarah so weak. He suddenly needed to focus on her, to do *something* that made sense to him. He grabbed her and lurched to his feet, his head still spinning as he turned her toward the pile of rocks where Thano was swinging his halberd through the base of the fountain, sending pieces of rock cascading though the air. Sweat was streaming down his body, and his muscles were flexed with the effort, but there was no water. "Damned fountain," Thano said as he paused to check.

Ryland sprinted over to Thano and slammed his machete into the rock. The rock splintered as the two men tore it apart, but there was still no water.

Kane lurched to the fountain, and fell to his knees, Sarah's need pulsing through him. Had to find the water. Had to help her. Had to save her. Had to focus on Sarah, not the taint screaming through him. He stared at the fountain and opened his senses to the rock. He breathed in scents so subtle that they were like secrets carried in the droplets of air. He heard whispers of sounds, the almost imperceptible gurgle of water. He felt the dampness on his skin...and he knew exactly where to go.

He called out his flail and dragged himself to a flat rock several yards south of the fountain.

"No," Thano shouted. "Over here, Kane!"

Sarah pulled herself beside him and put her hands on the ground. She stared at him, disbelief in her eyes. "I can feel it, too."

His body screaming in pain, blood cascading over his face, over his chest, and down his legs, Kane reared back and slammed the flail into the earth, summoning every last bit of strength in his body. The impact was tremendous, and the earth shook beneath them as the weapon decimated the rock and plunged out of sight beneath the ground, leaving a gaping wound in the earth almost three feet wide.

He didn't have to look. He knew he'd found the water. He grabbed Sarah, scooped her up in his arms and rolled them over the edge without even checking to see what lay below. The edge of the rock dug into his back and then they were over, plummeting straight downwards. Sarah gasped and sucked in her breath, and then the cold water closed over their heads.

The moment it touched Kane's skin, he knew it wasn't just for her. It was for him as well.

* * *

The relief from the water was instant, surging over Sarah with a life-giving purity that jolted her body into awareness. It had been years since she'd been fully submerged in the water, and it felt incredible. She closed her eyes, letting the current toss her as the cleansing water poured into her body, firing up her cells, infusing her with the healing energy and power she'd needed so badly.

Strength surged into her, and with that came hope. New life. Chances. She had time again.

Kane grabbed the wall of the underground tunnel, jerking them to a stop against the current of the underground river. He turned her in his arms so she was facing him. His face was dimly lit by the sunlight that was streaming through the hole in the tunnel's roof, but they'd already drifted far enough from the hole that the sun was faint and distant, casting his face in shadows swathed in light.

His gaze was intense on her, his eyes dark, and she became viscerally aware of his hard body locked down around her, holding her ruthlessly tight against him. The water slid over her skin, like a sensual caress, igniting all the nerve endings in her body.

Kane's eyes were hooded, fierce with pain and agony, but also a desire so intense that her entire body vibrated in response. "The pain inside me is gone," he said. "What is this water?"

She realized that he'd been washed clean of the blood, and he wasn't bleeding anymore. She touched his head, and he didn't wince. "It shouldn't affect you like this," she said. "Only me."

"What is it?" he asked again.

She shook her head. "It's the life force of angels. It's hope. It's faith. It's all those good things in life that give people the strength to get up each day and cope with what they have. It's the blood that flows through me."

He narrowed his eyes, holding her tight as the water gently bumped them against each other. "So, why did it take my pain away?"

She shook her head. "I don't know." She raised her eyebrows. "I don't suppose you're part angel, are you?"

He laughed softly. "You really think there's a chance of that?"

She didn't need to answer. They'd both felt the evil consuming him. "Demons and angels are cut of the same cloth," she said. "We just go in different directions." She frowned. "But angel water would burn a demon."

"You mean, like this?" He held up his hand, revealing a crimson streak across his palm. "I got this when I was feeling the mist from the water."

"Oh..." Foreboding rippled through Sarah. "But it's not burning you now."

"No. It's not. It burns me one minute, heals me the next. I feel like I'm near death, and then a minute later, I'm raging with violence and pain. My head feels like it's splitting in two, and I don't know what the fuck is going on." His eyes darkened then, and he shifted position, pinning her up against the wall of the cave. His pelvis pressed against hers, his hand locked down on the rock next to her shoulder, blocking the water for both of them. He was so imposing, his broad shoulders gleaming and wet as the water cascaded off his skin. "But you do. Tell me now, Sarah. Tell me who I am."

She swallowed, aware that they were alone in the tunnel. She could hear her grandmother shouting at them, asking if they were okay. She could hear the rumble of Thano and Ryland's deep voices as they checked out the hole.

"We're good," Kane shouted. "We'll be out in a few minutes. Sarah needs to recover."

There was a whoop and a holler of victory from Nonny, and Sarah heard her ordering Thano and Ryland to back off and give them space. Sarah's heart began to pound at Kane's closeness, and suddenly she didn't want to be in there with him. All she could think about was the night he'd saved her from her brother, the intensity of the physical connection between them, the way he'd stripped through her defenses and made love to her so passionately and so intently that she'd fallen completely under his spell.

The angel water had marked him. It would only mark demons. *Only demons.*

"No." Kane moved closer, his bulk blocking out the sunlight. He grabbed her wrists with his free hand and pinned them over her head. "No more games, Sarah. No more shutting me out." He bent his head, his mouth inches from hers, so his breath was warm and tempting against her lips. "Who the hell am I, and why in God's name can I think of nothing else right now except tearing off your clothes and driving into you until you scream my name and become a part of my soul for all eternity? You have an answer for that one, too, I bet."

So much was raging through Kane's mind that he could barely think. The violence that had been haunting him had eased the moment they'd hit the water, and the pain had settled, but in its place was a rising lust that was nearly crippling in its intensity. He pressed Sarah's wrists more tightly against the rock, breathing in her scent. He felt alive, more alive than he ever had been in his life. The emptiness was long gone, and he was filled with desire, lust, passion and life, and it all centered on the woman in his arms.

His blood was thundering through him, and he was viscerally aware of her breasts crushed against his chest, of her hips pinned by his, of the desire pouring off her.

All he wanted was answers, and yet all he could think about was her body pinned beneath his. With a low growl, he caught her lower lip in his teeth, needing to touch her, to own her, to make her his. "Tell me what you know." He wasn't moving, wasn't letting her up until he had answers. To all of it.

She took a breath and met his gaze. "Kane, I don't know for sure—"

"No more excuses, Sarah." He tightened his grip on her, his adrenaline beginning to race. It was time. He knew it. Right now, he was going to get the answers he'd been seeking for so long. "Tell me what you know. Why do I fit in here? What did I see in your woods and why did it affect me like that? Why did that water burn my palm, but no one else's?" His voice vibrated with urgency. "What the fuck are my scars from?"

Sarah stared at him, and he knew then that she was going to tell him. "There are demons in our woods, Kane. What you saw was a demon."

He narrowed his eyes. "An actual demon?"

"No, well, a Calydon—"

He swore. "I already told you, I'm not a demon—"

"All Calydons were originally created by demon taint, and you know it. The water that the original warriors drank two thousand years ago was from a fountain poisoned with demon taint. It turned those men into powerful warriors who were always haunted by their dark side, always on the edge of going rogue."

Kane had to acknowledge the truth of her words, because all the Calydons since the original crew were burdened with that violent side hidden beneath banners of honor and protection, even the Order members. "That doesn't mean we're demons."

"The Calydons outside our village, like your teammates, are generations away from the original demon source, so they're not demons," Sarah said, cutting him off. "But the ones who hunt this town are different. This town was originally created as a haven for angels. We were drawn to it, and so were the demons. They came here to destroy us, and they conscript the men from our village into doing their work. The Calydons in our village are first generation, and the demon taint runs thick in their blood."

Kane narrowed his eyes at the information, already planning to share that with his team back at the mansion. "And what does that have to do with me? You called me a demon, but I'm Order. I'm not from this village—"

"Let me finish." She put her hand on his lips to shush him, and sudden heat rushed over him at the feel. Lust. Desire. Raw, burning need for this woman in his arms. He began to rub her shoulder, sliding his thumb past the edge of her collar so he touched her bare skin.

Sarah jumped and caught her breath. "Don't do that," she said. "I can't concentrate."

"Can't stop." He bent his head, trailing his lips over her throat. "Keep talking."

Sarah leaned her head back against the wall, not trying to shove him away. "God, Kane, how can you be the same man? How can you be two different men like this? I should never respond to you like this—"

"Yes, you should." Kane fisted her hair and brought his mouth down over hers. Now that he knew he was going to get the answers he wanted, suddenly, the urgency was gone, replaced by a thrumming anticipation and a heady sense of power. He had what he wanted, and it was coming now. "Talk to me, Sarah." He brushed his lips over her jaw, all too aware of how passionate they'd been together that night. "Who am I?"

She pushed at his shoulders, trying to get space. "I think you might be Los Muerte."

"Los Muerte?" Kane paused in his seduction, rolling the name over in his head. It didn't sound familiar. "Who is Los Muerte?"

"Death. A Calydon in our village who killed his own wife and son and murdered over five hundred people, mostly angels. Los Muerte destroyed this entire town, Kane, in one murderous frenzy and wiped out almost an entire race of beings."

Kane went still, staring at Sarah as her words crashed through him like the black night of hell. Visions suddenly stormed through his head. Death. Bloodied bodies. A small boy cowering in the corner of a bloodstained floor... Jesus! He jerked back from her, denial racing through him. "That's not me."

Her face was strained, shadows erasing her features as she kept talking. "They couldn't kill Los Muerte. Everything they tried didn't work. He healed every time and would come back. The last time they were able to incapacitate him, they carved the talismans in his body, symbols of protection against the demons, frantically marking up his skin before he could recover and attack again." Sarah touched his arm, running her fingers over his scars, a touch so soft and so incongruous to the story she was telling. "They covered every last bit of his skin, trying to contain the demon within."

Kane shook his head, trying to clear the visions. "There's no way that was me."

"They dumped Los Muerte in another city before he woke up, praying that he wouldn't be able to find his way back," Sarah said softly. "They were hoping that when he woke up, the markings would have contained the demon, so only the parts of his soul that weren't a monster would remain."

Kane leaned back against the wall of the tunnel, trying to process Sarah's information. The story fit with what he knew of his past, with the scars and waking up in an alley with no memory. Was he a murderer? Did he murder his own son? Disgust and revulsion pulsed through him, but Kane forced himself to look inside, to see if it fit him.

It didn't.

He opened his eyes and looked at Sarah. "I'm not Los Muerte. It's impossible."

"Your scars match the talismans carved all over the village," she said. She touched his chest. "I can feel the darkness inside you, Kane. The violence. The evil. And that void—it felt like death, like your soul was dying. That could have been from the talismans keeping your true self buried. Maybe they were killing your soul."

"And it's coming back to life because of you? That's the darkness and the pain, my true self trying to come back to life?" He swore, pressing his hand over hers, knowing exactly what she was talking about. His need to attack Ryland. The darkness swirling inside him that had been getting worse and worse. The restlessness. "Shit."

Sarah moved closer, the water rippling between them as it streamed past them. "But I also feel the goodness inside you. I feel both, Kane." She looked up at him, and there was wariness in her eyes, but also warmth and acceptance. "I don't know what you are. I don't know how you can be Los Muerte and still be the man who averted his weapon so quickly when I moved in front of it."

Kane braced his hands on either side of Sarah's neck, pulled her close, needing to feel her against him. "Shit, Sarah, of course I'd move my weapon away from you—"

"No." She touched his mouth again. "There's one more thing about Los Muerte, Kane."

Kane slid his hands over her hips, drawing her tighter against him. "What?"

"He was created to wipe out the angels in the village." She raised her chin to meet his gaze. "I'm the last one left, Kane. If you're Los Muerte, then you've come back to this town to kill me."

Kane stared at her, and for a split second, a vision flashed in his mind of Sarah dead, her body floating on the river, eyes closed, stretched out like the angel of death had wiped her out. Panic hit him, raw uncontrolled fear at the thought of her dying, and he yanked her close. She barely had time to yelp before he slammed his mouth down onto hers and kissed her.

* * *

Kane's kiss was frantic and desperate, almost violent, nearly consuming Sarah from the intensity of it. It was nothing like the kiss the night they'd met, which had been about emotional connection and trying to uplift each other's souls.

This was raw, untamed possession. Desperation. And it crashed through all the shields she'd been trying to hold so tightly to protect herself from him. With a frantic moan, Sarah threw her arms around him and kissed him back, just as desperate as he was for the kiss, for the connection, for the feel of his mouth on hers.

She didn't know how he could affect her this way, how she could dig her fingers into his scars and not feel unbridled terror, but she didn't. She just felt the raw strength of his body surrounding her, the steel of his arms as he locked her down against his solid frame, and the burning need of his soul for hers.

His hands gripped her hips and he pushed her against the rock wall, his body pinning her against the rough earth. He was so dominant, so powerful, and her entire being wanted more. She wanted to feel his mind the way she had before. She wanted that connection. She wanted to feel him burning his way into her soul and igniting the light buried within her—

"God, Sarah," Kane whispered against her mouth. "You're like this burst of white light into my soul."

She laughed softly. *Well, I am an angel—*

Kane broke the kiss suddenly, slamming her against the wall. He loomed over her, his eyes dark and turbulent. "I'm not here to destroy you," he ground out. "When I see you, I'm consumed by the need to protect you. These last two weeks have been hell, wondering where you were, terrified that those bastards had found you and I hadn't been there to protect you." He gripped her hair, his voice fierce and raw. "My only mission for the last five hundred years has been to find out who I am, until I met you, and then it became you." He tightened his grip and lowered his mouth to hers, almost touching, not quite. "I need to breathe the air you breathe. I need to feel your skin against mine. I need to feel your mind in my head. I burn to make love to you until the very earth itself explodes from the intensity of our passion." He lifted his gaze, his eyes blazing with fire. "Those are not the words of a man brought into this life to destroy you, Sarah. I will never, ever believe that I'm meant to destroy you. *Never.*"

And then his mouth descended on hers and he took her as his own.

Tears filled Sarah's eyes as Kane kissed her, her heart aching as his words reverberated through her. How could he say those words? How could he mean them? How could she trust him? But it felt so right. It felt true. Her entire soul wanted to reach out to him and enfold him into her heart— "Stop!" She pushed him away, struggling to get free. "Don't—"

"What?" He didn't let go, didn't release her, didn't give her space. His face was stark and raw, and she felt his horror at what she'd told him, at the possibility that he was who she'd said. "Why are you so scared of me, Sarah? What do you see in me?"

Sarah heard the desperation in his voice, and suddenly she just wanted to cry. She didn't want to hold this man at arm's length anymore. He'd saved her life three times already, between her brother, her fading light, and now the fountain. He'd averted his weapon when she'd moved in front of it. He'd touched her heart. And he'd said the most beautiful things to her, the kind of things that made the aching wound in her soul want to heal.

But how could she trust him? How could she trust another Calydon again?

"Sarah." His grip was desperate. "You've been inside my soul. As God is my witness, what did you see in there that makes you so afraid of me? Did you see Los Muerte? Did you?"

"No!" she blurted out. "I saw my husband!"

Kane sucked in his breath, and his fingers dug into her arms. His voice went deathly cold. "You have a husband?"

"No." She closed her eyes, fighting against the memories trying to consume her. "I did. He killed my parents, our daughter, and almost me." She tugged her shirt up and showed him the eighteen inch scar across her abdomen. "I was in the hospital for eleven months," she said. "He came as close to killing me as anyone has ever come."

Kane felt shock roll through him as he stared at the raw, brutal wound transgressing Sarah's torso. There were a multitude of lines, crisscrossing in several different directions. Claw marks. Swearing, he spread his palm over her belly as if he could take away the memory and the pain. "Shit, Sarah. What happened?"

Sarah looked at him, and he saw the immense pain in her eyes. Not just pain. Betrayal. The same as she'd felt with her brother. "Mason and I lived next door to each other in the village as kids," she said. "Back then Akara was pretty populated, and it had begun to thrive again after the destruction."

Kane grimaced at her reference to Los Muerte, but he quickly shut it out when another wave of Sarah's pain hit him. "Sarah—"

"No." She shook her head. "I want you to know." Her eyes were shimmering with tears. "Mason and I had been best friends since we were kids. We were so tight. Connected in our souls."

Jealousy shot through Kane at the idea of Sarah being connected with another male, and he cupped the side of her face with his palm, needing to bring them together in the present. He was the one here now. Not anyone else. He was the one who'd made love to her until the earth had shifted. "What happened?"

She set her hand on his wrist, wrapping her fingers around his arm to keep him from releasing her, pleasing Kane. "We fell in love when we were teenagers." She looked at Kane, searching his face for understanding. "I knew that the Calydons were hunting us. I'd grown up having to bar my doors at night to keep them out. I knew that boys who were my friends could turn, husbands, brothers...it happened all the time. Sometimes, they didn't. Sometimes they came into their powers and remained loyal, protecting the rest of us at night. Other times, they crossed that line into monsters. Sometimes it happened as soon as they came into their powers, and sometimes years later. We all knew not to trust our men."

Kane narrowed his eyes as he digested that information. "Did they turn rogue because they were bonded with females?"

"No. There was never a reason we could find." She closed her eyes, and he felt the sudden swell of her pain. "I knew I had to be careful, but I trusted Mason. I'd known him my whole life, and we loved each other. I knew I could believe in him, that our love would be stronger than the curse that had taken so many of the others." She opened her eyes, and tears filled them. "After he came into his powers as a Calydon, we realized I was his *sheva*. We bonded, and it was amazing. I felt safe with him, Kane. He was my soul mate. He couldn't turn on me, right?"

Kane swore. "Fate requires that he turn rogue—"

"No," she shook her head. "That never applied in our village. The bond didn't have that effect—"

"What?" He gripped her arms. "You're serious? How many times?" Then he saw the pain on her face, and suddenly it wasn't about the details. It was about her. The village could come later. "What happened?"

"We had a daughter." Her voice broke, and Kane felt sudden emotion swelling in his own chest. "Her name was Abigail. She was so beautiful, Kane. Such a treasure."

Kane was stunned by the depth of love in her voice. He'd never heard anything so beautiful. He lived a life of violence and honor. He'd spent half a millennium cutting down males who had turned on their women. Kane had no basis for even understanding the kind of love in Sarah's voice. He had no memory of his childhood or a mother, and nothing in his life had prepared him for the enormity of emotion in Sarah's voice. Something inside him moved, something so deep and so buried he didn't even know what it was, something that hurt almost unbearably. He touched Sarah's hair, unable to speak, unable to respond. *Sarah. The way you talk about her is beautiful.*

Then she raised her eyes to his, and he saw the most agonizing loss in them. Pain that went so deep it had torn her soul to pieces. *She died, Kane. I couldn't protect her. I saw Mason's eyes when he came into the house that night. I knew that he had changed, but I couldn't believe he would turn on us. I went right to him, intending to pull him back from the edge. I should have grabbed Abigail and run, but I didn't. I believed I could save him.* Her voice broke, and tears flooded his mind, drawing him into her story.

And suddenly, Kane was in her memories, and he could see what she was remembering. A young man, early twenties, strong and strapping, his eyes glowing red, claws extending from his fingers. Around his neck was a talisman in the same shape as the ones on Kane's body. He felt Sarah's horror as viscerally as if he was living it. He felt the stab of pain as Mason jammed his claws into her belly. His body shook from the impact of Sarah being flung to the side, the crash of her body against the wall. Her anguish, her desperate cry as Mason strode across the room to the little girl, who was watching her daddy without the slightest bit of fear.

Kane could smell the trail of blood as Sarah lunged across the room, throwing her body over her daughter as Mason reached for her. He felt the agony of his claws coming down and slamming all the way through Sarah's body into the child she was protecting beneath her.

"No!" Sarah screamed, her voice ripping Kane out of her thoughts. Caught in the memories, she was pounding on Kane, hitting him, fighting against the enemy that was long gone. "Abigail! God, not my baby—"

"Sarah." Kane enveloped her in his arms, pulling her tightly against him. "It's over. You're here with me now. You're safe now."

"No, no, no!" Still she fought him, screaming for the child she hadn't been able to protect, for the man who had betrayed her so brutally.

She was lost in the memories of a hell worse than anything Kane had ever lived.

He had no idea what to say to take away her anguish. He didn't know how to help. He'd never trusted anyone enough to be betrayed by them, and he had no basis for how to help her, for what to say, how to take away her pain.

He swore, holding her close, stroking her hair, whispering to her everything he could think of to make it okay. But as she trembled in his arms, sobbing desperately, he knew his words made no difference. No words would ever take away what had happened to her. No words would ever give her daughter back to her. No words would ever rebuild the emptiness of her heart. "Sarah," he whispered, brushing his lips over her temple. "It's not your fault."

"It is," she gasped, trying to suck in air. Tears were streaming down her cheeks, the agony and guilt of her loss eating away at her. "Don't you understand? I trusted him instead of going first to Abigail. If I'd grabbed her and run—"

"It wouldn't have made a difference." He kissed her lightly, not for sex, but for comfort, for reassurance that she wasn't alone in her grief, that he had her. "I've fought the men from your village. They're tough and strong. You couldn't have stopped him—"

"But I did." She leaned her head against his chest, gripping Kane's waist desperately, as if she were trying to ground herself. "I killed him," she whispered. "I used my white light to kill him, but it was too late. I couldn't believe he was beyond hope like that, and I waited too long." Her guards were down and Kane was able to touch her mind.

Again, he was back in that room, feeling Sarah's agony as Mason yanked his claws out of her. Before she could move, two older people rushed into the room, and he knew instantly from Sarah's memories that they were her parents. He felt Sarah's horror as they attacked Mason, her scream of anguish when he cut them down with two quick blows, and finally, her absolute betrayal and loss when he turned toward her again, his eyes blazing red.

"Sarah," Mason said, his voice a growl of hate and death. "Now you die."

Kane went still, staring into his eyes as Sarah remembered them. There was something wrong with Mason's expression. Something different. Something off. Then Mason dropped his head and charged Sarah. Instinctively, Kane's weapon exploded into his hand, trying to protect Sarah even in her memories. He yanked her close, his soul screaming in defense of her as Mason swiped his claw at her—

A blinding white light exploded through Kane's mind as Sarah killed Mason. Kane recoiled from the pain as it ripped through him. It burned his eyelids, seared his mind, made his skin scream. He jerked his mind from Sarah's, cutting the connection. The white light vanished immediately, but the pain didn't. Swearing, he jerked his eyes open, and saw Sarah staring at him, tears pouring down her cheeks.

Sweet Jesus. Her grief was unbearable. Ignoring the pain from Sarah's attack, Kane pulled her against him, burying her in his arms. Sarah came willingly, her body pliant as she clung to him, her body shaking with the trauma. Kane pressed his lips to her hair, trying to absorb the trembling of her body into his, offering his strength. "It's over, Sarah," he said. "You did the right thing by killing him. You had no choice."

"I loved him," she whispered against Kane's chest. "How could that not have been enough to save him? How could I have let my family die because I thought I could save him?" She pulled back and looked at him, the guilt in her eyes so heavy. "My beautiful Abigail," she whispered. "She died because I trusted Mason. How could I make that mistake? And I still had to kill him. I had to use my powers that are supposed to be for good. I used them to kill the man I loved. How did I screw up so badly, Kane? How?"

"Shit, Sarah." He kissed her forehead and framed her face with his hands. "Mason made his choice. There was no stopping him." He laid his hand over her heart. "It's beautiful that you loved him that way, that you offer the world that kind of love. That's never a mistake."

"But my daughter—"

"You did protect her," he said. "You offered your life to save hers, and it was Mason's decision to kill her. You can't take the blame for what he did." He gripped her shoulders. "I can't imagine what in God's name could make a man so weak that he could make that choice, no matter what was going on.

She shook her head. "No, he didn't make the choice. He loved us. He never would have made that choice. He was crazy. The choice was taken away from him."

Kane's mind flashed back to that moment when Mason had looked at Sarah, and he recalled the way he'd dropped his head and charged her for the final kill. Suddenly, Kane knew what had been wrong in that moment: Mason had not been rogue. His eyes had been red, yeah, but they'd been clear and focused.

He'd known exactly what he was doing, and he'd done it on purpose.

Son of a bitch. What was going on in this village? "You're sure he was your soul mate?" He didn't understand how it was possible for a male to attack his own soul mate unless he was rogue. It was simply impossible.

"Yes." Sarah took a deep breath, still gripping Kane's arms. "I had his mark on my arms. They've been there ever since, as a reminder never to trust another male again." She rubbed at her arms, as if they were suddenly itchy.

Something dark twisted inside Kane at the idea of another man's brands on Sarah's arms. He set his hand over her arm, as if he could cleanse it from her...

Her skin was hot. Burning right through his palm. Recognition pulsed through him, an intense sense of ownership and possession that reverberated right though his core. And then he knew. His mark was on her arm. She was *his*. He jerked his gaze to hers, and saw the sudden flash of fear in her eyes. Of knowledge.

"Jesus!" He yanked her sleeve up, his hands almost shaking from the intensity of it. On her arm was a set of thin silver lines that were an exact match for the handle of his flail. "Mother of God." Rightness rippled through him, and then as he watched, another line formed, traveling up her arm toward her elbow. Sarah was his *sheva,* and she carried his mark.

"Trust," he muttered. "You told me your darkest secret, that you fear you caused your daughter's death. Sharing that with me satisfies your half of the trust stage." He didn't need to ask about the other lines. He'd been there when they'd made love. He knew damn well that they'd completed that stage. "Son of a bitch." He jerked his gaze to Sarah's and saw the guilt on her face. "You knew?" How had he not sensed it? How in God's name had he been with her and not sensed it? Ryland and Thano should have known as well. "How did you hide this from me? And why?"

"Mason," she whispered. "Mason is why I hid it. I used my magic to hide it." Tears burned in her eyes. "I can't go through all that again, Kane. I can't." She touched his chest where the scars were missing. "For all we know, you're Los Muerte, the man who killed his *sheva* and child. If you are, you'll do it again. To me." Her voice broke and she clutched her chest. "I can't go through that again, Kane. I can't."

Denial roared through Kane. He gripped her shoulders, his body vibrating from the force of his anger. "As God is my witness, Sarah, there is no chance in *hell* that I would ever hurt you. I don't know what Mason's deal was, but I'll find out." The stark terror in her eyes broke through some of his anger, and he softened his grip, struggling to find a place of reassurance for Sarah's sake. "I swear on the grave of Dante, my mentor, that never in this God-forsaken existence of mine would I *ever* fail to protect you..." His words stumbled. "Or any child that we might have."

Sarah's face turned ashen. "God, no, don't even say that about children, Kane. I can't do that again. I can't!"

"Okay, okay, okay." He dropped his head, fighting for control. Struggling to let go of the anger and rage that she doubted him. Fighting to reach the place of control that would comfort her.

She didn't move from his arms, and for a moment, there was no sound in the tunnel except the sound of their breathing, as they each tried to regain their equilibrium. Finally, Kane raised his head and met Sarah's gaze. "I swear to you, Sarah, that I will not become like Mason. I'm not that weak. I'm just not."

She met his gaze, such betrayal and anguish in her eyes. "Mason wasn't weak either. He loved me, Kane. You don't even love me. What do you have to stop yourself?"

"Shit, Sarah, I don't need a crutch!" He pulled her against him and opened his mind to hers, drawing her in. *Can't you feel it? My need to protect you and keep you safe? It's burning so strongly in me that I'd strike down my own teammates before I'd hurt you.* He took her hand and pressed it to his chest, right over the spot where she'd erased his scars, where there was nothing blocking who he really was. *Can't you feel it?*

Sarah dug her fingers into his skin, and a small furrow formed between her eyebrows. *I can. But I can also feel darkness inside you. Something terrifying.*

Kane ground his jaw, because he knew exactly what she was talking about. It was the darkness that had made him almost strike out at Ryland. It was the violent images coursing through his mind. It was the pain knifing through his body.

But he *knew* he couldn't hurt her. He took her hand and pressed it to his lips. But he'd been in her mind, and he knew the level of trauma, and he understood why she would fear him. And in the back of his mind, he couldn't quite get her stories about Los Muerte out of his head. He also couldn't ignore the scars on his own skin or the fact that he'd connected to whatever had been in those woods.

He belonged here. He could tell he did. Somehow, some way, this was his world...so if there was a chance, any kind of chance, that he was the man she was talking about, that Los Muerte was lurking beneath his scars, then he needed to make sure she was protected. *Okay, Sarah, let's make a deal.*

She met his gaze, biting her lower lip as he brushed a kiss over her knuckles. "What deal?"

I promise that I will never hurt you, and you promise me that if you ever think I'm going to, that you will kill me before I can hurt you. Don't hesitate the way you did with Mason. Just kill me.

Her gaze snapped to his. "No, I can't. Using my powers to kill will destroy me—"

"You survived killing Mason. You can do it again if you have to." He cupped her face. "You're an angel, Sarah. Angels always find a way."

Tears shined in her beautiful blue eyes. "I can't do it, Kane. I can't do any of it again.'"

"Yes, you can." He lightly kissed the corner of her mouth, and then the other. And again, until she finally stopped fighting him and kissed him back. It wasn't a kiss of violent passion, it was a kiss of connection. *I'm going to find out what's going on in this village, Sarah. I'm going to find out who I am, and I'm going to keep you safe.*

She looked at him, and he saw hope flash in her eyes. True hope. The kind that she'd been searching for so desperately. Respect flowed through him. She was battered, but not broken, and he knew how strong she was. "I know the Order kills rogue Calydons," she said, "but will you promise not to kill the men in our woods? They're good men. They're just a mess at night."

Kane couldn't help but smile at her question, and a part of him softened. It was just like her to ask him to spare the lives of the very creatures who wanted her dead. "Yeah, I'll do my best."

Sarah took a deep breath, and he saw her summon the strength that he'd already come to recognize as hers. "Well, if you're going to help save our village, then we have a lot of work to do."

He grinned. "I'll bet we do." He eased back from her, swishing his arms through the water. "After you, my dear."

She managed a small smile, and then started to swim past him. Just as she neared him, though, he grabbed her arm and tugged her against him. Her eyes widened. "No kissing." She braced her palms against his chest. "I can't go there with you again, Kane. I really can't."

He swore at the pain in her eyes, and he dropped his hands, giving her a respite.

For now.

But as she turned away and began to swim back toward the opening in the tunnel, he let his gaze settle on her arm. On his mark. She was his. *His.*

A sense of deep, masculine satisfaction pulsed through him...and a flicker of dark anticipation. Swearing, he looked down at his chest, and he saw another patch of scars had disappeared on his stomach. A ripple of unease went through him.

What if he really was Los Muerte, and the only things keeping the monster at bay were his scars? And those scars were disappearing...

Shit. He needed answers, and he needed them fast.

He would get them tonight, when the sun fell and the moon brought the nightmares of this village to life.

Chapter Ten

Kane paused outside the Akara general store, letting Nonny, Thano and Ryland enter first. Sarah stopped beside him, watching him carefully. "What is it?"

He shook his head "I don't know." He touched the door frame, running his hand over the talisman carved in the wood. Smoke rose off his fingertips, and he jerked his hand back. "What does that one mean?"

Sarah moved up beside him. "I'm not sure. It's just one of the many carved everywhere to protect against the Calydons who hunt at night."

Kane looked around, studying the abandoned village square, searching his mind for some sense of recognition.

Nothing.

He swore under his breath. "Nothing looks familiar. I don't remember being here."

Hope flashed over Sarah's face. "Maybe you weren't. Maybe you haven't been here before. Maybe—"

"He was."

They both turned, and Sarah saw Javier, the old guardian of the village, leaning against the edge of the house. His face was in the shadows, his body lean and wiry, his jeans faded. Sarah hadn't seen him up close for years, and he never spoke. Until now. "When?" she asked.

Javier fixed his black eyes on Kane. "He knows."

Kane stared at Javier, and there was no mistaking the hope gleaming in his eyes. "I don't remember anything."

"You will—"

"Javier!" Nonny came out on the front porch and set her hands on her hips. "For heaven's sake, man, if you're going to come out of your cave and join humanity, you need to come in here—"

But Javier was already gone, drifting away in the shadows as quickly as he'd come.

"Blasted man." Nonny held the door open. "He never sticks around. Drives me nuts. Come on in, folks. Let's get some food. I opened the store for you guys, but the afternoon rush will be coming soon."

Sarah rolled her eyes at her grandmother. "There hasn't been an afternoon rush in years, Nonny."

"An old lady can always hope." She gestured at Kane. "Come on, Kane. Let's move it."

Kane glanced at the shadows one last time. He thought he saw something move, but when he looked more closely, there was nothing but stillness. A chill rippled over his skin, and he looked over his shoulders at the woods. He could sense nothing, but he got the distinct feeling he was being watched. Shit. "Someone's out there," he said as he walked inside.

"I know." Sarah looked past him. "There always is."

"The place is haunted," Thano announced, already lounging comfortably in a chair by the fireplace. "Lots of creepies." He jerked his chin at the fireplace. "That's the village's body count, my friend. All the innocents and rogues who have died over the last six hundred years, since the Los Muerte destruction."

Kane stiffened at Thano's casual reference, realizing that Nonny must have filled them in on the town's history, but there was no edge to Thano's voice. The warrior didn't know about Kane's possible connection to the town's history yet. Relieved not to have to address that with his team yet, Kane looked past Thano and saw rows and rows of hash marks carved into the old mantle. Thousands of marks.

More than the Order had killed during that time. Far more.

"Every man who has succumbed to the dark side, and every person they've killed," Sarah said softly, running her hand over it. Her finger touched on a small one in the corner, and she looked at Kane. "Abigail," she said softly.

Kane reached out and took her hand, and Sarah's throat tightened at his gesture. God, it had been so long since anyone had given her comfort, or since she had even considered accepting or seeking it. She'd just put her head down and kept on pushing, refusing to give up, refusing to grieve, because she couldn't afford it. Nonny never gave her sympathy, just told her to get herself together and move onward, which is what they both knew she had to do.

But it felt different with Kane, as if she could afford to feel that pain and grief, and yet somehow, he would provide a buffer to keep it from destroying her.

But she couldn't rely on him. She couldn't let her guard down. She had to remember Mason and Abigail—

I'm not Mason, Kane said.

Sarah bit her lip. *I know, but—*

"So, this is a night gig," Ryland said, pacing around the room. None of the men had commented on the fact that there was no one else in the general store besides them, or that the few remaining inhabitants of the town had vacated when the Order had appeared on the premises. Kane knew it was because they were Calydons, distrusted completely, and it was an odd sensation to be distrusted by the innocents that they had taken an oath to protect.

Were the villagers jaded, or were they the wise ones?

Jaded. It had to be jaded. He and his team would never attack innocents. They just wouldn't.

"These guys are close to sane and normal during the day, but at night they attack. Is that right?" Ryland asked.

"The level of daytime sanity varies, but basically that's correct," Sarah said. "It used to be really bad, but for the last few hundred years, it seemed to stop. But in the last fifty years, it's been virulent again. Most people have moved away, hoping to protect the men that way, but many of them still become Calydons and go rogue, and come back here."

"Yep, only us stalwarts remain." Nonny was perched on the edge of the counter, drinking a beer. She pointed it at Kane. "You've got a job to do, young man. My granddaughter needs to survive, or this town goes down, and so does hope and light as the earth knows it." She shrugged. "And of course, whoever it is she's assigned to."

Kane frowned. "What do you mean?"

"All angels are assigned to someone to protect," Sarah explained.

Thano raised his brows. "We have guardian angels? Damn. That's cool."

"No, not exactly," Sarah said. "I don't go out and hover over the shoulder of the people I'm connected to. My life force is linked to theirs, so that when they need hope and faith, they can tap into mine, even though they don't realize where it's coming from." She shrugged. "I'm like this great fountain of hope."

"And if you don't have anything to give them?" Kane asked, studying her closely.

She met his gaze. "Then they're on their own. Most people are these days. There aren't many angels left."

"Well, shit." Thano looked over at Ryland. "That explains you.

Maybe we can put in a request for you to get one. Think it might help?"

Ryland's black eyes glittered. "No, I don't."

"We need to stop the Calydons." Sarah stood up, pacing the room, impatient to get the men back on track. "That's our only chance. They'll keep hunting me otherwise, and I'm all that's holding that river open right now." She looked at Kane, Ryland and Thano, who were exactly what she was trying to defend against. They were massive, much larger than those who hunted in her woods, but they were the same race. How could they resist the allure of whatever it was that took the Akara men? "We need to stop them at the source. We need to find out what is turning them and destroy it. It's our only chance."

"I like mysteries." Thano was sweeping his blade over the doorframe, as if he were using it to sharpen the edge of his halberd. "I'm in." He jammed the blade into the floor and grinned at the guys. "Let's go kick some ass, shall we?"

Ryland grinned. "I'm in. I still owe them for almost taking us out a couple weeks ago."

Sarah noticed that Kane said nothing. He looked directly at Nonny. "How old are you?"

Nonny's eyebrows shot up. "Why is it that everyone seems to think I've got age issues now? Did my eye cream suddenly stop working?"

"Nonny, you're the hottest firecracker I've ever seen," Thano said. "You don't need any eye cream, sweetheart."

Nonny winked at him, "Keep it up, young man, and you'll find out exactly how much pep there is in this old girl."

"Were you present during Los Muerte's attack?" Kane asked, not taking his attention off Nonny.

Sarah frowned. "Of course not. She's not immortal..." Then her voice trailed off when she saw the gleam of anticipation on Nonny's face. "Nonny?"

Nonny laughed softly. "I am highly offended that either of you think I'm that old." She raised her brows. "And yes, I was there."

Sarah stared at her grandmother. "But you're not immortal—"

"No? Don't make judgments, young lady—"

Kane leaned forward, his voice urgent. "Was it me? Am I Los Muerte? Am I the danger that's going to bring this village down?""

Nonny's eyebrows shot up. "Why are you asking me? You know the answer to that question."

Kane swore. "I don't remember anything—"

"Of course you do. Everything you've ever lived is inside you. You know exactly who you used to be, and who you are now. It's your choice to decide when you're ready to know."

"I don't remember a damned thing."

"You can't erase what's in your mind, boy. You just have to decide you want to hear it." Nonny stood up. "Come on, Sarah. We need to get you out of here. There's no need for you to spend the night in the village and endanger yourself. Let the boys do their thing."

Kane blocked the door "No," he said fiercely. "Sarah stays."

Sarah frowned. "I can't stay here. They know I'm here and they'll come get me. Without Jacob to track me, I can hide outside the village—"

"And if they do find you outside the village, who will protect you?"

"My brother is the only one who can find me, and he's dead—"

"He's not dead."

Sarah went still, and Nonny sucked in her breath. "What?" Sarah had suspected her brother might have survived when she'd realized that she and Kane hadn't done the death stage of the bond, but she hadn't dared to hope it was true, not when Jacob had failed to reappear. She'd simply tried to focus on keeping herself strong so that his death and betrayal couldn't kill her as well. But now... "He's really alive?" Joy leapt in her heart for her brother, at the same moment that fear trickled through her for the assassin he was planning to be.

"He's not dead. He's unconscious. They're keeping him at the mansion until they can figure out how to hold him. The minute he wakes up, he'll find you, won't he?" Kane's eyes flashed the challenge, and Sarah closed her eyes as rekindled fear simmered through her.

Kane was right.

She opened her eyes and looked at her grandmother. Nonny's face was grim, but at the same time, there was a glimmer of hope. As long as Jacob was alive, they might be able to save him. Resolution poured through Sarah, and she clenched her fists. "All right," she said, "I'm staying." But she knew there was no hiding. If Jacob was alive, he could teleport right into the house, right past the lights. There was nowhere safe to hide from Jacob. The only man who could keep her safe was Kane, which meant that when he went hunting tonight, she had to go with him. "This has to end tonight. I can't keep this up."

Nonny set her hands on her hips. "How is it going to end? What ends tonight?"

Sarah took a deep breath. "Tonight they... we... are going to follow them home and find out what happens to them at night to make them crazy. Tonight, it ends." She glanced over at Kane and the others, and knew this was her best chance.

As long as they didn't go crazy, too. Oh, God, what if they went rogue once they were exposed to the village?

Kane grinned at her, flashing a decadent smile. *I won't go crazy until after we complete our bonding, sweetheart.*

Desire pulsed through her, and fear. *We will never complete our bonding—*

Oh, but we will. There was no other choice in the matter.

* * *

Hours later, Sarah huddled beside Kane, crouched low in the cave on the side of the mountain near Akara. She watched the sun dip lower in the sky, and her heart began to pound. She hadn't been outside in the village at night before, not in her whole life. It was terrifying, but at the same time, exhilarating. This was her village, her town, and she was taking it back.

No longer was she hiding. No longer was she quivering in fear. Kane had given her the power to stand up and fight for her village, for her brother, for herself.

She glanced over at Kane. He was on his stomach in the dirt, hunkered down behind the rock ledge. His weapons were at the ready, a flail in each hand. His body was streaked in mud to make him blend into the night, and his muscles were taut with alertness.

Out in those woods right now were Ryland and Thano, hunting Calydons, herding them toward Kane, trying to sweep for the darkness that Kane had sensed earlier. The powerful one. The one that had nearly brought him down by flooding him with those terrible visions, and by drawing blood from Kane without even touching him. She'd felt the darkness that had attacked Kane on other occasions, and she'd felt it earlier today. It was laced with a depth of evil and depravity that made her blood turn to ice in her body. She'd always been certain that was the energy signature of the leader. Kane and the others agreed.

He was the one they needed to find, and Kane was going to try to find him by following a trail of blood...literally.

Sarah looked down at the scars on Kane's arm and saw another clear spot on his forearm. The talismans were definitely disappearing. Whether he was Los Muerte or not, those talismans were on him for a reason, and she was scared of what would happen if he was stripped of their protections. What would happen if he imbued himself with tainted blood from one of Akara's rogue Calydons? She touched his arm, and he jumped, before turning his head toward her. "Your touch ignites something inside me," he said, his eyes hooded. "Every single time."

Heat burst through her, and suddenly the cave seemed to disappear, consumed by the enormity of his presence. She swallowed and pulled her hand back. "Kane—"

He grabbed her hand and kept it pressed against his skin. "Don't let go," he said, his voice low and sensual. "I need it."

Ohh... Desire rippled through her, a calling for him, for his touch, for his possession. His grip was tight, his skin burning hot as if he were trying to melt through her flesh right to her soul. Involuntarily, her fingers tightened around his arm, and she felt his body shudder in response. How could she have that much power over him? "Is this from the *sheva* bond?"

"Hell if I know." He bent his head and brushed his lips over her knuckles, his gaze never leaving her face. "All I know is that I've been inside this fucking shell for the last five hundred years. I feel nothing. I just exist. And yet when you touch me..." He lifted his head, his mouth almost touching hers... "Or when you kiss me..." He brushed his mouth over the corner of hers, and she went still, her heart hammering in her chest. "Or when I touch you..." He slipped his hand beneath her shirt, spanning his palm across her lower back. "My world literally changes, and I come to life."

Sarah's breath was tight in her chest, and she felt like she couldn't get air. The current was electric between them, and Kane's emotions were rolling over her. Desire, passion, and something else. Something she couldn't read. Something so human, so vulnerable, so endearing that she wanted to cry that this powerful, rugged warrior who lived a life of such violence could be so broken inside. "Don't do it," she whispered.

"Do what? Kiss you?" He caught her chin and kissed her, his lips so tender and gentle that tears filled her eyes. *I have to kiss you, Sarah. You're like my oxygen. I don't know how to make my heart beat unless you're inside my soul. It didn't beat before. Not until I met you.*

"Kane," she gasped, pulling away. She gripped his hair, desperate to hold onto this man who was breaking through the shields she'd kept around herself for so long. "Don't do the blood bond with one of the Calydons from our woods. They're evil. You shouldn't have their blood in you."

His eyes glittered, and she felt a pulsing heat from him. A burst of raw, sensual desire. "You're worried about me?"

"Well, yes..." She glanced at the talismans on his body and felt a ripple of fear at the thought of what their purpose was. "I mean, we don't know exactly what we're dealing with here and—"

"Shit, woman. No one worries about me. It's an insult." Then he locked his arm around her waist and kissed her again. Hard this time.

Like he wanted to possess every inch of her soul and own it forever. *But I fucking love that you said that anyway.*

She almost laughed at his reply, even as heat tore through her body at his kiss. *You big strong guys are just liars. You want to be coddled, don't you?*

"No." He pulled back, his gaze so intense it seemed to bore right through her. "I want to make love to you until you can't move. I want to be inside you, on top of you, wrapped around you on every level of our being until our spirits are so intertwined that everywhere I go, for every second of every day, I feel your spirit inside me, keeping me alive."

"Oh." She could barely manage to squeak a response, she was so overwhelmed by the mixture of emotions flooding her. His. Hers. Passion. Lust. Protectiveness. Darkness. Desperation. She didn't even know whose emotions were whose, but it was an unbelievable feeling. Suddenly, she knew what he meant when he'd claimed that she made him come alive, because he was doing the same thing to her.

She'd shut down her own emotions the day her daughter had died in her arms. She had closed herself off to any emotions, including the hope and faith that was so necessary for her to live. "I was dying, too," she said quietly. "But you're giving me hope again. You're not letting me shut you out."

He grinned. "Good. I hate being ignored."

"No. It's not good." She groaned and closed her eyes, resting her cheek against the cold stone of the cave floor as she realized the implications of what she was feeling. "I can't go through it again. If I hadn't trusted Mason so completely, it wouldn't have devastated me so badly. I can't do that again." She sighed. "I know, you're this big, tough badass who's at least five hundred years old, and Mason was only twenty-two, so you should be able to resist what he couldn't and not go insane, but it's not that easy, Kane."

Kane was silent for a moment, his hand rubbing small circles on her lower back. "Sarah. There's something I need to tell you about Mason."

"What?" Sarah inched closer to him, checking her flask of water from the river. She couldn't afford to think about Kane or how he made her feel. She couldn't afford to let down her guard. She had one job, and that was to find out what was poisoning the village and stop it before it destroyed her.

The water was a reminder of what she was about to face, of the need to recover if she had to strike offensively with her powers. She had two flasks on her hip, and several more on the ground beside her. Kane had forced her to bring them, ordering her to be prepared to use her powers to save herself if she had to. With the water at her side to help her recover, Kane was determined that she would be able to protect herself and not die from it.

She had other plans, and they involved not hurting anyone. She'd had enough of that. Tonight, it would be different. Kane and his team could fight the battle. She was going to find the source of the taint and end it. Now.

Kane had told her to stay close, that he would teleport her to safety if she needed it, and she knew he meant it. He would take her out of the battle, even if she wanted to stay. Heat went through Sarah at the memory of how he'd saved her before. The intensity of their lovemaking, the power of their connection. She missed that. She wanted it again. She wanted to fall into what he offered her and forget about everything else. She wanted to believe his words and his touch and stop trying to stand on her own, but she'd done that before, and how wrong she'd been.

She couldn't lose sight of what mattered. She couldn't make herself so vulnerable that she lost the ability to do what she was supposed to do. The darkness that was encroaching on the village had to be stopped, and falling into ecstasy with Kane wasn't going to do it.

"Mason's eyes were clear," Kane said quietly. "He knew what he was doing when he attacked you and Abigail. He wasn't rogue." He glanced over at her. "Is it always that way? Do they always know?"

His words plunged straight through her shields, and suddenly Sarah was back in that moment, staring into the face of the man she'd known her whole life. Into his eyes. Glowing. Red. And aware. Shock rippled through her, icy cold shock, as she realized Kane was telling the truth, and that she had known it all along.

Betrayal bit deep, even deeper than ever before, and she bowed her head, fighting against the swell of despair trying to take her. It was one thing for someone she loved to go insane and try to kill her. It was worse, so much worse, for him to turn on her and know what he was doing. Like Jacob. They both had known, and she knew it. She took a deep breath, fighting to steel herself to the emotions that would never serve her. "Yes."

Kane swore and shifted position, moving closer to her until his hip was against hers. "Then they're not rogue. They're something else."

"Evil." God, it hurt just to say the word, to acknowledge that two men she'd loved dearly for her whole life were evil, but it was true. She knew it was. There was no other word for someone who would kill those they loved in ruthless, cold blood.

Kane looked at her in surprise. "That's a strong word."

"I know." She looked out into the dusk, at the yellows and oranges lighting up the sky, beginning to sink the woods into darkness. "But can't you feel it? The woods change at night. The air becomes stagnant. It smells like sulfur and rot. It hurts to breathe. It's as if there is a layer of death on the earth, and each night it gets stronger, encroaching upon the village." She looked down at the old fountain, at the river that Kane had opened earlier today. "It will be closed up in the morning," she said. "We won't be able to get to the water. We'll have to hunt for it again. Each time it gets harder."

Kane touched her shoulder. "We'll find it."

"Someday we won't." She stretched out next to him on her belly, resting her shoulder against his. For some reason she couldn't understand, touching him seemed to ward off the fear haunting her. If anyone should scare her, it was Kane, with his scars, his darkness and the fact she carried his mark on her arm. But right now, as she looked into his eyes and felt his strength, she knew he was not going to hurt her. He would protect her, and that was a gift.

Kane made her feel safe, and it was incredible. She couldn't remember ever feeling safe. Even as a child, her parents had told her stories about the forest at night, trying to terrify her into never daring to sneak out. It had worked. She hadn't. Ever.

Until tonight. Until Kane and his team had given her the freedom to stand outside while the sun went down and look directly into the demon's mouth. "That's why we have to find out what happens at night." It was thrilling being out here, not being afraid. She knew that as long as she stayed close to Kane, he would teleport her out of danger and kill everyone who needed to be stopped.

Kane gave her the power to be the person she wanted to be.

They fell silent for a moment, watching the woods. Sarah felt content. Safe. In control. Kane gave her that luxury. It was heady and amazing. Brilliant. A gift. As long as she didn't think about Mason or Jacob, or the scars on her belly, she was good.

"I talked to the guys at the mansion," Kane said. "Jacob's still out, but they're going to try waking him up at dawn, since that's when he's most likely to be somewhat sane."

Sarah clenched her fists against the sudden fear in her belly, an emotion that shouldn't be associated with her brother. What kind of man would he be when he woke up? Would he have a moment of being her brother, or would the evil consume him right way? Would he vanish from their hold even in the light of day and track Sarah right to their home? She couldn't lie to herself anymore. The time for false hope was over. She had to accept that Jacob would come after her instantly. "So, tonight is our last chance," she said. "Once Jacob's out, he'll be hunting me ruthlessly."

"Yeah." There was an undercurrent of blackness in Kane's voice, and she looked sharply at him. There was a black stain across his shoulders, spreading slowly through his scars, like a river of taint oozing through the maze of ridges on his back.

She sat up quickly and put her hand on his back. Kane jumped and sucked in his breath, his whole body rippling. "What?" she asked. "Did that hurt?"

"No." He spun toward her suddenly, his eyes dark with passion.

"Oh..." She sat up, startled by his sudden reaction. "Kane, we're about to engage in battle."

"No." He grabbed her by her ankle and hauled her over to him, his eyes blazing with lust, and something else. Something dark. Something that made chills of fear ripple over her skin.

"Kane—"

"Sarah," he growled, as he grabbed her around the hips and yanked her against him. "You're mine." And then he kissed her, a voracious kiss that seemed to consume her and suck her very spirit right out of her.

Fear arced through her, and a sense of belonging so powerful she couldn't stop it. Kane felt so right, even at the same time that she was so terrified of what lay beneath the surface—

He growled, a deep-throated growl that sounded nothing like him, and fear ran more thickly through her as he upped his assault on her senses. His kisses were a torrent of desire and aggression, flooding her defenses, arousing her to levels beyond her ability to resist.

Then suddenly, he was in her mind, rushing her with all his emotions. Fear, lust, darkness, passion and something else...something in the very depths of his being...a light? Warmth? His real soul? She hadn't felt it before, and it slithered out of her grasp before she could access it.

Panic assaulted her as it disappeared, as if it was her job to find it and hold onto it, keeping it from disappearing. She gripped his shoulders, kissing him back frantically, desperate to reach inside him, to find what she'd lost. She felt like she could help him, that she was supposed to help him, that she was supposed to find that light inside him. *Kane. Let me in. Let me find it.*

Pain suddenly rocked Kane, shooting through his body like a violent stab. She felt his body shudder, but he didn't break the kiss. His hands went to her throat, her chest, over her breasts, as if he could lose himself in her and spare himself the pain. *What is this, Sarah? Why does it hurt like fucking hell to kiss you?*

I don't know, she gasped, reeling from the pain that was hitting him. *I*—

Suddenly, there was an unholy scream of terror, and Kane threw her off him, whirling to his feet as several Calydons rushed into the cave, howling a blood-thirsty cry of assault.

Eyes red.

Claws out.

The night had begun.

Chapter Eleven

Kane leapt to his feet and immediately engaged, aggression howling through him as he shoved Sarah behind a rock, out of the way. Behind the intruders, he saw Ryland and Thano, acting fast as well. The three of them worked as a team, taking down the local boys, but not killing them, not this time. Within moments all four of their targets were incapacitated, but not dead.

"I'll blood bond with the big one," Kane said, immediately targeting the largest, oldest one. That was the one he wanted. The male was practically bleeding poison, and his taint was so thick that the air around him was churning with black and purple and a thick yellow. If Kane blood bonded with him, there was no doubt he'd get a good inside look at the source of the taint destroying these men.

Thano swung hard and took the big guy out, and the warrior dropped. Kane sprinted to his side, and immediately jammed his flail into the downed Calydon's arm. The blood poured forth as Kane sliced his own arm open. Then, while Ryland and Thano hauled the other Calydons out of the way, Kane pressed his wound against the other male's and chanted the words of the warrior blood bond, Thano and Ryland's voices raised to accompany his.

The moment the words were complete, bonding the two warriors, Kane's entire body began to vibrate. Searing pain rushed through him, dropping him to the floor of the cave as the warrior's blood cut through his veins like razor blades. "Jesus," Kane gasped, as his body began to shake, and his muscles began to convulse.

"Shit, man!" Ryland was beside him immediately. "This isn't supposed to happen!"

Pain tore through Kane, along with darkness, and visions of

demons with claws and dripping fangs. Skin stretched across his body like parchment over hell itself. His insides felt like they were being clawed to pieces, his muscles ripped from his bones, his lungs torn from his chest, his bones crushed by a force so great it bowed his spine.

"Jesus, man!" Thano grabbed his shoulders, trying to hold him down. "If you want more attention, just ask for it!"

Images flashed through Kane's mind. Bodies. A boy. A young boy looking up at him, with dark brown eyes, trusting him. Then the child was bloodied, sprawled across the floor, slashes ripped through his small frame. "No!" Kane screamed, the anguish tearing through him. He tried to get to his knees, to crawl away from the nightmare, to escape from the hell—

"Kane!" Suddenly Sarah was in front of him, holding his shoulders. "Come back to me!"

He screamed again, and suddenly her face changed. Her hair seemed to turn a glossy white, drifting in floating tendrils around her head. Her eyes were pale blue, her pupils pitch black. He touched her face, and his fingers seemed to drift right through her skin, skin that was so pale and fragile it was like silk threads dangling in the breeze. She was wearing a pale blue dress, the color of a full moon on a clear night, shimmering as if a thousand stars had been woven into it. Her lips were pale, a pink so fair he could barely even register it. Her cheek bones were high and flawless, and she was wearing a thin silver chain around her neck with a single diamond hanging from it. "My angel." He touched her hair, and the shimmering tendrils wove around his fingers as if they were alive.

She smiled, her face glowing with love and hope, and Kane felt his own heart come to life, beating with a vibrant light of triumph and salvation.

"What's he doing?" Ryland asked, but his voice was distant, a faint rumble.

"His eyes are white," Thano said, his voice drifting through Kane's mind. "I have no clue. Kane. Kane!"

He didn't even need to acknowledge them. They just floated out of his mind, until all that was left was Sarah. There was a white glow behind her head, growing brighter and brighter. "Kane," she said again, only this time, her voice was raspy...harsh...

He stiffened, and suddenly streaks of black tainted her hair. Her lips turned black. Her skin turned to ash, crumbling in gray flakes from her body. Her mouth opened and a violent scream tore out of her. She raised her palm, and he saw a flail in it. His own weapon. To be used against him. "No!" He lunged for her, his hands going for her throat, knowing there was only one answer, one choice, one way to live.

She had to die.

* * *

Sarah screamed as Kane lunged for her, his fingers locking around her throat. "Kane!" She clawed at his hands as Ryland and Thano leapt on him, trying to pull him off. But his muscles were rigid, locked down, and they couldn't stop him.

Thano called out his halberd, but Kane flung him across the cave. He hooked Ryland in the neck and tossed the other male aside, as if he were nothing but a rag doll. Then he was back on her, lunging for her. Just like before. Just like Mason. Just like Jacob.

Sarah gasped, fighting for air as Kane loomed above her, his hands around her neck. His eyes were black. Not red. *Black!* He wasn't rogue! He was like her brother and Mason. Sane, and trying to kill her. "Kane!" She scrabbled at his arms, clawing at his fingers, and still he pressed tighter.

Dear God, he was going to kill her!

Use your white light to stop him. The voice burst through her mind. A male voice, hard and lethal...not Kane. Someone else was trying to force them to destroy each other.

No! She screamed the thought and then the world started to spin as she began to lose consciousness. *Kane, don't do this. Please, God, Kane. Don't!* Tears poured down her cheeks as she fought for air. This couldn't be happening again. It couldn't. She thrust her mind into Kane's, and then almost screamed from the darkness that consumed her the moment she connected with him. It was a miasma of poison and death, of evil, of *hell.* It sucked her in instantly, flooding her with despair and hopelessness. She saw her mother, her father, her daughter, all dead. She saw herself, lying on the floor, her hand on her belly as Mason crashed to the ground beside her, his skin blackened and destroyed from her attack. Death and murder between people who loved each other. No one alive. Everyone dead.

There was nothing left. No hope. Just failure. Just love that wasn't strong enough.

Sarah. Kane's voice distant in her mind, so faint, but she heard his desperation. *We have to break through it.*

Her heart ached at the sound of his voice, and she tried to find him, but there was too much chaos and darkness. So much death. So much loss. *I can't.*

You can. Suddenly, she felt a thrust of power from Kane, a rush of electricity so fierce she screamed from the pain. He forced his strength into her, and suddenly there was a flash of black light and a crack so loud it sounded like the cave itself had shattered. Then Kane's flail appeared in her hand, the twin spiked balls spinning wildly. He'd made her call his weapon into her hand!

She had no time to think, no time to react, as Kane forced his will through her, until she could almost feel his hands closing around hers, his intentions so powerful that she had no chance to resist them, no chance to second guess. She simply grasped the weapon and swung it as hard as she could.

It slammed into his chest, flinging him off her. She had a split second to see relief in his dark eyes, and then he landed in a slumped pile against the wall of the cave. Horror reeled through her, and she flung the flail aside as she stumbled to her feet, nausea churning in her belly as the blood streamed down his chest. "Kane?" Dear God. Her hands started to shake, and her legs gave out. The rocky floor dug into her knees as she fell to the ground, staring in agony at him. Her neck was burning from the pain of his attack, and it hurt to swallow, the truth of his attack undeniable.

Tears burned in her eyes. Kane had failed. He'd succumbed like the others. There was no way to trust him. To trust anyone. And now she'd killed him.

"You're his *sheva?*" Ryland was on his feet now, staring at her, his face aghast with horror. "That's impossible. You're an angel. It would destroy you to be linked with one of us."

Sarah couldn't even look at him. She just couldn't take her eyes off Kane. *Breathe, please, breathe.*

"Damn, woman, that was a slick move." Thano was on his feet now, striding across the cave to check on Kane. "You activated the transference stage of the *sheva* bond to use the weapon against your own mate. That's a good one. I gotta admit, I like the irony of that."

"I didn't call it," she whispered. "He made me." She suddenly realized the significance of that statement. Kane *had* forced her to call his weapon. He'd been clear enough in his mind not to let the evil take him. He'd stopped himself by making her strike first.

He *had* been strong enough.

"Kane!" She scrambled to her feet and stumbled across the floor. She fell into him, grabbing his shoulders.

To her disbelief, Kane groaned and grabbed her, shifting her to the side. "Not on the broken ribs, sweetheart. Give me at least a minute to heal."

"You're okay?" She couldn't believe it. "You're serious?"

His eyes flickered open, and she saw the pain in them, but also the smug triumph. "Of course I'm okay. I'm immortal, remember?" He raised his brows. "Are you still going to doubt my ability to resist the bogeyman?" Then his gaze went to her throat, and his amusement vanished. "Jesus, Sarah." His voice was raw with fury and pain. "I did that?" He set his hand on her neck, and she couldn't help but flinch.

"Fuck!" He lurched to his feet, his hands clasped on his head, his face almost ashen. "I hurt you. Son of a bitch. *I hurt you.*"

"Kane, no, it wasn't like that." She leapt up and grabbed his arm. "You stopped it. Don't you understand? I felt the poison inside you, all that violence and despair, and it took me, too. I had no defenses against it, and I'm an angel! But somehow, you were able to summon the strength to make me call your weapon. Don't you get it? You *are* strong enough."

"No." He pulled free, backing away from her, self-loathing and disgust still etched on his features. "Look at your throat. You're bruised. Because of me."

"Dude," Thano's hand came down hard on his shoulder. "Give yourself a break. You were seriously fucked up there for a minute, but all you did was give her a few red marks on her skin? Shit, that's practically a love bite." The humor left his voice, and he turned Kane toward him. "Do you realize how easily you could have snapped her neck? And yet you didn't. In the five seconds it took for Sarah to call your weapon, you could have killed her a thousand times, but you didn't." Thano held out his hand, revealing a blackened palm. "That's what I got from touching you, big guy. That's how much shit was going through you, and yet you didn't hurt her."

Kane pressed his hands to his forehead and paced away from them. His shoulders were trembling, and Sarah felt the waves of fear rippling over him. True fear. The kind of fear that could tear a person's soul to pieces and destroy the very nature of who they were. "Kane." She hurried over to him and pressed her hands to his chest. "Look at me."

He dragged his gaze off the far wall and looked down at her. There was so much anguish in his face that her own heart ached. *What if I'm Los Muerte, Sarah? What if I really am here to destroy you? What if that was just the start?* He slid his hand through her hair, his touch so soft and gentle, as if he were afraid to even touch her. *What if I am the monster?* He looked down at his chest, at the smooth expanse of skin that now stretched halfway across his chest. *What if when these scars disappear, Los Muerte comes back to life?*

"No!" She shook her head, clasping his face between her hands. *You stopped yourself, Kane. You don't understand how significant that is. No one has ever done that.* Tears filled her eyes. *No one has ever done that for me.*

Hell, Sarah. He fisted her hair, but didn't pull it. *You deserve more than to be grateful that all you got were a few bruises. That's so fucked up. You should be kicking my ass.*

Life is so much more complicated than that, Kane. She pressed her lips to the wound in his chest that had already stopped bleeding and was beginning to heal. *For the first time since Mason's attack, you give me hope that maybe there's a way to be stronger than the evil trying to take us.* She took his hand and set it over her heart. *Can you feel that? My heart is beating again, truly beating. I have hope, and you gave it to me.*

Kane closed his eyes, spreading his hand across her chest, and she felt him reach out for her with his mind. She let him in, and merged her spirit with his, allowing him to feel the hope in her heart, the gift he had given her. He let out his breath, and then opened his eyes, his gaze meeting hers. "I have no idea who the hell I am," he said.

"According to Nonny, that's actually a lie. You know exactly who you are," Thano chimed in.

Kane glared at him. "Shut up, Thano. You have no idea what it's like—"

"I do." Ryland was lurking in the shadows, his machete clenched in his hand. He was leaning against the wall, but his body was rigid, and Sarah felt a ripple of menace flowing from him. "I know what it's like to spend every minute of every day wondering if this is the moment when I finally snap. To walk behind my teammate and know exactly what it would feel like to sink my machete between his shoulder blades, and to wonder when the day will come that I'm going to do it."

"Shit, Ryland." Thano let out a low whistle. "You serious? I knew you were cranky, but—"

"You live like that?" Kane was staring at him, a hooded look on his face.

"Yeah." Ryland shifted, and he seemed to almost disappear into the shadows, as if he'd turned into a specter himself. "I know that there's a fucking monster inside me that will come out some day. I know what it's like to sit in my room every night with my machete in my hand, debating whether the only right choice would be for me to cut myself down before I can destroy the world." His eyes glittered. "I know what it's like to have a monster inside you, Santiago, and if you want, we can kill each other right now, and then it's over."

"No!" Sarah leapt between them. "You can't! I need you! Both of you." She pressed her hand to Kane's chest, and held out her other hand to Ryland, her heart beating frantically. She could feel Ryland's despair and lack of hope. It plunged inside her, nearly devastating in its intensity.

"Stop!"

"The angel's right," Thano said. "We can't do this without you, Ry, and if you're about to turn into a monster, your timing is right." He toed his boot against one of the Calydons still on the ground. "We've got a battle, and we might need a monster on our side to win it."

Sarah stared at Kane, worried that he still hadn't moved, hadn't responded to Ryland. The two warriors were facing each other, their gazes locked on each other as if they were communicating silently. "Kane?" She touched his chest again, and he started, jerking his gaze toward her. For a moment, he looked confused, and then he took a deep breath.

"I'm not walking away from this." He shot a long look at Ryland. "You kill yourself, and who's going to protect the angel when I turn into Los Muerte?"

Ryland's eyes glittered, but then he looked at Sarah. The intensity of his gaze was almost scary. He said nothing, but nodded once and walked out of the cave into the night.

Thano let out a low whistle. "That dude's in bad shape, Kane. We need to watch him."

"I know." Kane stepped back as the Calydon he'd blood bonded with began to stir. He grabbed Sarah, and the three of them moved into the shadows at the rear of the cave. They went deathly still, and she felt Kane do a faint mental push to direct the Calydons' attention away from them.

The one Kane had blood bonded with woke up, shook his head, then roused the other three. The quartet quickly slipped out of the cave, still holding the wounds the Order had inflicted upon them. The moment they were out of sight, Kane stepped forward. "Let's go." He took Sarah's arm and led his team out into the night to track the male Kane had blood-bonded with.

Sarah caught her breath as they emerged from the cave, and she was hit with the full darkness of the evening. She was really outside the village in the night, a target for all who had been trying to kill her. She glanced around as Ryland materialized out of the shadows and took his place by her left side. Kane was on her right, and Thano was tight on her heels. A triangle of protection by three massive warriors as they escorted her into the midst of the very hell that had been trying to kill her and her kind for the last thousand years.

Her heart started to pound, and then she felt Kane's hand settle on the back of her neck. *Sarah.*

She glanced up at him, but he wasn't looking at her. He was searching the night vigilantly as they moved forward. *What?*

When you called out my weapon, that completed another stage of the bond. We're getting close. His satisfaction vibrated through her, the male appreciation of claiming his woman.

She swallowed and placed her hand over the brand on her arm, knowing that she was being pulled inextricably into his web. Eventually, she wouldn't be able to get out. A part of her loved it and felt the absolute rightness of it...and another part of her thrummed with a fear so ingrained that it was almost paralyzing.

The bond will keep you safe from me. I can't hurt my sheva. He brushed his fingers over the back of her neck and sent her a mental push of warmth.

But beneath his strength, she felt a ripple of uneasiness. Kane's.

Because he was no longer so certain that he wasn't meant to kill her.

Sarah thought of the bruises on her neck, and prayed that she was right to trust him.

* * *

An hour later, Kane crouched low, peering over the cliff as he watched his quarry descend into the valley flanked by the forest. The earth seemed to descend into a V, and at the bottom of the crevice was pure darkness, so thick that even Kane's preternatural vision couldn't penetrate it. The Calydon they'd been following seemed to literally vanish into the crevice.

"Where's he going?" Thano asked. "You think there's a beauty salon down there? Maybe he's getting a manicure."

"Probably," Kane replied. "What else do you have to do in these woods other than get beautified?"

"No." Sarah was crushed up against his side, sandwiched between him and Thano so tightly that not even a breath could come between them. Ryland was at her back, guarding her from anything coming up behind them.

Their trip through the woods had been uneventful. Nothing had come after Sarah or the rest of them. But the woods had been too silent, devoid of even the smallest animals. They were being hunted, and they all knew it.

"I've been near it during the day," Sarah said. "It's pure evil. I can't even get close to it without getting violently sick. The only ones who can get near there are the men. The women all get sick, but I'm the worst." The townspeople had all heard rumors about the existence of the place, but no one had ever been able to find it. Sarah had searched for it for years, always during the day. And then one day, she'd stumbled across it, and she'd known instantly what it was. The evil had crept over her like some insidious taint, and she'd barely made it back to the village before falling into a fever that had lasted for weeks.

She'd never gone back, though she'd spent many hours watching it from afar, trying to figure out what it was and what she could do about it.

"Oh..." Thano said, anticipation humming in his voice. "That sounds like just the kind of place we like."

Kane looked over at her. "Did Mason or Jacob ever go in there?"

Sarah nodded, remembering all too well how she'd warned them to stay away. "They couldn't sense anything wrong with it. They went in and out all the time, and said there was nothing in there but grass and plants. They didn't believe me that there was something wrong with it."

Kane looked at his team, and Thano and Ryland both nodded. "We need to go in there."

Sarah grimaced, and a cold chill shuddered over her. "I don't know—"

You can do it. Kane's voice washed over her, and she felt his strength wrapping around her. *I can shield you, and you've got the water. And if you start to crash, I'll get you out.*

He was right. She knew she wasn't on her own this time, and she did need to get in there and find out what was going on. Sarah took a deep breath and nodded. "Okay." She pulled the flask off her belt and poured some in her hands to rub it over her skin. Her skin tingled when she did it, energy surging through her.

"Let me." Kane poured some into his hands and ran his palms over her arms. His touch was like fire, electric and sizzling, and she instantly sucked in her breath.

"Hell," Ryland stepped back, his face contorted. "I can feel the lust between you guys. Jesus, Kane, she's an angel. You can't think about her like that."

Sarah felt her cheeks heat up in embarrassment. *He can sense that?*

Ignore him. Kane poured more water in his hands and ran his hands over her head, drenching her hair. His touch was hot and sexy, and she had a sudden urge to simply throw him down and attack him. *He's got some issue with you being an angel.*

Ryland and Thano turned their backs, staying close, but giving them privacy, which embarrassed Sarah even further. *It's not like we're having sex.*

Kane's eyes were gleaming as he ran his hands over her hips, spreading water over her jeans. *Sweetheart, every time I touch you, I can remember every detail about having you under me, about making love to you, and feeling our bodies and spirits intertwined. So, yeah, we're not having sex, but it's there, in the currents in the air, in the electricity jumping between us, in the heat burning my palms, and they can feel it just as much as we can.*

Sarah swallowed, her heart thudding in her ears. *We're in the middle of the woods, Kane, about to go down into the crevasse of hell, or whatever it is. How can there actually be chemistry leaping between us right now? I'm an angel! I'm not a sex maniac!*

Kane laughed, a deep, rolling sound that seemed to catch her embarrassment and roll it up into a cocoon of warmth. *You're my* sheva, *sweetheart. It comes with the territory.*

It does not! It was never like this with Mason!

Kane's eyes darkened, and a flicker of something dangerous lit them up. *It's a damned good thing it was never like this with Mason. And if it was, you'd better keep that from me.*

Sarah stared at him, her insides curling into a warm knot at the lethal expression on his face, on her behalf. *You're jealous of a dead man who betrayed me so badly I almost died?*

No. Kane poured the last bit of water down the back of her neck, the water trickling over her spine like invisible fingers caressing each vertebra. *I want to kill the bastard who betrayed you, but I want you to be thinking about only me when it comes to getting naked.* His fingers clamped around the back of her neck, hauling her against him. *You may have had a man before, a child, a family, but you are the only thing I've had in my entire life worth living for, so I can't even begin to handle the idea of you looking past me at someone else, even in your mind.*

His desperation was so fierce, so raw, so unbearably agonized that Sarah forgot all her fear, all her embarrassment, all the noise in her head, and it simply became about Kane. She knew what it was like to be lost, to be buried in loneliness, to go to bed at night and feel the silence of the world closing in on her. Unlike Kane, she had a past, yes, but everything that had mattered to her had been stripped away, leaving her as isolated and alone as Kane was. *Kane.* She threw her arms around his neck and kissed him. It wasn't a kiss of desire or lust, it was the only way she could show him that she *got* him.

He growled and yanked her against him the minute she kissed him. His kiss was raw and possessive, so full of need and desire that it burned through her like fire, igniting every cell and spiking through her very soul. It was even more than the night they'd made love, because this time, she was kissing the man, not a gallant, sexy rescuer.

His hands went to her hips, and she could feel his erection grinding against her belly. It got hot fast, hands moving, kisses wandering, her heart racing—

"Stop it!" Ryland roared with fury and yanked them apart. "Just fucking stop it!"

Kane whipped out his flail and Ryland called out his machete, and they locked weapons instantly, both men tense with the need to kill.

Sarah froze, afraid to move and trigger them. *Kane. He didn't hurt me. It's okay.* She could feel Kane's intensity raging though him, his instinct to protect her, which was great, of course, and far better than an instinct to kill her, but there was so much violence laced through his energy that she knew there was serious danger going on.

"Hey, old guys." Thano moved between them, but she could see he was moving with caution, and he was keeping his hands free to call out his weapons if he needed to. "We all know you're both fucked up, but the angel that we've all sworn to protect is going to get killed if we don't all play nice with each other and take out the bad guys instead of the team."

Ryland swore, and his gaze went to Sarah. Not taking his gaze off her face, he sheathed his weapon, making it clear to all of them that it was Thano's reminder of Sarah's situation that had brought him back. He wasn't doing it for Kane.

Kane, however, didn't stand down. "Do not covet my woman," he said, his voice rippling with such anger that chills popped up over Sarah's skin. "Unless you want me to kill you."

Thano set his hand on Ryland's shoulder. "You know he's right," he said quietly. "There's no Calydon alive that could watch another male with a hard-on for his female and not react. What the fuck are you doing, man? She's his *sheva*. You shouldn't even be able to notice her as a woman, let alone *want* her."

"She's an angel," Ryland said, his voice grim.

"So?" Thano asked.

Ryland finally looked at Thano, and there was something in his eyes burning so fiercely that Thano actually lifted his hand to call out his weapon. "So, she is my salvation. She's my only chance."

"No." Kane stepped between them and carefully placed the flail at Ryland's throat. "She is my salvation, Ryland. Not yours. Never yours."

Ryland's eyes flashed. "No one claims an angel for their own."

"No?" Kane grabbed Sarah's arm and shoved up her sleeve, showing Ryland her brand. "Those are my marks, Ryland. No matter what you think about how the world should be, destiny has chosen her for me. That doesn't mean she doesn't serve the greater good, because we all do that every damn day. But as a woman, she is not available, and if you can't get that, we have a major problem because I'm no damn saint, Ry, and we both know it."

Ryland stared at her arm, his lip curled in a snarl. Sarah felt a brush of darkness from him, something evil, something terrible, and then he spun away. "Let's go then," he snapped, striding down the slope straight toward the crevasse.

For a moment, no one moved to follow him.

"Hell, man," Thano said. "It's impossible for him to want another male's *sheva*. How is this happening to him?"

"I don't know." Kane slipped his hand around Sarah's and gripped tightly. "But it has to stop or we're all going to be in serious shit."

"I'll talk to him. Later." Thano moved ahead of them, striding to catch up to Ryland.

Kane didn't hesitate, pulling Sarah quickly along to catch up to his team. Without a word passing between them, Thano and Ryland parted, allowing just enough space for Kane to push Sarah between them. Kane locked down her back side, setting up the triangle of protection once again.

But this time, the tension rippling between the men was so thick she could almost touch it. How in heaven's name were they going to be able to fight?

Because we have one mission, Kane said. *To protect the greater good from rogue Calydons. Whatever these bastards are, they're a threat against innocents, and we are sworn to protect that. You included. Everything is secondary to that.*

Sarah glanced back over her shoulder at Kane, and he flashed her a grim smile. In the shadows of the moon, in the darkness of the night, he loomed huge and muscular, a force powerful enough to destroy anything that came at him. Including her. *How are the scars, Kane?*

He didn't look away from her. *They're still fading, Sarah.*

Fear rippled through her, and she touched the bruises on her neck. Then, there was a flash of black light and a crack, and Kane's weapon appeared in her hand. She jerked back, startled, and Ryland shot her a look of such agonized yearning that her heart broke for him.

No. Kane's voice eased through her mind as they neared the edge of the crevasse. *Don't think about Ryland. Don't think about the bruises. Think only about the fact that I made you call my weapon, and you did it. I have the power to resist, and you have the power to defend yourself.*

She nodded, her mouth suddenly dry as they reached the edge. One step over it, and the assault on her senses would start.

Kane set his hand on the back of her neck, his touch strong and protective. "Focus only on your strength, Sarah. Trust your team. There is no other way."

Thano raised his halberd over Sarah's head, and Kane did the same with his flail. The weapons clinked as they made contact. *Sarah?* Slowly, she raised Kane's other flail and let it rest against the other two.

They all looked at Ryland. For a long moment, he simply stared into the blackness of the pit. He took a step, one foot disappearing into the blackness. Literally. His foot was gone. Ryland cursed under his breath, then raised his machete and slammed it against the other three weapons. The crash ripped through the night and vibrated all the way down Sarah's arm, but she immediately felt a shift in the air between the three men.

They were a team again, to the death.

They lowered their weapons, then as a unit, they moved forward. Kane slipped his fingers around her wrist, locking his grip in an iron band that she knew nothing would be able to break through. He was making sure there would always be physical contact between them so he could teleport her to safety. She glanced up at him, and he shot her a brief smile before looking past her into the darkness.

Sarah paused as they reached the edge, concentrating on the wetness of her skin from the water and Kane's grip on her arm. Then she took a deep breath, embraced the nightmare that had been stalking her for her entire life, and stepped off the edge into the void.

Chapter Twelve

His stallion's feet were silent on the forest floor, the iron-shod hooves leaving no prints in the dirt. Warwick Cardiff bent low over his steed's neck, the animal's black mane whipping against Warwick's chest. Beneath him, his mount's muscles strained, sweat caked on the horse's neck and shoulders. The power of the beast was extraordinary, and Warwick urged him onward, riding hard, both the mount and the rider exhilarating in the display of strength and power. Deathbringer had been Warwick's mount for over a hundred years, and the partnership was far tighter than simply man and beast. It was an intertwining of souls, the one living entity on the earth that Warwick could trust.

They burst out of the woods, and the animal leapt over the rubble of buildings that no longer stood, his hooves silent even on the rocky pebbles. Before him, stepping out from the shadows was the man...the creature...Warwick had come to see.

Warwick reined his steed to a halt, stopping inches from the man lurking in the shadows. He looked down at the creature whose eyes were like bottomless pits of hell, whose skin was stretched across his skeleton like the burned-out hide of an animal long dead. "Luc," he said, not dismounting. He knew better than to trust these creatures who roamed the woods.

Luc Acostos went down on one knee, bowing to Warwick while Deathbringer danced restlessly, his massive hooves thudding dangerously close to Luc's feet. "My lord," he said. "The pieces are in place."

"You lost him," Warwick said, dripping his disdain over the demonic creature before him. "You had him, and you let him go."

Luc's head snapped up, his eyes glittering dangerously. "Santiago is strong. That's why he's the one I need."

"I don't give a shit about what you need." Warwick glared down at him. "The angel must die. Santiago is the key to that, and you need to make sure it happens." He pulled a rose out of his black cape, crumpled it in his hand, and then flung it at Luc's feet. "Or she will be gone forever."

Luc made a noise of agony, of such distress, that Warwick smiled. He knew that kind of pain, and he knew Luc would do whatever it took to save the woman he loved. Warwick knew it, because that was what had driven him for the last seven hundred years. Redemption for the woman who had died in his arms.

Disgust curled Warwick's lip as Luc gathered the crushed red petals, cradling them in his hands as if they were the greatest treasure known to humankind. "Tonight, Luc."

Tonight was when the Order of the Blade was going to begin to fall. Finally. Completely. Until it was nothing but ashes and smoldering vomit, as it deserved to be.

Luc looked up sharply. "Tonight? It can't be tonight. Santiago found the river, and Sarah's strong again—"

"He did?" Enraged, Warwick whirled his mount around toward the fountain. It lay in a pathetic pile of crumbled stone, so dry he could taste the dust on his skin. "Where—" Then he saw it. The massive hole in the ground. Furious, Warwick urged Deathbringer over to the opening. Beneath it flowed the pure, clear water that kept Sarah alive, giving life to the angel who had to die.

Warwick reached beneath his cape and pulled out his wand, a supple, pliant stick of highly polished wood from the tree that marked the grave of his beloved Audrey. He summoned his magic into the wand, and violet and silver sparks crackled violently from the end of it. For a split second, he almost hesitated, grimly aware that if he destroyed the river completely, it wouldn't affect only Sarah, but the entire earth would be profoundly impacted.

The he laughed softly at the irony of his thoughts. "Sacrifice one to preserve the greater good," he said bitterly, mimicking the Order of the Blade mission statement that still made fury and disgust burn through him. "No longer," he said. "Today it is sacrifice the greater good to preserve one."

Then he pointed his wand at the river, and he invoked the power of the demons in his incantation. A bolt of light streaked from the end of his wand, and neither he nor Deathbringer flinched when the earth erupted in a shriek of agony, and then collapsed, burying the river beneath a ton of rocks so tainted that they bled black as they fell into the water.

He spun his mount back toward Luc, who was clenching the rose petals in his hand. "Now, it is up to you. Do not dare to disappoint me."

A slow, insidious grin stretched across the face of the creature masquerading as a man. "Have no fear, my lord. It will be done." He turned his head away from Warwick, scenting the air. Then he stiffened and went into high alert.

"Did you find him?" Warwick asked, stroking Deathbringer's shoulder as his mount shifted restlessly.

"I did. He is mine." Then the demon-man dissolved into a tendril of thick, noxious smoke that immediately streaked through the night and disappeared into the woods.

For a long moment, Warwick did not move. He simply closed his eyes and breathed in the silence of the night, the freshness of the air, the freedom of the breeze rippling over his skin. Anticipation hummed through him, and he smiled, the first true smile he'd felt in over seven hundred years.

Slowly, he shoved up his sleeve and looked at the markings on his arm. The brand of his own weapon, the battle axe that he hadn't bothered to call out in over five hundred years, since he'd walked away from the Order and their mission. And there, woven into his own brand was the name Audrey, carved there with his axe the very last time he'd ever called it out.

He raised his arm and pressed his lips to her name, unable to suppress the same well of grief that had been haunting him so relentlessly for so long. But this time, with the grief was the raw, unbridled promise that her death would finally be avenged. After centuries of planning, her time, their time, had finally come.

He raised his arm to the heavens, reaching up toward the stars that mocked him with their levity. "Tonight, it begins, Audrey Beckett. Tonight, it begins!"

Then he grabbed the reins, whirled his mount to the right, and then the two of them galloped into the night, swallowed up by the darkness, soon to be far, far away from the hellhouse, long before the nightmare was unleashed.

* * *

The moonlight vanished the moment Kane and his team stepped over the edge of the cliff into the crevasse. It was total and complete blackness as they skidded down the rocky shale, down toward a destination they couldn't identify. The air was thick and noxious, making it feel like they were trying to breathe a fetid swamp itself.

Sarah coughed, and he tightened his grip on her wrist. *Talk to me, sweetheart.*

I'm okay so far. Just hard to breathe.

Kane wrapped his arm over her shoulder and tucked her against him, holding her face against his chest. *Better?*

Sarah's body shuddered with relief. *Yes.* Excitement rippled through her. *I've never been able to come in here before.*

Kane tightened his grip on his flail as they descended deeper. He reached out with his senses, searching for any sign of life, but he could sense nothing. Just the overwhelming stench that overrode all other smells, and the ominous, deathly silence. *What do you think is in here?*

The source of the evil, Sarah said. *It has to be.*

Then we better be ready. The darkness seemed to pulse and swirl through Kane, a cold, clammy sensation of fingers trying to peel off his skin ever so carefully.

"I don't feel anything weird," said Thano. "What about you?"

"Nothing," Ryland said. "The air is just regular. I'm scenting trees and some scrub brush and rodents. An owl."

"You get the frog off to the right?" Thano asked.

"Yeah, and the fly it just ate."

Kane swore under his breath, straining to pick up the scents that his teammates were smelling, but his senses were overwhelmed with the thick, pungent fumes of sulfur and rot. He could hear nothing, except the sound of his team. Not a single flutter of feet. Not a whisper of an owl. Nothing but silence that was so loud that it seemed to beat at him. Shit. Why was he sensing things the others weren't? *Sarah? What do you smell?*

Smell? The woods. Dirt.

Something began to pulse inside Kane, a dark foreboding. *What do you hear?*

I hear a whisper, like two giant pieces of sandpaper rubbing against each other.

He shot a sharp look at her, but it was too dark to see her face. *Merge with me.* He reached out with his mind as they continued to skid down the shale slope. Sarah instantly opened to him, and he wove their minds together, enabling each of them to see and hear what the other was experiencing.

Oh, God, Kane. That silence is horrible. Sarah put her hands over her ears. *It hurts.*

He heard the rasping that she'd mentioned, and it sent chills rippling down his arms and over his spine. He jerked suddenly, realizing that he could feel it on his body, that the scratching sound was from something that was rubbing against him. He swore and slapped at his arms, trying to clean them off. Thick black sludge peeled from his skin, tearing from his flesh like glue that had adhered to him.

Sarah jerked back, her face barely visible. "What's that?"

"No idea." It was creeping up his legs now, like tendrils of black smoke wrapping around his legs. He kicked his foot, and it got even thicker around him.

"What the hell's going on?" Ryland slashed at the black vines with his machete as they tried to grab Kane. He tore through them with his blade, but even as he did it, more seemed to come out of the air, wrapping around Kane.

"Shit." He scraped more of it off with his flail, and then Thano was attacking it as well, all three warriors slashing at the black smoke that kept wrapping tighter and tighter around Kane, like living tattoos sinking into his flesh.

"Shit." Thano finally stopped, leaning on his halberd. "It's faster than we are."

Sarah's eyes were wide with horror. "Does it hurt?"

"No." But Kane could feel it seeping through his skin, like thousands of microscopic needles piercing his flesh. The malevolence was thick and tainted, and his skin crawled from the sensation of it closing around him. "Let's keep going."

Thano raised his brows, but didn't bother to question him. Ryland just nodded, and they began to move forward again.

Kane swatted at the back of his neck, and he felt something fall off his skin and drop to the earth. "Shit. Something bit me."

"I'm not getting anything," Thano said. "I always thought you looked like you tasted better than the rest of us." But his voice was grim, with none of the levity he usually had.

"Let's speed this up," Ryland said. "I'm getting a bad feeling about this."

As a unit, the team broke into a jog. Kane kept his hand on Sarah's back, letting her set the pace and keeping her close. The skin on the back of his neck prickled, and he jerked around, searching the darkness, but finding nothing. "We're being hunted."

"I know," Ryland said. "I can feel it."

"Stupid bastards," Thano muttered. "Don't they know that we're the good guys? We do the hunting."

"It's the Calydons," Sarah said. "They're hunting me."

"They're hunting all of us," Kane replied. His brands were burning, warning him of the danger coming in all directions, and he clenched his fists, his mind rapidly assessing their situation and trying to come up with a solution. "Sarah," he muttered, stepping in front of her. "Get on my back."

Without a moment of hesitation, she grabbed his shoulders and leapt up, locking her legs around his hips and her arms around his neck, after handing him the other flail. He made sure she was secure, then he muttered one word to his team. "Run."

The three of them broke into a dead sprint, racing down the hill at a speed very few living creatures could match. They leapt over rocks and crevices, tore past boulders, and raced deeper and deeper into the crevasse. Silent, the three massive warriors were like streaks in the night, in high conceal mode as they sprinted down the hill. Sarah was secure on his back, holding tight, giving them the freedom to cover ground at a pace she could never match.

They ran for eleven minutes. Eleven minutes straight down into the earth at breakneck speed, until Kane felt a lessening of the sensation of being watched. "We're losing them," he told the team. "Keep going."

Barely breathing hard, they upped their speed, their muscles contracting with fierce intensity, their legs churning so fast that most eyes would not be able to track them. But even as he ran, Kane felt his muscles stabbing with pain, as if the black sludge on his skin was eating away at his body. Swearing, he dug harder, fighting to keep up with his team—

Suddenly there was a loud-pitched scream, and a black shadow sprang out of the earth directly in front of Thano. Thano shouted and swung his halberd as it swooped around him. It jerked him off his feet and began dragging him along the earth.

"Shit! Thano!" Ryland and Kane sprinted after him, as Thano hacked at the shadow with his weapon, but the blade was going right through the black smoke, as if it wasn't even there.

"Fuck!" Thano's muscles were bulging as he fought, as his body tore a furrow through the rocky terrain. "Let me go you bastard!"

Ryland and Kane ran harder, but Thano was moving faster than either of them could go. "Teleport," Ryland shouted. "Get the bastard!"

Kane swore, and tore Sarah off him. "Keep her safe!" He tossed Sarah at Ryland, not breaking stride. He started to teleport even as she flew out of his arms—

The moment he wasn't touching her, agony ripped through him. He bellowed with anguish even as he dematerialized. He reformed ten feet in front of Thano, his body screaming with agony as he spread his feet to block the path of his teammate. Kane reared back with his flail as the tentacle neared and brought down his flail with tremendous strength just as the black streak moved between his feet.

But it simply parted around his weapon, streaking past him, still dragging Thano. "Thano!" Kane dove on Thano as the warrior was ripped past him. He locked onto his teammate, and instantly dematerialized, taking Thano with him. But as he faded, he felt Thano's body resisting the teleportation, his cells refusing to disintegrate. "Shit!" Kane rematerialized, still holding onto Thano as they were yanked and dragged, tumbling across the earth as they were sucked along.

"Get out of there!" Ryland shouted, pointing past him.

Kane turned and saw a gaping black hole in the earth. The air above it was murky, roiling with violent green, purple and black. "Son of a bitch." He concentrated his energy on Thano, who was still relentlessly hacking at the thing wrapped around him. "Thano! Don't shut me out!"

"I'm not," he yelled back. "It's not me. Get us the fuck out of here, Kane!"

Swearing, Kane gripped Thano tighter and opened his mental connection to his teammate. They weren't blood bonded, but when they were close, they could talk mind-to-mind like any Calydons. Thano's mind met his, and he sensed the warrior's grim desperation. They locked onto each other, and Kane made sure they were tightly connected.

"Now!" Ryland shouted. "Now!"

"Kane!" Sarah yelled, her voice frantic. "You're almost there!"

With a furious burst of power, Kane poured all his energy into Thano, tearing apart his cells and yanking him ruthlessly into the dematerialization. They began to fade, and Kane felt a surge of triumph—

Then Thano was torn out of his grasp, and both warriors bellowed in fury as they were ripped apart. Kane lunged for Thano as the younger warrior plunged over the edge of the hole. "Go," Thano shouted as he was yanked over the edge. "This isn't about me! I'm not your mission!" Then he was gone, and Kane was hurtling over the edge after him—

Kane! Sarah's voice ripped through his mind. *You can't save him that way! Don't go in there!*

With a roar of agony, Kane dematerialized, and he landed beside Ryland and Sarah, his body screaming from the effort. He landed hard on the earth, his body shaking as the black taint rushed over him, eating away at his skin. Son of a bitch. He'd lost Thano. *He'd lost him.*

He stumbled to his feet, as Ryland and Sarah hurried over. "We have to get him," he managed, barely able to stand through the pain. It felt like his skin was being torn off his body, like his flesh was being ripped from the bone. "Now!"

Ryland was already racing toward the hole, his machete out as he bellowed his rage. Kane grabbed Sarah, and they sprinted after him. But even as they raced after him, Kane saw another black tendril spring out of the earth right at Ryland. "Ry!" he shouted. "Watch out—"

Ryland vaulted over the tendril, hacking at it with his machete. It twisted and turned, trying to track him as he leapt over it. "Stupid bastard," he yelled. "You don't get to have me—" It grabbed at his ankle and hauled him back toward the hole, tearing through the air as Ryland shouted his rage.

Sarah let go of Kane. "Get him," she shouted. "Go!"

Kane didn't waste any time. He immediately dematerialized and teleported to mid-air where Ryland was being dragged down toward the hole. Ryland met Kane's gaze, and Kane saw his teammate's eyes were blood red. Pure, raw evil was pouring out of Ryland, so thick that Kane's hands burned where they touched his flesh. "Fuck that bastard, Santiago," Ryland snarled. "Get me the fuck out of here."

Inches from the churning miasmas of smoke spewing out of the hole, Kane dematerialized again. He felt a scream of rage from the smoke, and he felt Ryland's body resist the dematerialization just like Thano's had. But then, something violent and evil ripped out of Ryland. There was a flash of crimson light, streaked with putrid brown and black slashes. It lit up the night, and the smoke that had been gripping Ryland so tightly screamed in agony and suddenly Ryland's body was released and he disintegrated with Kane.

Kane teleported them to the hill just below Sarah, both men landing with a staggering impact. Kane braced his hands on the earth, fighting against the pain, his body vibrating with the shock of whatever Ryland had unleashed. "What the hell was that?"

Ryland was on his stomach in the dirt, not moving, his head turned toward the side, away from Kane.

"Ry?" Then Kane saw Sarah's expression. She was on her knees on the other side of Ryland, staring at Ryland's face. She was frozen in sheer terror, her eyes wide, her mouth open, her body trembling.

"Sarah?" Raw dread pulsed through Kane and he saw Ryland's body twitch. Violent black, brown and red slashes appeared on his skin, as if he were being flayed with an invisible whip before their very eyes.

"Oh, God." Sarah began to back away from Ryland, and he felt the raw coldness of terror so deep it could destroy one's very soul. "Kane," she whispered. "You need to see this."

"What? *What?*" Kane lurched to his feet and vaulted over Ryland's twitching body, tackling Sarah and yanking her back from Ryland. Once he had her a safe distance from Ryland, Kane shoved her behind him as he whirled to face his teammate.

Then he saw what Sarah had seen, and his blood ran cold. "Hell, man," he whispered. "What the fuck are you?"

Ryland's face was gone. In its place was a smoky, turbulent facade of shifting shadows. Black, red, green, purple. Where his eyes should have been were two black abysses, bottomless pits of raging fire, of spirits screaming in agony. Thousands and thousands of spirits, trapped in the abyss, screaming to be saved, suffering agony beyond words.

Kane held up his flail, reaching behind him to make sure Sarah was still within reach. "Ryland," he said quietly. "Come back to us. We need your help."

The warrior didn't move, but his body was still twitching, and more and more slashes were appearing on his skin, tearing his clothes, ripping chunks out of his flesh.

"Ryland!" Kane yelled. "Get the fuck back here! Your angel needs you!"

Still no response, and the ground beneath Ryland began to churn, spewing bits of dirt and earth into the air. "Shit," Kane swore.

"This isn't the pit that's doing it," Sarah said, her hand tight on Kane's back. "I've never seen that before. This is him."

"Ryland!" Kane shouted. Shit. What would Dante do for Ryland? Dante had been their leader, the only one who'd been able to provide peace to Ryland. Thano had seemed to have a connection with Ry, but... Guilt and grief welled through Kane. Thano was gone. Kane was all Ry had left, but he had no idea how to help him. How to bring him back—

His brands suddenly burned in his arms, and Kane jerked his attention back to his surroundings. He became aware of massive amounts of smoke pouring out of the hole in the ground now, so dense with evil that it permeated his pores.

Sarah gripped the back of his shirt. "This is it," she whispered, her voice pulsing with anticipation. "This is what I feel at night. It's coming out." She stepped up beside him, keeping close to him, her heart pounding. "This is the source."

Kane fisted his weapons as he watched it swirl. The pain in his flesh was almost excruciating now, but he shut it out, focusing his adrenaline on the shapes swirling above their heads. "Touch me and don't let go," he instructed Sarah. "I need to be able to take you out of here, but I need my hands free."

Sarah set her hand on his waist and twisted her fingers in the waistband of his jeans. Her skin was cold, too cold, and he glanced over at her. Her face was pale, and there was a sheen of perspiration on her forehead. Protectiveness surged through him, and he whirled back to face the smoke, intensely focused. This was the source of the threat to his woman, and it ended now.

Chapter Thirteen

Sarah caught her breath as the smoke began to take shape, the swirling getting faster and faster, like a tornado of doom and rot—
Click click click.
A triple clicking noise sounded from her right, and she jerked her gaze off the mass that was accumulating above them. Two red eyes glowed at her from the side of a nearby tree: a Calydon ready to attack. A triple click to her left. More glowing eyes. And to her right. And behind them. Suddenly, the night was alive with clicking, and the woods took on an eerie red glow. She felt for the flask at her hip, her last one. *Um, Kane.*
I know they're here. I knew they'd come. They were waiting.
She swallowed hard, frantically scanning the woods. The triple click always preceded an almost instantaneous attack, yet nothing was coming at her. She braced for the assault as the clicks became louder and louder. The crescendo rose to a thundering din, and the woods began to glow so brightly. It was as if a forest fire was raging around them, ready to burn them all to a crisp.
"Holy shit," Kane breathed, pulling her attention back just as the clouds above them began to take the shape of a face, of a man, a distorted, tormented male.
The wind began to howl around them as the massive face took shape above them, whipping Sarah's hair around her cheeks so violently it felt like it was cutting her skin.
Kane pulled her more tightly against him, crushing her against his side, protecting her from all the directions that he could. "Ryland," he muttered. "Get the fuck up."
But Ryland was the same, his body bleeding now from all the slashes, convulsing violently as the earth was chewed up around him,

chopped up by invisible blades.

Suddenly there was a flash of red light so bright that Sarah yelped and covered her eyes. Black spots flashed in her vision as she struggled to see. The clicking grew louder, closer, and she jerked her eyes open as shadows began to shift around her, Calydons moving into position, surrounding her, getting tighter and tighter. "Oh, crap," she whispered.

"Who the hell are you?" Kane demanded.

Sarah jerked her gaze off the woods and gasped in shock when she saw a man walk out of the red light, striding toward them. He was tall and heavily muscled, wearing a black leather shirt cuffed to the elbows and unbuttoned to his navel, showcasing angry red marks across his chest, as if someone had tied him down for centuries and the cables had become permanently carved into his flesh. His muscular legs were encased in black pants and his leather belt that seemed to undulate as if it were alive.

The man fastened his gaze on Kane, and there was a glow of intense satisfaction in his eyes. "You returned."

Kane stiffened as the man's voice rolled through him. His voice was grating and harsh, as if he'd spent centuries screaming and had nearly destroyed his ability to speak. His voice carried pain, anguish, despair, and a violence so dark and so dangerous that all of Kane's warnings began to sound. Kane tightened his grip on Sarah, pulling her back. He was vigilantly aware of all the Calydons surrounding them, ready to leap, and he knew he'd have only a split second to get Sarah out of there once they launched their attack.

Swearing, he began to edge to the right, toward Ryland. He would not leave two men behind. Not today. *Thano, if you can hear me, stay alive. We're coming for you.*

"Kane Santiago," the man said. "You're more than I ever thought you might be."

Kane's adrenaline bolted into high gear as he kept moving Sarah toward Ryland. "You know me?"

The male's eyes narrowed. "You don't remember?"

Kane went still, all his senses on high alert, racing through everything he could pick up. The scent of sulfur and death on the man, the taint of blood on the claws that reached halfway to the ground, the raspiness of his breathing. The male bled evil. He was thick with power, corruption and torture. Kane's brands burned, and he felt his upper lip lift in a snarl, disgusted by the creature before them.

"No!" The man shouted his rage. "You know me! Think about it, Kane! Bring it back!"

Kane swore as something nudged at the back of his mind, but he couldn't place it. But even as he thought it, pain began to streak through his body again.

Sarah gripped his arm. *Kane. Your arm!*

He glanced down, and saw the skin on his left arm was completely flawless. Not a single scar from his shoulder to his fingers. But as he watched it, it began to ripple, as if there was a black poison beneath his skin, being stirred by an approaching storm.

A thin smile stretched across the man's face, and he raised his hand. A streak of red light flashed out of his hand spiking right toward Kane's heart. Kane instinctively blocked it with his flail. The man smiled, his face pleased. "You're good."

There was movement from his right, and Kane sensed Ryland dragging himself onto his knees. He glanced over and swore when he saw that Ryland's face was still the distorted hell that it had been. Ry's eyes were fixated on Kane, on his hand where he was holding onto Sarah. Kane swore. Threats coming from all directions. Too many to defend against. "Who are you?"

"Luc Acostos," the man bowed deeply, and Kane saw black markings on his right shoulder, markings that made the hair on the back of Kane's neck stand up.

Because he had those same markings. They were barely visible beneath the scars, but they were there. And this man had them too.

"Jesus," he said softly. "What are you?" The man carried no brands. He wasn't a Calydon.

"You know," Luc said, moving closer, his gaze locked on Kane. He didn't even seem to see Sarah or Ryland or anything else. "You *know.*"

Kane's mind filled with flashes and images. A woman. Brown hair, blue eyes. Kindness. Warmth. Something shifted inside Kane, something that tightened in his gut and seemed to reverberate through him...then the pain began again. Not his skin this time. Deeper. Inside his soul. The kind of pain that stripped a man raw and left him to die.

Luc's eyes glittered. "Elizabeth," he breathed. "You see Elizabeth."

"Who is she?"

"Your mother."

And suddenly Kane was back there in the room. He could smell the fire in the hearth, the scent of food cooking. She was rocking in a chair, humming to herself as she knitted. Kane closed his eyes at the sound of the song. He knew it. Sweet Jesus, he knew that song. She held up her project, and he saw it was a small blue blanket. A baby blanket. She smiled and pressed the blanket to her heart, and he felt the waves of love pouring off her, filling the room with warmth and a golden energy that seemed to wrap around her.

Kane. Sarah's awed voice was in his head, and he realized that she could see what he was seeing. *She's an angel. The gold glow. Your mother was an angel.*

An angel? His mother was an angel? His entire body shuddered in disbelief. This was his past? This was his world? His mother stood up suddenly, and he saw she was heavy with child. She patted her belly, and again, he felt her warmth. It plunged straight into his chest so fiercely, he couldn't breathe, and he realized that she'd sent that love into him. *Jesus, Sarah. She's pregnant with me.*

And she'd loved him. Son of a bitch. She'd loved him—

His mother staggered suddenly, and waves of violent energy began to pour off her. She screamed and grabbed the back of the chair while she slid to her knees, grasping her belly. "No!" Kane leapt up, reaching for her, for the woman who wasn't really there. "What's happening to her?"

She screamed again, and a black stain began to spread over her skin. Violence spewed off her, turning her golden light to a mutated taint of poisonous smog. She fell to the ground, and her body began to convulse as smoke poured out of her fingers, blood oozing from her pores, cuts appearing on her body. "No!" Kane screamed, lunging for her, but his hands met only earth. Her body began to shake, and others rushed into the room, people shouting and holding her. Some staggering and gagging from the taint in the room. The vileness of the atmosphere was palpable, and some ran out, shouting for help.

People surrounded her, cutting off his view of her, and Kane bellowed his rage, trying to get to see her—

Then someone stood up, carrying a baby. A boy. Him? The crowd parted, and he saw the outline of his mother's body beneath a tattered black blanket. Seeping from the edges of the blanket, inching its way through the crevices in the wood was a thick, black stain, eating away at the very fabric of the home.

Kane stared in horror at his mother, bile rising in his throat. "What happened to her?"

"You did," Luc's voice was dripping with disgust, with disdain, with hatred so thick that it tore through Kane's memories and jerked him out of the past.

Kane looked up in shock. "What?"

"You killed her." Luc spat on Kane, his lip curled in disgust. "You destroyed her, you bastard cretin. I was coming back for her. We had a plan. And you fucking killed her."

The truth of Luc's words reverberated through Kane, and pain stabbed through him, tearing through his flesh and his soul. "Son of a bitch." He bent over and braced his hands on his quads, fighting for breath. How could he have killed his own mother? But he felt the truth of it. He knew that taint was his. He'd poisoned her before he had even been born.

Kane, Sarah said. *Don't listen to him. He's trying to torment you—*

"No!" He gasped. "I can feel it. It's true."

"And now you pay for it." Luc lashed out suddenly, and Kane felt his heart stutter. He looked down and saw a black shadow had pierced his chest and was trying to rip his heart out of his body.

"Stop it!" Sarah called out Kane's flail and hurled it at Luc. He glanced over at her too late, and it slammed right into his chest, hurling him backward and ripping his shadowy arm out of Kane's chest.

Kane gasped for breath, his mind reeling as he fought for clarity. He had to focus. Had to concentrate—

Luc was on his knees now, glowering at Kane, but he didn't attack again. "In due time," he snarled. "But first you suffer."

More visions flashed into Kane's mind, thundering through his consciousness. He was in a small cabin in the woods. The night was beating at the doors, the windows rattling, but there was a fire in the hearth. He was restless, pacing the room, his skin on fire. He reached for the door, and then a soft voice called his name.

He turned as a woman walked out of the bedroom. She had white blond hair, blue eyes, and a smile so tender that Kane nearly choked. She was young, shit, so young, barely eighteen. She smiled at him, and he saw brands on her arms. His brands. His soul mate. "Son of a bitch." He didn't know her name. He had no clue who she was, but those were his brands. She belonged to him. "Jesus." His chest hurt, his lungs hurt, he couldn't breathe. This was who he was. His past. His family.

Kane. Sarah's hands were on his shoulders, and he gripped them tightly, trying to pull himself back from the images. But he couldn't. He didn't want to. He wanted to find out about his past. To know the people who had been important to him.

Another scene now. The same woman. Working outside in the garden. She turned toward him, and a smile lit up her face. Not just a smile. Love. Son of a bitch. She'd loved him. He'd been *loved.* He reached for her, and then there was a shout from around the corner of the house.

His *sheva* turned and held out her arms, laughing as a young boy toddled toward her. The boy Kane had seen before in his dreams. Tousled curly hair. A muddy red shirt. The woman swept the boy up in her arms, their laughter echoing through the yard. God, they were happy. Then the boy looked toward Kane, and his heart almost stopped. The boy had his eyes. Sweet Jesus. "Is he my son?"

"He is," Luc said, violent disgust making his voice vibrate. "Do you feel their love? Do you feel their innocence?"

"God, yes." Kane tried to reach for them to touch them, but his hands just passed through air—

Then suddenly, his *sheva* whirled around, facing the woods. Her smile vanished, fear flickered across her face. She began to back toward the house, clutching the boy to her chest. She had her hand out, as if she was trying to ward off something.

Slowly with great dread, as if he knew what was coming, Kane turned his head to see what she was looking at, and he went rigid when he saw himself sprint out of the woods. His body was clean, not a scar to be seen, his muscles leaner with youth. He couldn't have been more than eighteen, barely a warrior.

But his eyes were glowing black, and he was wielding both his weapons as if for battle. She screamed and tried to run, and Kane leapt on her, raising his weapon and bringing it down toward her head—

Stop it! Sarah blasted through his mind, shredding the image.

Kane gasped, his mind whirling, agony constricting his heart. "I killed them." Jesus. He couldn't breathe. He couldn't swallow. His emotions were tearing apart his insides. "I killed my son—"

"No!" Sarah grabbed his shoulders, forcing him to look at her. "It's not real, Kane! Luc is projecting them into your mind! It didn't happen! You wouldn't do that! It's not real."

He gripped her shoulders, his fingers digging into her in desperation. "Get away from me, Sarah. Get away before I do it to you."

"No!" She screamed at him and hammered on his chest. "Stop it!"

Then the images flashed. His *sheva* on the ground, blood pouring from a wound in her chest. His son on the ground next to her. Eyes closed. His face angelic even in death. Grief roared through Kane, and he staggered to his feet, unable to focus, to think. He'd killed them. He'd killed them all. Jesus Christ. He was the monster. He was the one who should have been struck down. It was him. He was the one. "No!" He bellowed his rage to the night, unable to contain the hell filling him.

"Kane!" Sarah grabbed his arm, and he felt her trying to build a connection between them, to call upon their bond to bring him back.

"Don't!" He yanked his arm out of her grip, staggering as the world spun around him. Everything he believed in was a lie. Everything that he'd purported to honor for his whole existence meant nothing. He was the protector. The guardian. The harbinger of relief to innocents. And it was a lie. A fucking lie. He was the monster he'd claimed to protect the world against for the last five hundred years. He was the one who deserved to die. Not the others. Him.

Sarah threw herself in his way, blocking his path. The anguish rolling off Kane was unbelievably intense, a thousand times worse than she'd ever felt from anyone. He couldn't see that it could be a lie, he couldn't fathom the concept of hope or faith that it was wrong. He was drowning in despair, pure unadulterated, heart-wrenching despair. He was sunk in the hopelessness for who he was, for what he had been, for what he could be.

It was so intense, so much stronger than it should have been. She felt it tearing at her, invading her own soul, burdening her. "Dammit, Kane! Stop it!" A flicker of fear rippled through her, fear that maybe he was the man brought to destroy her, and she grimaced, knowing full well that it was the loss of hope and faith that was making her afraid.

Somehow, Kane had given her back hope and faith, and now it was slipping through their fingers, torn apart by the magnitude of what he was feeling. A sudden chill rippled over her. The river. Something had to have happened to the river, and it was affecting Kane, tearing him apart.

She knew then that they had to get out of there now. She didn't know what game Luc was playing, but he was winning. "Kane!" She grabbed his wrist. "Teleport us out of here. Take us out—"

There was a sudden howl of victory that sent chills down Sarah's arms. She whirled around just as a Calydon's blade closed in on her face—

"No!" Kane's flail slammed into it, knocking it aside. Sarah whirled toward him. His eyes were wild and strung out, and anguish was pouring off him, but his eyes were clear now. "You don't get to hurt her!" He bellowed, tearing past her as the forest erupted with Calydons attacking her. He tore through them with his weapons, fighting with unbelievable speed and force, beyond what any male should be able to summon. The others had no chance against him, and—

"Sarah." A cold hand closed around her throat, and Luc yanked her over to him, his claws digging into her flesh, and cutting off her breath. His eyes were glittering with black rage, as she scrabbled at her neck, trying to pry his hands off. She couldn't call Kane's weapons, because it would leave him defenseless against the dozens of attackers.

His eyes glittered. "Kill me, Sarah. Try."

She realized then what he was trying to do. He was trying to destroy her. He was the one behind it all. He wanted her to use her powers to hurt him. Damn him! "No," she hissed. "You don't get to destroy me!"

His claws tightened on her throat, and she couldn't breathe. The earth started to spin, and her arms went numb. Panic hit her, and she fought desperately. *Sarah!* She heard Kane's roar of outrage, and suddenly he materialized beside her. He grabbed her and started to dematerialize—

But her body wouldn't go with him. It was the same thing that had happened with Thano and Ryland!

"Shit!" Kane reformed, and he struck hard against Luc, but her captor simply dissolved into smoke, allowing Kane's weapon to pass through him before rematerializing again.

"Kane! Behind you!" Kane whirled around and blocked another blow, but the Calydons were on them, attacking swiftly and aggressively. Sarah screamed as another blade came down toward her. Kane deflected it, and then someone hit him in the back of the head. And another came at her. Too many, from all directions.

Sarah screamed as a blade jammed into her belly, trying to twist free of Luc's ruthless grip, but she was nothing more than a rag doll in his grasp.

"Stay away from her!" Suddenly there was a roar of fury, and Ryland leapt to his feet and hurled his machete at Luc. His face was human again, his body thick with muscle as he charged Luc. "Get the fuck off the angel," he bellowed.

But again, Luc simply dissolved himself where the machete had struck, and then he reformed, a broad grin widening on his face. "You can't beat me," he shouted. "Now is when the suffering begins, and I get what I want." He raised her up by her neck, leaving her feet dangling above the ground. "Kane Santiago," he shouted. "Come save your *sheva!*"

Then he hurled her right at a team of Calydons, standing there ready with their blades. "No!" She instinctively summoned her white light, and she struck instantly, igniting the night with her light just as she reached them. But before she hit them, Kane materialized and grabbed her. "Oh, no!" She tried to turn off her white light, but it was too late, and she smelled the stench of burning flesh as Kane tore her away from them, the smoke rising from his own body as she torched him.

Kane gasped and stumbled, and they reformed right in the middle of the carnage. Calydons descended upon them, and Kane leapt up, fighting to protect her, even as the white flames flickered on his body, and he fell to the ground. Ryland rushed in beside them, cutting down their attackers as Sarah crawled over to Kane, who was trying to lurch to his feet. "Kane! Just take us out—"

He grabbed her and tried again, and again, nothing happened. They didn't disappear. Kane swore, and she saw that same black shadow winding around their legs, the same one that had taken Thano, the one that had made it impossible for Kane to teleport him out of there.

They were trapped.

Then more Calydons attacked Kane and Ryland. The moment her guardians were engaged, Luc grabbed her again, grinning at Kane's howls of fury as he tried to get to her, but couldn't, his teleporting stripped from him by the smoky tendrils. Sarah gasped as Luc dragged her across the dirt toward him and locked his claws around her throat. "I'm sorry you need to die for this," he said, and Sarah saw real humanity in his eyes for a split second. "But I have to save her."

Her? Who? "We can help—"

Real pain flickered in Luc's eyes. "No," he said. "You can't. There's only one way, and that is for Kane to take my place and free me from the bondage that has kept me here for seven hundred years." And with that, he whirled her around and flung her into the pit that had sucked down Thano.

* * *

Kane!

Kane whirled around as Sarah tumbled through the air, heading straight for the black hole. "Son of a bitch." He broke into a dead run, straining with everything he had to teleport, but there was no response from his body. No tingling from his cells. "Shit!" He ran harder, plowing through the Calydons, not even flinching as the blows rained down. His entire being was centered on Sarah, his entire soul focused on the woman falling into the pit.

He reached the edge of the pit and launched himself into the air. Sarah reached for him, and he caught her wrist. He tried to dematerialize instantly, and again, nothing happened. Son of a bitch! He yanked Sarah against him, locking her against his chest as they tumbled through the air. Kane looked below them and saw only a bottomless pit of blackness. Smoke swirled beneath them, and there was the most horrific scent of rot and suffering, of death, of evil, bubbling up from the earth.

He knew then that they would die if they went in there.

There was no rescuing of Thano. Nothing could survive that. *Nothing.*

I will. Sarah's voice was grim. *That won't kill me.*

Kane realized suddenly what she was saying. She wouldn't die from that. She would live an eternity of torment and suffering, unable to die to escape from it.

"Unleash the beast!" Ryland shouted as he raced down the hill toward them. "Let it go, Kane!"

Kane suddenly remembered how Ryland had broken the spell. By turning into a monster. Sarah gripped Kane tighter and met his gaze. *I trust you, Kane. Do it.* The heat from the inferno was raging now, and Kane could feel it burning his skin. They were inches, seconds from hell.

He kissed her hard, then he stopped fighting the darkness within him. He embraced it. He embraced the nightmare that he'd seen in the vision. He allowed the darkness that had been hunting him to simply take over.

The pain tore through him with violent force, erupting from him. Violence, hate, death, a thousand murders, bodies strewn across the earth, the joy of seeing such destruction. Kane embraced it all, and he opened himself to it. Suddenly there was an explosion of red light from his body. He screamed from the evil spewing through him, but at the same time, he felt sudden lightness in his cells, and he knew that he'd broken free of the dark tendrils.

Sarah gasped and gripped him tightly. *Now, Kane, now!*

Kane immediately tried to teleport again, and this time, he felt both of them begin to disintegrate.

"Wait for me!" Ryland launched himself off the edge of the pit and dove straight down toward them, narrowing his body like a spear to slice through the air. He reached for Kane as they began to dissolve. Kane lunged for him, and their fingers touched as they vanished, making contact just in time.

Kane had a split second to revel in the triumph of their escape, when he heard Luc's laughter, and he realized that somehow, they had just played right into a trap that Luc had set for them.

It wasn't a victory. Not for them. But what battle had they just lost?

Chapter Fourteen

Sarah tumbled to the hardwood floor of her grandmother's house, her body aching as she landed, still wrapped in Kane's arms. Ryland crashed beside her, and Kane landed with a thud.

For a moment, none of them moved. Her body was shaking violently from the aftermath of using her powers, and the two warriors were bloody and ragged.

Kane rolled over, pulling her under him, his dark eyes searching hers. *Sarah? You okay?*

Sarah nodded, still trying to catch her breath. Kane's body was warm and heavy on hers, filling her with a sense of safety, of respite. She wrapped her arms around his shoulders, clinging desperately. She could still see that pit, bubbling with things so awful that she couldn't even imagine them. "That was so close."

"Nah," Ryland said, his voice strained. "It was a piece of cake."

Sarah turned her head, and she was relieved to see that Ryland's face was still human. His body was still streaked with the slashes, and his clothes were torn. But the nightmare that had consumed him was gone.

"You okay, man?" Kane asked, still not moving from Sarah, as if he couldn't bear to separate them, which was fine with her.

Ryland sat up and propped himself against the wall, draping his arms over his knees. "Yeah."

"What happened to you out there?"

Ryland's eyes glittered with something dark. "Nothing."

"Nothing? Shit, man, you were—"

"Nothing." Ryland interrupted again. "You imagined it."

Kane narrowed his eyes, and then he nodded once, giving Ryland his space. "For now, I imagined it, but eventually, I'm going to realize I didn't, and I'm going to want answers."

Ryland's eyes were haunted. "Thano," he said quietly.

Kane's sudden grief beat at Sarah, and his body shook with the effort of containing his emotions. "I know."

"Luc has to die," Ryland said. "He has to."

"Damn right he does." He met his teammate's gaze. "Any ideas?"

Ryland said nothing.

"Sarah!" There was a clatter from the kitchen, and Nonny flung open the living room door and raced inside. She took them in with a quick sweep and then swore. "Good God, what kind of defenders are you? I thought the Order of the Blade was tough!" But there was kindness in her voice, and she immediately went to the closet and pulled out a stack of Navajo patterned blankets.

She draped one over Ryland's shoulders, and Sarah was surprised to see the surly warrior accept it silently, giving Nonny a nod of appreciation. Nonny wrapped one over Kane, who grudgingly rolled off Sarah, and wrapped it around her instead, pulling her tight into his arms.

The blanket was warm, encasing Sarah like a cocoon. She felt it tuck itself around her, a protective energy that tingled through her skin, easing the tightness in her chest. They were the same blankets that Nonny had wrapped around her so many times growing up, the ones that Nonny had kept on her for months and months after the attack.

Kane ran his hand over her arm, and squeezed lightly on the brands. She looked at her arm and saw another line had joined the others. The handle of his flail was done, and one of the spiked balls was outlined. Another stage had been completed, tightening the bond. When? What had they done? Fear rippled through her at the realization that he was drawing her more and more tightly under his spell, like Mason had.

When I dove over the pit to save you, Kane said, his voice low and satisfied in her mind. *I risked my life to save yours, so that's my half of the death stage.*

Sarah swallowed, her throat tightening as she remembered how he'd launched himself into the air after her. At that point, he couldn't even teleport, and he had no way out once he was airborne, but he'd done it anyway, willing to risk his own life for the chance of being able to save hers. And it had worked. *Thank you.*

He pressed his lips to her arm. *There can be no other path but for us to bond and for me to protect you.*

Sarah watched his face, but she saw no danger in it. There was none of the monster that he'd unleashed to break Luc's hold on him. He just seemed like Kane, and she relaxed, suddenly realizing how exhausted she felt. For the moment, she was safe in his arms.

Nonny eyed Kane, but she made no comment as she draped another blanket around his shoulders. Kane shuddered as she wrapped it around him, and Sarah knew he was feeling the same impact as she did from the blankets. "They're special wool," Sarah explained.

"I can tell." Kane tugged the blanket around his shoulders, wrapping his arms around Sarah, and pulling her back against his chest more securely.

Nonny looked around the room, one more blanket dangling from her hand. "Where's my young stallion?"

Sarah felt the wave of grief from Ryland and Kane, and her own chest tightened. No one spoke, and Nonny's face suddenly became old. "My dear boy," she said quietly as she turned away and set the blanket on the table.

She picked up a candle from the window sill and set it on the floor between Ryland and Kane. Then she held her palm over it and whispered a prayer. A light breeze drifted over Sarah's cheeks, and then a small flame flared to life, flickering gently in the dimly lit cabin. "May Thano's spirit be at peace," Nonny said.

Kane made a sound of pain, and he held out his hand to the flame. "May Thano's spirit be at peace," he said gruffly.

"Fuck that." Ryland lashed out with his foot, knocking over the candle. "It's not over until I see his body." He lurched to his feet. "I'm going outside."

"No." Nonny rose off her haunches, blocking Ryland's exit. "It's not dawn yet. It is not time. Now, you rest. During the day, you plan. Tomorrow night, you go out. It is then that you will get your reprisal."

Ryland's eyes flashed, and his lip curled in a snarl. "Oh, trust me, you don't need to worry. I'm not going to get myself killed. The bastard can't get that lucky. Tomorrow, he fucking dies." Then he slammed his heel down on the candle, crushing the flame, and stalked out the front door, slamming it behind him.

Nonny sat down heavily on a chair, and peered at Sarah and Kane. Sarah felt the weight of her grandmother's worry in the hunch of the old woman's shoulders and the lines around her mouth. "Bad night," Nonny observed. "Did anything worthwhile occur?"

"We found the source," Sarah said, leaning her head back against Kane's shoulder, needing to feel his strength around her. She knew her body was drained and depleted, and it felt good to be able to let Kane support her. "We found the leader."

Anticipation gleamed in Nonny's eyes, and excitement danced

across her features. "You found him? He showed himself to you?"

"Yes. He said his name was Luc Acostos, and that he needed a replacement."

"Luc Acostos?" Recognition flashed across Nonny's face, and then fear, real fear.

Sarah sat up. "You *know* him? What do you know?"

"I have heard rumors, but I didn't believe them. I didn't think they were true."

Sarah frowned. "What rumors? I've never heard of him."

"Javier told me about him, and even he said they were rumors." Nonny's gaze shifted between Sarah and Kane, and she seemed to hesitate. "Luc Acostos is the link between the demon world and the angels," she said. "He was once an angel, but he made a bad choice and was condemned forever." She looked at Sarah. "He was once like you."

Kane shifted, his body tensing. "What did he do?"

Nonny sat down in front of them and picked up the candle again. "He was an angel of death, and he came to our village to claim a young woman. But he fell in love with her instantly, and he refused to kill her."

Sarah thought of how Mason hadn't had that same aversion to killing her, and anger rippled through her. How come Mason hadn't been that strong? "Can an angel of death do that?"

"No. It is impossible for an angel to ignore a death call, so what he did was unthinkable. He shifted the death call onto someone else." Nonny set Thano's candle upright. "He used his love for his woman to overrule his compulsion to kill her and killed an innocent instead. It was the first time that an angel had ever been able to do that, and the repercussions were extraordinary."

Sarah glanced at Kane, and thought of the *sheva* bond and how Kane managed to break through Luc's hold on him to save her. Was Kane the kind of man who could do that?

"The demons were able to claim him instantly, and they did, turning him into a demon more powerful than most because of his angelic origins. Because of his connections to angels, they were able to use him to prey on angels. He became their tool to destroy this village and the angels, and to free up the land so that demons could cross over. He guards the link between their world and ours, and his job has been to weaken the barriers between the worlds until the demons can pass over." She met Sarah's gaze. "He is bound to these woods forever."

Sarah thought back to what Luc had said. "He wants to be free of the bondage." She looked at Kane. "He said he needs you to do it."

Kane narrowed his eyes. "Me? Why?"

They both looked at Nonny, but she shook her head. "That I don't know, but if Luc Acostos truly is the one haunting our woods, then he has the immortality of a demon. This is not good." She held her hands over the candle and lit Thano's flame again.

The orange light flickered and danced, casting shadows on the walls.

For a long moment, no one spoke, and the only movement in the room was the flickering of Thano's candle.

Eventually, Nonny stood up, walked over to the closet and pulled out a stack of linens. She set it on the couch, then opened the door to the spare bedroom, the one Sarah had slept in when she was recovering from the attack by Mason. "You both need sleep. Tomorrow, we will talk." Defiance flared in her eyes. "Tomorrow, we will plan." She walked over to Sarah and pressed a kiss to her forehead, and Sarah reached up to hug her.

Nonny's arms wrapped around her, a fierce hug so much stronger than an old lady should be capable of. Sarah clung to her, to the wiry body that had been her sole support for so long. God, she wanted to be a little girl again so her nightmares could be washed away by Nonny's special blanket and a glass of warm milk. Not anymore. She wasn't a little girl. There was no magical solution. "I'm sorry, Nonny," she whispered. "I'm sorry for letting you down."

Nonny pulled back and shook her head. "Apologies are for the weak and pathetic, Sarah. You owe me nothing." Her gaze went between them. "Sarah, you—" She hesitated suddenly, indecision flashing across her face. Then Nonny shook her head and stood up. "Rest well, both of you."

"Wait!" Sarah sat up as her grandmother headed toward her bedroom. "What were you about to say?"

Nonny didn't look back. She just waved her hand. "You aren't ready for it." Then she walked into the bedroom and slammed the door shut.

* * *

Kane leaned his head back against the wall as Sarah slipped out of his arms. She stood up and faced him. Her blond hair was tousled and tangled around her shoulders, and her eyes were heavy with shadows and weariness. Her skin was pale, the aftereffects of her using her white light on him. But in those shadows was softness, warmth, the woman he'd thrown himself into a pit for.

Somehow, the need to save her had given him the strength to do the impossible and break the bond. "You make me a better warrior," he said.

He felt drained and exhausted, and Thano weighed heavily on his soul, so heavily he could feel it almost crushing him. His body hurt, a sharp, throbbing pain that never seemed to cease, and even his soul seemed to be laced with acid, burning him with every breath he took. But somehow, despite all that, simply being in Sarah's presence made it all seem to fade into a throbbing ache. "You give me respite from who I am."

Sarah hugged the blanket tighter around her and smiled. Her gentle, endearing expression softened her eyes and made something tug in his heart. "You are not so bad yourself, Kane Santiago."

He smiled then, something twisting in his gut. A need to protect, to care for her, to be the man that Mason had never been. "You need to sleep."

"You do, too."

"Ten minutes and I'll be fine." He gripped the doorframe and hauled himself to his feet, surprised at how much his legs were aching. He looked down and saw black stains around his legs, the remnants of the tendrils that had been holding him, keeping him from using his powers. He frowned, surprised to see them. He'd felt something snap when he'd erupted, and he'd felt the distinct release of being freed from the bonds of something...but he didn't know what.

But the black was there still, and so were the scars. What had Luc felt so triumphant about? What had Kane missed?

Sarah walked over to the couch, drawing his attention. She was moving gingerly, as if her body was on the verge of crumbling. "I'll help you make up the couch—"

"No." He caught her arm. "We're sleeping together in the bedroom."

Sarah stiffened, but he didn't miss the surge of desire in her eyes. "Kane, that's not smart."

"Why not?" He let his blanket drop to the floor and grasped her hips, pulling her toward him.

Sarah put her hand on his forearm, bracing herself against him. "Because there's so much going on. I don't know what is happening, or who you are or what—"

"I'm me." He pressed his lips to the side of her neck and smiled when she sucked in her breath. But even as he spoke, visions of what Luc had showed him flashed through his mind. Kane immediately swore and dropped his hands from her. Sweat beaded across his brow, and he stepped back. "Shit."

"No!" Sarah came after him. "Don't think about that—"

He met her gaze. "That's what you were talking about, wasn't it? That I could have really murdered my own *sheva* and son, right? That I could be Mason all over again?" He held her arm, showing both of them the marks. "That these don't protect you from me." He gripped her shoulders, suddenly filled with revulsion for who he was. How could he even think about seducing Sarah, when he could be the very creature that she feared the most?

Sarah's eyes glowed luminous, and he saw in them the answer she didn't want to give. That she was afraid of that, too.

And how could she not be? They'd both be fools if they didn't acknowledge that as a real truth, as a real possibility, especially when he could feel that same darkness still swirling through him. Something had happened to him when he'd snapped in the air, and he didn't know what it was. Not yet. But something was changing inside him. "Can't you feel that, Sarah?" He took her hand and pressed it to his chest. "There's something happening inside me."

Sarah closed her eyes, shuddering at the rightness of what it felt like to have Kane's bare chest beneath her palm. How could he feel so right and be so dangerous? What was he? A part of her wanted to trust him so badly, but she'd been so wrong before. How did she know this time was right?

Sarah. Kane's voice drifted through her mind. Desperate. Dangerous. *Tell me what you see inside me. You were in there before when we made love. You saw parts of me I can't. Tell me what I am. Tell me what you see.*

She was suddenly filled with the power of his being as he opened the barriers between them. She tumbled into his aura, and this time, it was like a raging inferno. So many colors and emotions. So much black and red, and other angry colors. The icy chill of cold death hit her, and she froze, shocked by what she was sensing inside him. She could feel the pulsating gloom of death and pain, torture, violence, the raw need to destroy. It was so strong and powerful in him, rushing through him like a violent tidal wave of destruction. She instinctively jerked back, breaking their connection.

Kane was staring at her, his dark eyes grim with the realization of what she'd seen. His eyes were haunted, so weighted with the grief of Thano's death, with the visions of what Luc had showed him. The reality of who he was, and what he seemed to be. And suddenly, she didn't believe all the darkness swirling inside him. This was Kane, and there was so much more to him than the darkness. She didn't know how, she didn't know why, but there was *more* to him.

Violence and self-hate stormed in his eyes. "I'm going outside with Ry." He tore himself away from her and strode toward the door, currents of dark energy rolling off him in thick waves.

Sarah thought of the dark night, of the thick taint rolling through the woods, and she was struck with a sudden terror of what would happen to him if he went outside, if he exposed himself to it. "No!" She ran after him and grabbed his arm just as he reached for the door. "Don't!"

Kane whirled around, and his eyes were a maelstrom of violence, lust, and so much deadly contamination. He pushed her up against the wall, his hands heavy on her shoulders as he pinned her there. His eyes were flashing with something dark, something oppressive. It was as if all the guilt, death and unknown had broken through his shields and were crushing all the truth and good out of him. Again, she could see there was no hope in his eyes, none of the belief in the good that could keep the destructive emotions at bay. "Kane—"

"No," he snarled, leaning close against her. "Don't, Sarah. There's something happening inside me, and you don't want to be around when it goes—"

"I can help—" She grabbed him around the neck as he tried to pull away.

He swung around to face her again, and she saw the depths of agony in his eyes. And violence. And then, she realized what he was talking about. There was something else inside him. Something far more than either of them understood. Her heart started to race, and she pulled back. "Kane—"

"Too late," he growled, before he locked his arms around her, yanked her against him, and consumed her with his kiss.

His kiss was violent and dark, pulsing with desire so raw and carnal that it plunged right into her core. The kiss was dangerous and deadly. It wasn't a kiss of connection and support. It was the animal trying to erupt from him. Fear rippled through Sarah, but at the same time, her body trembled with desire, responding to his power, his strength, his unbridled need for her.

He locked his hand around the back of her neck, trapping her against him as he kissed her, kisses so deep and strong that they tore apart her very soul. It wasn't the man kissing her right now. It was the tormented Calydon warrior, no longer in control of who he was or his need for her.

Excitement raced through her, and her body trembled from the realization of how badly he needed her, how deeply his soul beat for her, how consumed he was by his connection with her. *Yes.* She whispered the word into his mind and laced her fingers through his hair, and committed herself to anything and everything that made Kane Santiago who he was.

Chapter Fifteen

Kane felt the moment Sarah accepted him. It was like this freaking white light going off inside his skull and streaking through his body. A white light of brightness and warmth, of salvation. He pressed her harder against the wall, crushing his body against hers as he claimed her mouth, trying to get closer to the salvation she gave him.

There was so much darkness inside him. So much pain. Visions of carnage and death flashing through his mind. Thano being ripped from his grasp and sucked into that noxious hell. *Thano!* Anguish tore through Kane, and he deepened his kiss, clinging desperately to Sarah as he fought the guilt and the grief of Thano's loss. All he could think of was Thano's cheeky attitude, the way the warrior brought levity and perspective into every situation. He was fucking *gone*.

Sarah broke the kiss and pressed her lips to Kane's throat. He closed his eyes, bracing his head against the wall, his breathing so heavy he felt like his chest was going to explode. He didn't move, all his attention riveted by Sarah's incredibly erotic and tender kisses along his throat. Over his collar bone. Over his chest.

Chills tore down his spine as she kissed him, his skin so sensitive that he could feel the warmth of her breath tickling over his skin. He could feel the seductive swirl of her tongue over his nipple. The sensual brush of her lips over his chest turned his blood into an untamed inferno.

Never had his skin been so sensitive before. It was a miasma of scarred flesh, so hard that he'd long ago given up hope of being able to feel a soft touch, a kiss, or a caress, and yet... Dear God... His body trembled and shook as Sarah's hands trailed down his sides, over his hips. Her mouth trailed lower, over his abs. His stomach quivered as she swirled her tongue in his belly button, a touch so erotic and tender he could barely even comprehend it.

He gripped her hair, threading his fingers through the decadently soft locks, straining to hold still as her kisses trailed lower toward the waistband of his jeans. It was so erotic, so intense to feel the lightest touch, the heat of her breath, the light scrape of her teeth. His cock was rock hard, his balls on fire, and still, he didn't let himself move.

He rested his forehead against the wall, his feet braced, his breath coming in sporadic jerks. His only movement was the frantic, almost desperate caress of her hair, the tresses like freshly spun silk against palms that used to feel nothing but the deepest cuts and the hardest hits. He shut out the pain and the visions of hell. He fought down the need for violence. He rebelled against the need to scent blood and inflict pain. He just focused every last bit of his soul, his consciousness, and his very being on Sarah's touch.

Her fingers went to the button of his jeans, and he sucked in his breath as she unzipped them, sliding them down over his hips. He even felt the cool brush of air against his cock as she freed it, a sensation he hadn't been able to feel his whole life, because of his deadened skin. Until now.

Then her hand wrapped around him, and his whole body jerked from the contact. *God, Sarah. You're going to break me.*

You're unbreakable, Kane. You know you are. Then her lips brushed over his cock, and he nearly climbed out of his skin.

Jesus, Sarah. He looked down at her as she closed her mouth around him. He nearly lost his control the moment he saw her taking him in, offering him everything she had. The mere sight of it was so erotic, combined with the unbelievable sensations she was evoking in him. He wasn't a man who could feel, who could be drawn to pleasures by touch, because he was so covered in scars, his skin so deadened. But with every move of her mouth, and the swirl of her tongue against his cock, he felt like his entire world was going to explode right then.

Her blond hair was tumbled around her shoulders, tangled and messy after their experience with Luc. Her shirt was dirty and torn, and her skin was too pale, with the faint hairline cracks by her temple. Protectiveness surged through him, and need, an unbearable need to bring her into his world where he could keep her safe.

He tightened his grip on her hair, and she looked up. Her blue eyes were hazy with desire, and his groin tightened at the raw need in her eyes. He tugged on her hair, demanding, not asking, her to rise.

He watched with growing need and desire as she let him pull her up, his cock brushing over her belly as she stood. *You're mine, Sarah.* There was no way to stop. No way to turn back from what he needed from her. What he needed to give her.

He locked his arms around her and hauled her against him as he slammed his mouth down over hers, making it clear that he was in control now, that she belonged to *him.*

Sarah wrapped her legs around his hips and kissed him back, every bit as fiercely as he was taking her. He tunneled his fingers though the hair at the nape of her neck, needing to control her and own her as he carried her across the room. He ignored the couch and strode into the bedroom, kicking the door shut without breaking stride.

He didn't toss her on the bed, because he couldn't handle being separated from her for that long. Instead, he simply fell onto the bed with her, never breaking the kiss, never letting her go.

The moment the bed shifted beneath their weight, providing a foundation, the animal inside Kane seemed to come unleashed. He needed more. He needed skin. He needed to touch her. He needed to feel her against him, around him, undulating for him.

Sarah was equally frantic, helping him yank off her clothes. Within seconds, they were both stripped down, nothing between them but skin, flesh and desperate kisses. He lowered himself on top of her, and almost lost it at the sensation of so much skin. He'd never felt it like that before, the intensely erotic feeling of so much flesh sliding against each other: her foot on his calf, her breasts against his chest, and her hips beneath his.

Kane kissed her everywhere, his hands roaming every inch of her body. He wanted to feel every curve, to taste every crevice, to feel her writhing beneath him, desperate for more of his touch, for more of his kisses, for more of *him.*

He gripped her thighs and slid lower, kissing his way down her belly, over one hip bone, then the other and then to the top of her pubic bone, then he pressed his thumbs against her most intimate parts, opening her to him. Sarah gasped and grabbed Kane's hair as he kissed her, one kiss, then another, a seduction of a type he'd never done in his life. He became aware of every nuance of her body, every movement, instinctively knowing exactly how to touch her.

Kane. She gripped his hair, her hips bucking against his grip as he held her still, locking her down at his mercy.

Give yourself over to me, sweetheart. As he said the words, Kane realized that he meant them. He needed Sarah to chase away all the crap going on inside him. He needed what she'd given him the first time they'd made love. He needed the beauty of her spirit.

But he felt her walls, the lock around her heart, and knew she was still holding back from him. There was the red hot burning of desire, and there was no mistaking the desperation in her kiss or the passion in her voice, but it wasn't enough. He needed all of her. *Now.*

Sarah. He growled her name as he kissed his way up her body. Her skin was slick with sweat as she gripped his shoulders. Kane palmed her waist as he shifted his hips over hers. She opened her eyes, and he saw the desire burning so deeply inside them. Not just desire. Need that was as powerful and desperate as his own.

She laid her hand on his chest, over his heart. *Kane. You have so many demons inside you, but I can feel this amazing heart fighting to beat. You should scare me, but instead, you give me hope that there can be light even amidst the darkest night.*

His heart began to thunder beneath her touch, and his lungs seemed to tighten. *Hell, Sarah, you're the one who gives me hope. Without you, I've got nothing.*

She said nothing, but she raised her arms to him, inviting him into her world, into her soul, and into the very essence of who she was. Rightness surged though him, and he caught her face, holding her still while he kissed her again. This time, it wasn't a desperate kiss of frantic need. It was a promise that he would protect her, that he would always find a way to make it right for her. That he would find a way to be the man she needed to have. Somehow, in that moment, with Sarah looking at him that way, Kane felt like he could make that promise, that he would somehow, some way, find a way to triumph over whatever was inside him and do it for Sarah.

Sarah kissed him back, a kiss so tender and loving that his own throat tightened up. Her fingers threaded through his hair, her touch so soft and loving that he felt it all the way to the depths of his soul. The intimacy was a gift, sweeping the two battered souls into a moment of such beauty and peace that Kane knew it had to be an illusion, an untruth that would never truly be his to experience.

No. Sarah's voice touched his mind, so beautiful and tender that it made his spirit ache with longing. *This moment is real, Kane. We don't know what is coming. I know that. But this moment, this connection between us, it is real.*

Disbelief hummed through Kane, and he pulled back enough to see Sarah's face. Her blue eyes were soft and smoky, and she slowly smiled, a beautiful smile that went straight to his heart, shattering the scars that had bound it for so long.

Sudden pain shot through him, the ache of a heart long since dead trying to wake up. He was filled with grief and loss. Sadness beyond words. Self-loathing so deep he felt it stain his cells. Emotions. His emotions. Painful, but also good, because they made him feel alive. But also, incredibly, he felt something else. Hope. Sunlight. Love?

Sarah's eyes widened. "I feel that," she whispered. "That's beautiful." Then she laughed. "Terrifying and awful, but also so beautiful."

"I know." He couldn't keep the awe out of his voice, and he bent his head to kiss her. He had no words to show his appreciation of what she'd done, of what it felt like to have all those emotions tearing through him, so he showed her the only way he knew how...by his kiss.

She kissed him back, a kiss that quickly turned from sweet and tender into something passionate and desperate. Kane moved his hips against hers as he deepened the kiss, needing to get closer to her, to lose himself in the beauty of her spirit, to lock his heart onto hers so it couldn't close up again.

Sarah shifted beneath him, her hips moving restlessly as the fire began to build between them again. Still passionate, still desperate, still so full of need and desire, but this time, there was more. There was that connection again, the fusing of their beings, the trust.

Kane. Please. Make love to me.

God, yes, Sarah. He moved his hips as she wrapped her feet around his calves. His muscles were straining with the need to plunge inside her, to make her his, and he fought for control as he slowly, seductively, slid inside her. Her body adjusted for him, and he ground his jaw, fighting for control as the sensation of being inside her overwhelmed him.

Sarah gasped and lifted her hips as he sheathed himself deeper inside her, her body shuddering as much as his as he brought them together. For a moment, he stilled his hips, meeting her gaze as the enormity of their connection filled both of them. Kane could hear the pounding of her heart, matching the thundering of his own. Never had it been like this, a mixture of sensations so intense that it was almost overwhelming. Never had anything in his entire life felt this right.

Slowly he withdrew, sending tremors through both of them. He reached the tip, and then plunged back inside again. Sarah gripped his shoulders, never taking her gaze off his face as he did it again. And again.

Desire coiled inside him, tighter and tighter with each move, and he felt it pouring off Sarah in hot waves, wrapping around them both and pulling them both in. "God, Kane,'" she whispered, as she moved beneath him, trying to draw him deeper.

Kane kissed her again as he increased the tempo, no longer able to keep himself slow, losing himself to the need burning through him, to the lust building within him. She kissed him ravenously, her own desire mixing with his, escalating them both, until he couldn't tell where his spirit ended and hers began.

His thrusts became furious and desperate, and Sarah gripped his shoulders as their bodies moved more and more frantically, until the desire tore them from reality and plunged them into a world that was only them and their connection. Gone were the past, the pain, the memories and the future, until it was only them: their bodies, their connection, their minds, and their spirits.

The orgasm ripped through Kane with sudden, brutal force. He shouted Sarah's name as the climax tore into her at the same time, vibrating fiercely through her body. She clung to him as it took her along with him. Kane held her in his arms, embracing the woman who he knew was his only chance at redemption, offering her everything he had.

Chapter Sixteen

Sarah never wanted the moment to end.

As she lay in Kane's arms, their perspiration-slicked bodies wrapped around each other, fear began to trickle in, seeping past the euphoria of the moment. She knew she was lost to him. He'd worked his way past all her shields right into her heart, taking root so deeply she knew she would never get him out.

The last time she had loved, the man she'd trusted had killed her daughter. How could she be so sure that she was right this time? She'd had a lifetime to know Mason, and she'd still been wrong. How long had she known Kane? How could she be certain the goodness in him would trump the vast amount of darkness amassing inside of him?

Because the violence inside him was definitely getting stronger. She'd been shocked when he'd bared his soul to her this time. The first time they'd made love, she'd felt darkness inside him, but there'd also been that gaping void of nothingness. Now, the void was gone. It had been filled with taint and violence, poison, all the things she'd sensed at the pit.

There was still that goodness, but it was almost buried now, being eaten away by all the darkness within him. She'd wanted to save him. She'd felt his despair, his loss of hope, and it had eviscerated her to know he was feeling such pain, and she'd wanted to bring light back into his soul.

She had, somewhat, but the moment she had, the darkness had begun to fight, trying to stake its claim on him. What was he? What would triumph? And would she know whether to trust him or not? She swallowed, reminding herself that there was no baby at stake this time, no added connection between them to blur the lines, to make her trust more than she should. Never would she have imagined it was possible for

Mason to murder his own baby girl, and that had been her downfall, that was why she'd been so slow to attack him with her light; she simply hadn't realized the extent of the danger. Maybe, without a child to protect, with only her own life at stake, she would be better able to judge.

Sarah took a deep breath, realizing the truth of that. She wasn't the same naive girl she'd been when she'd trusted Mason. She'd seen him turn. She'd seen her brother turn. She'd let herself see and feel the evil inside Kane. She no longer lived in a cocoon of naiveté.

She was not the girl who would make the same mistake again.

"Sarah." Kane's voice was muffled against her neck, where he'd nestled in after making love to her.

"What?" She ran her hand over his forearm, tracing the brand that defined him as a Calydon, the race of warriors that were brought to this village to wipe out angels. Part demon, part man, they had one mission, and that was to destroy the angels.

"We're going back to the pit," Kane said.

She swallowed, unable to stop the ripple of fear or the burst of adrenaline and excitement. "Yes."

"I almost lost you tonight when Luc tried to suck you in there." He set his hand on her belly, and Sarah felt a tremor of heat in response. "I can't let that happen again."

"It worked out fine—"

"No." He rolled on top of her suddenly, his eyes blazing. "If you had been drawn into that pit, I would have lost you forever. You say you wouldn't have died from it because that's not how to kill you, but by God, Sarah, I would have spent an eternity knowing that you were suffering the worst hell possible in there."

A cold chill settled in Sarah's bones, but she tried to push it away. She could not let fear debilitate her. "I can't worry about that, Kane. I have to go back—"

"*I* can worry about it." His eyes were shadowed and turbulent, filled with the darkness that was building inside him. "I need to be able to find you, Sarah. No matter what. If we blood-bond, I'll be able to track you."

"Oh..." She grimaced, thinking of how that could go against her if he turned out to be her greatest enemy. The blood bond was one of the stages of the *sheva* bond, and they had so few stages left to go before their bond was finalized and inextricable. Mason had turned on her after the bond was complete, and she was well aware of the Order's destiny of turning on their mates and going rogue. She didn't need the extra risk. She really didn't. "I don't think—"

"Your brother will be awakened in the morning by my team," Kane said. "He can find you, and he will. At dusk tomorrow night, if not sooner, he will teleport in here and try to grab you. I *have* to be able to follow you if he gets you away from me."

Sarah closed her eyes at the reminder of the threat coming for her. There was no way to lie to herself. Jacob would be coming for her. He, like Mason, was at the mercy of Luc Acostos, who was somehow, some way, turning them all against her. Would he also be able to turn Kane?

Kane gripped her shoulders. "Look at me, Sarah."

She opened her eyes. His eyes were blazing with heat and determination. In that moment, he looked like a warrior, a protector, not a male who would succumb to the hell trying to take him. She felt like she could turn herself over to him and he would make sure everything would work out okay. Crap! What was the right choice?

"I won't turn on you," Kane said fiercely. He grabbed her arm and showed her his brand on her flesh. "This mark is stronger than anything else. I'm incapable of hurting you—"

"What about the *sheva* destiny? That the moment the bond is complete you will go rogue and destroy everything we both care about. You'll kill me, Kane, and I will kill you, and everything that matters will be gone."

His eyes glittered. "I thought you said that doesn't happen in this town."

Sarah pushed him off her and sat up, hugging her knees to her chest. "It doesn't happen with the local males who are turned Calydon from our woods," she said. "But you're not from here."

Kane propped himself up on his elbow, studying her. "What are you talking about?"

Sarah pressed her lips together, thinking of how many thousands of hours she'd poured into the situation at the village, trying to understand how to stop it. "The original Calydons were created two thousand years ago, from that waterfall tainted with demon magic. You all are descended from those warriors, and you carry their bloodlines." She ran her hand over the mark on her arm, the mark that had erased Mason's. "But in this town, becoming a Calydon isn't genetic. None of these males came from Calydon lines. They were regular people who got turned by living here." She looked at him. "They're the next generation of Calydons, Kane."

"They're different," Kane agreed. "With the claws and their nocturnal tendencies. Plus, they can all teleport. With the exception of the original Calydon who was the progenitor of our race, I'm the only Calydon I know who can teleport except these guys—" He stopped suddenly, and she knew they were both thinking the same thing.

Was Kane a creation of Luc's? Was that why he could teleport like them?

"I don't have claws," Kane said. "And I don't change at night."

"But you teleport."

"I do." He rolled onto his back and draped his forearm over his face. "Did the original Calydons who threatened the village have claws? Were they nocturnal? The ones from six or seven hundred years ago? When I would have been around?"

"I don't know the details. It was long ago." Sarah bit her lip, and for a long moment, there was simply silence between them, the great unknown about what and who Kane really was. If he was Los Muerte, then whatever goodness was in his heart hadn't been enough to stop him from killing his own *sheva* and child the first time. If he wasn't Los Muerte... then what was he? She felt tension radiating off him, and suddenly she was filled with empathy for him. How terrifying to not know who you were, what you'd done, or what you were capable of. How did one live with that?

"I have a dream," Kane said quietly. "It haunts me almost every time I go to sleep."

Sarah turned her head so she could see him. He was staring at the ceiling, his face dimly lit from the spotlights shining outside the shuttered windows, the ones lighting up the grounds to try to keep the night crawlers away. "What dream?"

For a minute, he didn't answer, and she thought he wasn't going to tell her. Then, finally, he did. "I have a dream that I'm walking through a field. There are people having a picnic in the field. Lots of people. Mothers. Fathers. Children. Dogs. There are flowers. The sun is shining. Music is playing. It's..." She felt his struggle to find the right words. "It's like heaven in a little corner of the earth."

Sarah propped herself up on her elbow to watch him. "Is it a place you've been?"

Kane shook his head. "I don't know. I never know." He closed his eyes, and she could feel him willing away the emotions that were trying to surface. She could sense how hard he was trying to remain impassive. "I'm walking through the field," he said quietly, "And there's this little girl sitting by a stream. She's got blond hair and little pigtails."

Sarah tensed. Her daughter had had blond hair and pigtails. "How old is she?"

"Around five," Kane said.

Her daughter had been less than a year. Not the same. *Not the same.* "What happened?"

"I walk up to her," he said, his voice low and hoarse. "She looks up at me and smiles. She holds her arms up to me and gives me this huge smile. She's missing her bottom two front teeth, and I tell her she looks like a big girl."

Sarah's heart began to race at the waves of tension flooding from him, especially the raw terror he was struggling to hold back. "Kane?"

"She looks up at me," he said, grief thickening in his voice, "And calls me Daddy." He pressed his hands to his face, and suddenly Sarah could feel all his emotions as he got sucked back in that moment. The intense pride, the awe that he could have created someone so amazing, still unable to believe that she was his. "She's so beautiful," he whispered. "Dimples. These bright blue eyes. And so smart. Shit." His breathing became labored, his hands curled into fists. "My daughter," he whispered, and she knew in that moment that the vision was real, at least to him, truly. "So beautiful."

"What happens in the dream, Kane?" Sarah could feel the grief already welling up inside him. The self-hate.

"She's reaching for me, to hug me, and I call out my flail." His voice broke then. "I murder her, Sarah. In cold blood. I murder her. And as I'm sinking my weapon into her beautiful heart, she looks at me and says, 'But you promised, Daddy. Daddies aren't supposed to break their promises.' And then..." He swore and his voice broke. "I kill her, then turn and walk away. Jesus." He pressed his palms to his eyes, and Sarah felt his body shaking with grief, with the reality of his dream.

"Kane, it's just a dream—"

"How the fuck do I know that?" He sat up suddenly, his muscles shaking violently. He turned toward her, his face so stark and raw that her soul broke for him. "Do you have any idea what it's like to have that dream night after night, and to have no idea if it's actually a memory of who you once were? For over five hundred years, I've lived with that dream and wondered if that's who I really was." He called out his flail with a crack and flash of black light. Then he hurled it against the wall. It cracked the boards and sank into the wood, sending splinters all over the room. "I spent the last five hundred years trying to save every fucking innocent I could find, protecting them from rogue Calydons who were turning on their families. But the whole time I was doing it, I knew I might be the exact man that the Order was created to destroy."

His agony was heartbreaking, so deeply entrenched in his soul that Sarah knew then, in that moment, that she could trust him. No man could feel that level of pain and regret and still lose his heart to the blackness swirling around the village.

Kane was her man, and she could trust him. "Blood bond with me," she said.

Kane swung around to face her, his eyes bleak with despair. "What?"

She held up her arm, and as she did, she saw another line forming on her arm. "Trust," she whispered. "You trusted me with your deepest secret, didn't you? That was it."

He stared at her mark. "I've never told anyone."

Sarah pulled him close, his body so rigid he almost didn't even respond. "I trust you," she said. "Blood bond with me."

Kane couldn't believe what she was saying. After the story he'd just told, the one that seemed to provide further evidence for the fact he was Los Muerte and had killed his own son, Sarah should be running away from him. Not offering herself to him. "I don't understand," he said, his voice hoarse with emotion. "Didn't you hear what I said? Don't you realize that it confirms that I might be Los Muerte? That the images I saw at the pit were real?" He swore. "For God's sake, Sarah, I had that dream before I heard any of this stuff. Because it's there. It's a part of me. And it's been there all along—"

"If it has," she said, her voice strong and firm, "it's who you used to be, not who you are now."

Her conviction plunged straight past his shields, right into the very depths of his soul, where something slowly, ever so slowly, began to flicker to life. Hope. Hope that he wasn't the bastard he'd seen in his dream for so long. "How is that possible?"

She set her hand on his chest, over his heart. "Because your heart has become too strong."

Kane pressed his hand over hers, as if he could burn it into his chest. "Shit, Sarah, I don't know—"

"I do." She scooted over and straddled him, sitting low across his hips. Her eyes were clear and blue, blazing with fierce conviction. "This is what I know," she said. "We have to take out Luc tomorrow night, and we have to do it before Jacob finds me. After Luc is dead, maybe Jacob has a chance. Luc is...he's so powerful, Kane. Our only chance is for us to team up, truly team up, and do it together." She held up her hand, and Kane's flail worked itself free of the wall, streaked across the room and slammed into her palm with a loud smack.

Without saying anything, she dragged the spiked flail across Kane's palm, drawing blood. Adrenaline and disbelief rushed through Kane. His throat thickened as he watched Sarah do the same to herself.

"Shit, Sarah," he said, unable to keep the emotion out of his voice. "You shouldn't trust me like that."

"You don't get to tell me what to do," she said, determination bright in her eyes as she lifted Kane's palm to her lips and pressed a kiss to the center of it. Daring him. Offering herself to him. Putting her entire soul and her life into his hands. This woman, who had no reason to trust him, and every reason to never trust anyone ever, believed in him.

"What do you see in me? Don't you see the demons?"

I see you, Kane Santiago. I see every single level of who you are, and I believe in you. She was still pressing a kiss to his palm, still waiting, still giving him that chance, those blue eyes so full of trust and love.

She knew everything about him, she knew exactly what he was, and yet somehow, she believed in him. She had faith in him, that he was the man he'd tried to be for the last five hundred years. Rightness surged through him, and he knew he didn't deserve that gift.

But he wasn't going to give it up. It felt too damn good.

Keeping his gaze on hers, Kane slipped his free hand around her wrist and gently raised her palm. "I swear on the souls of my children, whether past or future, that I will never, ever violate that trust, Sarah. I give you my oath." He then kissed her palm, pressing his mouth directly over the injury and sucking her lifeblood into his body.

The moment he swallowed, his whole world seemed to vibrate. Intense satisfaction surged through him, a sensation that he had finally found his place, that he was exactly where he was supposed to be. The words tumbled from him, filling her mind and his with promises that would seal them forever. *Mine to you. Yours to me. Bonded by blood, by spirit and by soul, we are one. No distance too far, no enemy too powerful, no sacrifice too great. I will always find you. I will always protect you. No matter what the cost. I am yours as you are mine.* The moment the words were spoken, raw intense need and desire raged through him, a need to make her his, to cement the bond. *I swear to keep you safe,* he added. *Always.*

Sarah's warmth flooded him, filling him and spilling over into the air, making it glow with a faint white light. *Mine to you.* Sarah's voice echoed through his mind, as the words burned into his soul, branding him the way his mark had branded her. *Yours to me. Bonded by blood, by spirit and by soul, we are one. No distance too far, no enemy too powerful, no sacrifice too great. I will always find you. I will always keep you safe. No matter what the cost. I am yours as you are mine.*

Rightness exploded through him, and he pulled her down, consuming her with kisses he couldn't contain. The lust, the desire, the animalistic need to seal the commitment they'd just made to each other. "I swear I'll protect you," he said as he rolled her onto her back.

"I know, Kane. I know." Sarah shifted beneath him, giving him access, and he drove inside her, desperate to put his mark on her, to brand her as his, even though he'd already done it. He needed to make her his in the personal and private way of a male with his mate.

The lovemaking was violent and fierce, a dominant possession, a promise of safekeeping, a baring of his soul. Sarah accepted all he had to offer, giving him her warmth and her trust and her faith. They filled the gaps in the other's soul, as he drove into her, as he filled her the only way he knew how. Sarah clung to him, kissing him back while promises and emotions tumbled unspoken between them, held only in their emotions and their touch.

He thrust again, and this time it was Sarah who screamed his name first, her body arching from the force of the orgasm. The moment he felt her reach her climax, he allowed himself to join her, shouting her name as he held her in his arms, offering her everything he had.

As the climax faded, Kane collapsed beside her and pulled her into his arms. He enveloped her with his body, tucking her tightly against his chest, using his arms and legs to create a shield around her, cradling her head with his palm. This was how he wanted to keep her forever. Safe. Protected. And in his arms.

As God was his witness, he would not fail her.

No matter who he was.

* * *

"Kane!"

He bolted out of bed, arising instantly from sleep to vigilant battle-ready, his flails clutched in his hands at Sarah's startled cry. He scanned the room, and instantly realized there was no immediate threat...until his gaze went to Sarah.

Her eyes were wide, her face in shock as she stared at him. The sheet had fallen to her waist, revealing the same curves he'd made love to all night long. Desire pulsed at him, but he didn't acknowledge it. He jerked his gaze back to Sarah's face, his adrenaline screaming its readiness to take on whatever threat was endangering her. "What's wrong? What is it?"

She pointed to him. "Your scars. They're gone."

Kane quickly glanced down at his body, then he swore, shocked by the sight. There wasn't a single scar left on his body. Every inch of him was smooth, unblemished skin. His arms, his chest, his legs, *everywhere.*

"Son of a bitch." He ran his hand over his stomach, unable to believe the sensation of his hand sliding across his body without resistance. His blood was racing through his body, humming so powerfully that he could actually hear it rushing through him. His lungs were loose and free, and he sucked in his breath, taking in more air than he'd ever inhaled in a single breath before. His heart was thumping so loudly he could feel it reverberating in his chest. It was as if there hadn't just been scars on his skin, but inside him as well, and they were all gone.

"How do you feel?" Sarah crawled across the bed and ran her hands over his shoulder. "Your skin is so soft. It's flawless."

"I feel..." He couldn't even begin to express it. He felt more powerful than he ever had before, as if he could tear the roof of the house off simply by thinking about it. "Like a fucking king."

Sarah looked up at him, her brow furrowed. "How did this happen?"

"You." He grabbed her hand and pulled her against him, their bodies hitting with a thump that seemed to vibrate all the way to his feet. "It started when I met you." He couldn't keep the awe out of his voice. He kissed her, burning with desire a thousand times more powerful than anything he'd felt before. He felt like he had a thousand years of fire amassed inside him, waiting to be unleashed onto the world.

He pinned her up against the wall, adrenaline and desire raging through him so fiercely it took him over, and he unleashed all of it into his kiss. He knew his kiss was almost violent, almost over the edge, but the moment he tasted her lips, he was totally lost to the power raging through him, and when Sarah locked her arms around his neck, giving him permission, he gave himself over to it.

Sarah was shocked by the intensity of Kane's passion. It was as if he was a man on fire, burning with a need that had exploded within him. His kisses were frantic, consuming her very soul, sucking it right out of her body with each kiss. His grip on her hips was fierce, holding her still, giving her no chance to move as he braced his knee under her thigh, shoving her legs apart.

She gasped as he thrust his fingers inside her, an invasion that tore an orgasm out of her throat. She convulsed in his arms, her own passion ignited by his, her entire being capturing the violent need of his essence. Again he thrust into her, stretching her widely, and again, an orgasm exploded through her, so powerful she felt like it was going to rip her apart. "Kane—"

He gave her no mercy, capturing her protests with his bruising kiss, driving into her again with his fingers and coaxing another orgasm from her trembling body, giving her no respite, allowing her no breath. And she didn't want one. She was sucked hopelessly into his spiral of sex and lust, and when he grabbed her hips and pulled her down onto him, she bucked violently as he sank into her.

"God, Sarah," he gasped as he thundered into her, slamming her against the wall, his thrusts so fast and so deep that she screamed from the intensity of it.

He didn't stop, she didn't want him to, and he took her again and again and again over the edge, every orgasm more violent than the last, until she felt like she was going to come apart in his arms, until she felt like she had nothing left. And again, he took her, driving deeply and violently, his eyes so black she couldn't see anything but the darkness. Dear God, he wasn't even getting tired. He would never stop! He was going to kill her. "Sarah," he growled, and he bent his head and bit her neck.

"Oh, God." The climax exploded through her, and this time, she grabbed hold of Kane and mimicked the love bite he'd just given her, placing it in the exact same spot as the one that had undone her, frantically trying to get him to climax before he drained her completely.

Kane roared in response, and the climax exploded through him, rocking him against her. Sarah clung to him as the orgasm took both of them, spiraling again and again, an endless loop that would never release them.

"Kane," she gasped.

He groaned her name and pressed his face to her neck as his body gave one final, violent shudder, and then it was over. Sarah collapsed against the wall, and Kane caught her in his arms, cradling her against him as he carried them back to the bed, both of them tumbling helplessly onto the mattress.

Kane landed with a groan beside her, his arm wrapped around her waist as if even that hadn't been enough for him. "Son of a bitch," he muttered. "That was a first."

"You and me both." Sarah's body was boneless, exhausted, and sore in a thousand places. She'd been satisfied dozens of times, and her body still vibrated with the need for more.

"I feel it, too." Kane rolled onto his side and propped himself up, his hand cupping her breast. "I need more."

"You'll kill us both," she gasped, even as her nipples turned hard beneath his touch.

"What a way to go, though, huh?" He said with a grin, his eyes dancing with mischievousness that made her skin tingle in anticipation.

"Wait." She braced her hand on his chest, trying to catch her breath. "I know I'm really hot and everything, but this isn't normal, Kane. There's so much power pouring off you that I feel like you're about to explode."

"I know." His eyes were blazing again, and she felt her whole body clench with need as he pulled her toward him. "I'm making you mine, Sarah," he said. "*Mine.*"

Mine. There was something in the way he said it that sent chills down Sarah's spine, and not the kind that were begging for more kisses. The kind of chills that screamed a warning that something wasn't right. That something was terribly, terribly wrong—

"Sarah!" The door was flung open and Kane yanked her under him, shielding her beneath his body. He growled as he positioned her beneath him, swinging his head around to glower at the person who'd barged in.

Sarah went still, aware of the lethal violence coursing through him. "Kane?"

There was no response from him, other than another low growl. She couldn't see his face, because he had her locked down under him, but his muscles were like steel rods, ready to attack.

"Kane Santiago." Javier spoke from the doorway, and Sarah peeked under Kane's arm, shocked to see the old man in her bedroom. Javier's cheeks were streaked with black paint, and he had talismans painted all over his bare chest. In his hand were two spears, Calydon weapons. He pointed them at Kane and Sarah. "The time has come," he said. "Both of you, in the living room. *Now.*"

Chapter Seventeen

Sarah perched on the edge of the couch in Nonny's living room. She was wearing a heavy sweatshirt as she watched Kane pace restlessly around the small space. She was cold, even though it was warm inside the cabin. Even the steaming mug of tea Nonny had made wasn't warming her up, and she knew it was because something was so wrong with Kane that she couldn't settle.

Ryland was standing in the open doorway, letting the morning sun stream in. His eyes were narrowed as he watched Kane pace, and she could feel the absolute readiness in Ryland's stance, prepared to react the moment Kane moved too quickly.

Javier was sitting cross-legged on the coffee table, his dark eyes fixed on Kane, while Nonny was handing out bagels and muffins that she'd prepared for them.

They were all waiting for Javier to speak, but he hadn't said a word since he'd ordered them to the living room. Now he was just watching Kane and Sarah, his sharp gaze going back and forth between them.

"For God's sake, Javier," Nonny said as she slammed a platter of pastries down beside him. "Start talking."

Kane spun around then, meeting Javier's eyes. "I'm Los Muerte, aren't I? I can feel it."

Javier gave Kane a long look. "Los Muerte is the name for the demon who will destroy our village and wipe out the angels," he said. "It can be anyone."

Kane swore and paced the room, restlessness rolling off him like a dark cloud. "Were you there?" he asked. "Were you there the day Los Muerte came to life and killed everyone?"

Javier nodded once. "I was."

Kane strode across the room then and bent over the old man, gripping the edges of the table so tightly that the wood cracked.

"Hey!" Nonny batted at his hands. "I like that table. Get off it."

Kane didn't move, staring down Javier. "Was I the man who murdered everyone? Was I the man they tried to kill and couldn't? Was I the man they carved up and tossed in a gutter to try to save the village?"

Javier lifted his gaze to meet Kane's, and Sarah leaned forward, her heart racing. "You know the answer," Javier said. "You tell me."

Kane stared at him, and then his face hardened. He looked over at Sarah, and she saw the pain in his eyes. "It was me." There was finality in his voice.

"No—" Sarah started to protest, then swallowed her words when she saw Javier nodding his approval. "What? That's impossible."

"He is a wise man," Javier said.

"So I'm right." For a split second, Kane's face went ashen and he bowed his head. "I'm Los Muerte, and I murdered my son."

Goosebumps prickled over Sarah's arms, and she hugged herself. She didn't know what to say, how to comfort him. The man standing before her had really murdered his own son and his own *sheva*, just like Mason? But she'd seen inside his heart. He had goodness. Was she so wrong? Nausea churned inside her belly and she lurched to her feet, suddenly needing space to think, to process, to get a handle on her emotions. "I have to go—"

Kane's head came up and he looked at her. There was such darkness in his gaze, and she saw him struggle with the news. His pain wafted across the room toward her, and she knew how devastating it must be to have it confirmed that he was once a monster. If he could do the unthinkable once, he could do it again, right?

Don't lose faith in me, he said. *I need you, Sarah.*

Sarah's throat tightened, and Nonny flicked her fingers in Sarah's direction. "Sit," Nonny said. "You're not going anywhere."

Slowly, Sarah sank back to the couch, perching on the edge, ready to run. But at the same time, she wanted to go to Kane and offer him her support. To tell him she believed in him. She swallowed hard, trying to know what to do, to preserve herself or to trust her instincts. Which was the right choice this time?

Ryland shifted in the doorway, and she saw him flexing his hands, as if he were preparing to call out his weapons. As if he was seeing Kane only as Los Muerte and not the warrior he'd fought beside for so long.

Javier turned to Kane. "The scars are gone. There is nothing protecting you from the demon within. It's you and he at war. No one to save you this time."

Kane nodded. "I can feel it," he said, his voice strained.

"You're being called home," Javier said. "To take over your role as the anchor of our village."

Kane frowned. "You mean as a destroyer or as a protector?"

"Both." Javier leaned forward. "Luc Acostos is a formidable foe, Kane. Do you know why?"

Kane shook his head. "Tell me."

"Because he is motivated by love. If he can find a replacement for himself, he will be free to leave this place and find the spirit of the woman he loves and connect with her. But his replacement can be only someone with enough strength to survive the pit. You have his blood. You are the one he has been waiting for."

Kane stiffened. "I have his blood? What do you mean?"

Javier raised his brows. "Your mother was an angel, Kane. Where do you think the demon comes from?"

Kane went still as Javier's words sank in, as the meaning took root. "You mean, I'm Luc's *son?*"

Sarah sucked in her breath as Javier nodded. "He is going to reclaim you, Kane. It is the only way for him to be free to be with the woman he loves."

"Jesus." Kane stood up and strode across the floor, his tension bleeding all over the room. "My father is a demon," he said. "I'm a demon. Jesus." Sweat trickled down his brow, and Sarah suddenly couldn't stop herself.

She scooted off the couch and wrapped her arms around him. Kane immediately locked his arm around her waist, pulling her tightly against him and burying his face in her hair, as if she could chase away the truth.

"Luc is here to destroy the angels," Javier said. "The village is a conduit to the Afterlife, and it is a weak link where the demons want to access the earth, but they need to cleanse the area of angels before they can do it. They've been working on it for hundreds of years." He looked at Sarah. "There is one angel left, standing in their way."

Sarah swallowed. "Luc's job is to take me out?"

"No. He can't kill you, not directly." Javier looked between them. "His job is to find your weak spot and use it to destroy you. It's a trinity, Sarah. Mason was the first part. Jacob is the second. Kane is the third and final element."

"No." Kane tightened his grip on Sarah. "I won't bring her down—"

"It's more dangerous now," Javier interrupted. "Because of the baby."

Sarah bit her lip as she thought of Abigail. "Why was Abigail important?"

Javier looked at her. "Because she was the next generation of angels. She needed to die before she became powerful. That was why she had to be killed. The next generation had to be stopped before it began. So, the stakes have gone up this time."

A dark feeling of foreboding started to beat through Sarah. "This time?"

Nonny pushed on Javier's shoulder. "She doesn't know. I didn't think she could handle knowing. It's too soon, Javier. Let it go."

Sarah shoved herself away from Kane, her heart pounding. "What are you talking about?"

Javier looked at Nonny. "They need to know."

"No, they don't."

"Hey!" Sarah grabbed her grandmother's arm. "Nonny. What do you know?" She didn't want to hear it. It couldn't be true. *It couldn't be true.*

Nonny sighed and looked at her, and in those eyes Sarah saw a thousand years of burden. "Sarah, you're pregnant."

Sarah felt the blood drain from her face, and her legs started to shake. She was vaguely aware of Kane grabbing her and holding her up, but her body was so numb she couldn't feel it. "But that's impossible," she whispered. "It was just last night. It couldn't happen that fast—"

"It didn't," Nonny said gently. "Sarah, sweetheart, when you showed up here, it was already done."

The night in the woods. When Jacob had been trying to kill her. "Oh, my God." Sarah couldn't breathe. The room was spinning. Her hands were shaking violently. She was cold. So cold. She didn't doubt Nonny for an instant. Her grandmother had always known things like that. It was her gift. Sarah was pregnant. Again. By Los Muerte. "I can't—"

Nonny raised her eyebrows. "You obviously can, my dear."

"But—" Sarah clutched her belly, fighting against the sudden pain in her stomach. "Mason tore me open. He made it impossible. It can't happen—"

"Sarah!" Nonny's voice was sharp. "Pull yourself together! You have to cope with this! There can be no mistakes this time."

No mistakes. No mistakes. No mistakes. No mistakes that would wind up with her baby killed. Again. "Oh, God."

"No mistakes from either of you," Nonny said. "Hell, Kane, you look like you're going to be sick."

Sarah jerked her gaze to Kane, who was on his knees beside her. His face was stricken, absolute terror in his expression. He looked up at her, and she saw visceral fear on his face. "Sarah," he said hoarsely. "I killed my own child before." He stumbled to his feet, staggering back from her as if she were a monster. "I can't risk you. I can't risk it. The talismans are gone. There's nothing to stop me. Jesus, Sarah." His gaze went to her belly, and suddenly she felt so exposed and raw.

"My baby," he whispered, and there was so much agony and grief in his words that tears filled Sarah's eyes.

"Stop." Javier rose to his feet in a swift movement. "There is no time for this. Luc must be stopped. Sarah is at tremendous risk now that she is pregnant."

"From me," Kane said. "She's at risk from me."

Sarah was shaking so violently she couldn't stop, and Kane was staring at her with a gaunt face.

Ryland called out his machete suddenly and charged Kane. Kane whirled around and called out his weapons. They clashed hard, Ryland's eyes blazing with fire. "You don't get to kill the angels," he snarled. "Let me kill you, Santiago. You're the monster now. Let me end it before you destroy it all."

"No!" Sarah shouted as Nonny yanked her back from the men. "Stop it! Don't kill him!"

The weapons clashed and Kane fought back. It wasn't a spar. It was a battle, a battle to the death. Ryland was raging with focus, with his need to protect Sarah, and Kane was fighting back. The warriors were violent and powerful, slashing at each other. "Stand down, Ry!" Kane shouted. "This isn't about you and your damned hero complex about angels!"

"You don't get to kill her!" Ryland shouted back, and he lunged at Kane. The machete sank deep into his shoulder, and Kane roared with fury. Then, suddenly, she saw Kane's skin begin to glow deep red, as if he had become hell itself. He lunged at Ryland, moving with twice the speed he'd been moving before. His strikes were violent and fast, cutting Ryland as the warriors battled. But the more they fought, the greater the glow emanating from Kane's skin.

"Stop it!" Sarah shouted, desperate to make them stop. "We need to fight Luc, not each other!"

But they simply roared with fury, unleashing the full extent of their battle skills upon each other. It was as if they saw no other solution. Killing each other was the only answer... "Oh, God!" She grabbed Nonny. "They have no hope or faith that they can make it work! Without hope, there's nothing to fight for. Crap!" It was the same as what had happened to Kane the night before. "Why are they losing faith like that? Why is it so bad?"

Javier looked over at Sarah, then back at the men. "Sarah," he said sharply. "Come over here."

She rushed toward Javier just as Kane threw Ryland into the wall. Javier grabbed Sarah's wrist and dragged her over to him as Ryland crashed through the plaster and onto the grass outside.

Sadness filled Sarah's heart as she watched Kane leap through the wall to attack Ryland. The two teammates, trying to destroy each other. She could feel the despair of both warriors, their complete lack of faith in each other, their inability to see the man who was on their side. She felt it in every cell of her body, all the way to the very depth of her spirit. Their loss, their utter loss of faith and hope, the absolute emptiness of their souls. "Dear God," she whispered as tears filled her eyes, as their pain overwhelmed her. She was filled with a sudden need to help them, to break them out of their hell, to infuse them with the hope that would make their hearts beat again. "Don't give up," she shouted. "Don't—"

"Touch them," Javier said. "Now!" And he threw her against the two men.

Sarah crashed into both of them. There was a split second of sheer, overwhelming despair coming from them, and then her entire body billowed with energy. Sudden power burned through her, a golden light of extraordinary brilliance, burning so brightly she felt her skin ignite.

Nonny gasped in astonishment, and Javier grunted with approval as the golden light filled the air, flooding the entire house with the glittering golden aura. It blasted into Kane and Ryland, the impact catapulting them across the clearing and into the trees. She heard the crash of their bodies through the branches, the thuds of their bodies hitting the earth, and then silence. Stunned, she scrambled over the rubble from the decimated wall and raced after them. "Kane! Ryland!"

Ignoring Nonny's shouts, Sarah ran through the bushes, calling for the warriors. Had she killed them? Panic filled her heart as she ran. She'd never done golden light before. She had no idea what it was. "Kane! Where are you—"

Then she saw him. He was sitting on the ground, his arms draped over his knees, rubbing his forehead with one arm. Beside him, Ryland was in the same position, blood dripping from a wound in his shoulder. Sarah stopped, staring in shock at the men. "You're not fighting. And you're not dead?"

Kane lifted his head to look at her, and she saw his eyes were gleaming brightly. The darkness was still there, yes, but not the despair.

Ryland looked over at her, and she saw that his expression was back to normal. Edging on violence and darkness, but not insane. "What did you do?" Kane asked.

"I don't know."

"I do." Javier walked up beside them, the black paint glistening on his chest.

Sarah looked over at him. "What?"

"They're your assignment." Javier's eyes were hooded and dark as he looked at her. "You're their guardian angel, Sarah."

Sarah frowned, shocked by his words. "Kane and Ryland? But I can have only one—"

"Not always." Javier rubbed his jaw. "An angel can be assigned to an entity, as long as it is considered a cohesive group. Like the Order."

Sarah stared at him in shock, as Kane shot to his feet. "No," he said. "We protect her. She doesn't protect us."

Ryland was staring at Sarah, a look of awe on his face. "We have a guardian angel? Sarah is our guardian angel? *Sarah?*"

"She's your angel for hope and faith," Javier said. "That's what she gives you. She gives you the ability to believe in the future. Without that, you wouldn't be able to kill all those who you kill. She gives you the ability to believe in what you do. She is the essence of your very mission."

Sarah stared at him in shock. How could she be responsible for the entire Order? But even as Javier spoke, she felt the truth of his words, and there was no way to deny the golden light. "Why did it happen?"

"Because they needed you, and you happened to be there." Javier nodded at her. "But it cost."

Sarah looked down and saw her skin was fragmented again, hundreds of microscopic tears in her skin. "It's because of the effort it took to pull them back from the edge," she said softly. "They were so far gone."

"Because you are so far gone," Javier said. He walked over to her and set his hand on her arm. His touch was cool, easing the discomfort from the cracks. "You have so little reserves left, Sarah, and the river is closed off again. You barely have enough to support them, and that's why they're crashing like this." He looked at Kane and Ryland. "If Sarah dies, the Order will disintegrate. You will be lost to the darkness. It will end, and all of you will die. What just happened is merely the start."

Kane swore as he looked at Sarah, protectiveness swirling through him. "We'll keep her safe." But even as he said the words, he felt the darkness still percolating inside him. Who was he? Her protector or her destroyer?

Javier met his gaze. "You are both, Kane. You have the potential to be either." He looked at the sun that was still rising in the sky. "And you have very few hours left to make your choice."

Kane swore and looked at Ryland. "We need the rest of the team."

Ryland nodded. "Call in the army. We're going to war."

Kane pulled out his phone and dialed Quinn. Without the blood bond, Quinn was too far away for Kane to communicate with mind-to-mind. His interim leader answered on the first ring. "We lost Jacob," Quinn said. "We got nothing out of him before he teleported. He's gone."

Kane's adrenaline kicked into an even higher gear at the news, even though it wasn't unexpected. "Quinn. We need the team." He looked across the room at Sarah. "You need to be prepared to kill me."

Protest flared in Sarah's eyes, along with a grim reality. Who was Kane, and what was going to happen to him when the sun went down?

No one knew.

They had to be prepared for anything.

Chapter Eighteen

The Order of the Blade invaded the village like ancient warriors descending upon Akara either to destroy it, or to save it.

Ryland's hand was tight on Sarah's arm as Kane materialized by the old fountain with seven massive warriors clothed in leather and steel. They were well-muscled, and their faces were grim with readiness for battle. They were like the Calydons who haunted her woods, the ones that had been hunting her for so long, only these men carried with them the wisdom, focus and skills from centuries of battle. These were the men she was supposed to protect? These were the men counting on *her*?

Along with the men were three women, who Ryland had explained were the *shevas* of three of the Order members. Two of the women had dark hair and silver eyes, and were clearly sisters. The other woman had white blond hair, and she was wearing pressed jeans and a tank top. She had a computer with her and was reading the screen even as she materialized with the rest of the team.

The moment they were all present, Kane broke away from the group and walked over to Sarah. He exchanged a long look with Ryland, who grudgingly released his grip on her arm, but he didn't move away from her side. Kane's eyes were dark and turbulent, and she could feel the growing restlessness in him. *It's getting worse, isn't it?*

Kane nodded as he set his arm around her shoulders and pulled her close, staking his claim on her in front of all the others. *Each time I pass through shadows, it gets worse.* His voice was grim, his body was tense. *Darkness accentuates it, and that's never happened to me before.*

Sarah looked at the sun, still high in the sky. *So, tonight...*

Kane tightened his grip on her. *Tonight we will know.*

Sarah looked down at his hand gripping her shoulder so securely, at the raw strength in his forearm as it was draped over her shoulder. At his brand gleaming so defiantly on his skin. Would he be wielding that on her behalf, or against her, once the sun went down? Her stomach churned, and she set her hand on her belly, on the life she was supposed to protect once again. Who was she supposed to trust this time? *Who?*

"Most of you have met Sarah before," Kane said, his voice calm and powerful, not revealing any of the torment he'd shared with her.

"She's our angel," Ryland said. He already had his machete in his hands. "It's our duty to protect her."

A muscular blond male stepped forward. He had to be close to seven feet tall, and his blue eyes were stark and radiant in his angular face. Then, to Sarah's shock, he went down on one knee before her and bowed his head. "Sarah Burns," he said. "My name is Gideon Roarke. We are in your debt for all you have done for us. We will keep you safe. You have our word."

Then, the rest of the warriors all followed suit, and Sarah was shocked to see all of them down on one knee, their heads bowed. After a lifetime of having Calydons hunting her ruthlessly, of having to fear every one of them, of having each of them turn on her, it was overwhelming to receive that kind of response, that kind of promise. Tears filled her eyes as Kane tugged her closer and pressed his lips to her head. *It's different now, sweetheart. You don't have to fight this battle by yourself anymore.*

Sarah felt Kane's warmth pulsing at her, and she looked up at him. There was so much possessiveness and protection in his expression that she wanted to melt right into his arms. *You can't be Los Muerte,* she said. *You can't turn against me. I don't understand how you could.*

Kane's face darkened, and he spread his palm over her belly. His hand was pulsing with heat that spread through her, filling her with his strength. *I will not hurt you,* he said.

But the grim resolution in his voice told her that he was willing to do whatever it took to make sure that happened, even if it meant having his team take him down.

The team wasn't there simply to take on Luc. They were there to kill Kane if that needed to happen. They were there to assassinate the father of her baby, if it became necessary. What kind of sacrifice was that? A father killing himself to protect his own child? The mere fact Kane was willing to do it told her everything she needed to know. She locked her hand around his, and shook her head as fierce denial roared through her. "No," she said. "You aren't that man." She turned to the team, who was still kneeling. "Don't kill Kane," she said. "Luc is the one who is the problem."

Seven impassive faces stared back at her, and not one gave her reassurance.

And suddenly, the brightly lit clearing seemed fraught with tension and doom. What had she done by allowing Kane to bring these warriors here? They didn't understand about everything that was important in life. They didn't understand about believing in people, about hope and faith. The hope and faith she gave them was so they could slaughter others in the name of the greater good. What kind of hope and faith was that? That wasn't what she was really about!

"So, hi." The woman with the computer stepped forward, breaking the tension with a warm smile. She held out her hand. "My name is Lily Davenport. I've got a bit of expertise regarding Calydons, so they brought me along for my mind." She winked. "Not my body. No one ever notices my body."

"No one better notice your body except me," Gideon growled. "Or I'll carve out his eyes."

At first Sarah was startled by the exchange, but when relief rippled through the team, she realized it had simply been teasing banter designed to cut the tension. Everyone rose to their feet as the low murmur of male conversation began to hum through the air as the men figured out their plans for the attack.

"Sarah," Lily said, patting her arm, giving her another friendly smile. "How are you doing?"

Sarah blinked, wanting to follow the conversation with the men. "Um, I'm..." She glanced over at Kane and Ryland, who were huddled down with the team. "I need to—"

"You need girl talk for a minute," one of the other women said as she walked up. She smiled. "My name is Grace, and this is my sister, Ana."

Sarah managed a distracted smile. "Hi, but I need to—"

"Sarah." Lily's voice was firm, jerking Sarah's attention back to her. "We have all managed to successfully bond with males who were destined to kill us. You might want to take a moment to chat before heading out into those woods."

Sarah stared at Lily, and in her moss-green eyes, Sarah saw compassion and understanding of such depth that her throat tightened. She looked at the other two women and saw similar expressions of warmth on their faces. Suddenly, she realized she was not standing in the company of strangers. She'd been blessed with the friendship of women who knew what it was to suffer and had somehow found their way out.

They were the ones who understood about hope and faith. They were the angels sent for Sarah. A huge weight seemed to lift off her shoulders, a realization that she wasn't alone. Not anymore. That there was someone out there who understood what she was going through. Tears welled up in her eyes, and for a moment, she couldn't talk.

Lily immediately threw her arms around Sarah and hugged her. "It's hell to love these men, Sarah," she said quietly. "But the only way to make it work is to believe in them, even when they don't believe in themselves."

Sarah pulled back, her heart aching as she looked at the three women standing around her. "My first soul mate murdered our daughter," she said. "And Kane murdered his first soul mate and their son. And now I'm pregnant, and his scars have disappeared." Her hands began to shake again, violently this time, as she put into words the facts that damned both of them. "I believed in my first soul mate, and I was wrong. How do I do it again? What if I'm wrong again?"

Grace's silver eyes were watching her steadily, and there was compassion in them. "Screw the past, Sarah. You can't change it, and no one has to be bound by it. You own your life today, and so does Kane. You can't be bound by what happened before. Don't use that as an excuse to roll over and give up."

Sarah stiffened. "I'm not, but I have a baby that I need to protect. That changes things."

"It sure does," Lily said with a grin. "It means we get to see what the men look like when they're trying to change a diaper. Can you imagine? I can't wait to see it."

Sarah stared at Lily, not understanding how she could joke. "But—"

Lily slung her arm over Sarah's shoulder. "You have two choices, Sarah. Laugh or cry. Laughing is always better. It helps you see things more clearly."

She stared at Lily, trying to understand. "But—"

Ana stepped forward. There was so much suffering in her eyes that Sarah's powers began to simmer in response, wanting to protect the woman before her. "Sarah," she said. "Elijah had a terrible, terrible past when I met him. There was so little left of the warrior he once was, and he had so little faith in himself. He couldn't even trust his own mind."

Sarah frowned. "That's like what happens here, when the darkness consumes the men. They do things they wouldn't normally do." She looked over at Kane, who was drawing in the dirt with a stick, sketching out the woods to his team. Her heart warmed as she watched him talking intensely. He was so handsome, so powerful, radiating a strength that seemed to always wrap around her and keep her safe. He looked up and caught her staring, and flashed her a quick smile that went straight to her heart. "I know he'd never kill me or our baby if he had a choice. I know that. But he might not be Kane anymore once the night comes."

"Sarah." Ana took her hand, drawing Sarah's attention back to her. "Do you see the warrior on Kane's right? The one with the scars on his face around his eyes?"

Sarah looked back over at the men and saw the warrior Ana was talking about. His body was heavily muscled, but he was leaner than the others, and scars covered his body. Not the artistic designs that Kane used to have. These were battle scars, indicative of a body torn apart by violence. As she watched him, she noticed that every couple seconds, he looked over at Ana, as if needing to reassure himself that she was still there and still okay. Her heart tightened at his evident need to connect with his woman, at his complete acceptance of his stark need for his woman. "I see him. He loves you, doesn't he?"

"Beyond what words could ever express. That's Elijah Ross, my soul mate." Ana smiled at him, and Elijah's face softened with such love and affection before he turned his attention back to Kane. "The scars around his eyes were self-inflicted, because he was trying to stop himself from seeing the nightmares that were turning him into a monster."

"Oh," Sarah said. "I'm so sorry—"

"No." Ana shook her head. "There's no place for pity, Sarah. I told you that so you could look at Elijah and see a man who completely lost his sanity to the extent that he killed people he loved."

Sarah looked sharply at Ana. "He did?"

"He did." Ana looked across the clearing at Elijah, and he looked up again, smiling when he saw her watching him. "There were times when I was the only one who believed in him, but I was right." She looked at Sarah. "You're Kane's soul mate, Sarah. You're always right."

"I wasn't right about Mason."

Ana lifted her eyebrows. "I disagree. I bet you were dead right about him, and you just weren't listening to your gut at the time. I think you knew all along that you couldn't trust him. You had to have known." She ran her hand over Elijah's brand that was on her forearm. "The bond is incredibly powerful. It connects us to our mates in ways we can't even imagine."

Sarah bit her lip as she watched Kane and the others talking, trying to think back to the night with Mason. To the moment when she made the choice to go to him instead of running to her daughter to protect her. Again and again, she'd run that night through her mind, trying to determine if she'd missed some sign that she should have seen that would have told her what he was capable of, but again, she saw nothing. "How could I have known in my heart that he was going to kill my daughter, and ignored it?" She looked at Ana. "There's nothing more powerful than a mother's instinct to protect her child. If there was *any* sign I was wrong to believe in Mason, I would have heeded it. That's how it works, Ana."

Ana met her gaze. "Or maybe you don't want to admit you failed to listen to the truth that you knew what Mason was like in your gut, that you ignored evidence that cost your daughter her life."

Sarah gasped, shocked by Ana's words. Grace grimaced, and Lily sucked in her breath. "Ana, don't push Sarah like that—"

"No." Ana spun toward her, her eyes blazing with challenge. "I love Elijah more than words can express, and if Sarah is the one responsible for giving him the hope that had brought him out of that awful spiral, then as God is my witness, I'm not going to let her screw it up by being afraid to face things."

Anger fired up inside Sarah. "I know I made a mistake," she shot back. "I live with that every minute of my life, the truth that I made the wrong choice and it wound up killing my daughter. Don't *ever* accuse me of not facing that—"

"I'm not," Ana said. "I can see the guilt in your eyes, and I feel your suffering. But what you're not facing is the fact that there were signs all along that you refused to see because you *wanted* the fairytale of the man loving you. You wanted to be loved, and I know that because I wanted it, too. We all do!"

Grace set her hand on Ana's arm. "Ana, I don't think this is the time—"

"It is the time," Ana snapped. "Because Sarah is about to go in there and has to make the right choice about who Kane really is. She has to have the courage to see with her heart and not to have her perception distorted by her fears, her desires or her needs." She faced Sarah. "Lily told us what you're going to be facing in there, Sarah. You're the anchor for this whole team, and if you can't find the truth in your heart and see it, then none of the men will be able to either." She shook her head, gripping Sarah's hand fiercely. "We all have so much to lose if the Order goes down," she said. "Not just the protection of innocents at large and the very foundation of what they represent, but the man I love with every fiber of my being is going into those woods to help you, Sarah, and to end the creation of all these rogue Calydons, and you're it, Sarah. You're the glue holding all of them together."

Sarah stared at her, the responsibility of what she was facing welling up like a great weight. "I don't have any heart left," she finally said, her voice raw with the agony of so much loss. "It died so long ago."

It had died that night with Abigail.

"Find it," Ana said fiercely. "*Find it.* Open your heart so widely that if it breaks, it will rip you to shreds, because if you don't, the man I love will die, and that is just not acceptable to me." Tears gleamed in her eyes. "Don't be a brave warrior, Sarah. Be a woman, with all the emotions and vulnerability and tears that make us the rock that keeps our men alive." Then, she spun away, striding across the rubble toward the men.

Elijah looked up, and he held out his arm as she approached. Ana instantly slid into his embrace, tucking herself against him. Sarah saw Elijah's body visibly shudder and then relax as he wrapped his arms around Ana and rested his chin on her head. Neither of them tried to hide their need for each other, and their vulnerability was evident to anyone watching. But no one seemed to mind the badass warrior needing his woman so badly. The battle discussion didn't break stride, and none of the men even seemed to notice Ana's arrival. She had simply become part of Elijah, and they all accepted that.

Sarah hugged herself as she watched Ana and Elijah together, an aching sense of loneliness welling up inside her. "I don't know how to be like that anymore," she whispered, unable to keep the tears out of her voice.

"I know." Grace wrapped her arm around Sarah's shoulder and squeezed. "I had no idea how to be all soft and vulnerable. I'd been on my own fighting for far too long."

"Me, too." Lily moved in close to Sarah's other shoulder. "And I had reasons not to trust Gideon. Personal, deep reasons that were very real and very true."

Sarah looked over at Lily. "Really? What were they?"

Lily smiled gently. "No," she said. "That is Gideon's past, and it is no longer who he is, so it doesn't matter anymore. Even though I had no reason to believe that he was a different man than he'd once been, I did believe in him, and that's why we were able to defeat the *sheva* destiny that the male will go rogue and destroy everything they both care about, until they both die." She hugged Sarah. "Who he once was doesn't define who he is today...not necessarily."

Not necessarily. Which meant that Kane might or might not be the same man who murdered his family before. And she was supposed to figure it out?

Sarah bit her lip as she watched the men finalize their plans. She already knew the plans, because she had helped Kane and Ryland figure them out before Kane had left. Kane was leading the discussion, and his authority and strength were evident in the way the team listened to him.

He had an aura of indomitability about him...one that he hadn't had when she'd met him.

He had changed.

He was still changing.

Kane looked up at her and caught her gaze. Simmering in those dark eyes were violence and danger, and it was getting more and more turbulent with each passing moment. Her heart tightened for the suffering she saw in his face, for the tension emanating from him. His fear of what he was and what he might do. But she also felt his fierce determination not to succumb to the darkness within him. His steady commitment to protect her and their baby.

His voice filled her mind as he reached out to her. *I will not fail you, Sarah. I swear it.* The sheer force of his promise, his unyielding focus on who he wanted to be, pulsed through her like the thud of a bass drum, like the slow beat of a massive heart coming to life.

She knew that she was staring into the face of a man more powerful than any she'd ever met, a warrior capable of destroying an entire town... and of saving one. He may have once been the man who did the former, but today? Who was he today?

Sarah set her hand over her belly, and for the first time in seven years, she tried to open her heart again. The moment she did, she felt the anguish of her daughter's death and Mason's betrayal consume her, driving into her with such destructive force that she couldn't breathe. It swept through her mind, ripping away at her shields, stealing from her the hope and faith that was so necessary to keep her alive.

Instinctively, she started to fight it, to shut it down, to shove it back into that locked box where it couldn't hurt so badly, where it couldn't tear away at the fabric of who she was...and then she saw Ana look over at her.

And Sarah knew what she had to do.

Instead of fighting the pain, instead of trying to survive it, she dropped her shields and let it destroy her.

* * *

Sarah's emotional devastation blew through Kane with brutal force. Before he'd even registered what he was feeling, he was on his feet and sprinting over to her. He caught her in his arms just as her legs gave out, and she started to fall to the ground.

He swept her up against his chest, his soul vibrating with the depth of her anguish. "Sarah. What's wrong?"

She had no words for him, but she wrapped her arms around his neck, holding desperately to him as the sobs wracked her small frame. He pulled her closer, burying his face in her hair, trying to offer her comfort. *Sarah. I'm here. I've got you. It's okay.*

She still didn't answer, but she gripped him tighter, as if he were her only anchor holding her down. Her anguish rolled through him, and he saw flashes of what was going through her mind. A small girl with blond pigtails, smiling with such radiance he felt his own heart stop as he looked into those blue eyes. It was the same girl he'd killed in his dreams, only she was much younger. Not even a year old. But there was no mistaking her impish expression, the radiant blue of her eyes, and the shade of her hair. *Sarah.* He could barely keep the tension out of his voice. *Is that your daughter? Is that Abigail?*

Yes. Her grief washed over him, and suddenly the world began to blacken and darken around him. His skin burned. Pain crawled down his legs. And a deep-seeded, brutal violence began to burn inside him.

That's the girl in my dreams. The girl I murdered.

Sarah sucked in her breath and jerked her head up, her tear-streaked gaze pinned to his face. "That's impossible. You said the girl in your dreams was five."

"She is. But it's the same girl." Kane's body began to vibrate, violent energy racing though him.

She tightened her grip on him. "I don't understand. How could you see her in your dreams? You never met her. She was never that old."

"I don't know." But shit, what did it mean? That he was going to kill her daughter? That he'd somehow contributed to Abigail's death— "Jesus." He set Sarah down suddenly, stepping backwards. "What if I'm the one who's causing all the Calydons to go rogue? What if I'm the catalyst? What if I already killed your daughter once, through Mason?"

Sarah's face was ashen as she stared at him. "That's impossible," she whispered. "It can't be—"

"Why not? We were already assuming Luc was turning the men in this village rogue. What if we were wrong? What if it was me all along, even though I wasn't actually here at that time?"

Sarah's mouth opened, but nothing came out, and he felt the true depths of what she'd suffered through the loss of her daughter and Mason's betrayal. Her pain was so brutal, so extreme, he couldn't believe she was still standing. Sudden, fierce protectiveness rose inside him, beating away the darkness. "Fuck that, Sarah." He strode over to her and caught her wrist in his hands. "No more," he promised. "No more suffering for you. Not ever." He meant it with every fiber of his being. His oath pulsed past the darkness trying to consume him, as they both battled for dominance within him. "I swear it, Sarah. I won't let you suffer like that again."

Sarah stared at him, her eyes red and puffy as she searched his face. He felt her reaching out for him with her mind, and he let her in, allowing her to see every part of who he was. Her warmth wrapped around him, and he closed his eyes at the sensation of being connected with her. It felt so right, so perfect. He knew it was where he was meant to be. *Sarah,* he whispered into her mind. *This has to be right. I'm not meant to destroy the beauty of your soul.*

I know.

Kane opened his eyes and saw the warmth and trust glowing in her blue eyes, and he felt his heart stutter at the depth of her love. It was even more powerful than the love his mother had offered him...just before he'd killed her.

He hadn't been worthy last time.

This time, he wouldn't make the same mistake.

Sarah had made her decision to trust him, and he wasn't going to let her down. He didn't give a shit who he might have once been, or who Luc Acostos wanted him to be. Kane had one mission, and that was to be the man worthy of his mate, and he would accept nothing less. He took her hand and squeezed it. "Are you ready?"

She took a deep breath and nodded. "Let's do it. We have only a few hours until the sun goes down. Not much time."

"Not much time," he agreed. And then, because he wanted to and because he didn't give a shit what anyone else thought, he wrapped his arms around Sarah and kissed her.

It wasn't a kiss of ownership, to tell his team that she was his. It was the only way he knew of to show her how committed he was to being stronger than whatever curse would try to bind him. And when she threw her arms around his neck and melted into the kiss, he knew that she'd accepted his promise.

Which meant he was bound.

Good. That was exactly how he liked it.

As he drew back, he pressed his lips to the brand on her arm, the one that was almost complete. *Only one more stage, and then we're bound forever.*

Sarah's eyes widened. *The death stage, right?* At his nod, she shook her head. *I really, really hope that I don't have to kill to save your life, or offer my own to save you.*

She didn't need to explain further. He knew the cost to her of taking a life, and with the river inaccessible, she had no way to restore herself if she did it. And as to offering her own life? He laughed softly and wrapped his arm around her shoulder. "Sweetheart, there is no chance I'm putting you in that position." But even as he said the words, his soul vibrated with the need to complete the bond and seal her to him for all eternity.

Which he would never do. There were too many risks and costs associated with that final step, and they had enough to deal with already. Today was about victory, not about succumbing to his ages-old instinct to make her his forever.

He tucked her against him and surveyed his team. "Ready?"

As a unit, the members of the Order of the Blade nodded. They were ready. Luc Acostos was going down before sunset. He wouldn't even have a chance to come back to life and destroy them.

It ended now, because now they were going right into that pit and pulling the damned plug.

Chapter Nineteen

They were being hunted.

Kane kept Sarah close between him and Ryland as he led his team down the embankment toward the pit that had sucked down Thano. The sun was streaming brightly through the trees, dappling the ground, illuminating even the darkest shadows, and yet Kane's weapons were burning his arms and his senses were on fire. Beneath the smell of fresh earth and trees was the ever-strengthening scent of death, rot and sulfur. *Anyone smell that?* He reached out with his mind to his team, able to connect with them all because they were close.

He got a negative from everyone, and he swore under his breath. If no one else could smell it, then it was up to him to track it. It was daytime. Nothing should be out in these woods except nature...unless *he* was the evil he was scenting.

Oh, man, because that was a good thought.

He took Sarah's arm, bringing her more tightly against him as they reached the edge of the pit. He hadn't known what to expect during the day, whether the seething cauldron of hell would still be there, but he hadn't expected this.

Quinn let out a low whistle as he walked up beside Kane. "I've never seen anything like that before."

Stretching out below them was a seemingly endless stretch of green grass that seemed to descend into the very depths of the earth itself. It looked almost as if something were sucking the field straight down into the center of the earth.

"Last night it was hell," Kane said, recalling that Sarah had said her brother and the other males in the town had claimed that the pit was only grass and flowers. Apparently, that's how it really appeared during the day.

"I bet it still is," Quinn replied. "I'm not buying the grassy fields for one second." He gestured to the team, and as a unit, everyone called out their weapons. Everyone except Drew, who called out two swords, a battle axe, a spear and a dagger.

Kane shot a surprised look at the youth. "Five?"

Drew shrugged, giving Kane a cocky grin that showed exactly how little he understood about what he was dealing with in the aftermath of the evil that had tainted him a few months ago. "I still have the ability to call Ezekiel's twenty-one weapons," he said.

Kane looked at Quinn, who nodded. Ezekiel was the bastard of pure evil who had given birth to the entire Calydon race two thousand years ago, and he'd tried to take them down a few months ago. Drew had been caught in the cross fire and he'd absorbed a lot of the ancient evil that had bled through Ezekiel, as well as the warrior's affinity for twenty-one different weapons. It wasn't a good sign that Drew was still carrying so much of Ezekiel in him, not when he was so young and didn't have the defenses against taint and temptation that the rest of them had.

I had to bring him, Quinn said. *Vaughn went off with Ian.*

Let's hope he uses them for us and not against us, Kane said.

He's my responsibility. I'll manage him. Lead on.

Kane gripped his weapon and looked back at his team. Ryland was right next to Sarah. Gideon and Elijah were covering the rear, armed and ready. Zach and Gabe were covering Kane's right flank, with Quinn and Drew on the left. Lily was back at Nonny's house doing information management, researching each detail they found and then replying to Gideon with anything she could find on it. Grace and Ana had stayed behind to provide protection for Lily.

Although Ana and Grace's Illusionist talents made them formidable in battle by being able to create offensive illusions that were so deadly that they could kill people simply because people believed they were real, neither of their soul mates was all that fond of putting them on the front lines. Given that Jacob and the others could teleport directly into houses past the spotlights used to guard them, in this particular situation, even Nonny's house wasn't safe, so they'd all seen the wisdom of keeping them back to protect Lily.

But Quinn, Gideon and especially Elijah were on edge about leaving their women behind when they were so close to the action. Kane knew they had to be back before nightfall, or the trio would be too distracted to work. Kane checked his watch. Less than an hour until sunset, and the monsters came to life. In and out in sixty minutes.

"Can you teleport us down there?" Ryland asked. "It'll save time."

Kane studied the grassy hills below, the ones that had been a roiling tomb of rot the previous night. He could see a spot at the very bottom, where the valley seemed to disappear into the earth that seemed clear. "Yeah, I can..." he said, not moving to do it yet.

"Kane." Sarah came up beside him.

"Hey, sweetheart." He tucked his hand on the back of her neck, searching with all his senses to try to get a lay of the land below them. When he teleported, he had to know where he was going, or he could wind up lodged in a tree with his cells fused with the bark. It looked clear below, but it didn't feel right. "What do you see, Sarah?"

"I see meadows, but I don't believe it."

He glanced over at her. "Yeah, me neither." He'd had too much experience with illusions lately to automatically assume that what he saw was reality. "I can smell the sulfur."

Sarah nodded, her hand tight in his. "I feel nauseous, and I can't breathe. Like last night."

Kane ground his jaw. "So, we're standing on the edge of that same damn pit we saw last night. It just looks all pretty during the day."

"Maybe," Sarah said, "but we can't be sure."

"Well, let's figure it out." Ryland turned and hurled his machete into a nearby tree. It sliced off a branch that crashed to the earth with a thud right next to Gideon. "Toss that to me, will ya?" Gideon lobbed the massive branch to Ryland as Ry called his machete back to him. Then he turned toward the meadow. "Let's see what we have going on here." He took the branch and heaved it into the air, launching it way out into the middle of the meadow.

It spun around in the air, twirling around as it fell down past the level of the ledge they were standing on. The moment it fell below the edge, into what would have been the pit last night, it exploded mid-air, shattering into thousands of fragments that showered over them. Kane held out his hand and caught some. The wood was burning with a flame that was green, black and brown. A noxious stench was emanating from it.

"Well, shit." Gideon said. "That's not very polite. We could have gotten hurt."

Kane snorted, and then realized it was the kind of snarky comment Thano would have made, and his amusement faded. "Thano's in there, and so is Luc. You guys ready?"

The team moved closer, and heavy hands descended on Kane's shoulders. He let out his breath and gripped Sarah's hand, locking her down against him. He was going to take them down there, but hell only knew what they were going to land in. It wasn't going to be a meadow and flowers. That much he was sure about.

"Jesus, man." Ry said quietly. "What the hell are we going to meet down there?"

Kane met his gaze. "Hell, I think."

Ryland nodded. "Me, too." He looked at Sarah, and his eyes darkened. "I don't think the angel should go down there. Why bring her?"

"Because we can't leave her behind," Kane said.

"I'll stay behind with her," Ryland said. "It feels wrong to take her in there. I'm feeling it."

Kane scowled, his adrenaline rising to a fast peak at Ryland's interference. "It's not your call, Ryland—"

"I'll make it mine." Ryland stepped back, holding out his machete. His eyes were gleaming back. "The angel should not go down there, Santiago. I know it."

Kane was about to argue, when he felt a pulse of darkness in his mind, a nudge of violence that told him to resist Ryland, to shut him down. It was his thought, but at the same time...it wasn't. He hadn't thought that. Something else had tried to put the thought in his head. Son of a bitch. What the hell was going on? All he knew was that something or someone wanted him to bring Sarah down there, and that was enough of a reason not to. Ryland was onto something. He was sure of it. "Fine. Sarah stays."

Sarah shook her head. "No, Kane—"

"Yes." Kane quickly scanned the crew, dividing them in half. He gripped Sarah's arm and pulled her close. *You swear to me that you will use your powers to kill anything that gets you. I'll come back for you, so don't restrain yourself. Got it?*

Sarah gritted her jaw. "I need to go with you, Kane. I'm the one he wants."

"And me."

"Both of us," she acknowledged. "It doesn't make sense to split us up."

Kane ground his jaw. "He's got to be hiding down there right now, Sarah. He can't come out until sunset. I don't want you down there now, but I swear I'll be back before it gets dark."

Sarah bit her lip, but finally she nodded. "Keep your mind open to me, and come back if I call you."

He nodded and pulled her close, giving her a long kiss. She melted into him, and Kane let himself get lost in her kiss. He didn't want to let her go. He really didn't. But he had to, and it wasn't simply because of what he'd told her.

The truth was, he didn't know what he would become when he went down into that hell, and he didn't want Sarah anywhere near him when he arrived in it. He met Ryland's hard gaze, knowing that the warrior had some kind of connection to Sarah that would keep her safe with him. "Ryland, you stay here with Sarah. Quinn and Elijah, you come with me. The rest of you stay."

Quinn shook his head. "Drew stays with me."

"Yeah, fine." Kane met Ry's gaze and understanding passed between them. An understanding that Ryland would unleash that same monster as before if necessary to save Sarah. Kane had no clue what Ryland had turned into last night, but he knew that it had been called out in defense of Sarah. Ryland wasn't Sarah's soul mate, but there was something he had going on with the angels that Kane couldn't deny.

He was going to have to trust that, and trust his woman with the man that no one on the damn team trusted to do anything except to go rogue. *Keep her safe.*

Ryland's eyes narrowed. *I will.*

Kane nodded and looked down at Sarah. She lifted her chin and met his gaze. "Kane," she said, touching his arm. "I just thought of something."

He raised his brows, unable to tear himself away from his woman. Dammit. He didn't want to leave her behind. "What's up?"

"How are you planning on killing Luc? Your weapons didn't work on him before."

He shrugged. "We'll find a way—"

"I can kill him. My light can kill demons. You know it can." She sighed, and met his gaze. "I have to go. There's no other choice."

Kane swore. "No—"

"This isn't your decision," she snapped. "This is my town, and it's my child I have to protect. I'm going in, and you can come or not."

"It's my child, too—"

"Then make the right choice." Then she tore herself free of his arms and sprinted down the slope into the grass.

Kane swore as noxious smoke rose up around her, sucking her out of sight instantly. "Jesus!" He immediately opened his blood bond connection with her and locked down on her location instantly. "Come on," he shouted. "Now!"

Everyone grabbed him, and Kane teleported, his entire being focused only on one thing: the woman who made his heart beat. The woman who was going to get herself killed.

* * *

Sarah's body was screaming with pain as she landed on the seething earth. The rocks were glowing with orange heat, black with burned ash, and the air was so thick she could barely breathe.

Her skin was on fire, and she stumbled with dizziness. She immediately unleashed a quick pulse of her white light, and it cleared an air pocket around her. There was dark smoke swirling around, and shadows undulating in and out of focus. Dark trees were waving over her head, the branches slashing as if there were a brutal wind trying to tear them out of the earth. It felt like she was in a place of eternal night where darkness was a constant protection for the evil festering beneath the earth.

"Oh, no," she whispered, realizing that's exactly where she was. Nothing was asleep down here. Nothing was resting until sunset. Down here, the atmosphere was buzzing and humming with the lethal energy that would be unleashed onto her village when dusk hit.

Cold pain wrapped around her ankle, and she looked down to see smoky black tendrils creeping up her leg, the same thing that had grabbed the men last night. "No," she said, and she lit up her leg. The white light burned the smoke off, freeing her. Sweat beaded across her brow, and she knew she was draining herself each time she used her powers, but she didn't care.

She was at war now, and she would fight until the end. She pressed her hand to her belly, and sent warmth into the life she was supposed to protect. "This time, it's going to work out okay," she whispered fiercely. "This time, I'm going to get it right—"

"Sarah!" The air pressure shifted, and suddenly Kane and the rest of his team materialized around her. He grabbed her arm, his face frantic with worry. "You're okay?"

His fear for her safety was so intense it brought tears to Sarah's eyes. She nodded, and remembered Ana's advice. That somehow, she had to look past the exterior and *know* the truth about who he was. But as she looked at him, as she opened her heart to him, she saw his eyes turn black and a wave of darkness flooded her.

Kane dropped his hand and turned away from her, staring into the woods. "He's here," he said, his voice low and guttural, unlike she'd ever heard it before.

"Who?" Gideon moved close to Kane, his weapon out. All the men were scanning the woods. No one was moving until they had a sense of what was going on.

Kane moved restlessly. "Luc—"

The earth suddenly erupted below them, turning from solid footing into a seething, bubbling swamp of noxious fumes. Sarah screamed as she fell in, and all the men were sucked in with her. Kane lunged for her hand, and her fingers touched his as it sucked her down, closing over her head. *Kane!* Her fingers slipped out of his grasp, and then she was sucked away.

Sarah! Kane's anguished bellow filled her mind, and then it was gone, and all she could hear was the mindless screams of thousands of people being sucked to their doom.

* * *

"Sarah!" Kane bellowed with raw terror as she disappeared into the muck. He immediately opened his mind to her. He found her instantly, and he tried to dematerialize...and nothing happened. "Shit!" He frantically charged through the sludge and dove into the mess where he'd seen her go down. The mud was thick and toxic, burning his skin as he fought to swim through it. The mire was blocking his path, not letting him through. Panic assaulted him, and he fought harder against the muck. "Sarah!"

A cold hand suddenly grabbed him around the neck, yanked him out of the mire and flung him into the woods. He landed on hard ground, and immediately began swinging his flail at the earth to dig through it to Sarah. *Sarah! I'm coming!*

No response. It was as if she were dead. "No!" He screamed his rage, his desperation, his fury as he fought harder against the earth that had suddenly turned hard again. Taunting him. Not letting him through. He tried to dematerialize again, and nothing happened. "Shit!"

"Sucks, doesn't it?"

Kane whirled around and saw Luc lounging against a blackened tree trunk. His body was in shadows, undulating in and out of focus. His hair was streaked with soot, and his skin looked noxious and poisoned. His face was bony and haunted, but his eyes were glittering with power and intention. "I sat there and fought for Elizabeth after you killed her, but I couldn't save her." Luc's eyes narrowed. "Do you know why I couldn't save her?"

Kane clenched his flail, quickly assessing the situation. His entire team was gone, sucked into the muck with Sarah. *Ryland, you find her under there and keep her the fuck alive.* No answer. It was as if they were all dead to him. The only living creatures were Kane and Luc. "No. Tell me." His instincts were screaming at him to attack, to destroy Luc, but he didn't move. He knew Sarah would still be alive. Toxic swampland couldn't kill her. He knew it. He kept telling himself she was okay, trying to hold his shit together long enough to figure out how to get to her.

He was too experienced as a warrior to make a move without a plan, and he forced himself to stand still as his mind frantically sifted through possibilities.

"Because I'm bound to this hell," Luc spat out. "I can never leave, until I find a replacement."

"So I hear." Kane looked down at the earth that had swallowed Sarah. It was solid now. Locking her away from him. Fuck that. It couldn't be solid. There had to be a way through.

Luc hadn't moved, and he was watching Kane with an interested gleam. "There's no way through. I control the earth." And at his word, the earth began to seethe again. Kane dove into the earth, and it went solid before he hit it.

Kane! Sarah's voice burst into his mind, and it was torn with agony. Pain. Suffering. *Hell.*

His adrenaline went haywire, and he gripped his flail. *Sarah! Call me to you!* He felt a sharp gasp of pain as if she'd been struck, and then she screamed. His entire body began to shake with the need to save her, and he felt dark, brutal anger rolling through him. "Let her go, you bastard!"

Luc grinned. "Make me."

Sarah screamed again, and her suffering broke through the last reserves of Kane's control. He launched himself at Luc, and slammed his flail toward the male's head—only the demon turned to smoke and disappeared as Kane reached him. Kane landed and whirled around as Luc reformed behind him. Sarah screamed again in his head, tearing apart the last of Kane's sanity.

He bellowed with rage and attacked Luc, swinging ferociously. Luc howled with maniacal glee and attacked him, striking with hard, fast blows that inflamed Kane even further. He couldn't even think, couldn't plan, couldn't focus. Darkness just streamed through him, giving him strength and power, ripping through his controls until he was nothing but pain, violence and destruction.

He welcomed it. He let it consume him. He allowed it to infuse his body with power. His muscles strengthened, his speed quickened, and his body magically turned from flesh to smoke. Luc struck at Kane, but he had already turned to smoke and the older warrior's blade went right through where Kane used to be. Kane threw back his head and roared with victory, basking in the sensation of power tearing through him. He channeled the demon power into his cells, and his entire body turned to smoke.

Luc turned to smoke as well and then streaked through the woods and went straight down into the earth that had sucked down Sarah. Kane bellowed with power and rage and followed him, plunging straight into the ground, his body separating into thousands of smoke fragments as he finally, fully embraced exactly what he was.

* * *

Sarah unleashed another flash of white light as another demon tried to sink his claws into her belly. It wasn't just Calydons. They were full demons. They were—

"Sarah." Jacob threw the demon aside and strode up to her.

Sarah gasped, rolling onto her side, holding her arms protectively over her belly. Her brother's eyes were rogue red, and his claws were out. Just like before. *Just like before.* "Jacob," she gasped. "Don't—"

He didn't hesitate. He just struck right at her stomach and this time, God, this time, Sarah didn't hesitate either. She unleashed every ounce of power she had at him, and he screamed with agony as she torched him.

He fell to the ground beside her, writhing in agony as death sank its claws into him.

She'd killed him this time. She hadn't held back. She'd killed her own brother, who she loved so dearly. Because she didn't believe she could bring him back anymore.

Her own brother.

"Oh, God." Her body began to shake, and nausea churned in her belly as she tried to crawl away from him. "I'm sorry, Jacob," she gasped. "I had to make a choice—"

"Sarah." He rolled onto his side, his eyes brilliant blue.

Sarah gasped, staring at him. "Jacob," she whispered. "Is it you?"

"Yeah." He held out his hand. "You did it. You broke me free of Luc's hold."

Tears filled her eyes, and she crawled over to him, taking his hand. His hands were cold and clammy with the onset of death. "Jacob, God, I'm so sorry—"

"Me, too, Sarah." He held out his arms. "But thank you for saving me, for bringing me back." He smiled, that same, beautiful smile he'd given her so many times in his life, the one that had always melted her heart for her baby brother. "For giving me one more chance to see you with my own eyes, and to tell you that I love you."

"Oh, Jacob!" She fell into his arms, hugging him desperately as his life force began to fade. "Don't die, Jacob. Please."

"I'm not going to."

There was an edge to his voice that sent a chill through Sarah, and she froze, staring into his face. "Jacob—"

"You shouldn't have made the same mistake twice, Sarah," he

said. "I thought you were smarter than that." And then his eyes turned red, and he jammed his claws right into her belly and twisted them.

And in that moment, the white light inside Sarah died for good.

* * *

Kane streaked through the earth, emerging just in time to see Jacob plunge his claws into Sarah's abdomen. Fury tore through Kane, and he erupted into a blinding frenzy of outrage. He tore across the clearing and ripped Jacob away from Sarah. The warrior started to dematerialize, and Kane turned his hand to smoke and wrapped the tendrils around the youth's throat, spreading his taint through the kid's body and latching onto every cell, holding onto it, refusing to let it go.

Jacob's eyes widened with fear when he realized he couldn't teleport, and Kane lifted his lip in a snarl. "And now you die!" He swung his flail and sank it deep into the kid's belly—

"Kane," Luc snarled.

Kane whirled around as Luc lifted Sarah by her hair, holding her above the earth like a rag doll. Blood was pouring from her belly and her skin was covered in thousands of microscopic fractures. She wasn't even bothering to hold onto Luc's arm or get away. She was just dangling, all fight, all hope, everything utterly gone, her life ebbing from her.

Raw, unbearable anguish ripped through Kane. *Sarah!*

Kane dropped Jacob and sprinted across the cave toward Sarah, but Luc turned them both to smoke and streaked away from him. "Sarah!" Kane turned into smoke and streaked after Luc, his entire body screaming with agony as he raced after them, trying to get to her, trying to save her. Sarah. Their baby. "Sarah!"

Luc got further ahead, and Kane saw a glowing red light up ahead, the opening to a cave. He suddenly knew that he would never find Sarah if Luc got her to that light. He tried to teleport again, and again, *nothing happened.* The same tendrils that he'd used to bind Jacob were holding him back, locked down in his cells.

Get her, you bastard. Ryland's voice echoed through Kane's mind, and he turned to see Ryland sprinting out of the forest behind, weapons out, followed by the rest of the team. *Unleash the monster like you did before.*

Kane didn't hesitate. He closed his eyes and came to a complete stop. He opened himself to the darkness within him. He accepted the violence. He looked into the soul of the man who had killed his own child and his own *sheva,* and he accepted him. He slowed his breathing and allowed himself to access the power that had consumed him and given him the strength to wipe out a town and kill his own family. He invited it into his body. He allowed the demon taint to coat his heart and poison his cells. He gave himself over to the very thing he'd been fighting for five hundred years to deny, and he gave it free reign over who he was.

He became the man he truly was, the one who had killed his own child.

The moment he did, power exploded through Kane, streaking violently through him, tearing apart his soul. He felt all the bonds holding him shatter, and he knew he had returned to life, truly and completely.

He was who he was destined to be.

Los Muerte had returned.

Kane fixated on his connection with his *sheva,* and he allowed his predator mode to go into full force, and then he went after her.

Chapter Twenty

Sarah was falling, failing, dying. There was nothing left inside her. She'd failed again. She'd chosen wrong again. And her brother had killed her in cold blood. There was nothing left—

A burst of power exploded in her body, ripping her from her emotional spiral as Kane materialized and tore her from Luc's grasp.

Sarah gasped as her body turned to flesh again, as the smoke fled from her cells. Kane tossed her to the ground, barely noticing her as he launched himself at Luc. Sarah rolled onto her side, her body shaking violently, her muscles drained and weak as she lifted her head to look.

What she saw made her blood run cold.

Kane's skin was black, stretched across his bones like dried snakeskin strung up to bake in a hot desert sun. His muscles were like metal coils beneath his skin. And long, deadly claws protruded from the ends of his hands as he slashed at Luc. The two men circled each other, claws out. Kane wasn't even using his flail. He was hunched over like an animal, reverted to the same state as the monsters that had haunted her for so long.

His eyes were glowing red, but there was grim awareness in them, an embrace of the violence toiling through him. Not rogue. Pure evil. Los Muerte. There was no doubt. Not anymore.

Sharp pain sliced through her belly, and Sarah gripped her

stomach. She tugged her shirt up to look at the damage, expecting to see a gaping hole like there had been after Mason. To her shock, her skin was intact, but the puncture wounds were deep and jagged. Had Jacob missed the baby or not? Tears filled her eyes, and she began to shake, barely aware of the violent confrontation between Kane and Luc.

She knew Kane was lost to her, their connection severed. He hadn't even noticed her lying there, and he hadn't tried to come to her aid. Los Muerte was fighting for dominance, to take his place, and the Kane she knew was gone forever.

Despair filled her, but she fought to keep it at bay. If there was any chance her baby had survived Jacob's attack, she had to find a way to survive. But even as she rolled to her side and tried to crawl away, she felt the devastating weakness of her body. Her body shook as she collapsed on the earth, and she realized that she was dying.

Her last hopes had died. Killed by Jacob. Killed by the sight of the man she loved becoming consumed by the evil that had taken so many from her.

"Dammit." Sarah dug her fingers into the dirt, struggling to drag herself a few inches. She had to get away from Kane before he noticed her. Before he finished what he'd been brought here to do—

A howl of triumph tore through the night, and Sarah saw Kane plunge his claws into Luc's heart and rip it from his body. He held it over his head in triumph, Luc's black blood pouring down his arm. Sarah went cold, horrified by the image of the monster Kane had become. "Dear God," she whispered. How on earth would anyone stop him?

Beside him, Luc fell to the earth, clutching his chest. But as he fell, Sarah saw a smile flood his features, a smile of triumph and relief. It made him look like a man, a human being. As his eyes closed, he whispered, "I'm coming, Elizabeth, my love. I'm finally coming." There was such pure serenity in his voice that Sarah felt her own soul respond.

And then his soul left, and his body vanished, leaving Los Muerte behind, basking in his victory.

Sarah tried to crawl away as Kane lowered his trophy. He scanned the clearing and then his gaze came to rest on her. There was no recognition in his eyes, simply violence and death. Sarah froze, afraid to move, terrified of triggering him into action.

For a long moment, neither of them moved. Her mouth parched and dry, Sarah dug her fingers into the dirt. *Kane. Are you in there?*

No response from him. No connection.

Then he dropped the spoils of his kill and began to circle her, his red eyes glowing like the demons of the night. Dear God. There was nothing left of Kane. Nothing at all. Adrenaline rushed through Sarah, the instinct to survive fighting to give her strength.

Did she have enough light to kill him? Could she make herself do it? And then what? Would Ryland find her? Would he drag her back to the village and find a way to uncover the fountain? And would the water be able to bring her back after she'd used her powers against Kane? There was nothing left inside her. She could feel the emptiness, the utter betrayal.

"Kill her, Los Muerte. Kill her now."

Kane spun around, his movements quick and jerky like a creature possessed, as a massive black horse stepped out of the woods. On his back was a rider, his face obscured by a black hood, his body draped in a long cape as black as his horse's coat. The horse pranced restlessly, his huge iron-shod feet making no sound on the packed earth.

The rider leaned forward, his heavily muscled body moving easily with his mount's restless dance. "The baby she carries," the rider said, his voice haunting and eerie, "will replace you if it lives, Kane. It will take your spot. It will dethrone you. You must kill it before it can destroy you."

Kane whirled around to face Sarah, and her stomach dropped at the expression of raw hatred on his face. His gaze went to her belly, and his claws lengthened.

"Oh, shit." Sarah's heart began to pound and real terror shot through her. "Kane. It's me." Her voice was shaky and terrified, and she saw Kane's body shift into attack mode, seeing her as prey. "Kane! I'm Sarah. Your mate. You aren't this creature! You're the man who has nightmares about killing his child! You're stronger than this!"

Kane let out a hiss and hunched over. His claws were out, his body primed for the attack.

"Yes, Los Muerte," the man encouraged. "Destroy her. Destroy the child. Do it *now.*"

Agony filled her as she watched Kane move into a crouch. Every line of his body was taut, his eyes utterly devoid of humanity. This was the monster who had killed his own family. She knew it. *Kane!* But she knew he couldn't hear her. He was so far away from the man—

Dammit, no! The man had to still be in there. Los Muerte had owned his soul before, but once the talismans had held it at bay, the real Kane Santiago had emerged, with his beautiful amazing heart and courage. He had to still be in there, just like before. She just had to get it out of him. "Kane," she shouted, pulling herself to her knees. "You dumb ass! You are madly in love with me, and you will never forgive yourself if you kill me!"

The rider laughed as Kane readied himself to attack. "He's nothing but scum! There's no valor in these Order members," he shouted. "There's no honor! You'll see what he's made of. You'll see why they all need to be destroyed!"

"No, he's not! He is honorable!" Fury raged through Sarah at the man's insults. "Kane is the most beautiful soul I've ever met," she shouted. "I wouldn't love him if he wasn't!" As the words left her mouth, she realized that she did love him. Truly, deeply with all the power in her very soul. Kane had given her life and hope again, because he really was the man she wanted him to be.

She met his gaze as he stared at her with those glowing red eyes. "You love me, you stupid man. Why can't you see that?" But even as she said it, she saw the marks on his arms, the brands, and she thought of the ones on her arms. One more stage to complete the bond. Would the *sheva* connection be strong enough to break through the hold that demon had on Kane? Or would it end like it had with Mason? As an Order member, sealing the bond would doom them forever, but if Kane was truly Los Muerte and born of this village, then the bond wouldn't destroy them in that way. Which was he? Was he Kane, an honorable Order member? Or was he the monster brought from hell to kill her?

As she stared at the man she loved, the father of her baby, she knew that she'd never loved Mason like she loved Kane. Mason had been her childhood friend. Kane was power, desire, passion and tenderness. Kane was her savior, and she would be his.

She met his gaze, and saw only monster in them. No Kane. No humanity. But she knew it was in there. *It was.* And she knew that Kane was strong enough to find it. She also knew she was the only one who could help him. He loved her, truly loved her, and that was going to save both of them.

Click. Click. Click.

Her only warning before his attack. "I love you, Kane!" she shouted as she called out his weapon. Kane launched himself at her, claws out, as his flail appeared in her hand. She positioned it over her heart and she drove it deep into her own body, into the one place that held onto hope and faith, the one spot where she could be killed.

As she fell to the ground, gasping in pain, she felt the final lines of the brand burn on her arms, sealing their bond forever as she completed the death stage by giving her life to save him as the man she'd given her heart to descended upon her to kill her. Triumph exploded through her, and she knew that she'd sealed their connection forever.

Nothing was stronger than the *sheva* bond, at least not the one that she and Kane shared.

It was done. The rest was up to him.

And like she'd done seven years ago, she didn't call out her white light to attack her soul mate. She simply let him come.

* * *

Pain tore through Kane as he careened through the air, and he screamed from the sudden physical agony. Golden light flooded his mind, tearing through the darkness blinding him. The darkness screamed its protest, digging its fingers into his soul as the battle raged inside him. But in the darkness, he sensed something warm. Something light. Something soft. Something calling to him with kindness and love, and he flung his soul toward it, catapulting through the darkness toward the light that was flickering so far away. *Sarah!* He gasped, suddenly recognizing it. *Sarah!*

Her entire soul flooded him, all her hope and her love, as well as her pain and her loss. Her emotions filled the void that had been baking inside him for so long. They stripped away the darkness and the pain, they eviscerated the grip of evil, and her spirit settled inside him with such rightness, such peace and such beauty that everything simply fell away. The bond was complete. She was his. He was hers. Locked together for all eternity, and eradicating all the darkness trying to consume him.

He was free, and she had saved him. Their love had saved him—

"Sarah!" He suddenly became aware of her body beneath his, and he was jolted back into reality as he realized that his claws were plunging straight toward her belly. "No!" With a roar of fury, he stopped himself just before he hurt her, throwing himself off her and slamming into the ground beside her, the impact so violent that the earth shook from the hit.

Kane shoved himself back up and spun back toward Sarah, horror striking him when he saw her holding her hand to her bleeding belly, her deathly-white skin fragmented with a thousand hairline fractures, his flail embedded in her chest. "Dear God," he gasped as he recalled his flail, jerking it out of her body. "Sarah? Can you hear me?"

She didn't move.

Sarah! He gathered her into his arms, pulling her against him, sending all his strength into their connection. *I'm so sorry—*

Kane? Her voice was so faint in his mind, but Sweet Jesus, she was alive.

Sarah. He framed her face, his heart hammering in terror. *Come back to me.* But even as he connected them and reached into her mind, he saw only darkness. There was no light. No white light. It was gone. Her soul was dying.

Fuck that. He knew how to save her now, and he was going to do it. This woman was his, and he wasn't letting her go. Kane pressed his forehead against hers and opened his mind to hers. *You want a story of hope and faith, Sarah? You want me to tell you about something I love? This time, I have an answer for you.* He pulled her closer and pressed his lips to her cold forehead. *I love you, Sarah. You are the oxygen that I breathe. You are the beat of my heart. You are the spirit that keeps my soul alive.*

As he spoke, Kane let her feel the true depth of his emotions, the pure, beautiful love that he'd never known how to feel. It now resonated through him with a force so strong he knew it could never be silenced. Something flickered inside Sarah, a faint white spark trying to come back to life, and his throat tightened, knowing that she was coming back for him. *I was empty for five hundred years, because the talismans kept the real me at bay. When they vanished, the demon came back, but it was too late. You'd already showed me what love was, and you believed in me.*

Kane thought about how she'd let him attack her, how she'd lay there defenseless as he'd leapt on her, because she had believed that he had the strength to call upon his love for her and break through the grip that the evil had on him. He pressed his cheek to hers as tears burned in his eyes, unable to express how much her faith in him meant. *You believed in me, Sarah. You believed in me even when I didn't, and your faith pulled me out of it. It broke the spell that had bound me for so long. You have shown me what hope and faith really are, and I will love you every second of every day from now until eternity. I love you, my sweet angel, and even if you have to keep the rest of the team in line, you'll always be mine. Always.*

And our baby? Her voice was weak, but there, alive, filling him with the most incredible sensation of hope and love.

Kane immediately transferred his attention to the life she was carrying inside her, calling upon the blood bond he had with his own child. He felt a pulse of warmth from her, and he knew the baby was okay. Of course it was. It had the immortality of a demon, an angel and an Order member. *Jesus, Sarah. Our baby.* He had no words to express the sudden surge of love that overwhelmed him, and he felt Sarah's answering warmth.

Do you feel that, Kane? We're both thinking about our child, and there's no fear from either one of us. We're not afraid of being parents anymore. Her joy leapt through him, and he hugged her tightly, knowing that she was more than his guardian angel.

She was his life.

* * *

Warwick snarled in disgust as he watched Los Muerte bring the angel back to life. "Son of a bitch!" Beneath him, Deathbringer stomped restlessly, his powerful body chafing at having to stand still for so long. For a moment, Warwick contemplated trying to destroy Sarah with magic, but even as he had the thought, he heard the almost-silent approach of the rest of the Order as they charged after Kane.

Swearing, he reined in Deathbringer, taking the stallion back into the shadows as the rest of the warriors emerged from the woods. His lip curled in disgust as he watched them surround Santiago and the angel.

He knew them all. Ryland Samuels, the bastard who was on the edge. Gideon Roarke. Elijah Ross. Quinn Masters. Men who had found their *shevas* and got to keep them, because the Order hadn't slain them the way they'd killed Warwick's. He narrowed his eyes, bile spewing through him as he watched the undeserving bastards celebrate the victory.

"Enjoy it while you can," he snapped quietly as he stroked his mount's neck. "You may have protected one of your guardian angels, but there are two more in the trinity of guardian angels that protect you, and you won't save them."

He knew that because he already had both of them, along with Thano Savakis. Warwick had wanted Sarah to die first, because he'd wanted to bask in the downfall of the Order. He wanted to enjoy every minute as the Order lost hope and spiraled into the emotional hell of despair and loss. Yes, Sarah had survived and was now under their protection, but it wasn't close to being over. Warwick would make sure the Order suffered plenty before he wiped them out. And when the other two elements of the Order's guardian angel trinity fell, then Sarah would go too.

It would all work, and then—

A younger warrior emerged from the woods to join the Order, one Warwick didn't know. He narrowed his eyes as he watched the youth stride up to the team. There were dozens of brands on his arms, and he was carrying five different weapons. The youth paused as he passed the heart that Kane had torn from Luc, and he looked down at it.

After a moment, he crouched beside it, studying it with great interest. Warwick carefully opened his mind to the youth, and he felt a surge of violence in the younger warrior, a lack of connection to the rest of the team. Warwick smiled, knowing that he had just found what he was looking for: the warrior that would join him in his quest, the one who would help him give birth to the new Order, once this one was destroyed. *What is your name?*

The youth looked up, searching the woods, but Warwick knew the boy would never find him.

Who are you? The youth's response was sharp and aggressive, not giving away anything.

What is your name? Warwick repeated the question.

The boy stood up quickly, and gestured to Quinn, who immediately broke away from the others. "What's up, Drew?"

Drew. Now he had a name.

"There's someone in these woods," Drew said. "A Calydon. An old one. Older than my dad."

Quinn swore and looked right at Warwick, and Warwick realized the warrior had somehow located him. Within a split second, the rest of the Order was on the run, sprinting through the woods directly at Warwick.

Not that they would ever catch him. He was so much more than that. So much more than them. With a burst of laughter loud enough for the entire team to hear, Warwick whirled his mount around and raced into the woods, leaving them behind.

Leaving them wondering what was still to come.

* * *

Sarah stood on the front steps of her grandmother's house, hugging herself as she watched the sun set in Akara for the first time in her life. Tears tightened her throat as she watched the sky fill with oranges and reds, so beautiful, but at the same time, she felt so empty.

Luc Acostos was dead, and Kane had broken through the Los Muerte curse. There was no one left to poison the men of the village, and she knew that eventually people would start to come back. Jacob had been gone by the time they'd returned, and she was holding out hope that he was still alive out there somewhere, that he was finding himself again. Kane and the others were ready for him to come back and try to kill her, and they all hoped he would so they could catch him and try to help him. They had no idea how he would be now that Luc was gone. Other men had started emerging from the woods, men who had gone missing over the years. Men who were battered and confused, but finding their way back. With them would come families and people, and the town would begin to rebuild again.

But not Jacob. Three nights had passed, and Jacob hadn't appeared. "Where are you, Jacob?" she asked. "Please come back. Please." She tried to open their connection, but all she felt was that same wall that she'd felt before, blocking her from reaching him. "Dammit, Jacob!" But even as she grieved the loss of her brother and feared for whatever he was facing, a sense of power warmed her. She'd been so certain that his betrayal and his death would destroy her by finally crushing all hope for goodness, but it hadn't. She'd found hope and faith on her own, and by finding it, she'd been able to reach out to Kane and love him, and help them save each other. Jacob and Kane had taught her that she was stronger than she could ever have believed.

She and Kane had managed to find the river again, using the same skills they'd used before, and she was restored and healthy...but sad, because it had come too late for Jacob. For Mason. For Abigail. But then she put her hand on her belly and knew that there was hope for the future. Life was beginning again.

Inside, Nonny was preparing food for the team, and the warriors were in deep discussion about who had been in those woods after Luc had died. Who was the male on the black horse? The warrior who had spat such vileness about the Order as he'd tried to convince Kane to kill her? Thano was still missing, and the weight on the team was heavy.

Lily had found evidence of an angel trinity protecting the Order, and it gave Sarah goosebumps to think of the fact that there were two others like her. The Order was worried that they were in danger as well, and Lily was searching hard to find out more information about them and the Calydon on the horse.

The Order hadn't heard from their teammate Ian, and they were beginning to suspect that his missing *sheva* might be one of the angel trinity...a woman who was being repeatedly murdered. Could an angel survive that? Sarah didn't know, but she shivered at the thought of that woman's suffering, regardless of whether she was part of the angel trinity or not. There was so much death and violence still to come, even though Luc was dead, happily dead. Was he finding redemption in the arms of the woman he'd loved? Was there a chance for redemption for a man like that?

Then she thought of Kane, and she smiled, knowing that yes, there was always a chance for redemption.

"Sarah." The front porch squeaked as Kane walked out, and he wrapped his arms around her, resting his cheek against hers as he clasped his hands over her belly. The puncture wounds were gone now, healed by the water, and she could feel the life pulsing within her. This time, her child would have the protection of both parents.

She turned in Kane's arms so she could look at him. His eyes were so bright, filled with softness and warmth. "Thank you," she whispered as she laced her fingers behind his neck. "Thank you for giving me back my hope."

He laughed softly and kissed her. "Shit, woman, I'm the one who owes you." His smile faded, and he ran his fingers gently through her hair. "You gave me the strength to break the curse that had held me for so long. Your love. My love for you." He kissed her again, and the kiss quickly became passionate and heated. *I love you, Sarah Burns.*

I love you, too—

"Santiago."

Kane broke the kiss as Javier came out on the porch. The old warrior had washed off the war paint, and his black eyes were intense.

"Thanks for your guidance," Kane said. "It helped."

Javier nodded, and he handed Kane a black cord threaded through a red stone. "This is for you."

Sarah smiled, and Kane felt a wave of warmth from her as he studied the necklace. The stone was carved with a design he didn't recognize. It wasn't one of the ones that he'd carried on his body for so long. "What's this?"

"That, my boy, is something we've been holding onto for a long time." Nonny walked out behind Javier. She was wearing a hot pink tank top and a pair of flowered shorts. Behind her filed the rest of the team, all of them wearing shit-eating grins.

Kane frowned as Sarah slipped her hand into his. "What's going on?"

"Hold it in your fist," Javier instructed. "Close your hand around it."

Kane glanced again at the panel of smug faces watching him, but he did as Javier instructed. His palm immediately began to throb with heat, a pulsing beat that seemed to echo through his entire body.

"Now, open it."

His knuckles were stiff and protesting, but Kane managed to pry his hand open. On his palm was a red mark, burned into his skin. Another scar.

Nonny grabbed his hand and peered at it, then she grinned at Javier. "It worked."

"Of course it did," Javier said.

"What is it?" Kane couldn't keep the impatience out of his voice. Having another scar on his palm made him uneasy, as if once again he was being cut from the town and branded a monster.

It was Sarah who answered, a smile lighting up her face. "When this village was founded originally as an enclave for angels, a team of guardians was assigned to protect the angels from demons. The original protector was conscripted by the demons, and he left us with no one."

"Legend said that the new one would come," Nonny said. "And that the stone would mark him as ours."

Javier tapped his palm. "That design is the same one that is burned into the top of the fountain, which is the center of our town. It means that you and this town are one."

"Kane stared at him. "What do you mean?"

"It means," Sarah said. "That you're home, Kane. You're finally home."

Home? Kane tore his gaze off his hand and looked around the crumbling village, the one that had once been his. The place he'd been searching for his whole life. The one he'd destroyed once...it had welcomed him back? His chest felt tight, and he had to take a deep breath.

"Kane." Sarah stood on her tiptoes and framed his face with her hands. "Welcome home." Then she threw her arms around him, and Kane hauled her against him, burying himself in the amazing sensation of all that she was. As his team pounded on his back and congratulated him, Kane knew that after five hundred years of searching, he'd finally found what he'd been looking for. Himself. His home. His heart.

He kissed Sarah's head and met Ryland's gaze across the porch. They exchanged a silent nod of agreement. The battle wasn't over. Not even close. Next up? To find Thano, Ian, and two other angels before the horseback rider from the woods made his next move. And as Kane watched Ryland survey the woods, he had a feeling that Ryland, with his connection to the angels, was going to be the man to lead them.

Sneak Peek: FOREVER IN DARKNESS
(The Order of the Blade, Book Four) (Novella)
(Dark & Sexy Paranormal Romance, Available Now)

It wasn't her.

Ian gritted his jaw, fighting against the need to sprint across the room and grab the woman standing beside the bar. It couldn't be true. There was no chance that the woman thirty feet away from him was Catherine Taylor.

Catherine Taylor was dead. She'd fallen into his arms, stared at him for a fraction of a second, and then Ian's teammate had struck her down. Dead. Done. Over. She was history.

And the second woman he'd buried earlier in the evening? He was sure now that it hadn't been Catherine. It had been a woman who looked like her, and his screwed-up mind had mixed them up.

The curse was trying to work him over. There was no reality anymore. Just delusions.

It's not her.

Sweat beaded on Ian's brow, and adrenaline surged through him. His entire body shook with the effort of staying where he was instead of responding to the siren call of the woman by the bar. His head pounded with the strain of trying to control his thoughts, to keep from hauling ass over there, sweeping her up in his arms and carting her off to his place to make love to her until neither of them could move.

He ground his jaw, focusing his attention on an old wooden sign on the opposite wall. *Be a Man. Play with Sharp Objects.*

Be a man. Stand with honor. Shit. What was he doing hiding in the shadows?

Honor didn't mean he was supposed to shrivel in the corner, afraid to look at an auburn-haired woman. It meant he stood tall, faced down that damn curse and defeated it. The curse had come to claim him, and it was time to step up and fight it. He needed to challenge what it threw at him and prove himself stronger.

He had to face it.

Ian clenched his jaw and slowly turned his head back to the woman. He steeled himself for the impact of seeing her, but the moment he saw her again, he felt like he'd been sucker-punched in the gut.

It was Catherine. It was her. *It was his woman.*

He would never forget those strawberry-gold highlights in her hair, the upturned slant of her nose, the way her lips pressed together in tension. Her skin was paler than he recalled, but her hips had that same curve of muscles and femininity. He would never forget the feel of her hips beneath his hands when she'd fallen down that damned cliff and he'd caught her. He knew exactly how they felt, precisely how they curved, and he knew just how her jeans caressed them.

Her hair was tossed over her right shoulder in a tumble of waves, and her white tee shirt hugged her body like it was put on this earth to torment him. The plain cotton was almost innocent in its simplicity, but the curve of her breasts beneath it made Ian's thoughts go to places that were far from innocent. On her left wrist was a thin gold bracelet that matched the gold hoops in her ears. No other adornment, no other flash. Not even any makeup. Just the pure, sensual beauty of a woman who was simply who she was, and that was more than enough for him.

She was searching the room now, her face tense with worry as she scanned the crowd. Her tension made his protective instincts pulse deep. Adrenaline rushed through him, and his weapons burned in his arms. This time the urge to arm himself was not to impale himself like some weak-willed embarrassment to his kind, but to protect her. To make her safe. To keep her from the fate she'd already suffered twice—

Twice?

Ian swore and gritted his teeth. What was he thinking? It made no sense that this woman was Catherine Taylor, that she was some reincarnation anomaly who could come back to life hours after he'd buried her. What the hell was his problem?

He knew the answer to that one. The curse was his problem. It was going to keep trying to make him relive the death of his *sheva* until it finally broke him.

Well, fuck that. The woman across the bar wasn't his *sheva*. He was going to prove it, and then cut himself free from her influence.

She turned her head and met his gaze. His gut jumped as her green eyes met his, and he felt himself sliding helplessly under her spell. She stiffened, then took a step back and glanced over her shoulder toward the door.

She was leaving? *Unacceptable.*

Urgency coursed through Ian, and he broke from the corner, heading right for her.

Her eyes widened when she realized he was approaching, and her cheeks flushed. But she didn't back away. She lifted her chin and waited for him to approach.

Anticipation roared through him as he neared her, and an urgent lust rose within him as he closed the distance between them. The scent of lilac and lavender filled the air, so subtle, so faint that he wouldn't even have noticed it if he hadn't been searching for it so relentlessly.

Lilac and lavender. Hot damn. She smelled *right.*

Her green eyes searched his, and in them he saw pain and fear, so deeply etched it had become a part of her soul. But at the same time, they flashed with defiance and courage, a woman who had not surrendered to the burden she carried. Respect surged through him, igniting his lust even further.

But it was more than respect and lust. It was a raw, burning need to drag her over to him and make her his, in any and every way that he could.

She swallowed, and he felt her rising nervousness. "What do you want?" she asked.

Sweet Jesus. Her voice was like the choir of angels. Desire exploded through him, a yearning so powerful he could barely contain it. He had spent his life fighting the carnal urges that were a part of being a Calydon male, determined not to let it rule him and put him in a position where a woman could bring him down. But with those four words, this woman had unleashed all the raw sexual need he'd held at bay for so long.

She had to be Catherine. She had to be his *sheva*. There was no other explanation for the intensity of his response...but Catherine had died eight months ago. Her spirit couldn't have been reincarnated into a twenty-something body that was already alive.

What the hell was going on?

He needed answers. He had to know. He wanted to feel her body against his, to crush her into him and feel their bodies come together. He needed to dive deep into her soul and see who she really was, and he needed it *now*. The pulsing of music from the band vibrated through him, the deep base thudding in every cell in his body. "Dance with me," he said hoarsely, his voice raw with lust and need. "Dance with me."

Sneak Peek: ICE
(Alaska Heat, Book One)
(Romantic Suspense, Available Now)

Kaylie's hands were shaking as she rifled through her bag, searching for her yoga pants. She needed the low-slung black ones with a light pink stripe down the side. The cuffs were frayed from too many wearings to the grocery store late at night for comfort food, and they were her go-to clothes when she couldn't cope. Like now.

She couldn't find them.

"Come on!" Kaylie grabbed her other suitcase and dug through it, but they weren't there. "Stupid pants! I can't—" A sob caught at her throat and she pressed her palms to her eyes, trying to stifle the swell of grief. "Sara—"

Her voice was a raw moan of pain, and she sank to the thick shag carpet. She bent over as waves of pain, of loneliness, of utter grief shackled her. For her parents, her brother, her family and now Sara—

Dear God, she was all alone.

"Dammit, Kaylie! Get up!" she chided herself. She wrenched herself to her feet. "I can do this." She grabbed a pair of jeans and a silk blouse off the top of her bag and turned toward the bathroom. One step at a time. A shower would make her feel better.

She walked into the tiny bathroom, barely noticing the heavy wood door as she stepped inside and flicked the light switch. Two bare light bulbs flared over her head, showing a rustic bathroom with an ancient footed tub and a raw wood vanity with a battered porcelain sink. A tiny round window was on her right. It was small enough to keep out the worst of the cold, but big enough to let in some light and breeze in the summer.

She was in Alaska, for sure. God, what was she doing here?

Kaylie tossed the clean clothes on the sink and unzipped her jacket, dropping it on the floor. She tugged all her layers off, including the light blue sweater that had felt so safe this morning when she'd put it on. She stared grimly at her black lace bra, so utterly feminine, exactly the kind of bra that her mother had always considered frivolous and completely impractical. Which it was. Which was why that was the only style Kaylie ever wore.

She should never have come to Alaska. She didn't belong here. She couldn't handle this. Kaylie gripped the edge of the sink. Her hands dug into the wood as she fought against the urge to curl into a ball and cry.

After a minute, Kaylie lifted her head and looked at herself in the mirror. Her eyes were wide and scared, with dark circles beneath. Her hair was tangled and flattened from her wool hat. There was dirt caked on her cheeks.

Kaylie rubbed her hand over her chin, and the streaks of mud didn't come off.

She tried again, then realized she had smudges all over her neck. She turned on the water, and wet her hands...and saw her hands were covered as well.

Stunned, Kaylie stared as the water ran over her hands, turning pink as it swirled in the basin.

Not dirt.

Sara's blood.

"Oh, God." Kaylie grabbed a bar of soap and began to scrub her hands. But the blood was dried, stuck to her skin. "Get off!" She rubbed frantically, but the blackened crust wouldn't come off. Her lungs constricted and she couldn't breathe. "I can't—"

The door slammed open, and Cort stood behind her, wearing a T-shirt and jeans.

The tears burst free at the sight of Cort, and Kaylie held up her hands to him. "I can't get it off—"

"I got it." Cort took her hands and held them under the water, his grip warm and strong. "Take a deep breath, Kaylie. It's okay."

"It's not. It won't be." She leaned her head against his shoulder, closing her eyes as he washed her hands roughly and efficiently. His muscles flexed beneath her cheek, his skin hot through his shirt. Warm. Alive. "Sara's dead," she whispered. "My parents. My brother. They're all gone. The blood—" Sobs broke free again, and she couldn't stop the trembling.

"I know. I know, babe." He pulled her hands out from under the water and grabbed a washcloth. He turned her toward him and began to wash her face and neck.

His eyes were troubled, his mouth grim. But his hands were gentle where he touched her, gently holding her face still while he scrubbed. His gaze flicked toward hers, and he held contact for a moment, making her want to fall into those brown depths and forget everything. To simply disappear into the energy that was him. "You have to let them go," he said. "There's nothing you can do to bring them back—"

"No." A deep ache pounded at Kaylie's chest and her legs felt like they were too weak to support her. "I can't. Did you see Sara? And Jackson? His throat—" She bent over, clutching her stomach. "I—"

Cort's arms were suddenly around her, warm and strong, pulling her against his solid body. Kaylie fell into him, the sobs coming hard, the memories—

"I know." Cort's whisper was soft, his hand in her hair, crushing her against him. "It sucks. Goddamn, it sucks."

Kaylie heard his grief in the raw tone of his voice and realized his body was shaking as well. She looked up and saw a rim of red around his eyes, shadows in the hollows of his whiskered cheeks. "You know," she whispered, knowing with absolute certainty that he did. He understood the grief consuming her.

"Yeah." He cupped her face, staring down at her, his grip so tight it was almost as desperate as she felt. She could feel his heart beating against her nearly bare breasts, the rise of his chest as he breathed, the heat of his body warming the deathly chill from hers.

For the first time in forever, she suddenly didn't feel quite as alone.

In her suffering, she had company. Someone who knew. Who understood. Who shared her pain. It had been so long since the dark cavern surrounding her heart had lessened, since she hadn't felt consumed by the loneliness, but with Cort holding her...there was a flicker of light in the darkness trying to take her. "Cort—"

He cleared his throat. "I gotta go check the chili." He dropped his hands from her face and stood up to go, pulling away from her.

Without his touch, the air felt cold and the anguish returned full force. Kaylie caught his arm. "Don't go—" She stopped, not sure what to say, what to ask for. All she knew was that she didn't want him to leave, and she didn't want him to stop holding her.

Cort turned back to her, and a muscle ticked in his cheek.

For a moment, they simply stared at each other. She raised her arms. "Hold me," she whispered. "Please."

He hesitated for a second, and then his hand snaked out and he shackled her wrist. He yanked once, and she tumbled into him. Their bodies smacked hard as he caught her around the waist, his hands hot on her bare back.

She threw her arms around his neck and sagged into him. He wrapped his arms around her, holding her tightly against him. With only her bra and his T-shirt between them, the heat of his body was like a furnace, numbing her pain. His name slipped out in a whisper, and she pressed her cheek against his chest. She focused on his masculine scent. She took solace in the feel of another human's touch, in the safety of being held in arms powerful enough to ward off the grief trying to overtake her.

His hand tunneled in her hair, and he buried his face in the curve of her neck, his body shaking against hers.

"Cort—" She started to lift her head to look at him, to see if he was crying, but he tightened his grip on her head, forcing her face back to his chest, refusing to allow her to look at him.

Keeping her out.

Isolating her.

She realized he wasn't a partner in her grief. She was alone, still alone, always alone.

All the anguish came cascading back. Raw loneliness surged again, and she shoved away from him as sobs tore at her throat. She couldn't deal with being held by him when the sense of intimacy was nothing but an illusion. "Leave me alone."

Kaylie whirled away from him, keeping her head ducked. She didn't want to look at him. She needed space to find her equilibrium again and rebuild her foundation.

"Damn it, Kaylie." Cort grabbed her arm and spun her back toward him.

She held up her hands to block him, her vision blurred by the tears streaming down her face. "Don't—"

His arms snapped around her and he hauled her against him even as she fought his grip. "No! Leave me alone—"

His mouth descended on hers.

Not a gentle kiss.

A kiss of desperation and grief and need. Of the need to control *something*. Of raw human passion for life, for death, for the touch of another human being.

And it broke her.

Sneak Peek: KISS AT YOUR OWN RISK
(The Soulfire Series, Book One)
(Humorous Paranormal Romance, Available Now)

"Let's get it done." Blaine grabbed her arm and began to propel her down the sidewalk.

"My car is the other direction—"

"We'll take mine." He nodded ahead, and Trinity saw a large, black motorcycle parked up beside the curb.

She stopped. "I can't ride on that."

He frowned. "Why not?"

"It's...dangerous." It was the best word she could think of. She didn't take risks right now. She kept all emotions tucked deep away inside, held tight like steel netting was wrapped around her. The motorcycle...too wild. Too adventurous. Too passionate. Too everything she didn't dare to be.

"Been riding for over a century. I'm good." He strode toward it, not bothering to wait for her. "I'll keep you safe."

"No." She was already walking toward it. She had to touch it. To feel what that kind of freedom felt like. She laid her hand on the seat. The leather was soft, but it felt tough at the same time. The chrome was gleaming. The wheels were immaculate. It was the ultimate expression of daring to take on life, of refusing to go gently, of feeling the passion and fire burn through her until she wanted to explode. Of embracing risk and danger.

It was everything she couldn't afford.

Not in this moment. Not with the spider edging so close to the line.

Right now, she needed to keep a stranglehold on her emotions. It was about self-control. It was about showing she could manage the cravings and desire burning inside her. It was about driving her Subaru below the speed limit while wearing her seatbelt.

Blaine swung his leg over the seat, straddling the huge machine like he owned its soul. Like it was a demon he controlled by his mere presence. "Just got it. Nice, huh?"

"I can't ride that."

"You're my ticket to freeing Christian." He held out his hand to her. "Trust me, I'll protect you. No chance you're getting hurt with me around."

"It's not that." She clasped her hands behind her back, against the urge to climb on there with him. She could almost feel the wind blowing through her hair, that sense of being utterly free in a way she never had been. Ever.

He turned the key, then punched the ignition button. The engine roared to life, so loud it drowned out the thoughts in her head. It thundered in her chest, made her body vibrate, reducing her to nothing but a physical, visceral reaction to the power and freedom it offered.

He didn't bother with a helmet. He didn't bother to shout above the din. He just jerked his chin at her and revved the bike with a twist of the right handlebar.

She saw the determination in his eyes. He was man who wasn't going to lose his race for Christian's life.

He wasn't even considering it. He'd do whatever it took, and he'd succeed.

She wanted to be like that. She wanted to be so sure, so confident, so certain in who she was and what she wanted that she never doubted herself again, never feared the monster within. She wanted to wake up in the morning with that same expression that Blaine was wearing. The one that knew, without a doubt, that she could have anything and everything she wanted.

Maybe she'd been going about it the wrong way. Maybe fighting her passions had been a misguided approach. Maybe the right choice was to embrace her inner fire and let it shine.

Blaine grinned, a smug look that told her that he knew she'd changed her mind.

Even as she started toward the bike, even as she slid her leg over the seat behind Blaine, even as she wrapped her arms around his muscled waist, she knew was using the logic as an excuse to get on and feel that fire, a choice she knew in her gut was the wrong one, the dangerous one, the choice of an addict unable to ditch the high.

Blaine let the engine idle, and it subsided to a quiet roar. He pointed to pegs poking out of the bike near her feet. "Rule number one. Your feet never, ever come off those pegs unless I tell you. Not even when I stop. Your feet get in my way, and we could crash, or you could burn your leg off."

Her heart started to race, but she put her feet on the rods. What was she doing, riding this bike? This wasn't her. But it was too tempting. She wanted to live, just once. How could a bike ride trigger her into going crazy and becoming a murderer?

By stripping her of what little self-control she had left, that's how. What if she liked the high too much? What if she wanted it again? What if—

He twisted around so he could look at her. "Second rule: you tuck up against me and let your body fall in with mine. When I lean into the corners, you relax and go with me. Got it?"

Oh, man, she so couldn't do this. Release all resistance and let the world take her? "I—"

"If you need to stop, tap my side with your left hand. Other than that, just keep your feet on the pegs and let your body move with mine and the g-forces of the bike, and you're good." He grabbed her knees and crushed her thighs against the outsides of his.

Heat began to throb through her inner legs. An awareness of his strength. Of the intimate feel of his body between her thighs.

He flipped a grin at her over his shoulder. "The name of the game is submission, Trinity."

She stiffened. Submission was a dirty word in her vocabulary. Submission meant giving into the curse.

"Surrender yourself to the bike and to me."

"I can't surrender to anything—"

He revved the engine with a flick of his right wrist, drowning out her protest. She frantically hit him on his left side to tell him to stop, but all he did was raise one eyebrow at her. Then he ditched the kickstand and the bike began to roll.

She lunged to get a grip around his waist, hugging desperately with all her strength. What had she been thinking—

She suddenly became aware of a deep vibration echoing up from the bike, like the pulsing of a bass drum throbbing in her core, down her legs, in her belly, along her thighs where she was pressed so tightly around Blaine.

And then the bike lurched forward with a squeal of tires. She tightened her grip around his waist, and then she felt the earth move beneath her. As the bike roared down the street, the cold wind whipped at her face, yanked at her hair, and her whole body shook with the vibration of a thousand pounds of force, she felt her soul come to life in a way she never had before.

She raised her face to the sky, felt the sun fighting to warm her against the wind's coldness, felt the heat of Blaine's body between her thighs. He turned a corner and they leaned as one with the bike.

She looked down as her right knee skimmed just above the pavement. They were going so fast, the ground was nothing but a gray blur, rushing past. Another inch closer and her kneecap would turn into a Frisbee. So close to utter destruction, dancing on the edge—

He straightened the bike and they moved upright again. Away from danger. She'd threaded the edge, but she'd never really been at risk. She could feel Blaine's complete control of the machine of the power beneath them. One wrong move and the bike could be an instrument of carnage and lost dreams. But in Blaine's grasp, it was a tool of pure, unadulterated freedom.

To be able to control death so easily? To turn it from hell into joy? Tears filled her eyes as she pressed her cheek to Blaine's back. The heat from his body pressed at her inner thighs, burning through her jeans. Her hair knifed at her cheeks, her shirt flapped ruthlessly, as if the fabric wanted to rip free from her body, to fly through the air. She hugged tighter, suddenly afraid.

Blaine tapped her wrist and held his right arm up to the sky, like he was reaching for the sun. "You can let go," he shouted over his shoulder. "Try it!"

She shook her head and held tighter.

She felt the laughter rumble in his chest, and then he leaned over the handle bars and the bike leaped forward, as if he'd unleashed a wild cat from a cage. She felt his muscles flex, felt a sudden energy pulse through his body, like sparks were jumping from his skin onto hers, and then he whipped the bike onto the highway, and let it all out.

And all she could do was hang on.

Sneak Peek: DARKNESS AWAKENED
(The Order of the Blade: Primal Heat Trilogy, Book One)
(Dark & Sexy Paranormal Romance, Available Now)

Quinn Masters raced soundlessly through the thick woods, his injuries long forgotten, urgency coursing through him as he neared his house. He covered the last thirty yards, leapt over a fallen tree, then reached the edge of the clearing by his cabin.

There she was.

He stopped dead, fading back into the trees as he stared at the woman he'd scented when he was still two hours away, a lure that had eviscerated all weakness from his body and fueled him into a dead sprint back to his house.

His lungs heaving with the effort of pushing his severely damaged body so hard, Quinn stood rigidly as he studied the woman whose scent had called to him through the dark night. She'd yanked him out of his thoughts about Elijah and galvanized him with energy he hadn't been able to summon on his own.

And now he'd found her.

She'd wedged herself up against the back corner of his porch, barely protected from the cold rain and wet wind. Her knees were pulled up against her chest, her delicate arms wrapped tightly around them as if she could hold onto her body heat by sheer force of will. Her shoulders were hunched, her forehead pressed against her knees while damp tangles of dark brown hair tumbled over her arms.

Her chest moved once. Twice. A trembling, aching breath into lungs that were too cold and too exhausted to work as well as they should.

He took a step toward her, and then another, three more before he realized what he was doing. He froze, suddenly aware of his urgent need to get to her. To help her. To fill her with heat and breathe safety into her trembling body. To whisk her off his porch and into his cabin.

Into his bed.

Quinn stiffened at the thought. Into his bed? Since when? He didn't engage when it came to women. The risk was too high, for him, and for all Calydons. Any woman he met could be his mate, his fate, his doom. His *sheva*.

He was never tempted.

Until now.

Until this cold, vulnerable stranger had appeared inexplicably on his doorstep. He should be pulling out his sword, not thinking that the fastest way to get her warm would be to run his hands over her bare skin and infuse her whole body with the heat from his.

But his sword remained quiet. His instincts warned him of nothing.

What the hell was going on? She had to be a threat. Nothing else made sense. Women didn't stumble onto his home, and he didn't get a hard-on from simply catching a whiff of one from miles away.

His trembling quads braced against the cold air, he inhaled her scent again, searching for answers to a thousand questions. She smelled delicate, with a hint of something sweet, and a flavoring of the bitterness of true desperation. He could practically taste her anguish, a cold, acrid weight in the air, and he knew she was in trouble.

His hands flexed with the need to close the distance between them, to crouch by her side, to give her his protection. But he didn't move. He didn't dare. He had to figure out why he was so compelled by her, why he was responding like this, especially at a time when he couldn't afford any kind of a distraction.

She moaned softly and curled into an even tighter ball. His muscles tightened, his entire soul burning with the need to help her. Quinn narrowed his eyes and pried his gaze off her to search the woods.

With the life of his blood brother in his hands, with an Order posse soon to be after him, with his own body still recovering from Elijah's assault, it made no sense that Quinn had even noticed the scent of this woman, let alone be consumed by her.

His intense need for her felt too similar to the compulsion that had sent him to the river three nights ago. Another trap? He'd suspected it from the moment he'd first reacted to her scent, but he'd been unable to resist the temptation, and he'd hauled ass to get back to his house. Yeah, true, he'd also needed to get back to his cabin to retrieve his supplies to go after Elijah. The fact she'd imbued him with new strength had been a bonus he wasn't going to deny.

But now he had to be sure. A trap or not? Quinn laughed softly. Shit. He hoped it was. If it wasn't, there was only one other reason he could think of to explain his reaction to her, and that would be if she was his mate. His *sheva*. His ticket to certain destruction.

No chance.

He wouldn't allow it.

He had no time for dealing with that destiny right now. It was time to get in, get out, and go after Elijah. His amusement faded as he took a final survey of the woods. There was no lurking threat he could detect. Maybe he'd made it back before he'd been expected, or maybe an ambush had been aborted.

Either way, he had to get into his house, get his stuff, and move on. His gaze returned to the woman, and he noticed a drop of water sliding down the side of her neck, trickling over her skin like the most seductive of caresses. He swore, realizing she wasn't going to leave. She'd freeze to death before she'd abandon her perch.

He cursed and knew he had to go to her. He couldn't let her die on his front step. Not this woman. Not her.

He would make it fast, he would make it efficient, he would stay on target for his mission, but he would get her safe.

Keeping alert for any indication that this was a setup, Quinn stepped out of the woods and into the clearing. He'd made no sound, not even a whisper of his clothing, and yet she sensed him.

She sat up, her gaze finding him instantly in the dim light, despite his stealthy approach. They made eye contact, and the world seemed to stop for a split second. The moment he saw those silvery eyes, something thumped in his chest. Something visceral and male howled inside him, raging to be set free.

As he strode up, she unfolded herself from her cramped position and pulled herself to her feet, her gaze never leaving his. Her face was wary, her body tense, but she lifted her chin ever so slightly and set her hands on her hips, telling him that she wasn't leaving.

Her courage and determination, held together by that tiny, shivering frame, made satisfaction thud through him. There was a warrior in that slim, exhausted body.

She said nothing as he approached, and neither of them spoke as he came to a stop in front of her.

Up close, he was riveted. Her dark eyelashes were clumped from the rain. Her skin was pale, too pale. Her face was carrying the burden of a thousand weights. But beneath that pain, those nightmares, that hell, lay delicate femininity that called to him. The luminescent glow of her skin, the sensual curve of her mouth, the sheen of rain on her cheekbones, the simple silver hoops in her ears. It awoke in him something so male, so carnal, so primal he wanted to throw her up against the wall and consume her until their bodies were melted together in single, scorching fire.

She searched his face with the same intensity raging through him, and he felt like she was tearing through his shields, cataloguing everything about him, all the way down to his soul.

He studied her carefully, and she let him, not flinching when his gaze traveled down her body. His blood pulsed as he noted the curve of her breasts under her rain-slicked jacket, the sensuous curve of her hips, and even the mud on her jeans and boots. He almost groaned at his need to palm her hips, drag her over to him, and mark her with his kiss. Loose strands of thick dark hair had escaped from her ponytail, curling around her neck and shoulders like it was clinging to her for safety.

Protectiveness surged from deep inside him and he clenched his fists against his urge to sweep her into his arms and carry her inside, away from whatever hardship had brought her to his doorstep.

Double hell. He'd hoped his reaction would lessen when he got close to her, but it had intensified. He'd never felt like this before. Never had this response to a woman.

What the hell was going on? *Sheva*. The word was like a demon, whispering through his mind. He shut it out. He would never allow himself to bond with his mate. If that was what was going on, she was out of there immediately, before they were both destroyed forever.

Intent on sending her away, he looked again at her face, and then realized he was done. Her beautiful silver eyes were aching with a soul-deep pain that shattered what little defenses he had against her. He simply couldn't abandon her.

It didn't matter what she wanted. It didn't matter why she was there. She was coming inside. He would make sure it didn't interfere with his mission. He would make dead sure it turned out right. No matter what.

Without a word, he grabbed her backpack off the floor, surprised at how heavy it was. Either she had tossed her free weights in it, or she had packed her life into it.

He had a bad feeling it wasn't a set of dumb bells.

Quinn walked past her and unlocked his front door. He shoved it open, then stood back. Letting her decide. Hoping she would walk away and spare them both.

She took a deep breath, glanced at his face one more time, then walked into the cabin.

Hell.

He paused to take one more survey of his woods, found nothing amiss, and then he followed her into his home and shut the door behind them.

Stephanie Rowe Bio

Four-time RITA® Award nominee and Golden Heart® Award winner Stephanie Rowe is a nationally bestselling author with more than twenty published books with major New York publishers such as Grand Central, HarperCollins, Harlequin, Dorchester and Sourcebooks.

She has received coveted starred reviews from Booklist and high praise from Publisher's Weekly, calling out her "...snappy patter, goofy good humor and enormous imagination... [a] genre-twister that will make readers...rabid for more." Stephanie's work has been nominated as YALSA Quick Pick for Reluctant Readers.

Stephanie writes romance (paranormal, contemporary and romantic suspense), teen fiction, middle grade fiction and motivational nonfiction.

A former attorney, Stephanie lives in Boston where she plays tennis, works out and is happily writing her next book. Want to learn more? Visit Stephanie online at one of the following hot spots:

www.stephanierowe.com
http://twitter.com/stephanierowe2
https://www.facebook.com/StephanieRoweAuthor

Select List of Other Books by Stephanie Rowe

(For a complete book list, please visit www.stephanierowe.com)

PARANORMAL ROMANCE

The Order of the Blade Series
Darkness Awakened
(Book One of the Primal Heat trilogy)
Darkness Seduced
(Book Two of the Primal Heat trilogy)
Darkness Surrendered
(Book Three of the Primal Heat trilogy)
Forever in Darkness (novella)
(Order of the Blade, Book Four)
Darkness Reborn
(Order of the Blade, Book Five)
Darkness Arisen
(Order of the Blade, Book Six)
Available Late 2012

The Soulfire Series
Kiss at Your Own Risk (Book One)
Touch if You Dare (Book Two)
Hold Me if You Can (Book Three)

The Immortally Sexy Series
Date Me Baby, One More Time (Book One)
Must Love Dragons (Book Two)
He Loves Me, He Loves Me Hot (Book Three)
Sex & the Immortal Bad Boy (Book Four)

ROMANTIC SUSPENSE

The Alaska Heat Series
Ice (Book One)
Chill (Book Two)

CONTEMPORARY ROMANCE

Birch Crossing Series
Dawn at Birch Crossing (Book One)

NONFICTION

The Feel Good Life

FOR TEENS

A Girlfriend's Guide to Boys Series
Putting Boys on the Ledge (Book One)
Studying Boys (Book Two)
Who Needs Boys? (Book Three)
Smart Boys & Fast Girls (Book Four)

Stand Alone Novels

The Fake Boyfriend Experiment

FOR PRE-TEENS

The Forgotten Series
Penelope Moonswoggle, The Girl Who Could Not Ride a Dragon (Book One)
Penelope Moonswoggle & the Accidental Doppelganger (Book Two)
Available 2013

Darkness Reborn

Made in the USA
Monee, IL
27 January 2022